THE COVENANT

Also by Thorne Moore and available from Honno Press

A Time For Silence
Motherlove
The Unravelling

THE COVENANT

The Life and Death of a Righteous Woman

by

Thorne Moore

HONNO MODERN FICTION

First published in Great Britain in 2020 by Honno Press

'Ailsa Craig', Heol y Cawl, Dinas Powys, Vale of Glamorgan,

Wales, CF64 4AH

1 2 3 4 5 6 7 8 9 10

Copyright: Thorne Moore, 2020

A catalogue record for this book is available from the British Library Published
with the financial support of the Books Council of Wales.

ISBN 978-1-912905-23-2 (paperback)

ISBN 978-1-912905-24-9 (ebook)

Cover photograph: Thorne Moore

Cover design: Simon Hicks

Text design: Elaine Sharples

Printed in Great Britain by 4Edge

Many thanks to everyone at Honno Press, especially my editor, Caroline Oakley, and to fellow authors Judith Barrow, Alex Martin and Catherine Marshall who read through it all and gave their verdicts and encouragement

Author's Note

My first novel, *A Time For Silence*, set the date, setting and characters for *The Covenant* in a description of gravestones in a chapel graveyard. *The Covenant* is set in the same cottage of Cwmderwen, amidst the same isolated community, so I naturally owe much of the inspiration for this story to the same sources, including the elderly locals who regaled me, when I first arrived in Wales, with tales of family life, of chapels and coracle fishing, service in big houses and slate quarrying. I was also inspired by the wonderful early 20th century Pembrokeshire photographs of Tom Mathias which had just been rediscovered when I moved here.

As before, I have drawn on a mine of information and opinions in old local newspapers, but I have been delighted to discover that many from the time of the Great War are now available on-line via the invaluable National Library of Wales.

I also owe a great deal to a PhD thesis available on-line: *The Social Impact of the First World War in Pembrokeshire*, by Simon Hancock.

I found the abominable sermon in Chapter 1 in *Revival Year Sermons* preached during 1859 by C H Spurgeon and my sincere sympathies go to all who had to sit through them at the time.

Assume that the members of the Owen family of Cwmderwen are Welsh-speaking (Pembrokeshire Welsh, too), even though I have written in English. As they frequently quote the Bible, I have used the King James Authorised Version as the most appropriate translation of the Bishop Morgan Welsh version that they would have read.

Most of the places mentioned in the book are fictional, including the village of Llanolwen and the nearby market town of Penbryn. In *A Time For Silence* their exact location is left deliberately vague, but I have been a little more precise in *The Covenant*. Penbryn is sited on the Cardi Bach, the branch of the railway that was extended to Cardigan from Crymmych in 1886, so you are welcome to deduce that it is somewhere in the vicinity of Boncath or Cilgerran. Haverfordwest was, of course, very real, but Rowlands Tea Rooms on Dew Street was not.

The wicked worketh a deceitful work: but to him that soweth righteousness shall be a sure reward.

Proverbs 11:18

Oakglen
Rochester NY
May 4th, 2014

Dear Sarah

Thank you for getting in touch. It's wonderful to have contact with our roots in the old country. I am so pleased you managed to track me down.

My grandmother was indeed Mary Ann Mackenzie, née Owen, so if you are the granddaughter of John Owen, yes we are related, as my gran was his sister. I am afraid I can't tell you much about Gran's life in Wales. She was a nanny here in America before she became a teacher and I think she may have been in service over there, too. It may interest you to learn that my uncle Jonathan has the old Welsh family Bible that was forwarded to Gran after the war. I am afraid I don't understand the language but there are names and dates, although they are not particularly legible because some entries have been blacked out. It seems there was a sizable family living in Cwmderwen, which, you tell me, is only a small cottage, though I never heard Gran speak of any of her relatives who remained in Wales, except your grandfather and an aunt called Leah, who died at about the end of the First World War, I think…

1

April 1st 1919

'Here!' The shout from John Jenkins is closer to a shriek, breaking in its intensity of excitement and alarm. The other men look up from the bloated remains of a cow, draped in seaweed from the night's high tide and, seeing Jenkins waving his arms wildly, they race across the dark wet sands to the tufted banks and muddy creeks of the estuary's salt marshes. Gulls and other water birds cackle alarm and rise in panicking battalions from the still swollen waters as the men spring into action.

A tree has come down on the flood. No telling how many miles the furious waters have carried it. Crashing against boulders on its journey, it has been stripped of lesser branches and roots, the larger boughs splintered and shattered. It has come to rest at last, as the flood subsided, wedged between two banks of flattened grass, its mauled stumps biting into the black mud, a dam holding back an arc of bushes and branches and other flotsam.

Entwined and impaled in its embrace is a woman.

At least it seems to be a woman, though battered beyond recognition. The eyeless face is one mangled bruise. One arm has been torn off, along with the sleeve that encased it, but the other arm still trails shreds of dark wool. Mud-soiled linen hangs about the torso. One laced boot miraculously remains in place. The other has gone, along with much of the foot that had worn it. Long strands of black hair wind themselves around the raw wounds of the tree and float on the salt water.

The men stare down at the sight, solemnly removing their caps.

3

'What to do?' asks John Jenkins, wiping his mouth. 'Do we send for Constable Thomas?'

The others nod and mumble agreement, but no one makes a move until Dai Edwards coughs, braces himself and steps down into the squelching creek, steadying himself to ensure he doesn't sink too deep. One hand for support on the skeletal tree, he untangles some of the black hair and eases the mutilated head away from the wood. The body is still caught fast. He eases the linen collar back from the swollen neck, sees something and leans forward to peer closer. Initials, embroidered in black. LO.

'Yes, send for Constable Thomas,' he says, straightening. 'And best send word to Llanolwen too. "LO". Seems like we've found the woman they were looking for. An accident, it must have been. Not something worse, not here, not amongst us. An accident, but no doubt, it's Leah Owen.'

THE SOWING

1883

'There's a storm coming.' Leah stood on the lowest bar of the gate, hanging over to gaze across the valley, while her sister Sarah fussed with a stone in her boot.

'I wish it would.' Sarah, squatting on the verge, was battling, red-faced, with the laces. 'It's hot enough. I can scarcely breathe.' She looked plaintively at the untied boot. 'Help me with this.'

Leah jumped down, kneeling on the grass to retie the lace. 'Why don't you loosen a button or two? Your frock's too tight.'

Sarah pouted. 'I can't go around unbuttoned.'

'Why not? No one will know.' Leah, at nine, was pragmatic. Sarah, three years older, was filling out in all directions, where she should and where she shouldn't, and seams were beginning to stain. Buttons would have to give or she'd faint. All fastenings were safely concealed beneath Sarah's shapeless pinafore. Besides, they were past the last cottage in Llanolwen, and their brother Frank had stayed behind at school, so there was no one around to see and snigger.

Sarah pouted again and took Leah's hand to struggle to her feet. 'All right. Just two.' Pinafore hoisted high, she unfastened two buttons and drew a deep breath of relief. Then she glanced over the gate into the adjoining field and saw what Leah had seen.

'Oh no!'

Above the heathery crags on the far side of the broad vale, clouds were piling up, ash and charcoal, heaving themselves into volcanic plumes, turning the late June sky to November gloom. Beneath them, distant veils of rain scythed down in biblical fury, dissolving rocks, forests, fields. Somewhere in the depths of the boiling clouds, lightning flashed. Thunder rolled, still so distant it was felt rather than heard.

Another of the sudden storms that came out of nowhere to hurtle around the countryside, and it was coming their way. Their side of the valley was still in afternoon sunshine, but it was an eerie light, too vivid, trying too hard to defy the advancing onslaught. Trying in vain. Along their deserted lane, the wind was beginning to whip up. The overhanging ash trees started to shiver and shake.

'I knew I shouldn't have waited for you to come out of school,' wailed Sarah. 'I'd be home by now.'

'We'd be home if we'd taken the chapel path.'

'I don't like that way. You know I don't.' Sarah had avoided the shortcut down through the woods ever since she had found herself stuck on one of the stiles, mocked and hooted at by passing boys. Another rumble of thunder and she shrieked. 'I'll be drenched!'

'Then run and beat it,' said Leah, setting the pace, her thin legs carrying her lightly along the rutted road, her bonnet flying in her wake. But she paused to look back, knowing that Sarah was sure to be far behind. Sarah, twice as heavy, was puffing and panting as she floundered, whining in distress.

'You run like Fegi Fawr,' said Leah.

Sarah was in no mood to be compared to their lopsided cow. As she caught up with her younger sister, her face began to crease again into a howl. At any moment, she was going to sit down and cry. It was Sarah's invariable response to most difficulties.

'Come on,' said Leah, tugging her.

And then the outriders of the storm rolled over them, gloom engulfing them like a candle guttering, and a moment later the rain came down, not a haze or a pitter-patter but a torrent, ice-cold and stinging, its hissing so loud that Leah could only see Sarah's wail, not hear it.

Sarah lunged for the shelter of an oak, solitary among the ash trees bordering the lane, but it offered little protection. The rain slanted like arrows through the leaves, determined to seek its prey. It pounded on the hard dry dust of the road, turning it to slurry and splashing up to soak them from beneath.

Leah saw no point in trying to hide. She was wet through, but she didn't care. The storm was glorious, thrilling, full of energy throbbing around her. Lightning flashed and Sarah screamed, but Leah just stood, open-mouthed, counting her heartbeats, one two three, till the great crack of thunder echoed up and down the valley. The voice of God, her father said, and so it was, surely.

'Deep calls on deep in the roar of Thy cataracts!' She raised her arms into the rain, wanting to fly like a hawk on the wings of the storm.

'Oh, stop it,' cried Sarah. 'You'll be struck by lightning!'

'You, more likely.' Leah shouted to make herself heard. 'Under that tree.'

With a squeal, Sarah slithered away from the oak and stood like a shivering lamb in the full force of the rain. Only for a moment. As suddenly as it had begun, the rain began to ease. It eased as if an invisible hand were releasing the pump handle, reducing the flow to a dribble. The storm heaved itself impatiently northwards, and the sun was already creeping back in its wake, breaking through the haze of lingering drizzle to glint on the puddles engulfing the lane and the raindrops hanging like diamonds from every leaf and blade of grass.

'Oh, look at it, it's mud everywhere!' howled Sarah.

'Keep to the grass, then.'

'Easy for you!' When Sarah attempted to follow Leah onto the narrow weedy verge above the sunken ruts of the lane, she overbalanced and nearly fell flat into the mud. Her face had twisted into a whine even before she had moved, yet she never learned that her whining got her nowhere. Sarah, thought Leah with a sudden flash of understanding, was like the little fledgling in the nest who squawked loudest and most persistently for food, only to see mother bird give it to another chick. Squashed in the middle, a second daughter of three, a third child of five. One day, if she only squawked loud enough, maybe someone would notice her.

'Here, take my hand.' Leah led Sarah as she tottered along, whimpering at every bramble that snatched at her.

A roar of laughter nearly had Sarah unbalancing again. Behind them, striding through the mud without a care, brushing the rain from his bright red waistcoat, came Eli John, son of the quarry manager, a big, brawny lad, leering at the sight of them.

'Fine little pigs! Can't manage a bit of mud? You want me to carry you?'

'Yes. No. Yes.' said Sarah.

'No!' said Leah.

'Just one of you then.' Before Sarah could think better of it, Eli had scooped her off her grassy perch and clasped her to him, striding on and laughing still. 'You're a big lass. Too big for your buttons it seems.' The saturated cotton of Sarah's pinafore was concealing nothing now. 'You want me to undo the rest?'

'No! Let go. Put me down.'

'Just one then.' Eli was pulling the pinafore up. Sarah tried, ineffectually to slap him, but he caught her hand and wrenched it back. She may have always longed for attention, but surely not in this manner.

'Now now, don't play cat with me. That's no way for a lady to repay a gentleman who's doing her a favour.'

'Put her down,' said Leah. She had leaped down into the lane, armed with a loose branch that she was wielding like a spear, ready to jab in Eli's face.

'Ach, to hell with you, damned parish beggars.' He sneered as he dropped Sarah into the mud. 'Snuffle your way back to your sty on your own.'

'We are not beggars!' snapped back Leah. 'Our father has land!'

'Ha! Because you've been permitted to scratch around like pigs on an acre or two, you think you're gentry?' Making a gesture that Leah supposed to be rude, Eli turned his back and strode on, spluttering invectives.

'Twenty-four acres, one rood and eight perches!' Leah shouted after him, as she helped Sarah to her feet.

Sarah was bawling fit for Armageddon, as much distressed by the mud that splattered her from head to toe as by Eli John's assault. 'Beast! He's a beast! Oh, look at me? Oh, I am covered.'

'Never mind, we are nearly home.' Leah relinquished her spear and encouraged her sister on. 'Look, there's the bend.'

Around the corner, the lane widened and in the bay between two gates lay a stone stand for milk churns. Leah sat Sarah down on it and began to mop her clean with handfuls of wet grass. 'That's the worst off.'

But Sarah only whimpered, ready to break into full-blown tears.

'Stop it!' Leah's patience had run out. 'You'll not get clean and dry with tears. Come on!'

Sarah stood up, sniffing, then her face crinkled again as she looked around. The gate on the right led onto broad open Castell Mawr pasture, but their way led through the left-hand gate, onto a track overhung with trees and running with liquid mud as it spilled down into the hollow harbouring their home. Cwmderwen.

Dragging Sarah, too impatient to waste more words, Leah guided her sister from tussock to rock to tussock till they reached the bend where the track doubled back towards their cottage and they both stopped short.

Their father was standing at a gate, his hand on their brother Tom's shoulder, gazing out over their top field. Doubtless he had come to see what damage the brief storm had done to the two and a half acres of oats that stood green-gold, rattling themselves free of the rain. The field was sheltered and there had been little flattening. That would be a relief to him, but it wasn't the oats that held him transfixed now. Their modest acres, spilling down a narrow cwm to the winding river on the valley's broad floor, were framed by dark woods on either side, with a hazy backdrop of misted hills where the rain still fell. But over it all arched a vast rainbow.

It caught Leah's breath, just as it held her father and brother mesmerised.

Sarah squirmed in her wet clothes, her boots squelching. 'Don't tell him about the buttons,' she whispered. Then her voice rose as if she couldn't resist calling attention to her state. 'I'm wet through!'

Her words brought Tada round. Thomas Owen was a tall man, seemingly rendered more so by his lank form and upright bearing. He was incapable of bending, as if he had made a vow, in a darker past, never to bend again – or so it seemed to Leah's fancy. His beard bristled as if he intended to brush the sky with it.

His dark eyes crinkled at sight of them. 'You are indeed, daughter. You too, Leah. Soaked to the skin. Get yourselves home before you catch chill. Your mother will be fretting for you.'

Sarah was only too happy to be released, stumbling on down the track to the house, wringing her pinafore as she went.

Leah, knowing she would be indulged, ignored the invitation, squeezing between brother Tom and Tada to peer between the bars of the gate, her eyes fixed on the translucent arc of glory as it slowly faded with the brightening sun and the receding rain.

12

Her father drew a great heaving breath. 'I will remember my covenant which is between me and you.' His voice was deep and triumphant. Like God. Sometimes Leah suspected he was God. God the Father. Or at least, God would be very like him. Stern but loving, caring, a safe refuge. Everything the Bible said.

Sixteen-year-old Tom took Leah's hand and squeezed it, so they were all linked, her father's hand on his shoulder, his hand around hers. This was the way it should be. And God set his rainbow in the clouds as a sign of the covenant between Himself and the earth. Their earth.

'Sojourn in this land, and I will be with thee, and will bless thee; for unto thee, and unto thy seed, I will give all these countries,' said her father, the roll of thunder in the words. How many times had she heard him say them, gazing out across his fields, clinging to the biblical promise like a warrior to his sword? 'Twenty-four acres, one rood, eight perches. Generation upon generation my forefathers held acres in Whitechurch, but they were snatched away so that my father received nothing, reduced to unjust penury. The sweat of his brow earned only profit for others. Such was my lot from the moment I could earn a crust, but God's hand is upon the righteous, and he brought me here, to hold this land, and to pass it, when my days are numbered, to you, my son. Owen land. Remember that. Owen land. We shall never again let it slip from our grasp.'

'No, Tada,' said Tom reverently. When Tada slipped into biblical language there was no help for it except to be solemn. 'I shall keep it to pass to my son and he to his.'

'If we keep the Lord's commandments, he will not abandon us.' Tada patted his youngest daughter's head. 'You understand this, Leah, my child? My bright one? Family, land, blood, soul. Bound together and never to be relinquished.'

'For ever and ever, amen,' she said devoutly.

13

He nodded, smiling down on her before his brows meshed together again as he peered back up the lane. 'Where is the boy?'

'You mean Frank?' Leah dreaded for a moment that he meant Eli John, but it wasn't possible that he could have witnessed that lewd scene.

'Who else should I mean but Frank? Do I have a third son I know nothing about? Why is he not with you? Did I not see you set out together for school?'

'He stayed behind for extra sums.'

'And what did he do this time to deserve such a punishment?'

'Nothing, Tada. He asked Miss Griffiths for more.' It was true. Leah's little brother Frank liked sums. So did Leah, though she had never stayed behind to beg for more.

Tada wasn't listening to her claims. He shook his head, convinced his younger son had earned rebuke, but then he smiled upon Tom. 'No prodigal here at least. The Lord has granted me a true blessing in my first-born.'

Tom looked down, blushing at such praise. Leah, still holding his hand, sensed the stifled trouble within him.

'Come now,' said Tada, turning to shepherd them before him. 'Let us get home before your mother thinks us all drowned.'

Cwmderwen might appear a fine modern house by daylight, with its upper rooms and iron range, its sash windows and slate roof. By twilight, though, as it prepared to embrace the night, it transformed. Its solid stones and heavy timbers seemed to sink themselves into the black earth and the darkening tangled oakwoods. Its ancient foundations made themselves felt, as old as Mr Pugh's cottage below the chapel, with its earthen floor, open fire and sagging thatch. But at least they didn't share the building with their beasts, as Mr Pugh did. Cwmderwen's cows had a barn of their own, and the pig had his pen across the yard. Tada was cleaning the pen now, his voice soaring like a bell on the notes of a hymn, drowning out the indignant squealing of the occupant. Mam and Sarah were rounding up the geese and hens, Sarah's squeals echoing around the cwm every time a bird evaded her. The daylight, still strong out in the broad valley, was already fading fast in their narrow dell. Soon Tada would come in to light the oil lamp and they would gather for prayers, but for now the only glow within the kitchen came from the failing embers in the range.

Leah wriggled herself into greater comfort, in a nest of Owen children. Tom had come in from tending the cows to slither wearily onto the comfort of the settle, under the massive beam of the chimney, and she was snuggled into the crook of his arm. Frank had laid himself across her lap, stockinged feet scorching themselves against the side of the cooling oven, squinting to catch the last light on the page of sums Miss Griffiths had given him. The embers in the fire shifted; sparking, fading, glowing against the blackened stones. A changing pattern on a permanent wall.

It was permanent, the wall. It surely must be, as old as time, Leah thought. This kitchen, where they gathered, cooked, ate, worked and prayed, was a fixed part of creation, permanent as the rock it stood on, with its nooks and crannies and creaking stairs, its cavernous fireplace and deep-set window and its pervading odour of smoke and broth, mutton fat and dried herbs. She couldn't imagine it not being there. Not being theirs.

'How did our grandfather lose his land?' she asked, as Tom stirred, drawing a deep breath of contentment.

He brushed away whatever daydream had been occupying him and gave a little shrug. 'I don't know. The parson and the landlord took it, so our father says. It was a long time ago. It was only a half a dozen acres, I think. We have this land now.'

15

'Twenty-four acres, one rood and eight perches,' said Leah.

Tom laughed. 'That is exactly right.' He had had it drilled into him since the day the growing family had taken up residence at Cwmderwen, a year before Leah's birth. 'Never forget the eight perches.'

'Will you keep it, after our father?'

'Yes, of course.' There was a weight of obligation in Tom's words. He sighed again but more in resignation this time.

'You wanted to be a soldier.' It was one of her earliest memories, Tom marching up and down the yard with a rake over his shoulder for a rifle. When Tada asked what he was doing, he'd said 'I'm going to take the Queen's shilling and wear a red coat.' She hadn't understood what he meant. She wasn't sure he had either, but Tada... What had their father said or done? She couldn't remember, only that there had been a sudden stillness all around them, a sense of transgression that had her infant self trembling. And then Mam saying softly, 'We are soldiers of Christ, my son, not of worldly Queens and Empresses.'

Tom gave a twisted smile and gazed up at the blackened timbers above. 'No, no, that was just childish fancy. I have put away such thoughts. I understand now that it is my duty to hold and work this land, Owen land, forever. As Tada wishes. We must all do our duty by our land and our family, Leah.'

'Will I live here too?'

'Owly wants to be a teacher,' said Frank, his face covered by his arithmetic book. 'She'll live in the school house.'

Leah slapped his hand lightly. 'I didn't say that.' But she had thought about it, picturing herself like Miss Griffiths, in a cramped cottage of her own, surrounded by books.

Tom squeezed her. 'I don't know about that, but maybe I'll let you stay here and keep house for me. Would you like that?'

Leah thought about it. Yes, even with a hundred thousand books, the little school cottage would not compare with Cwmderwen. 'We could have books here?' Books other than the Holy Bible and Mam's religious tracts.

'As many as you like. Except that you won't really want to stay here, little Leah. No, no, when the time comes, you'll be off with a house of your own to keep, and another man to care for.'

'You mean if I marry?'

'Women do, you know. Don't pull a face. When you have grown a little more, you'll be wanting a husband and children. One daughter kept home to mind the house is enough or there'd be no new generations.'

Leah wrinkled her nose – and found Mary staring across at her in the gloom. Mary, the eldest girl, stocky, plain, looking twice her fourteen years. She who had had barely a year's schooling before being kept at home to help her mother with the younger children. Mary, named for Mam; Mary their second mam who sewed and cooked and cleaned and carried and said next to nothing as she toiled. While they had sat comforting themselves by the fire, she was crouched on the bench on the far side of the chimney, silent as usual as she hunched over her sewing to catch the fading light, working through a basket piled high with mending.

But she broke her silence now. 'There's still light enough to knit, Leah.'

Obediently, Leah pushed Frank off her lap and raised her needles which had fallen beside her, to resume her work. The future was a strange country, but it seemed it was already mapped out, ordained by God and Tada. She had only to follow the road.

'Have you received forgiveness through the blood of Jesus? Are you glorying in His sacrifice and is His cross your only hope and refuge?

Then you are in the covenant. Some men want to know whether they are elect. We cannot tell them unless they will tell us this. Dost thou believe? Is thy faith fixed on the precious blood? Then thou are in the covenant. And oh, poor sinner, if thou hast nothing to recommend thee...'

Leah drew a deep silent breath. The chapel was pleasantly cool compared to the heavy heat outside. With high arched windows opened, the scent of cows and summer dust filtered in to mingle with the smell of beeswax and old leather. Summer chapel smell. In winter, it was pungent with musty damp clothing and sweat.

A bluebottle was buzzing somewhere over the heads of the congregation. Droning on and on, just like the Reverend Williams. He delivered the word of God, Mam said, but he never sounded like the voice of God, the way Tada did. Tada, in his place in the big seat below the pulpit with their neighbour William George and the other chapel deacons, would have read the sermon better, with *hwyl*, and then Leah might have learned what it was about. It was the third time she had heard this self-same sermon and she still didn't understand a word of it.

Leah raised her eyes, over the polished planks of the pew in front, over the black backs and bonnets, to the preacher perched up on his pulpit. All she could see of him was his little round balding head with its little round spectacles. The rest was concealed by Mrs Beynon, seated in front of her, bony shoulders erect, black straw hat motionless. The Reverend's head seemed to emerge from it. Maybe the rest of him was in Mrs Beynon's hat, sitting on her head. Leah dug her nails into her palms to stop herself laughing.

On her right, Sarah was busy arranging and rearranging the pleats of her skirt until Mary's hand reached across and slapped her fingers to still them.

'If thou art standing back and saying, "I dare not come, I am

18

afraid, I am not in the covenant," still Christ bids thee come. And when thou hast come to Him, and His blood has been applied to thee, doubt not but that in the red roll of election stands thy name.'

Leah felt her eyes drooping. That wasn't allowed. Mam would be disappointed in her and she couldn't bear that. Leah longed to love God and rejoice in his word the way Mam did. She just had to be still and listen. She must imitate Mrs Beynon – one of the true elect – who sat rigidly to attention, devouring every word, not stirring a muscle.

Steady breathing all around her, silent attention, nothing but the distant lowing of a cow and the persistent buzzing of the fly to interrupt the preacher.

'Canst thou read thy name in the bloody characters of a Saviour's atonement? Then shalt thou read it one day in the golden letters of the Father's election. He that believeth is elected. The blood is the symbol, the token, the earnest, the—'

An almighty roar erupted, so sudden, so startling, that Leah – like others around her – couldn't understand its cause for a moment. Then Mrs Beynon's black straw bonnet quivered as her own profound snore shook her awake, and her half-choked grunting gave way to a squeal of horrified mortification.

The minister stopped in mid-drone. Mr Beynon, white-haired beside his wife, didn't stir a muscle, still fast asleep, but Mrs Price, on her other side, tutted, breathing in through clenched nostrils, so that Mrs Beynon shrank down, shoulders tightening, praying for the pew to swallow her up.

Mam leaned forward and gave the poor woman's shoulder a reassuring pat.

From the pew behind, their stout neighbour Mrs George, straining in her Sunday black, leaned over to whisper 'She got there before me.'

19

Her daughter Florence, biting back a smile, nudged her to hush. The shuffling and shh of muffled whispers dried up.

The Reverend Williams blinked and continued. 'The blood is the symbol, the token, the earnest, the surety, the seal of the covenant of grace to thee. It must ever be the telescope through which thou canst look to see the things that are afar off.'

Down the line, little brother Frank put an imaginary telescope to his eye. Mam firmly pulled his arm down and gripped his hand in hers.

Leah wondered what it would be like to look at the world through a telescope filled with blood. She had no idea what it would be like to look through a telescope of any sort, but she thought this one would make things look very red. She looked at the wall of black serge in front of her and imagined her neighbours dressed in bright crimson. Maybe that was how heaven would be. She shut her eyes tight, trying to remember the scriptures and the precious stones of the holy city, jasper, sapphire, chalcedony, emerald, sardonyx. Was one of them ruby? She thought not. Rubies were red, she knew that. But maybe some of the others were red too. What colour was crysopras? It might be red. Not the gates, though. They were made of pearls, which were white. And there was gold... All precious stones and gold and bright light. How unforgiving heaven must be, without green fields or the shade of trees.

Something prompted her to open her eyes. Tom's arm was propping her up. He was smiling down at her. How long had she been asleep? There was a rustling all around her and she realised the Reverend Williams had stopped droning. Everyone was rising for a hymn, so she wriggled off the bench and dropped to her feet too, to sing with the rest. No droning now but fire and spirit to raise the roof.

'*Nes cyraedd hyfryd lanau'r nef*... Until I reach heaven's beautiful shores...' Were they such beautiful shores, all precious stones and gold and blinding light? Was that really what Tada desired as he sang? His rich baritone, reaching across the chapel from the big seat, sounded sincere, but he loved his own land so much, would he really want to relinquish it? Secretly, deep down, she thought she wouldn't care for heaven very much, not without dark oaks and meadows and fields of silver rustling barley. But perhaps she would never get to see it. Perhaps she wasn't one of the elect and Hell fire would await her instead, which would be even worse.

'Aaaaa-men.'

The sombrely clad families of Llanolwen filed out of chapel, nodding to their minister who stood at the door like an unwilling martyr preparing for the lions in the arena. It must be sad, thought Leah, to know that your congregation barely tolerated you, that in huddled clusters away from the door they were rejoicing that they were soon to be rid of you.

Out in the June sunshine, men were wagging their beards at each other, women bowing their heads together in hushed indignation.

'No soul, that man. Our cow could have read it better.'

Mam's soft voice, firm in her faith. 'It's the Word of God that commands our attention, not the man who speaks it. He is a mere vessel.'

'True enough, Mary Owen. Though I heard Dafydd Morgan preach once. Now there was a man.'

'Our reverend bought those sermons, you know. Little pamphlets.'

'Well, if the spirit was ever on him, it left him long ago.'

'Sooner he goes off to live with his sister, the better.'

'We'll have better soon, I hope.'

'Could hardly be worse.'

It was the same every week. Nothing was new, and the conversation soon moved on to other matters.

'So you think to start on another mow tomorrow? Yes, best to be about it before this weather spoils...'

'Two hoggets for market this week and the old ewe for the pot, I think...'

'Shameless! Hannah Griffiths saw her with her own eyes and if you ask me...'

Leah sidled away to where her brother Tom was standing with David George, their neighbour's son. They both smiled as she approached.

'Your father's going to put your old ewe in the pot,' she said.

David nodded gravely. He was always grave. 'Well, she's lost a lamb two years now. She's served her time.'

'We aren't put in the pot when we grow old,' Leah insisted.

Tom winked. 'How do you know? If we have another lean year, we might not even wait for you to grow old.'

'You will not cook me!'

'No, Sarah would be better. More meat on her.'

Sarah, yawning at her mother's side, caught them laughing at her and began to shift in their direction, demanding to know the joke. But before they could explain, the chapel crowd was forced to part down either side of the lane, like the Red Sea, but not by God. Jacob John, quarry manager, was more akin to Pharaoh, or the Devil. Here was a man who made even Mam frown with his ungodliness. Leah wasn't sure what form that took, except that it included playing cards and a housekeeper and not attending chapel on the Sabbath but attending to business instead. His wagon, rumbling along through their midst, was laden with picks and shovels, barrels and sacks. There were stony faces in the crowd and mutterings about iniquity and ale houses and God's wrath awaiting all sinners.

Jacob John, big and brawny, confident in his position, didn't give tuppence for their disapproval. 'Whoa!' He pulled up his horse by

William George's side. 'You wanted stone, that right, man? For the yard?'

'This is not the time, not outside chapel on a Sabbath,' said William George.

'Well, that's no matter to me. Do you want it or not?'

While they argued, Jacob's son Eli leaped down from the wagon and swaggered in front of the children, straw in his mouth. His waistcoat was green velvet today, with brass buttons the size of pennies. A peacock in their sombre sober midst.

'Finished your prayers then, good little babes? They won't help you, you know.'

David George laid a cautionary hand on Tom's arm, but Tom wouldn't be held. Tom the would-be soldier. 'What do you mean?'

'Breaking your backs on your miserable acres when you haven't got a hope, that's what I mean, Tom Owen.'

'We have hopes above your dirty dreams, Eli John. Things have been hard but the harvest promises to be good this year.'

'And what good will that do, when it merely brings the prices lower? You'll barely make a farthing from it.'

'We don't grow it to sell, but to feed our stock, so you know nothing about it.'

Eli laughed. 'And doubtless you all eat from the same trough. Leave it. Find proper man's work that pays. Come to the quarries or join the railway gangs: they'll take you for the new track to Cardigan. Too much of a weakling, are you? If you haven't the stomach for it, why don't you put your sisters to work instead? Sarah will make you a penny or two. If she hasn't already, flaunting herself half-naked in the road.'

Sarah screamed indignation, stepping back, fists clenched to her mouth.

Tom turned to her. 'What is he talking about?'

Sarah only shook her head, her face crimson.

'He tried to undo her frock,' said Leah.

'He what!' Tom span around to face the leering Eli.

'Leave it,' warned David, but Tom shook off his restraining hand.

'You dared to lay a finger on my sister?'

Eli grinned at the success of his jibe. 'Only to finish what she'd started. Isn't that right, Sarah Owen? How many buttons undone today? Let's see.'

Tom swung at him. Eli parried the first blow easily enough, but the second caught him in the eye. He swung back and they were locked in a brawl before David could come between them. Sarah retreated, squealing and waving her hands...

How did it happen? Leah saw Sarah stumble into William George as he stood at the wagon's head, and he in turn was shunted heavily against the hot, fly-pestered horse. The creature neighed in indignation, rearing, bucking the cart and a bucket and a pick slid loose, slamming onto the brawling boys.

Men stepped in to break them up. Eli was pushed away, nursing a bruised head and a bloody nose. Hands reached down towards Tom, offering to help him to his feet.

'Thomas Owen, here, man! Your boy's hurt.'

Leah ran forward, but her father, striding up, pushed her to one side.

'What's this, my son? Would you have your mother see you brawling, and on the Lord's day too?'

Tom was curled up in speechless agony, his fists clenched into his groin, gasping for breath.

'Pick caught him,' said an onlooker. 'In his privates, I'd guess. Painful.'

Embarrassed, Tom pulled himself up to a sitting position, his jaw clenched for a moment before he forced the words out. 'I'm all right. It's nothing.'

Tada, who had been about to bend over him, straightened to his normal posture, nodding.

'Tom! Tom, my boy!' Mam had come up, throwing herself through the crowd. 'What have they done to you? Let me see?'

'It's nothing,' Tom repeated, blushing, as Tada tugged his wife back.

'Hush, woman. Leave the boy be.'

'Not dead, then?' Jacob John peered round from his seat at the front of the cart. 'That's good. Eli! Get up!'

Eli hauled himself back onto the cart, grimacing in pain. Leah glared at him in loathing as the cart jolted forward at Jacob's whistle and rumbled on its way, leaving Tom surrounded by his curious neighbours.

'Get back now,' said Tada, waving them away. 'Leave the boy some privacy for decency's sake. Son, can you rise?'

'Yes, Tada.' With an effort that had the veins standing out on his forehead, Tom got to his feet. A whimper escaped between closed lips, and the sweat stood out on his forehead. He swayed, and Mam gasped.

'Dear God in heaven, look at him, he's bleeding! Tom, let me—'

'Leave him, woman!' commanded her husband. 'He's a man, not a boy. Is that not right, son?'

Tom nodded.

'Come, let us go home. This is no way to honour the Lord on his Sabbath. Frank! Attend your mother.'

Seven-year-old Frank had drawn close at the promise of trouble and was staring in open-mouthed fascination at the dark wet stains on Tom's trousers. 'Is he...?' He caught his father's eye and realised that questions were forbidden for now, so he shut his mouth and fell in between his mother and Mary, who dragged him after the men of the family. Tom hobbled on his father's arm, a whimper of

25

pain escaping him now and again, as his mother hovered behind him, hands rising repeatedly to catch him should he fall. But he didn't fall. Little by little, he straightened, to prove the agony was fading.

Leah and Sarah followed in the rear.

'They'll blame me,' whispered Sarah.

'Don't be silly. No one cares about you,' said Leah. It was herself they should blame. Why hadn't she held her tongue? Why had she told Tom about Eli's wicked behaviour?

David George came hurrying past them, nodding politely as he passed. It was a strange thing to see David hurrying. Everything about him was careful and paced, as if he gave thought to every step. Now he didn't quite run, but he bustled.

'Mr Owen, forgive me, but my father says if you will only wait a moment, he will take Tom home in the trap to save him the pain.'

His father looked at Tom. 'Well, boy, will you take our neighbour out of his way for your comfort?'

Tom shook his head. 'No, Tada.' He paused to catch his breath. 'Not necessary.'

Tada nodded. 'There. You see, David. Thank your father for his charitable offer, but we need not trouble him.'

David accepted the answer without argument and hurried back. A minute later, the Georges' trap slowed up alongside them and William George leaned down. 'Come on, man, let the boy ride with us, at least to the gate.'

Tada raised his palms as if to say it had nothing to do with him. Tom held himself erect, with a forced smile that brought the sweat beading on his brow. 'Thank you. Kind offer, Mr George, but...' His jaw clenched before he spoke again. 'No need. For me. Mere scratch. Healing already. I shall do–. Own two feet–.'

Shaking his head, Mr George flicked the reins and his piebald

26

pony trotted on. Mrs George looked back with an expression of exasperation at Mam, whose eyes gleamed with tears though she said nothing. Her husband had spoken.

It was a painful mile back to their cottage and once they had turned down Cwmderwen's rutted track, Tom's gasps, smothered with such determination till then, escaped with every step.

'Mary, run on, get the kettle heating,' ordered Mam. 'We'll need hot water and clean linen.' Without a word, Mary obediently hastened ahead, though, like David, she did not run. It was not seemly for a woman to run. *I'd run and not care,* thought Leah, but she didn't want to leave Tom.

By the time they got Tom through the low doorway of the cottage, Mary was tearing an old shirt into neat strips and the range fire was stoked under the great black kettle. Mam busied herself without delay, reaching down salves and herbs from the high shelf above the oak beam.

'Set him down here—'

But Tada was already guiding, half-carrying Tom into the parlour, into a wave of stale air. 'I'll see to him in here, Mary. No need for a bunch of women to go gawping at him.'

'Then let me—'

But Tada had shut the parlour door on them.

Mam stood there, wringing her hands. In all Leah's life she had never heard Mam argue with Tada. He was master and law in his own house, as the Lord commanded.

'Shall I finish this shirt?' asked Mary, still ripping neatly.

Mam stared at her, then recovered her wits. 'Yes. Leah, you can help me roll them up. And Sarah, fetch some fresh rosemary. It's a good cleanser.' She checked the kettle and brought out the big washing bowl. By the time she had poured boiling water into it, Tada had opened the door again.

'I'll take that. Fetch him clean clothes. And stop fussing, woman. He's fine. It's barely a scratch.'

Mam continued to pace with anxiety, hovering on the brink of rebellion, but when Tom emerged at last, in clean trousers from the settle cupboard, he did seem fine. A little pale, except when he blushed under their gaze, but he was smiling, his voice almost normal.

'I'm sorry for the distress I caused you all. It was my own doing. I should not have–'

Sarah gave a muffled yelp of alarm.

'I should not have risen to the likes of Eli John taunting me.'

'Or engaged in fisticuff with anyone, least of all on the Lord's Day,' said Mam. Now that she had seen Tom recovered, she could afford to scold, though her scoldings were always bread and milk compared to Tada's, leaving them more distressed for her pain than theirs.

'No, Mam.' Tom hugged her. 'It was wrong. Forgive me?'

She kissed his brow, smiling broadly with relief. 'You'll be the death of me.'

Tada's lips twitched into a smile. 'Now, woman, enough fuss over nothing. Are we to eat?'

That was that. They said grace and ate bread and the cawl prepared yesterday and set about the tasks that a farm demanded, even on a Sabbath. Tom got about with a limp, which was clearly more painful than he let on, so he was excused the return to chapel in the evening,

The new day brought with it the usual round of school and work, hens to be fed, house to be cleaned, supper to be eaten, prayers to be said. Tom, apart from an occasional wince and a hint of the limp, was his old self, smiling, teasing the girls, assisting his father. All the drama was forgotten and life returned to its usual pattern.

For two days.

Then Tom became flushed and Mam gave him peppermint tea. 'Let me dress the wound properly, Tom,' she said, but Tada was having none of it.

'It's all healed, isn't it, son? I'll take a look if you must fuss, woman, but leave the lad be. He was out in the sun all day, that's all that's wrong with him.'

Tom drank his tea and smiled away her concern. He was sleepy when they gathered at last for prayers. The girls filed up the steep winding stair to the bed they shared in one of the upper rooms. Mam and Tada gave Tom one last scrutiny by candlelight before following them up. The boys slept on the settle and bench by the range and Tom's face glowed with the last embers as he waved them all away.

It was Frank's voice that woke Leah. Frank who could seldom be roused from his hard bed. Even with the lure of school beckoning, he would linger, cocooned in his blanket when the rest of the household was up, washed, dressed and busy. But this morning there was still only the palest glimmer of light in the sky when she heard Frank speaking in the room next door. Mam and Tada's room.

Then her mother, instantly alert, gave a sharp reply. The sound of hasty movement, voices down below. Leah slid out of bed and hurried through, in time to follow her father down the steep stairs.

The house was dark, a mystery of moving shadows and an air of panic, until a candle was lit. Mam was crouching by the settle, her hand on Tom's brow.

'He's burning.'

Burning and shivering. Tom's eyes were half open. He was murmuring, very low, or was it groaning? Leah couldn't decide which, because her heart was thundering so loudly it was almost all she could hear.

Tada was staring down at his son. 'It's a fever. It will pass.'

Mam said nothing as she rose to dip a cloth in cold water.

Tom let out a louder moan, throwing himself over with sudden wildness on the narrow bed.

'It will pass,' repeated Tada.

Still Mam said nothing. She pulled back the rough blanket that Tom had already thrown aside and made as if to raise the sweat-soaked nightshirt, but Tada's hand stopped her. 'Leave it, woman. Would you unman him?'

'I'm his mother. It is my job to nurse him. Let me see the wound, see that it is clean.'

'I'll see to it. Not here. He cannot stay here. This bed is no good for him.' He stepped back. 'Leave him to me. Don't touch him.'

It was a command. Mam stared at the parlour door as it closed behind him, her lips moving in prayer as she pleaded to understand her duty.

They heard the scrape of furniture moving, the clank of iron. Leah realised what Tada was doing. Reassembling the iron bed that had stood in the corner against the wall for the last five years. That was when a true, black sense of doom descended on her. The parlour was never used, except when the minister called, or the landlord, or when someone...

That bed had stood, dismantled and propped up out of the way, since Mamgu Owen had died in it, a sickly smell pervading the room while Mam and Mary had prayed and sniffed as they closed the blank eyes and tied up the gaping jaw. Her coffin had stood in there, while sombre pious neighbours, hats in hand, had filed past to pay their respects to the waxy withered wisp of an old woman laid in it, before the lid was nailed on, the coffin taken away and Mamgu was gone forever.

To Jesus, Mam said.

Leah felt a sickness welling up inside her. She didn't want Tom in that bed, in that room. She wanted him out in the fields with her, mocking her, chasing her, sweeping her onto his shoulders like Tada sometimes did, holding her hand, tickling her to make her giggle so hard she couldn't breathe.

She couldn't breathe now. But she would force the breath to come, because this was nothing, just her fancy making her terrified. Old memories and nightmares. Tom had a fever, that was all. He'd get over it as they all did, especially if he took Mam's peppermint tea and yarrow cordial and had a comfortable bed. It was only a bed.

When Tada had finished setting up the bed and unrolling the mattress, he carried Tom to it. Tom thrashed as he was carried, unaware, but Tada ignored the blows, laying him down before taking the water and bandages, ointments and cordials that Mam had gathered, her jaw and shoulders clenched. Tada would do everything. He was master of this house, master of this family, master of all, while God was with him. He would suffer no other hand to help. Leah handed him the candle as he shooed them from the parlour and shut the door again.

In the darkness of the kitchen, Mam gave a single sob. Leah took her hand.

Daylight was strong when Tada emerged again. He was wiping his hands. 'I've redressed the wound. It is nothing, Mary. Nothing to fuss about. Just a scratch as he said.'

'Let me see it,' said Mam. An expressionless request.

'No! He's a man. He doesn't want you or any woman fussing over his privates. Don't shame him, woman! He'll be fine. He's taken some cordial. The fever is already subsiding.'

'Can I see him?' asked Leah.

'In a while. It's sleep he needs, by God's mercy. We must let him rest for now, all of us.' Tada turned his back on the parlour door, to set an example. It was an injunction even he could not keep. In an hour he was back from the barn where he worked, making good solid furniture for the surrounding farms. He had to look in on his boy.

The rest of the family were gathered, pretending that they would be about their normal tasks as soon as they had been allowed to say good morning to Tom.

Tada opened the parlour door and they filed in. Leah struggled not to shiver as she entered the cold, tomb-like room with its smell of damp and disuse. Darkness seemed to well up from every corner, but then she saw Tom's eyes open, sleepily, and he managed a bewildered smile, his finger twitching in her direction. She crawled in between her parents and planted a kiss just by his ear. Though he looked hot, his skin was clammy against her lips.

'That will do,' said Tada. 'You have seen him and already he's better. Now be off to school. We cannot all be sitting around idly all day. And no earning punishments from the teacher to keep you behind. Be off.'

Sarah had hated school, itching to be free of it, but Leah loved it, and Frank was the same. It was one of the things that bound them together, the youngest surviving siblings, secret and safe at the bottom of the pile. They shared a questing curiosity, a hunger for learning and knowing and understanding. Even when he had been a mere toddler and she little more than one, she had recognised that secret flame and had appointed herself her baby brother's guardian and companion, protecting him from the irritation and impatience of their elders, whenever his interminable questions or curious fingers needed curbing. She'd kept him close and been his playmate, exploring the world around them and its intriguing complexities.

Frank, she thought, would one day be a scientist, or an explorer, or a professor. A great man, anyway. And she too would love to be something; a teacher, no doubt. School offered the path to such a destiny.

Today, however, neither of them had any wish to attend the schoolroom tucked behind the old church in the village. They trudged silently down to the footpath that offered a shortcut in dry weather across their fields and through the steep woods, to the chapel on the outskirts of the village.

In the secrecy of the woods, Frank halted. 'Is Tom going to die?'

'No!' For once, she hated his compulsion to ask questions. She turned her face upwards, suddenly screaming denial into the overhanging branches. 'No! Don't say that! Don't say anything.'

Frank was scared. Leah never screamed. Then he took her hand and they walked on silently together. At school, they both sat staring out of the window at the clouds, unable to concentrate. Betty Phillips, sitting next to Frank, took sly note of his inattentiveness, and her hand shot up to summon the teacher. Frank got a rap across the knuckles, twice – once for not listening, and once for yanking Betty's hair as soon as Miss Griffiths had turned away.

Leah, across the row, could do nothing. She had always been a model pupil, less easily bored by repetition than Frank. But today she couldn't concentrate any better than her brother. For the first time ever, she too had her knuckles rapped.

'What is this, Leah Owen? Are you ill, or determined to be as lazy and ill-informed as your sister Sarah? Again, please. Deduct five pence and three farthings from two shillings and thrupence.'

'One shilling, nine pence and a farthing, miss.'

'That's better. Pay attention from now on.'

But Leah could not. She could only picture Tom, lying in that cold musty room where Mamgu Owen had died.

33

When they were released at last, she grabbed Frank's hand at the gate and pulled him after her. 'Let's run.' He obeyed for a couple of paces, then dug his heels in, pulling back, forcing her to stop. 'Come on!'

'I don't want to run. I don't want to go home.'

She saw the fear in his eyes. She understood. But this time she couldn't stand by him. She had to get home to Tom. She released Frank's hand and ran on, the air catching in her throat, the hard earth of the path jarring her limbs, a stitch knitting in her side. She was panting as she approached the yard. The doors of the workshop stood open, its floor thick with sawdust and shavings, but there was no Tada within, busy with his saw or his plane. Fegi Fawr, the lopsided cow, was pushing against the gate from the grazing, her calf beside her, as if waiting for news.

Leah hurried into the house. Tada was there with Mam, Mary and Sarah. There was a strained silence, as if a torrent of words were piling up against a dam that was about to burst. Mam's eyes were fixed on the kettle, not seeing it, just fixed. Her lips were pinched together.

The girls were folded back against the wall, Sara quivering as ever, Mary casting her eyes down, her hands clasped. Tada stood tall, motionless.

Leah's entry must have broken a spell. Tada turned, his brows knitting, though he barely glanced at her. 'I am going for the medic,' he said. 'Leave him be.' He strode out, pushing Leah aside.

'Is Tom still bad?' asked Leah, her voice small and breathless. Sarah let out a squealing sob.

Mam's eyes were still fixed on the kettle. Then her head rose and her chin stiffened as she drew a deep shuddering breath. Seizing the kettle, she turned to the table, suddenly all energy and iron determination as she poured steaming water into a bowl. 'Mary, fetch down the comfrey salve. Sarah, give me the bandages, and towels.'

'Tada said we mustn't...' Mary's objections died as Mam's eyes stabbed her with a fury none of them had ever seen in this gentle, dutiful woman. A master greater than Tada was guiding her now. With trembling fingers and bated breath, quaking at their own defiance of their father's wishes, her daughters did as Mam bade. Leah, doing nothing, felt her insides freeze. Never, in all her life, had Mam ever disobeyed Tada's commands. Until now.

At Mam's nod, Mary opened the parlour door. That smell. Sweet sickliness to turn the stomach. The same as when Mamgu Owen had died.

They gathered at the door, watching Mam lean over the bed where Tom lay. His eyes were shut but his lips twitched. He was flushed, glistening with sweat, his skin mottled. Mam drew back the cover and began to lift his nightshirt. 'Shut the door,' she said.

Locked out, they stared at each other in silence. They heard Mam's involuntary scream, subsiding into a choking sob. 'Oh my son, my son.'

Oh Absalom, my son, my son, would I had died for thee.

Tom was going to die.

Tom couldn't die. It wasn't right. Leah wanted to scream. Instead she stood there motionless, knots tightening and tightening inside her.

A flash of sunlight as Frank came in. He looked at them, dried tears on his cheek but also the stinging red of a slap. 'Why is Tada on the horse?' he asked.

Mary found her voice at last. 'He has gone for the doctor.'

'Oh.' Frank's mouth opened for another question. Leah shook her head, and he stopped, small, close to tears. He sniffed, then sank down on the settle, stripped of the thin cushion that was stained with Tom's sweat and blood, and glanced hopelessly at the table. There was no sign of food, not even a crust of bread. He was seven: whatever the crisis overwhelming the family, food was a matter of supreme concern that could not be ignored.

Mary, with a sigh of exasperation, fetched down the loaf, spread it with dripping and cut him a slice. Frank tucked in greedily, though his eyes were glinting with tears.

Leah crouched on a stool to wait, and wait and wait, while Frank munched and Sarah snivelled. Mary, having brought out the bread, slipped automatically into preparation of their tea, clearing the table and wiping its boards. Leah didn't want any. She just wanted this all to go away. She wanted the gurgled moans from the parlour to stop. She wanted Tom to laugh again instead. That was all. Just laugh.

At last, the parlour door opened and Mam emerged, her cheeks wet. The bowl she carried was thick with blood and pus. She nodded to Leah who jumped up to open the outer door and let her out into the yard to empty the contents and rinse out the bowl.

'There's nothing I can do for him.' Doctor Hargreaves sniffed as he shut his bag. 'It's too late. The poison is in his blood. You should have called me sooner. You're a chapel man, are you not, Owen? All I can suggest is that you say your chapel prayers and ask God for a miracle.'

They stared at him in incomprehension, as if his English were truly a foreign language. There was no doctor in Llanolwen. Tada had ridden to the far side of Penbryn to fetch him, had stood waiting an hour, cap in hand, humbly like a landless man, while the doctor finished his tea, and all for this. Nothing.

'I'll send you my bill,' said Dr Hargreaves, picking up his hat and gloves. 'Prayer. It's your only hope.'

36

He was gone.

Mam breathed out, her voice strong, though it shook. 'He is right. Our hope is not in doctors or princes nor any man, but in the Lord. Men are fallible,' she raised her chin to Tada, 'but God is not. In Him is our only refuge.' She sank to her knees beside the bed. Her daughters and Frank followed suit. Tada finally bent his knees and dropped, face in his hands.

Leah prayed. She prayed harder than she had ever done. She bargained: she would never be bad again, never impatient or disobedient or inattentive. She recited the Lord's prayer over and over until the words became meaningless. She begged forgiveness; she shouldn't have pushed Megan Rice at school, shouldn't have lied about dropping the eggs, shouldn't have fallen asleep in chapel. The droning sermon came back to her. *Covenant of blood, the blood of the Son.* Don't think about blood. Think on God, His grace, His goodness, His forgiveness. He was a loving Father. He would not let Tom die.

He let his own Son die.

She couldn't pray any more. Her mind was blank. Numb as the grave.

Tom died.

In the dark moonless night, his gasping breath ceased, his body shuddered and was still. His father was gripping his hand, his mother was stroking his brow.

One strangled cry escaped from Mam, before she shut her eyes and raised her face to heaven, but Tada was convulsed with silent sobs. Frank whimpered, Sarah began to wail and Mary sniffed convulsively, but Leah did nothing. She couldn't move, couldn't think, couldn't believe. Wouldn't. It all made no sense. She stared at the wall, at the fading stencilled dots on the yellowing plaster.

There was a crack. She had not seen it before. It was the faintest hairline, running down from the ceiling, a thing of no consequence but it was a crack in the fabric of the house. A crack in the world, which had swallowed Tom and closed behind him.

Mam rose to her feet, a shudder running through her. She, who was so much shorter than Tada, looked down on her husband. 'So it is over. I must prepare him. Am I permitted to touch him now? Now that my son is dead?'

Suddenly, Leah wanted to run. She had to run. She bolted for the door, out through the kitchen, into the yard and through the owl-haunted darkness, making for the other side of the crack, where Tom would be. But he wasn't: he was gone forever, and God hadn't saved him; He had done nothing. She hated God, who was cruel, not loving, and she would never trust Him again. She howled into the dark and stamped the cobbles and beat her chest, screaming like a petulant infant. But nothing would bring Tom back.

The Reverend Williams called, because he must, because it was his duty. Sick in her stifling grief, Leah watched him exuding that same impression of wanting to be somewhere else as he did in chapel, the words streaming out of him without passion or meaning.

'Mrs Owen, I grieve for your pain, but we must all submit to the Lord's will.'

'Amen,' whispered Mam.

'Owen, the Lord has tried you bitterly with this terrible tragedy, even as Job was tried, but I trust that you will keep the faith and will answer, as did the righteous Job, "The Lord giveth and the Lord taketh away. Blessed be the name of the Lord." And the Lord says to you, even out of the whirlwind of your grief, "Gird up now thy loins like a man." Do not fight the will of the Lord but let His grace be upon you.'

With the Reverend Williams, another man had come, another minister by his clothing though Leah had never seen him before. He was taller, young; not yet thirty, his dark eyes gleaming with compassion as they fell upon her, crouched in her corner. He crouched beside her and took her hands.

'I see, little one, that you are lost in grief for your brother. He was all the world to you, was he not?' She sniffed and nodded. 'But think of this, my child, was he suffering on his death bed? Did he feel pain and sickness and terrors? Did he know disappointment in his life, or the burden of hard labour? Did he ever go hungry or thirsty or weep for want of anything? Oh, I know he will have done, for we all do in this life. But only think, he has passed through that terrible dark gate into the light. Our heavenly father has released him from his suffering and brought him to a place where there is no pain or disappointment, no burden or want, only glory and joy. So we must wipe away the tears that are for our own selfish desires, and rejoice for him.' He smiled, his dark eyes full of sympathy, his voice melodious and full of reassurance.

Leah, looking into his eyes, felt a great stone lift from her chest.

The Reverend Williams' stream of dry piety ceased as he turned to regard his companion with blinking desperation, as if he had lost his place in his sermon. 'Owen, Mrs Owen, allow me to present the Reverend Matthew Vaughan, who will shortly take my place among our Christian community at Beulah.'

Mam forced a smile, rigid with pain. 'You are very welcome, sir.'

Tada looked at Mam. Almost. Not quite at her face. 'Shall we not offer our guests refreshments, woman?'

Matthew Vaughan had risen from Leah's side and raised his hands. 'Sister, I beg of you to forgive my intrusion at such a time. I came, as your new pastor, not to be tended by you but to tender any comfort that I can. If you will permit, shall we pray together, not for your son, for I have no doubt he walks now in Elysian fields, rejoicing, beyond the need of our prayers, but let us beseech the Lord to bring comfort and peace to you who are left abandoned on this barren stony shore.'

'Please. Pray with us,' said Mam, seizing his hand, and, one by one, they all knelt, heads bowed, leaving the Reverend Williams wordless and meaningless in the gloom.

Leah wandered down to the meadow to imagine Elysian fields, full of lilies and daisies and buttercups, and Tom running through them into sunlight. It was better than cities built of precious stones. She was glad Matthew Vaughan had come. She loved Matthew Vaughan.

1884

Frank should have known better. He should have kept the book out of sight. It was nothing wicked, only a volume of *The Accomplished Tutor*, heavy and stained, scattered with notes from Matthew Vaughan's pen and much older hands. If Frank had kept it in the settle box, wrapped in a shirt, Tada might not have noticed it. But there it was, lying for all to see, on the table.

'What is this?' Tada held it up as if it reeked of sin.

'A book,' said Frank. It wasn't that he was deliberately trying to sound insolent, but he succeeded all the same.

'You stole it!'

'I did not!'

'Do you dare to lie to me? This is not a school book for a boy of your age. You don't have the ability to read or understand. You are a mere jackdaw. You stole it. Admit it, boy! Admit it!'

'I did not! The Reverend Vaughan lent it to me!' Frank was already bracing himself for the inevitable blow, which caught him on the ear.

'Thou shalt not steal. Thou shalt not bear false witness. Wicked sinner, must I beat the evil out of you?'

'No, you'll beat it further in!' Frank couldn't resist increasing the aggravation, though he was weeping and cringing from the welts of the strap Tada was wielding.

'Heathen ingrate, you think to make a mockery of me!'

Mam didn't intervene. Once, without challenging Tada's role as head of the household, she would have offered gentle counsel that

41

he would heed, but these days she never spoke up, as if life had become too dark, too doom-laden to be worth fighting. So she said nothing as Tada's wild blows rained down.

Leah couldn't bear to watch. She ran up the stairs and through to the raftered room she shared with her sisters. She too was guilty. More guilty because she must have realised it was wrong, or why would she have concealed her book? And it was all down to her whispered complaints to the minister. She was ten. A year ago she would have thought this meant nothing. A year ago she and Frank had gone happily to school together, expecting to do so for four or five years more. Tada had paid their fees without a murmur, happy that two of his brood should be educated just like gentlemen's children. But in the black wake of Tom's death, Tada had taken against it with a vengeance. Llanolwen's was a church school, halfway to heathen, Tada declared, and he wanted no further dealings with it. Once Leah turned ten there was to be no more schooling for her. He'd have taken Frank out too, but for the threatened shame of the attendance officer. Sunday school at the chapel should be enough for both of them, said Tada.

It was at Sunday School that Leah had murmured her burning disappointment, and their new minister, Matthew Vaughan, had understood her plight. He had offered her a little tutoring and lent her volumes from his own boyhood stock, school books and even novels to feed her hungry mind. Leah had devoured *Mary Jones, the Welsh Girl without a Bible*, as well as *Uncle Tom's Cabin*, and now she was working through *Settlers in Canada*, though it was less easy, being in English. It was such an exquisite luxury to be able to disappear into words and worlds. Frank had begged books too, bored with the limitations of the village classroom, and Matthew, imagining such a bright boy surely destined for college, had obliged. But now, it seemed, Tada was set on forbidding this too, and if she

42

didn't confess, would Frank be left to bear all the punishment alone? She had appointed herself his guardian, so she must speak up.

Clasping the book to her, like a mother saying a wrenching farewell to her baby, Leah descended the stairs, where Tada was standing over the cringing boy.

'Why was I cursed with a son so lost to righteousness that he'd steal from another man's shelves?'

'Tada.' Leah's small voice was enough to draw his attention, though his arm remained raised. She proffered her book. 'It's true, Tada. The Reverend Vaughan lent him that book. See, he lent me one too. We did not steal.'

Tada stared at her, his beard twitching, his eyes...they were mad eyes, she thought, terrified.

'We meant no harm by it, Tada. The minister brings books to Sunday School and lets us choose.'

Tada took the book from her and she saw his hand was shaking. 'What business does he have lending my children such books as these?'

'It was because I am not allowed to attend school any more, Tada. That is all. Tada, if I could only go...'

Tada's finger was raised to silence her. 'Stop, child!' He turned and disappeared into the parlour. A moment later he returned, holding the great family Bible from which he read to them every night. 'Here!' He thrust it, open, towards her. 'Read this! Can you do so? Read!'

Shaking as much as he, she read aloud, her voice trembling as she sought to get the words right, for nothing would infuriate Tada more than impious stumbling on the Holy scriptures. 'Blessed is the man that walketh not in the counsel of the ungodly, nor standeth in the way of sinners, nor sitteth in the seat of the scornful. But his delight is in the law of the Lord...'

Tada snapped the Bible shut and finished the verse himself, his voice thundering around the room. 'And in his law doth he meditate day and night.' He glared at Leah; at Frank, whose arm was over his head, at Sarah, trying to shrink out of sight into a corner, at Mary who sat impassively with pinched lips, at Mam who stared blankly at the book in his hands. 'This is all the schooling that you need! To read the Word of the Lord and obey his commands. The rest is worthless vanity and idolatry.'

Leah thought of *Settlers in Canada* and *Uncle Tom's Cabin*. It was true they were not scripture but were they really idolatry? Were Frank's sums mere vanity? But there was one command the Bible had drummed into her from birth: children, obey your parents. She could not argue.

Settlers in Canada and *The Accomplished Tutor* were not seen again in Cwmderwen. Leah didn't know whether Tada had locked them up, destroyed them or returned them, with a rebuke, to the minister, but she knew that she ached for the opportunity to read something, anything. Something other than the Bible, though she would probably be struck down for her impiety. Struck down by Tada, if he suspected she had not submitted quietly to his law.

Frank did not submit quietly. When the truth sank in that he too would not be permitted to attend school beyond his tenth birthday, he sulked, resisted and he earned himself more beatings. In sheer petulance, he took to truanting from the little schooling that remained to him, asking what was the point? At Sunday school, Matthew Vaughan smiled sadly at them, offering sympathy but no more lessons in mathematics or geography, so Leah knew Tada had spoken to him. When Frank realised this, he refused to attend Sunday School any more.

'I don't want to learn the Bible! I hate it! I hate God!'

'Don't speak like that, Frank. It's wicked.'

'Well, so it is, but I don't care. Being good never did any good.'

'It might. If you behaved better with Tada, he might not get so angry.'

'That's not true. It doesn't matter how I behave. He hates me. And I hate him!' Frank ran off, punching the air, leaving Leah to ponder. She understood Frank's anger but how could it help to behave in a way that merely provoked greater wrath in Tada? Their father had changed in the year since Tom had died. He no longer laughed or relished life. He no longer sang hymns in a voice that made the rafters ring. Now they rang with the roaring of his rage. When he was not locked alone in the parlour with his Bible, he frowned and preached and found fault and beat. He had rarely used his belt or stick before, except for the gravest misdemeanours, but now he wielded them at the slightest irritation, with that mad look in his eyes. There must be a way to win him round, to bring back the father that Leah loved. If she were good, if she were obedient and obliging and willing in everything, surely he would calm at last and listen. Frank would never gain anything with his resentment and sulks, but she would play a different game.

Yes, she would be good. She would be ready, she would pre-empt his commands and even his wishes. He would see how good and obedient she was and he would love her again as he used to do. He would listen to her humble reasoning. If she had proper schooling, she'd say, she could become a teacher herself, and teach others to read and obey the word of God. Tada would see there would be no sin in that. He would answer her prayer, which was not wholly selfish but a prayer for both her and Frank. School could not be so very wicked just because the vicar came to catechise them once in a while.

Leah balanced the milk ladle gingerly as she released the gate into Dark Field, for fear more of the already tepid tea would slop out. She had lost too much at the last gate. Tongue between her teeth, she held it steady as she nudged the gate closed behind her. Tada neither requested nor expected tea to be brought to him, so surely he would see how much care she took for his welfare – if he were not in one of those tormented moods beyond reason.

Then she saw him, standing at the bottom of the field, his face to the sky, his hands raised. Leah walked on, picking her way with care, determined not to spill another drop, but suddenly unwilling to arrive at her destination. He was never in a mood to listen, she knew, when the fever of biblical rage was on him. In a moment his brain could turn and he'd become a monster of fury and howling grief. This was as it had been since Tom. But perhaps he was not raging, just praying as he used to, full of joy and triumph.

She was in earshot:

'...compassed me with gall and travail. He hath set me in dark places, as they that be dead of old. He hath hedged me about, that I cannot get out: He hath made my chain heavy. When I cry and shout, He shutteth out my prayer.'

There was an agony in Tada's voice that distressed Leah beyond measure, so much so that the tea slopped again and she gave a stifled gasp. It brought him round, and his face was a picture of grief and desolation. Then his eyes shut, he lowered his hands and was still for a moment. When he opened his eyes again, he looked on his youngest daughter with a bleak ghost of the affection he had once freely shown. A ghost of a far-off memory. 'Every good gift and every perfect gift is from above, and cometh down from the Father. My child. My last blessing.'

46

Leah offered the milk ladle nervously. Did he mean the tea was a good and perfect gift? She suspected he meant her, and his tortured love suddenly overwhelmed her, oppressing her. She was not fit to bear it. Nor was she his last blessing. That was Frank, surely.

Tada drank deeply, then handed the ladle back. 'You are a comfort to me, daughter, yea and will be so unto death, that I know.'

'Yes Tada.' She was never easy when he spoke like the Holy Bible.

'Though I have been tried like Job, still my quiver is not empty. See, daughter!'

Before Leah knew what was happening, he had swept her up and was holding her aloft, like an offering about to be laid on the altar, the ladle and its contents flung aside. She quaked with fear.

'See, Leah, our land that the Lord has given us. A covenant.' He was shaking. She could feel shivers rippling through the hands that held her. 'A covenant sealed in blood! Because thou hast not withheld thy son!'

'Tada...' Leah was gripped so hard she could barely breathe. But then his grip was released, so suddenly that she was dropped to the ground, stumbling onto her knees as Tada roared above her.

'Forgive not their iniquity, neither blot out their sin from thy sight! Get off my land! You and your foul breed will not step foot here!'

Leah picked herself up, bewildered, as Tada strode to the lower gate into the meadow. Trembling, she hurried after him.

The footpath that wound down through woods from the chapel crossed their meadow into Castell Mawr land, towards Plas Malgwyn. It was a path that many of the Llanolwen folk used, going to pay their rent, or to work at the big house, like Sarah who was now employed in the dairy there. The path had always been an afront to Tada. He resented trespassers on Owen land, but she had never heard him explode in such anger about it before.

47

Then she saw who the present trespasser was and understood his fury, though it turned her cold. Jacob John, the quarry manager, hands in pocket, pipe in mouth, was strolling across from the stile at the bottom of the woods as if he owned the earth he trod on.

Tada was over the gate now, striding towards him, fist raised, and Jacob John stopped in his tracks, taking his pipe from his mouth in a bullish gesture of appeasement. 'Now, man.'

'Get off my land, Jacob John!'

'So I mean to do, if you let me pass, but I have as good a right to use this path as you, as well you know.'

'I'll not have your murdering feet touch my soil!'

'You call me a murderer?'

'You slew my son!'

'Look to yourself for that sin, man. No!' Jacob raised a hand to catch Tada's wrist as a blow came at him.

Leah's terror doubled. Tada was taller, but Jacob John was twice as wide, all brawn, a famous pugilist who boasted that he could flatten any man in the parish with one hand tied behind his back.

'No,' repeated Jacob. 'I'll not fight a man still crippled by his grief, but you will not bar my way.' He was past Tada, whistling back at his son Eli who was trailing behind, only just clambering over the stile. 'See to your own business, man, and let me do mine.' He strode on, pipe back in his mouth.

Tada roared after him, 'Deliver up their children to the famine, oh Lord, and pour out their blood by the force of the sword! Let their men be put to death; let their young men be slain by the sword in battle!' As Eli loped round him, smirking, he struck out, smiting Eli's ear and sending him flying.

Jacob, almost at the next stile, turned, hands on hips, legs apart. 'You'd do better to provoke your God than provoke me, Thomas Owen. Or is that what you're doing? Eli! Get up. A knock on the head never hurt you. Come on, lad, and leave the old fool to his wittering.'

Eli scrambled to his feet, shooting a look of poisonous loathing at Tada, but he stepped well clear and ran after his father.

Tada was left standing, shuddering as if the earth quaked beneath him. Hopping over the stile onto Castell Mawr land, Jacob hauled his son over and pushed him out of the way as another figure appeared. A boy.

Frank, coming back from some errand to Sarah at Plas Mawr, stopped short of the stile, reading something dire in Eli's face, but Jacob picked Frank up and whirled him over the stile into the meadow. He set him down and leaned over to ruffle his hair, saying something that made him laugh.

Why did he have to laugh, thought Leah, in agony. Frank so rarely had anything to laugh about these days; it should have been a joy to hear him, but nothing in Tada's present state would be so certain to arouse his anger.

It didn't matter that it was an innocent laugh. Dawdling through their meadow, Frank was so absorbed in something that rustled or ran in the long grass that he hadn't noticed Leah and Tada yet. But then he raised his head and saw his father waiting. He paused in his stride, trying to read the situation, figure out what he'd done wrong this time, his smile twisting into hostility. Tada was motionless and silent, so Frank must have concluded there was no especial cause to fear. He approached them, breaking into a run and holding a jar aloft triumphantly, his eyes on Leah as he came to a halt, gasping for breath. 'Sarah sent some dripping and she said there's some good beef in it.' His grin of delight wavered. He was close enough now to feel the force building up and about to explode in the rigid figure beside them.

'That's good,' said Leah. 'Run home and—'

The stillness broke so suddenly that it almost stopped her heart, though she had been expecting it. As if galvanised by lightning, Tada was beating his son, thrashing and thrashing, his roars of denunciation drowning out the boy's screams.

'We wrestle not against flesh and blood, but against principalities, against powers, against the rulers of the darkness of this world.'

'Tada! Tada!' cried Leah, trying to catch his arm, but he thrust her away.

'You cannot drink the cup of the Lord and the cup of demons too! The devil was cast into the lake of fire and brimstone, where the beast and the false prophet are, and shall be tormented day and—'

'Thomas Owen! Hold your hand!'

It must surely be the voice of God thundering at them. Leah looked up, expecting to see the heavens opening, but it was the minister, the Reverend Vaughan, his hand gripping Tada's raised arm.

Tada made one furious effort to release himself, but the minister's grip was unrelenting. Tada gasped, like a man waking from a nightmare or an evil spell, uncertain where he was. Then he frowned, but before he could speak, the Reverend Vaughan was addressing him again, his voice as forceful as a river in full flood.

'How dare you speak the word of God with hatred in your heart and violence in your hand! On your knees, man, and beg forgiveness of our Heavenly Father before He strikes you down into the very lake of fire and brimstone you speak of.'

Tada trembled more violently than ever, then collapsed and buried his face in his hands, shaking with sobs.

Matthew Vaughan stepped back, looking down on him, invested with divine authority, ready to play an angel of vengeance again, but Leah saw him release a sigh of relief and silently mouth a prayer of thanks that Tada had fallen on his knees and not in rage on the minister.

Vaughan steadied his breathing, caught Leah's eyes and gave her a look of sorrowful pity before gesturing quietly for her to go.

She grabbed Frank's wrist as he crouched and cried, pulling him up and snatching up the jar of dripping that he had dropped. 'Come. Quickly!' she whispered and they ran, blindly, clumsily, until they were at the gate into Dark Field. She went to open it, but Frank was already scrambling over. There was blood running from his nose and from a gash on his forehead.

'Take this!' said Leah, passing him the jar.

Frank took the jar, stared at it, then hurled it in wild fury into the trees. It smashed and splattered among the stones and he was gone, to seek whatever comfort Mam could be roused to offer him.

Leah looked back. Tada was still on his knees, face still in his hands, but the Reverend was kneeling with him, talking, talking, talking.

Praying. Leah wanted to pray too. The only prayer she could think of was 'Thank you, God, for giving us the Reverend Vaughan, for we have nothing else.'

THE WEEDING

1887

Leah wandered down to the meadow, with a vague idea of being useful. With Mary and Mam bustling in the house, she felt superfluous. At thirteen, and with any hope of a future as a teacher long abandoned, she had supposed she would be sent to work at Plas Malgwyn, like Sarah, but Tada had decided he'd have none of that for her. The landed gentry were a godless lot and their ways were not the ways of the righteous. He was not a landless labourer who must go seeking employment for himself or his from such as the Herberts. He had land, twenty-four acres, one rood and eight perches of it, and his daughter would stay put where she belonged.

Leah was thankful Sarah had been at Plas Malgwyn when Tada had said this. He had had no qualms about dispatching his middle daughter to work amongst the heathens. It hurt Leah, on her sister's behalf, that Sarah was so disregarded. Tada paid her no attention but paid too much to Leah. It was inexplicable and troubling, but then so much about Tada was inexplicable and troubling if she let herself dwell on it.

She must not dwell on it but devote herself to helping on the farm instead. She fetched and carried and cared for the poultry, churned the butter, weeded the garden, helped to harness the horse. Now she could surely assist with the hay. She pushed open the gate, stepping from the cool shadow of the trees into bright burning sun. The long lush grass, mown yesterday, was already turning to crisp pale gold, the jewels of buttercups, clover and knapweed fading to brown. On the far side of the meadow, Tada was tossing the hay, aided by David George and Amos Absalom, for the Castell Mawr hay was already turned and their neighbours were ready as ever to assist the Owens.

The Reverend Vaughan had volunteered his assistance too, wielding his rake in shirt sleeves and straw hat, but when he caught sight of Leah at the gate, he straightened, waved, and snatched the opportunity for a moment's rest. He joined her by the hedgerow, dropping down onto the bank – where an overhanging elder offered a little shade – and stretching his arms.

'Your father will castigate me for the sin of idleness, I know.'

'You are not idle, Matthew.' Leah settled beside him, hugging her knees. He always addressed her as if she were his little sister, so she spoke to him with similar familiarity. He was the brother she missed. 'If you were idle, you wouldn't be here helping with the hay. The Reverend Williams never did.' She couldn't imagine their old minister, dusty and wiping the sweat from his brow in a hayfield. In times of heat and business he had always hidden himself away in his cool study, with books that dried out his soul, and no one had ever seen him without his tightly buttoned black jacket and high collar.

'Ah, but I expect he was not accustomed to such work,' said Matthew. 'Whereas I was brought up on a farm like this, and I know that when the hay is to be turned and wise women like old Mary Jane Lewis tell us their bones predict a turn in the weather, there is no time to be wasted.' He drew a deep breath, raising his face to the sun. 'Yes, I was raised further north, but ours was a farm very much like this.'

'But you never thought to be a farmer,' Leah said. 'You were educated.' She couldn't keep the wistfulness from her voice.

'Well, yes I was.' Matthew glanced at her, understanding, and patted her hand. 'It is true, my father set great store by it. Perhaps he thought to make me a gentleman, but you see I am not, for all my learning.' He smiled. 'Just a simple labourer for the Lord.'

'You studied at college,' said Leah.

'At Bala, yes, but that was not from school. I was put to work in business first, as a shipping clerk, as my brother is still. But the Lord sought me out and drew me to a different path.'

'Which led you here.'

He smiled. 'So far. And after this, it is in the Lord's hands. I trust my loving heavenly father to guide my steps.'

'Do you ever question God's will, Matthew?'

'His will, no. Only the wilfulness of His creation.'

'Mam says we should question nothing, only obey and find salvation in submission.'

'Never question the Word of God, Leah. Obey it with reverence and joy. But our heavenly father gave us curiosity and judgement, and they are not sins. Never cease to enquire into the world and question the ways of men. Only God is infallible.'

'He commands us to obey our fathers.'

Matthew opened his mouth as if he would respond with an alternative command. Then he thought better of it. 'Yes, he does.'

Leah gazed out across the meadow. Kites were wheeling overhead, searching for prey that the workers had disturbed. She saw one stoop, a blaze of amber cruelty. It was impossible to be in this meadow, with Matthew Vaughan, and not remember that day when Tada had been brought to his knees by the minister. Some wild madness in him had passed that day, and a semblance of sanity had returned, but there was still a darkness on Cwmderwen that no prayers had yet lifted. A cruelty in the soil and in the air. 'Is our heavenly father always loving?'

'Always,' said Matthew emphatically.

'Mrs Price says you speak too much of God's love and not enough of his stern judgement.'

Matthew's lips twitched, trying not to smile. 'I have heard her say it.'

'She says you are too young and green to serve. Ministers should have white beards, or they cannot be trusted.'

'Others doubtless think it too.'

'Oh no, only Mrs Price.' It wasn't true. Tada said it too. 'Nobody minds what Mrs Price says. They call her a sour old biddy.'

'That, Leah, is not a very loving or Christian thing to say, is it?'

'Is loving and Christian the same thing?'

'I believe so.' Matthew rose on his knees to face her and took her hands. 'Come now, my wise and solemn little sister. I know you are still nursing old pains. Are troubles at home no better?'

She looked into his dark eyes, hoping that she would see some sort of revelation there. She found none elsewhere. 'I don't know.'

'Tell me. Does your father still have savage fits of rage?'

'No. Not any more. But things have never gone back to the way they were, before.' She didn't need to say before Tom died. Everything was before or after that. 'There is no... I don't know.' She lied. She did know. There was no love in the house, that was it. The madness of grief had passed, but in its place had come a cold righteousness, a religion that was cold and harsh in its judgements, without any of the joy that Matthew found in it. All her life, the Bible and prayers and chapel had been at the heart of their family, but once it had seemed comfortable, a warm embrace.

It had been Mam who had been the consistently pious one, the ardent witness to God's grace, the bright unwavering torch that others turned to for reassurance of their own salvation. Tada, in those days, had been correct in his belief and practice, but sometimes Leah had thought it was as much out of respect for Mam as anything else. She'd heard it told, by Mrs George, that Tada had been a sinner in his youth, scarcely better than Jacob John, and had attended a great prayer meeting merely out of curiosity, but he had been so smitten there with young Mary Eynon that she had brought him to the Lord.

That was a time sealed in the past. With Tom's death, everything had changed. Mam had fallen silent, her prayers constant but kept to herself. It was Tada who had become the fire-breathing prophet, the Bible ever on his tongue. His readings kept them from their beds into the dark hours and his catechisms had them quaking with fear of Hell.

'Is God anger as well as love?'

Matthew drew a deep breath. 'God is all things, Leah, but most of all He is forgiveness, and that is the greatest wonder of all, for He has so much grievous sin to forgive in all of us and yet He never fails.'

'Tada doesn't forgive.'

Matthew studied his hands. He understood perfectly.

'Still he will not forgive Jacob John.'

'I know.'

'I know all the psalms about wicked enemies perishing, because Tada recites them whenever he sees Jacob or Eli. He accuses them of killing my brother.'

Matthew heaved another sigh.

Leah swallowed tears. 'I saw the pick fall. It was an accident, but Tada speaks as if Satan were in them, guiding their hands.'

'Leah, I think you understand well enough – I know you do – that your father's anger, against Jacob John and against fate, secretly perhaps against God Himself, is born of his own guilt.'

'Because he would not let Mam tend Tom?'

Matthew nodded. 'Your father is master in his house. That is a good thing, Leah. It is as the good book commands. But sometimes men accustomed to command find themselves overwhelmed by

59

their own certainties, and they don't know how to give way. They become fixed on a course from which they cannot turn, and the consequences can be too bitter to bear, so they lash out. They find a target for their wrath, and sometimes they are unjust in their judgements. Your father, I hope and pray, will finally come through his valley of the shadow, into the arms of Jesus, whose death has redeemed us all.'

'The covenant of blood.'

'It's a covenant of love, Leah. Ah,' Matthew looked to the gate and rose on one knee, as Mary appeared, with a covered basket, 'Miss Owen, if that contains what I think, I thank you from the bottom of my heart.'

Leah watched her sister's expression change from sharp irritation on finding Leah there before her, to blushing, simpering modesty at the preacher's words. There was scarcely an unmarried woman in the parish who didn't blush and simper at sight of Matthew Vaughan, but poor Mary's face, thought Leah, was not designed for simpering. Her blushes were blotchy crimson. At eighteen, she was short like her mother and growing stout like Sarah. She seldom opened her mouth, at least at home, but her eyes were speaking volumes as they fixed on Matthew. A dog's eyes, all soppy devotion. She set the basket down beside him and pulled back the muslin cover to reveal bread and cheese, a jug of lemonade and tin mugs.

'Where would we be without your concern for our welfare, Mary?' asked Matthew. 'I know I would be hard put to manage all my duties in Llanolwen without your inestimable aid. You are truly a God-send at the Sunday School, veritably my right hand.'

It was a generous thing to say, Leah knew, because Mary, for all her diligence, taught her lessons by rote, with many mistakes, because she could barely read.

The crimson blotches flared up with a vengeance, as Mary busied herself with the bread. 'I was delayed, searching for Frank. That naughty boy is not to be found and he should be here, helping with the hay as he was instructed.'

'Ah. I believe he is with some other boys down in the river.'

'He gives no thought to his duty or the family. He is a wicked sinful child.'

Leah had never heard Mary manage so many words in one go. There was a desperation in her voice, as if she had so much to spend and little time in which to spend it. But her prim disparagement of their young brother wasn't best calculated to win Matthew's approval.

'He's a boy,' he said. 'I know, none better, the lure of a cool river on a hot summer's day for a boy who would rather not be tending to his tasks. At his age, I fear I would have done the same.'

Mary's face worked through confused contortions. 'He will feel my father's ire tonight.'

'I fear so.' Matthew glanced at Leah as he spoke. 'Francis bears a heavy burden.'

'He would not anger my father so much if he were less idle,' said Mary, trying unsuccessfully to keep the complaint from her tone. 'We are all burdened with duties.'

Matthew nodded, not arguing, but Leah understood what he meant by Frank's heavy burden. Nothing Frank did would ever be right, because he was not Tom. Merely by breathing, he provoked Tada, and so, knowing he was doomed, he embraced provocation. On his remaining son, Tada wielded the rod as if its correction would summon Tom back to life.

Leah longed for her mother to intervene, but though Mam's frigid passivity, born of eviscerating grief, had passed, she had never regained her joyful certainty in the goodness of life. Joy was for the next world, which she awaited in patient silence, and if injustice befell her children, that was simply the way of an imperfect world. She embraced Frank with a weary sigh when he was reduced to tears, and tended his bruises and cuts, but said nothing against the punishments Tada administered with cold certainty of righteousness.

'Frank is not Tom,' said Leah sadly.

'No, he is not!' Mary sniffed. 'Not at all like Tom. Frank is all wilfulness and defiance, while Tom was all obedience and respect.'

'Tom could anger Tada too,' said Leah. 'When he wanted to be a soldier, not a farmer.'

'Oh that was nothing. Just a little silliness. He understood his duty well enough.'

Matthew took the tin mug that Mary handed to him, and a hunk of bread and cheese, raised his face to the blue heaven to murmur a word of thanks, then thoughtfully swirled the lemonade before drinking. 'A soldier understands duty. It makes demands on all of us, sometimes so contrary to our own wishes that we ache for wishing otherwise, but still we answer the call and do our duty, do we not, Mary? Leah?'

'Yes,' said Mary, in a curiously flat tone, before returning to her grievance, suddenly unleashed as if she had been a chatterer all her life. It was Matthew who wrought this. 'But duty is something Frank will never understand. He is naughty and careless and disobedient. No wonder Tada has to beat him.'

Matthew frowned sadly. 'I am sorry to hear that, Mary.'

She was confused. 'But the Bible says, doesn't it, that he who spares his rod hates his son?'

'Yes, that is true. But it also warns us that children driven to anger are discouraged. And I would not like to see Frank discouraged any further. I will consider it a task well done if I can bring some healing between father and son before I move on from Llanolwen.'

'Do you think God will call you to leave us?' asked Leah, drawing his attention. She felt bereft at the thought of losing him, but that was nothing to the anguish that Mary exhibited while his head was turned.

'I shall let you into a secret, little Leah.' Matthew smiled wistfully. 'I have for some time now felt a call to missionary work.'

'Will you go to India?' asked Leah, feeling a stir of excitement. Anything far away and other seemed thrilling to her.

'I believe God speaks to me of China.'

Mary's anguish turned to outright horror.

'That is the other side of the world!' said Leah quickly, pitying for her sister.

'Indeed it is, but all the world is held in God's hand.'

Mary's blotches had faded to pale grey. She said, 'I have sometimes dreamed of doing mission work in China.'

'Have you, truly?' Matthew turned back to her with delighted surprise. 'It is a noble calling, but not for the faint-hearted.'

'I am not faint-hearted,' said Mary.

'No, indeed. But you must be certain, Mary, that it is God guiding you towards this goal. We shall pray together about it, and if you are certain that it is His will, have no doubt, sister, that He will bring it about, and a way will be found.'

'Amen!' Mary mouthed, although no strangled sound managed to escape her lips.

Leah bled for her.

'You have come in good time, Mary!' David George was advancing on them in a halo of dust. 'We are dying of thirst.'

Tada was behind him. 'Lay out the cups, daughters, and then be back to your mother. There is no place for idleness on this farm, or the Devil will find use for you.'

In silence, Mary and Leah spread out the contents of the basket, poured the lemonade and, with a bob of farewell, retreated to the gate.

'You don't want to go to China,' said Leah, as they crossed into the rising pasture of Dark Field.

'You don't know what I want!' snapped Mary. There were unshed tears in her voice, swilling in her head. 'I've always wanted to be a missionary's... to do God's work. You know nothing about it.'

'Matthew—'

'The Reverend Vaughan! You have no right to be so familiar. You should show respect.'

'He doesn't mind that I call him Matthew.'

'That is because you are a child. He treats you as a child.'

No he doesn't, thought Leah, but she said nothing.

'He has asked me to pray with him, about China, about my vocation.' Mary, usually so self-contained, was choking as hope and terror fought it out within her.

'He thinks that you—'

'Hold your tongue! You don't know what he thinks. You know nothing about it. You're just a silly little child. Be quiet.'

So Leah was quiet, but she still felt sorry for Mary.

Mary had always been diligent in her assistance at the Sunday School, yearning for Matthew's favour. Now her efforts doubled. She stayed often to pray with him. If he met her on the footpath or the lane they would walk together, talking earnestly. She brought home pamphlets that she could barely read, though Leah devoured them, learning about missions and the faraway places that had always fascinated her.

Leah prayed that God would tell Matthew to stay in Llanolwen. She prayed that Mary would not be hurt or shamed.

God never answered her prayers.

In February, icy rain washed away the last grimy snow from the roots of the hedgerows, leaving even the top road a quagmire through which they had to wade, skirts lifted immodestly high. But still they attended chapel, Mam and Tada herding their children as if they were loving man and wife like any other. Not stern guilt-ridden man and silent resentful wife. They wiped their boots at the door and Tada made his way to his place in the big seat with the other elders, while the rest of them filed in to their accustomed pew. The Georges were already ensconced in the one behind them.

'We have a stranger amongst us,' wheezed Mrs George, as they settled themselves. She nodded to the front pew, occupied by a woman they didn't know. At least, they didn't know the grey bonnet bowed over a bible and the grey shawl across narrow sloping shoulders, which was all they could see of her. In a community where everyone knew everyone and any outsider had the congregation twittering like startled hens, her presence challenged their worried curiosity, but she didn't stir a muscle until the Reverend Vaughan climbed to the pulpit and raised his hands, his face aglow.

'Beloved brothers and sisters in Christ.'

Then the bonnet rose in his direction, and so did everyone else, after the briefest glimpse of an aquiline nose and a grey gloved hand patting the shawl into place.

Matthew's readings, as ever, were full of joy, his sermon, unscripted, full of passion, filling the chapel with the spirit of the Lord, but though he talked of love and grace and forgiveness, Leah sat and listened with a creeping sense of sorrow, as if instinct were speaking louder than his ringing voice. At last, his final prayer over, he looked down on them with a smile of pure delight.

'And now, my brothers and sisters, I must share with you my news. I have, two days since, received a summons for which I have

65

been waiting with, alas, less patience than God demanded of me. I am to leave you...' He had to pause while the grunting and murmuring and twittering died down. 'Though I will ever hold you all in my heart and my prayers and will never forget the kind reception you gave me, a stranger in your midst, or the trust you have placed in me these last four years, I must say farewell. I have been summoned to engage in the evangelisation of the world in this generation. I am to serve the Lord by joining a mission in China.'

Again he had to pause, to allow the swell of alarmed exclamations and explosions of astonishment to die down. Leah heard Mary draw in a deep breath and hold it.

As the hubbub subsided, Matthew's smile broadened. 'And I would like to share with you, too, the joyous news that I shall be accompanied, in the Lord's work, by my beloved sister in Christ, Miss Emma Davies, from Rhosarian, who has consented to be my wife and soul companion in this great work.'

The grey bonnet bowed modestly.

'I hope—'

'No!' Mary stood up, the pew shaking as she did so. All eyes turned to her, in time to see her drop in a dead faint.

As Sarah and Mam rushed to tend to her and Tada rose to his feet, frowning at the unseemly spectacle, Leah glanced up at Matthew and saw the faint blush on his cheek, the look almost of horror as enlightenment struck at last. How was it, she wondered, that he understood so much of other people's inner tortured thoughts, and yet he had missed this? He met her eyes and could only shake his head in desperate apology.

Along the pew, Frank snorted a laugh and was slapped for it.

Poor Mary, thought Leah. Poor Matthew, poor Miss Emma Davies, poor all of us.

Leah went, with Frank and most of the Beulah congregation, to the recently opened Penbryn station, to see Matthew and his bride depart for their new life on the far side of the world. Despite the green youth that Mrs Price had so deplored, the Reverend Vaughan had earned great respect in the area for his compassion, his pastoral energy and his earnestness in preaching. There was a general feeling that his calling to missionary work somehow encompassed his flock and bestowed a degree of grace on them all. He was their champion, bearing their Christian zeal to the furthest reaches of the earth, while requiring nothing more from them than to flutter bunting at the station. His departure had all the importance of a coronation procession.

The excitement wormed its way into Leah, despite the lack of joy in her soul. She gripped Frank's hand as the steam engine drew in, a great belching black monster, the first train she had ever seen at close quarters, though she had glimpsed one in the distance on a trip to Haverfordwest and Tom had told her – eyes shining in excitement – of seeing them at Crymmych. She gazed on the locomotive, enveloped in clouds of steam and smoke like a tamed dragon, thunderous and grinding as the traction engines that came to Plas Malgwyn at harvest time, and she understood Tom's excitement. So did Frank, for she felt his fingers squeeze hers.

Mr and Mrs Vaughan were attended on board, porters and chapel folk competing for the honour of manhandling their trunks and portmanteaux into the luggage van. Matthew leaned from the window as though he were still in the pulpit, hands raised, mouthing prayers that were drowned out by the hissing and grunting of the train and the clamour of his well-wishers. For a moment, over the crowd, his eyes held Leah's, a smile of apology and promise on his lips. He clasped his hand in a gesture of prayer, or union, in her direction and she raised hers, clasping them back, before joining the crowd in waving wildly as the engine let out a wild whistle and a roar, and the dragon train jerked forward.

She continued to wave until the end of the guard's van vanished from view and Matthew was gone, to Whitland, to Carmarthen, to London, to China, to World's End. Gone.

'That's it, then,' said Frank. 'He's off and we're here. Still.'

'Yes,' said Leah.

'We should have got on that train.'

'We have no money,' she said, before realising that what she should have said was 'No, we belong here.'

'One day,' said Frank.

1891

A fine day for a wedding. A very timely wedding, though not all would guess it. Sarah was so plump that any additional swelling would escape notice for a month yet. And not many would be as shocked as they should be, since it was a common enough occurrence, even among the chapel congregation. It was how so many marriages came about.

Sarah had ceased her employment at Plas Malgwyn with a suddenness that had suggested she'd been sent packing, though Leah was not given any explanation. She had been excluded from the whispered conferences between Mam, sadly disappointed, and Sarah, alternating between sulks and sheer panic. But she had been astute enough to guess what had happened. It had been no surprise when young carter, William Price, had come nervously to their door, egged on by a desperate Sarah with Mam's silent encouragement. He had stood like a quivering rabbit, turning his cap so many times in his hands that Leah thought it would shred to pieces.

'I have come... sir, I have come to ask... that is, I have come to beg... to beg permission to marry,' Leah thought he was going to pass out before he managed to finish the request, 'marry your daughter Sarah!' He ended on a squeak.

Tada, enthroned in his high-backed chair, perused the supplicant with a frown, while William Price's knees began to knock uncontrollably.

'And does my daughter wish to be joined to you in holy matrimony?'

'Yes, sir.' The squeak rose even higher.

'I have only seen you in chapel this last Sabbath.'

William's mouth worked as he fought to remember the lines that had been fed to him. 'S...sir, I...my mother favours...um...Soar in Felindre.'

Tada's frown refused to lift. 'No man will marry a daughter of mine unless he is a God-fearing man, washed in the blood of the Lamb. Are you such a man, William Price?'

'Yes sir!'

'Hm. I would wish to see evidence of this. In a few months, perhaps, if you attend diligently—'

'They have to marry now because Sarah is with child,' said Mary.

Sarah clasped her hands to her mouth, William almost collapsed, Mam shut her eyes in silent prayer and Leah felt her heart begin to gallop, but Mary's face remained impassive, as stony as her voice.

She had been silent, stony, impassive – her thoughts locked away from any other soul – since that day she had expressed too much, on Matthew Vaughan's announcement of his betrothal. When she'd been hustled home from chapel by Mam and Sarah, she had locked herself in the bedroom for an hour and then emerged as if nothing had happened. She had continued with her silent duties in the home, continued at the Sunday School under Matthew's successor, the Reverend Pritchard, a married man, and no one could guess that she had ever experienced a moment of passion or yearning. She shared nothing, and no one shared with her, not even Mam and Sarah, but she had eyes as good as Leah's, and seemed to know all about Sarah's predicament without being told.

'Is this true?' Tada rose, looking from William to Sarah as if he would burn them to ashes then and there. 'Have you played the harlot and dishonoured this family with this...this heathen?'

'Tada, I don't... I didn't...we...it was only once.'

Or twice or a thousand times, it would make no difference to

70

Tada. They all waited, not daring to breathe, until he pronounced judgement.

'You will marry, immediately, if that will diminish the disgrace that you have brought upon your sisters, but it will not wash your soul clean, sinful girl. You have rejected God's grace and are cast out, from this family and from the company of saints.'

Sarah looked as if she would melt into the flagstones, but Tada's thundering condemnation, predictable as it was, stirred something into life in Mam. Something that had been dead for years. She spoke up, her voice clear and adamant. 'It is for God alone to say who is cast out.'

'It is for me to say in my own house!' said Tada, as ever not quite looking at Mam. 'I am master here and I say,' he raised a finger of doom to point at Sarah, 'you will leave this house and contaminate it no more. Get out. Become this creature's wife and let him look to your sorry welfare. You are no daughter of mine.'

Sarah wailed in panic, and her future husband cowered.

Mam said, 'Come, Sarah. I bore you, I raised you, I will see you safe. Though you have sorely let me down, I will not abandon you, even as Christ our King will not abandon any one of us poor sinners in our guilt. Only God grants grace or denies it.' She took Sarah's hand and led her out into the yard.

William Price gulped in terror, then fled after them.

Tada remained standing, his righteousness deflated and his wrath frozen by Mam's response. At last his beard bristled. 'I am beset by Eliphaz, Bildad, and Zophar. My righteousness I hold fast and will not let it go: my heart shall not reproach me so long as I live.' He withdrew into the cold gloomy parlour to be alone with his Bible and whatever answers and excuses it offered him there.

Mary hadn't stirred a muscle.

'Why did you tell him?' asked Leah.

'It is the truth. Should the truth be denied?'

'It can be borne in our hearts and not proclaimed aloud. You, of all people, know that.'

'He is our father, the master in this house. Does he not have a right to know if his children sin?'

Leah gazed at her sister, trying to prise open the pages of that closed book and understand her intent. 'Aren't we taught that we are all sinners? We cannot sit in judgement on everyone all the time. Tada knew how it was with Sarah. He is no more blind than any of us, but he would have shut his eyes and ears to it and let them wed as if there were nothing amiss, if you hadn't laid it out so starkly.'

'He spoke of delaying for months. Sarah doesn't have months.'

'He said that to assert his authority. He would have relented in another moment and let them make haste.'

'What do you know? You speak as if you understand our father better than I do. You think you understand everyone.'

'No,' said Leah. 'I don't understand you, Mary.'

She understood Sarah, though, hungry for any sign of affection or even notice from anyone, and if she had always thought her sister foolish and frivolous, she still grieved to see her cast out in disgrace. Now she sat in chapel, head high, as Sarah made her vows, voice skittering between breathless whisper and shriek as terrified nerves and utter relief waged war within her.

The marriage was finalised at last and Tada had neither roared denunciation nor stormed out but maintained a stiff silence. He had not said a word in public about the marriage since William Price's visit. He had not repeated his insistence that Sarah was cast out from the family, because there had been no need. Mam had taken her to Castell Mawr farm and had left her in the care of Florence, the Georges' eldest daughter, who had charge of the house now that Mrs George had passed away.

Perhaps Mam had said something to Tada in private, or perhaps he had been shamed by her actions, but when the time came, he consented to attend chapel and hand his erring daughter to her new lord and master without a word. William Price looked as relieved as Sarah to be emerging unscathed, without black eyes or broken limbs, onto the chapel steps.

Sarah carried a posy, which she hurled so wildly that it almost caught in an overhanging ash branch, before descending on Leah. Leah reacted instinctively and caught it, as the gathered crowd laughed and winked.

Mrs Pritchard, the minister's busy useful wife, having a discreet understanding of how to paper over family rifts and social awkwardness in such situations, had prepared tea at Tŷ Capel, and a table had been laid out with a modest array of cold meats and bread and cakes, so that no hint of disgrace should sully the bride's day. Some crowded into the house to admire Mrs Pritchard's china and antimacassars, and others stood out in the sun or perched on the green banks surrounding the graveyard. If Tada turned his back on the merriment and strode over to stare down at the little wooden cross on Tom's grave, no one remarked on it.

Leah, too, remained outside. She could not enter Tŷ Capel without remembering Matthew in it, with his glowing faith and understanding eyes and the well-thumbed books of his childhood among his theological works. All they had of him now were occasional letters, forwarded by the mission and read out with pride in chapel. Letters that spoke of hope, blithe at first and lately, more determined. Leah detected a hint of resignation in them. He had lost a child. Converts were few. To go so far at God's summons and achieve so little, that was a sad thing...and this was not a day for sad thoughts.

'I am all of a flutter, you have no idea,' twittered Sarah, emerging into the open to clutch Leah's arm.

'Yes, I have. You are always in a flutter.'

Sarah pouted and Mary, standing behind her, gave a snort of contempt. Then Sarah giggled and tutted. She no longer had to care. She was no longer lost in the dark centre of a family that disregarded her. For once she was at the centre of her own glorious stage. 'Well, I may be aflutter today, may I not, because I am a bride?'

'And I hope the blessed joy of today will stay with you through all the years to come,' said Leah.

Sarah's smile lit up her face and she hugged Leah, kissing her. 'My little sister! Bless you.'

'I'll do nothing to mar it, if it's in my power,' said the groom, beaming like an idiot. Leah smiled. Very little was in William's power. He worked hard but earned little, and Sarah was a hapless manager, so the joy of simple poverty would be their probable lot. But for now, they had escaped terror and shame, and that was all that mattered.

'You'll be a fine husband,' said David George, who had stood as groomsman with William. He looked as grave as ever, though handsome and dignified in his good wedding clothes, and Leah could detect the hint of an impish smile as he added, 'And a fine father if God should choose to bless your union.'

Bride and groom both blushed. Mary turned her head away. Betty Phillips was standing near, with her back to them but all ears, ever ready for salacious gossip.

'Never doubt that every child is a gift that comes with God's blessing,' said Leah, and David's hint of a smile broadened, despite himself. Behind them, from the long grass, Frank, the child who came unblessed, popped up suddenly with a well-aimed pinecone that caught Betty Phillips on the back of the neck.

Betty was crimson with outrage and Frank collapsed in laughter. As he was unperturbed by her indignation, she turned instead on

Leah. They were of an age and had attended school together, but they had never been close friends. Betty was too full of herself and her own adamant opinions for Leah's taste, and Leah, she suspected, was too quietly clever for Betty's.

'You should control that little beast! He's a disgrace, and in a graveyard too. Where's the respect? I wonder you don't curl up in shame, Leah Owen!'

'Had I thrown the cone, I would,' said Leah. 'Frank, behave yourself.'

Frank shrugged, unrepentant. He shared Leah's opinion of Betty Phillips and made a point of tormenting her or mimicking her la-di-da ways whenever their paths crossed. 'It slipped out of my hand.'

'How...! How dare you tell such an untruth on God's land!' retorted Betty, swelling up.

David stepped in, the eternal pacifier. 'Frank, come here and apologise,' he said, calmly reasonable. 'Slip or deliberate, you distressed Miss Phillips, which no gentleman wants, so make amends.'

'I am mortified beyond endurance,' said Frank with a mocking bow.

'Frank!' said Leah.

'No, I am sorry. I beg your pardon, Betty.'

'Miss Phillips!' Betty seemed disinclined to accept the apology but a display of righteous anger in such a setting would have been unseemly, so she contented herself with a simpering smile at David. 'Thank you, Mr George, for your timely intercession, or I don't know what that wild boy would have done.'

'It might be a cowpat next, eh Frank? Just to teach the cow.' It was Eli John. Where he had come from, Leah didn't know. He hadn't been in chapel, but here he was now, in a brushed bowler and a silken cravat, with a slice of bread and ham from the wedding table, challenging them all with his leering smile. 'So, Will, you're a married man, and you've got your hands on Sarah Owen. You're a lucky man, believe me, I know.'

Frank barked with laughter, while Sarah turned crimson and William's discomfort was making him squirm. 'I know I'm lucky, Eli.'

'He is indeed,' said David. 'Because she's–'

'You!' Tada was upon them, his outstretched arm pointing at Eli as if to shoot lightning at him. 'Do you dare to show yourself on God's ground, in the very ground where those you have destroyed lie buried!'

'I'm here at my cousin's wedding,' Eli smirked, his eyes bright with spite. 'Will can't do without my blessing, can he, Rachel?'

A girl was hovering in the shadows behind him, tall, dark haired, starved thin despite her extravagant silk twill gown and velvet braid, her fine features thickly painted to conceal bruises. However Eli treated her, she seemed content with her lot, as she stared them down with contemptuous hostility, daring them to challenge her man.

'You insult God and his people, coming here with your harlot. You murdered my son and now you—'

'I murdered no one, old man. Your Tom attacked me. I didn't do him the injury that killed him. Look to yourself, if you want to point a finger of blame.' Eli leaned nonchalantly on a tombstone and provocatively took a large bite of his bread and ham.

'Leave this gathering or I'll horsewhip you!' said Tada. 'I'll not have you and your foul ways near me or mine!'

William, who had had Sarah's panicking whispers in his ears, tried to intervene. 'Perhaps, Eli, it would be for the best...'

'Best for whom?' asked Eli, still grinning. Then realisation dawned that he was being encircled by male wedding guests, none of them friendly. The godless Johns, Jacob and Eli – black sheep in an otherwise respected local family – were universally despised by this community. Jacob laughed off all the disapproval of his sins, his failure to observe the Sabbath and his scandalous housekeeper and his encouragement of wrestling and gambling among the quarrymen, knowing that they had to work with him and put up with his wicked ways. Eli, though, was driven by darker forces. He connived, he wrought malice, he simmered, storing up resentments and insults, just as he was rumoured to store up debts that others owed him. There was no one in the chapel gathering around him who wouldn't pay to see him excised from the parish.

Eli's eyes squinted in calculation for a moment. He knew when he was outnumbered and wouldn't risk a scrap that would see him ignominiously worsted. So he took another large bite, chewing noisily as he cocked his bowler and sauntered away, dragging his girl with him towards the trees behind the house, the shortcut to the quarry. At the last moment, he turned and winked at Frank.

Tada remained motionless, staring at the gravestone where Eli had been leaning, then, without warning, he turned and cuffed Frank around the ear. It was a blow hard enough to send the boy flying, rolling hard against a granite slab, and Frank cried out, whimpering out of shock. Tada's chastisements were seldom so public.

Tada strode away.

Leah knelt down beside Frank and offered her handkerchief to dab at the blood from his nose. 'Are you all right?'

'What do you think? Why must he always lash out at me?'

Because he must lash out at someone, she thought. 'Because you threw that cone at Betty Phillips.'

'He didn't see that. I made sure his back was turned first.'

'Oh Frank! You shouldn't have done it, whoever was watching.'

'I don't care. It was no excuse for him to strike me like that, just because I am not Tom. God, I hate Tom!'

'Don't say that.'

'Well I do. And I hate Tada.'

'That is a wicked thing to say.'

'Then I'm happy to be wicked. I've a good mind to be as wicked as Eli John and see how he likes it then.'

'Oh Frank.'

But Frank had had enough. He scrambled to his feet and thrust her soiled handkerchief back at her before darting off into the trees in Eli's wake.

She found David George waiting for her, beside Mary. 'Don't distress yourself, Leah. He'll calm down, everyone will, but perhaps it's better, for your sister Sarah's sake, if ill tempers took themselves off to cool down.'

'Yes, I know.'

'He will not be missed,' said Mary. 'He shames us all.'

'Indeed he does,' said Betty. 'It is as well we have you here instead, Mr George, to smooth the day.'

David bowed. 'I am glad to be of use. I am only sorry Flo could not come to the wedding too, but my father is so poorly at the moment that she cannot leave him. Alas, the inevitable duty of the daughter of the house.'

A visible quiver ran through Mary. 'I shall visit very soon and see if I can be of any use.'

'As shall I,' declared Betty. 'I'm sure Mary has more than enough to do at Cwmderwen.'

'I will always have time for our neighbour,' insisted Mary, with gritted teeth.

David held out pacifying hands. 'I thank you both. Your assistance will be greatly appreciated by Flo, I know. But for now, should we not all follow the happy couple?' He offered an arm. To whom, it wasn't clear, but Mary and Betty Phillips both leaped to it, so he was obliged to proffer both arms.

Following the fracas with Eli John, Mam had stepped in to urge the bride and groom away to the tiny cottage at the far end of the village that had been found for them. A procession was wending its way into Llanolwen to make sure they arrived safely.

Leah watched David accompany Mary and Betty towards the gate and surprised herself to find something like a small sad mouse squeaking inside her. Betty was always one to grab attention and bustle in where she wasn't wanted, and Leah need pay no heed to her. But Mary? Leah could see now how, for some months past, Mary had put herself out to be more sociable, more talkative, when David was around. Always saying what she thought might impress their young neighbour, knowing his character as she did. And now there was Mary on David's arm, and the world would look on them and see a pair perfectly matched in gravitas and thoughtfulness. A virtuous, devout Sunday School teacher who had shown herself to be practical about the house and farm, and a respectable young man with an ailing father who would inherit the lease of Castell Mawr, as prosperous as any farm could hope to be in these stricken times. It had even grown, through carefully management, absorbing a couple of neighbouring patches when the tenants could no longer struggle to survive on so little and when the landlord had reluctantly lowered the rent rather than let the land fall into total decay. Everyone would see it as a good match, even Tada, for David was an honest, God-fearing man, without vice of any sort, who would be sure to gain his unequivocal approval. And Mam's too. She was very fond of David.

Perhaps this time it would indeed happen as Mary so clearly wished, and Leah should be glad for her. But instead she felt a pang of...it was not jealousy. Loss. She was very fond of David, too. So fond that she felt easy with him in a way that she seldom was with any other, since Matthew Vaughan had gone. She did not want to lose him too, not even to her sister.

Mary's hand was clinging to his arm. She brushed close to him. Was he leading her or was she leading him? David stopped, forcing Mary and Betty to do likewise, and he turned to look back, smiling. That beautiful smile.

'Leah, you will walk with me too, I hope?'

A golden evening. David escorted them back to the top of Cwmderwen's deep-cut lane, Mary on one arm, Leah on the other. Mary spoke a few words now and again. Leah said nothing. She didn't need to. She was happy. She wasn't sure why, but it was there in her breast, a feeling of contentment as warm and comfortable as the feel of David's arm, strong and steady.

They said polite farewells and parted, the two women walking in silence down to their cottage. Leah sensed a tension in her older sister that was at odds with the peace within herself. Mary was winding herself up, just as she had over Matthew. Leah prayed the result would not be equally shattering. Having seen Sarah settled and smiling, all aglow in her own home with a fond husband standing by her, Leah wanted the day to end with a similar glow, with the remaining Owen family united in a semblance of the old lost love.

But when they gathered for prayers there was no unity, because there was no Frank. He had not been seen since he'd run from them in the graveyard. Tada waited, stiff and silent, as minutes ticked by and his womenfolk stood with heads bowed, waiting patiently, but there was no sign of him, and at last Tada took a deep dismissive breath and opened the Bible.

Prayers ended, Tada firmly bolted the door as they turned to climb the stairs.

Mary said nothing as she undressed, locked in her own silence again now there was no David to make little remarks to. Leah slipped her nightgown over her head and stared out over the darkening cobbles of the yard. 'Perhaps he'll bed down in the cowshed. At least there's straw there to keep him warm.'

'Where he belongs,' said Mary, tying her nightcap. She snuffed the candle without waiting for Leah to come to bed.

Leah slipped under the covers but now she couldn't sleep. She lay listening for Frank, but there was nothing except the usual night noises, rustles in the woods, an owl far off, a grunt from the pig, a pitter patter of something scurrying across the cobbles. The room fell into utter darkness before a waning moon rose to shed a ghostly grey and still there was no Frank.

She must have slept, but lightly, light enough to start awake at the sound of footsteps, though they were soft, as if someone were stalking prey. Then the footsteps stumbled. The angle of the moon told her it was well past midnight. She slid out of bed, pulled a shawl around her shoulders and, holding her breath, eased open the door into the adjoining chamber. Her parents lay side by side, untouching, a gulf between them, eyes shut, Tada's jaw clenched as he emitted the faintest snore, Mam's lips moving in her sleep, her hands clasped in prayer on the quilt. Edging past, terrified of the slightest squeak of floorboards, Leah tiptoed down into the chill kitchen, just as the front door was pushed, rattling the bolt.

There was a muffled oath outside.

'Sh!' she whispered, tongue between her teeth as she drew the bolt back. Frank was standing there, staring at her.

'Owly. Why are you awake?' He spoke too loud.

'Hush! I was waiting for you. Come in. But be quiet. Come through to the scullery.'

'I just—'

'Sh!' She drew him after her, through to the back room with its washtubs and buckets, the cold of the tiles biting into her bare feet.

81

'Where have you been?' she asked, with the door safely shut on them. Frank had stayed out many times before, but never this late.

'With friends,' said Frank, dropping onto a stool and folding his arms. 'Eli and Rachel. They're my friends. That's what.' As he spoke, she smelled something odd on his breath. Sour and herbal.

'What have you been eating?'

'Eating? Nothing. Drinking, that's all. Ale and gin.'

'Frank!' Her voice almost rose to a scream. 'How could you? You are pledged never to touch—'

'Well, I've unpledged myself.'

'You'll go to hell.'

'Can't be worse than this place.'

'Don't say that, Frank.'

'Why not? I can say what I like, and drink what I like.'

'This is Eli John's doing.'

'What if it is? Don't care what you say about Eli. He's a friend.'

'That's nothing to boast of. If Tada hears you, if he smells that evil stuff on your breath—'

'He'll beat me. Yes, Owly, but he'll beat me anyway. Except, not any more. You see? Not any more. Because I won't be here to be beaten.'

'What do you mean?'

'I mean I'm going. To sea.'

'You can't do that!'

'I can. Eli says there's a coal steamer for Ireland put in at Cardigan and—'

'But you know nothing of ships and the sea. You're only fifteen, Frank; you can't—'

'I learned a bit of navigation and such, didn't I? At least when I was allowed to learn anything. They take boys my age.'

'But the farm, Frank. It will yours one day. You can't leave.'

82

'I don't want the farm! I never wanted it. It's a useless patch of nothing, just something for us to break our backs on.'

'It's not nothing. That's Eli John talking, mocking us, whispering malice to try and poison you against us.'

'Whispering sense more like. Tadcu Owen had a brother, remember? Joseph. He went to America.'

'Yes, I know. What of it?'

'Do you know what they do in America? They farm.' His voice was rising. 'Hundreds of acres, or thousands. They grow corn and they raise beef and it comes here on great steamships and that's why we are nothing but bare-arsed paupers on our twenty-four acres, one rood and eight perches. We're fools to stick at it here, but I'm not going to be a fool. Not any more. I'm going to take ship and work my passage to America and do like great-uncle Joseph. I only came back for my things.' He swayed as he spoke.

'No! Don't go, Frank. You can't. It would break Mam's heart.'

'Her heart's already broken. It broke when Tom died.'

'But she needs you. I need you. Tada...Tada will mend. He will pass this land to you and you to your son, and you cannot walk away from that.'

'I can. No one wants me here.' There were tears in his eyes. He was leaning back against the wall now, incapable of walking away or towards anything. It was gin talking, she knew. She didn't know enough of drunkenness to tell how drunk he was, but it must be the gin, stoked by Eli's malice, bringing him to this.

'I want you here, Frank, you know I do. I don't want to lose you too.'

'You can have David George instead. We watched you making moon eyes at him, you and Mary, both.' He gave a high giggle. 'If you fight over him, you'll win. Mary won't stand a chance.'

Leah's skin crawled at the thought of Frank watching them all, out of sight, in company with Eli John. But she couldn't afford to think of Eli now. 'I don't know what might happen in the future, Frank, but you know I love you. My brother. My baby brother. I've always loved you and I thought you loved me.'

'Well I suppose I do, Owly. Of course I do.'

'And yet you'd run away and leave me?'

He thought about it, so deeply she suspected he was dozing off where he stood. 'You could come too,' he said at last.

'But I am not dressed,' she said, realising that he was beyond rational argument now, bendable to her soft suggestions. 'And it's a long way to Cardigan, in the dark. Why not sleep now, and start your journey in the morning, when the sun is up.'

'Maybe. I'm still going, though.'

'Yes, Frank, but in the morning. Wouldn't you rather sleep now?'

'Yes. Maybe. Yes, just an hour or two...'

'Come,' she said, guiding him back into the kitchen. He would have slumped onto his usual bed on the settle but she pulled him back, whispering in his ear. 'No, no, take your cover.' She picked up the thick blanket that was folded ready. 'Tada has locked you out. Come with me.' Tentatively opening the door, she led him out and across the cobbles. The cold air of night came near to rousing him, but as they slipped into the warm darkness of the cow byre, his eyes began to close again and his knees began to fold. She let him drop into deep straw and tucked the blanket around him.

'Night, Owly.'

'Good night, Frank.' He was snoring before she'd reached the door.

He wouldn't go. She knew Frank well enough to know that if flight had seemed wisdom in the evening, it would be a mere fancy by morning. He was obstinate in nursing his hurts but all his energy, such as it was, went into shows of resentful aggravation. Inertia invariably prevented him from doing anything to amend his situation. Place a mere pebble before him and he would give up.

Such weakness offended Leah, but he was as he was, and she was his guardian still. She could not let him wander off into God only knew what wilderness, slyly goaded by Eli John.

1896

The kitchen of Castell Mawr was the perfect place to fend off the November chill. Heat pulsated from the range as Flo George baked bread and pies. It was an old house with low ceilings, walls thicker than Leah's arm could reach, filled with the watchful whispers of past generations. The Georges had held this tenancy since the reign of King George II at least, and acted as if their bones had grown from its stone and their blood was drawn up from its well. They accepted, without any need to proclaim it aloud, that Castell Mawr, regardless of tenancy agreements and rent payments, belonged to them and they to it. Land was everything. It made them people of standing, pillars of the village community, because they belonged, rooted so deep into that community that none could oust them.

Leah, busying herself laying out plates and knives for the dinner the men would soon be wanting, could understand her father's desperation to establish himself and his family in the same manner. The man whose father had lost whatever little he'd had, who had been obliged to labour for the profit of others, in wind and rain and summer heat, now had acres of his own, however spare, however difficult, however few. Twenty-four acres, one rood and eight perches, to be passed on down the generations. Owen land. How many generations would it take, she wondered, before the Owens had the same social standing as the Georges?

Socially, they were not so very far apart. Georges and Owens were both tenants of the Herberts of Plas Malgwyn. They worked

86

their fields, tended their cattle with their own hands, shared the same worries over tumbling prices, poor hay and untimely weather. They attended the same chapel. But the Georges lived comfortably off their land, acquired more of it where they could, employed men and machines and were consulted by the Herberts' steward, while Tada worked alone like Adam with his rake and mattock, his scythe and lonely plough, eking out the scant earnings of their farm with joinery work. But good neighbours for all that. Love thy neighbour.

While Leah fetched the ham and jars of pickles and dishes of butter, and set out a new loaf, still warm, with the remains of the old, Flo was tending to old Mr George, with Mary's assistance. William George had shrunk a little with age and illness, but he was still a big man, difficult for them to manoeuvre when his limbs failed him. Persuading him of what was required was not always easy. Sometimes he grumbled, mocked, patted his daughter's hand in gratitude, and at other times he was lost, slumped, barely awake, recognising no one.

'Sit up, Tada, there's a dear. Come on, now. Mary, can you take that arm? We'll ease him back.'

'Eh?' Mr George looked up at his daughter in bewilderment, as she tried to prop him up with cushions on the great carved chair that had stood like a throne near the range for as long as Leah could recall. 'Why am I here?'

'You're going to have some dinner, Tada. Some nice broth I've made for you.'

'Where's John?'

'John? Uncle John? He's at his home in Penbryn, Tada. He's not here.'

Panic quivered through the slack folds of William's face. 'Where am I?'

'At home, Tada. At Castell Mawr, in the kitchen, with me. Your daughter, Flo.'

His face worked for a moment, then his eyes brightened. 'Of course I am. My Flo.'

'That's right, Tada.' Flo straightened and moved towards the range, where a pot of broth was simmering.

'Where are you going!' Panic again.

She turned back and took his hand, squeezing the flabby flesh. 'It's all right, Tada. I'm not leaving you. You know that, don't you? I'll never leave you.'

Leah glanced at Mary, who had remained standing silent by William's chair. Her face gave nothing away. For a second, her eyes met Leah's, then flitted away, expressionless, and she moved to the dresser to fetch cups and saucers.

It was the Castell Mawr dresser, at one with the family. Polished and fretted, its darkened oak gleaming as though it had absorbed the candlelight and firelight of centuries. Its brass handles were aged by generations of use, its high boarded shelves packed with modern china and past dowry offerings, its pot board below straining under good practical stoneware and ancient pewter platters. The dresser at Cwmderwen had none of such dignity or antiquity, but was a plain, battered thing that had come with the cottage, a discard excised from the kitchen of some big house, probably, though Mam tended it and did her best to polish it as though it were the most prized heirloom in the world.

The door opened as Mary was arranging cups on the table, and David came in, followed by Amos Absalom and Rhodri Davies who had been moving the cattle with him. Two busy collies rushed in with them and headed for the range.

'Out!' said David, and the two dogs smoothly looped around each other and headed back out.

The men's hands were still damp from washing in the porch, and Leah held out a towel. David smiled his thanks, reaching out, but Mary snatched it from her and placed it in his hands.

'Thank you, Mary,' he said, gravely. 'Good day, Tada. How has it gone with you this morning?'

'Oh, well enough. I've been to see John.'

David exchanged smiles and shrugs with his sister. 'That's good, Tada.'

A growing doubt crossed William's face, and with it a hint of returning panic.

'Tomorrow is market day. I'll bring Uncle John back with me,' suggested David, and the old man immediately perked up. They all knew it wouldn't happen. William's younger brother John was crippled by apoplexy and hadn't left his house in town for two years. Sometimes William remembered this.

David turned hastily to their guests before the proposal could be discussed. 'Will you stay and eat with us, Leah, Mary?'

'Leah only came for the goose feathers,' interrupted Mary. 'Our mother will be expecting her home.' In Castell Mawr, especially when David was present, she could be almost garrulous.

'No,' said Leah. 'Mam has gone to see Sarah and the baby while Tada is delivering the chairs to Felindre. She said I was to stay and make myself useful here.'

'I am doing that,' said Mary.

David was undeterred. 'But you are both here and the table is spread, so you will both eat with us. Yes, Flo?'

'Indeed they will,' smiled Flo. 'Please, be seated and eat, all of you.' She carried the heavy pot of broth to the table, ladled some into a bowl and carried it to her own chair, beside her father, while the others gathered around the table. She waited, spoon ready, until David had said grace, then she raised the spoon to her father's lips and smiled as he drank noisily.

Mary, at David's left, took charge of ladling out the broth. Leah, on his right, brushed her hand against his jacket as she reached for her bowl. 'Barely damp. Has the rain stopped?'

'It has, and there is even a break in the clouds. Summer may be far behind us, but there is still a gleam of sun now and again to be thankful for.'

'Amen,' said Mary. 'You will have some ham with your bread, David?'

'Thank you, Mary. Yes.'

'And there is some of your favourite damson chutney... Ah, Leah hasn't put it out. But of course she has no idea where to find it, as I do. Indeed, I think I know this house as well as my own.'

'You do, Mary,' said Flo, from her father's side. 'And I thank God for your daily assistance here.'

Mary gave a small triumphant smile as she placed the prized chutney on the table.

Flo smiled at her brother with a guarded expression that Leah couldn't quite translate. Was it encouragement? Warning? Sympathy? Florence George was a loveable and intelligent woman, still with a trace of her childhood prettiness, who might have married and become a doting mother of a dozen children, but she loved her father and her brother and never complained of her lot.

Flo did not kick against fate, as Mary did. Leah, twenty-two and a mature woman now, realised that though Mary hid her thoughts behind a mask of stone and never divulged her desperate inner dreams, she was kicking as hard as she could, yearning for something forever out of reach. Once it had been Matthew Vaughan, but that passion had long been buried alive. Matthew occasionally made kind reference to her in his letters, written to be read out to the chapel congregation, but Mary remained frigidly indifferent. It was to Leah that one or two private little notes had been passed by Mrs

Pritchard. 'I pray my little sister is still seeking answers and growing in wisdom.'

Mary didn't know about those notes. There was no need to tell her, for now it was David that she quested after. That made Leah sad, for Mary's quest was hopeless and Leah knew it. She knew because she understood matters that no one had yet spoken of, and when they were spoken of, Mary would suffer.

Mary fetched the teapot, which had been brewing beside the range, and Leah began to rise to help her, but Mary was quick to dismiss her. 'No, no. You're a guest here, Leah. I can manage. I have done this a thousand times, have I not, David?'

'Indeed you have, Mary. A true Godsend.' David laid his hand over Leah's. 'And you are always a truly welcome guest at my hearth, Leah Owen.'

She smiled, wincing within at the hurt that could not be far off, though David's regard warmed her heart. Mary was marking her territory as blatantly as a dog cocking its leg, and others seemed to have taken the message on board. Once they had eaten and drunk their tea, Amos and Rhodri rose and touched their forelocks to Mary as they did to Flo, before sidling out and back to work.

Mary nodded graciously to them, as if she were already the mistress of the house.

Flo glanced at her brother, eyes wide as if urging him on. David seemed to understand the message. He took a deep breath, then pushed back his chair and strolled over to the window, wiping the condensation from the pane. 'Yes, the sun has broken though at last, and it looks to be a fine afternoon. Fine enough, I think, for a stroll up onto the castle banks to admire the view. What do you say, Leah? Will you attempt it with me?'

Leah opened her mouth, hesitating in the consciousness of the iron silence around her.

David hurried to put her mind at rest. 'And Mary will come too, to chaperone us as usual. You will, I hope, Mary?'

Leah couldn't bring herself to look at Mary's face, but she could see her sister's hand, in the folds of her frock, working as if to draw blood from her palm. Flo was looking from one to the other, biting her lip.

At last, Mary spoke, her voice cold and steady. 'I'm afraid I must return to Cwmderwen. One of us must be at home helping our mother, and if Leah prefers to go gallivanting off for her own pleasure, then it must be me.'

Mam isn't there, Leah wanted to say, but she held her tongue, feeling the colour rise in her cheeks. Let Mary have an exit as dignified as possible. She grieved for her, but not as much as she rejoiced for her own sake. Within her, a quiet joy found wing like a song bird whose cage had been opened. Not wild ecstasy, but a gentle dissolution of bars. She felt Mary's pain but she could not find it in her to summon up the tiniest regret for what David had said.

Flo squeezed her father's hand in reassurance before stepping forward as Mary, with frosty rigidity, donned her coat and hat. 'Thank you as ever for your assistance, Mary. You know how much I value it. Shall I see you tomorrow?'

'No. I shall be attending market with my father. Perhaps another time.' Head high, Mary walked out. It was as well she would have time on her own. Mam and Tada were both out, and wherever Frank was, in their absence, it would probably not be on the farm. Mary could have the place to herself to howl out her grief and disappointment.

Am I cruel? wondered Leah. But if she were, so were David and Flo, and she couldn't believe that. They smiled at each other in quiet relief.

'I must tend Tada,' said Flo, 'but don't let that keep you. I don't believe Leah needs a chaperone.'

The ancient Castell Mawr, which crowned the hill above the farm, had no towers or moat and drawbridge but rings of grassy mounds cloaked in gnarled oaks. It had been built by the druids for their devilish sacrifices, so Leah had heard, but there was nothing heathen about it now. As the climb steepened, David offered his arm. Leah hesitated, but only for a second. She was fit and strong and had no need of support, but the gesture had a deeper significance, one they could have discussed if either had been of a mind to talk, but neither was. David was always one for speaking only when he had thought carefully what needed to be said and Leah had never been a chatterer. Owly was Frank's nickname for her. Owl still and silent, waiting for the mice to give themselves away. She was an observer like Mary, but whereas Mary kept her own thoughts concealed behind lock and key, Leah watched with an intelligent understanding that would instruct her words and deeds. She knew where she and David stood, without the need to spell it out. He had chosen her and, except for her sympathy for Mary, she would have chosen him long ago. It was right. It was God's will.

They emerged onto the highest bank at last, at a point where the tawny trees parted and their whole world was spread out before them, the green fields of Castell Mawr farm spilling down to the floor of the broad valley, the river twinkling silver as it meandered, the craggy hills beyond blue and brown as withered dragonhide. Down to their right, in a cluster of cedars and purple beeches, exotic among the native oaks and ash, the elegant façade of Plas Malgwyn gleamed pale gold. Away to their left, the thickly wooded cleft of Cwmderwen cut a dark line under the curving hilltop and the lane that zigzagged up to the chapel, its steep roof silhouetted against the pale autumn sky.

Leah rejoiced in what she saw, her arm still linked in David's as they drew deep breaths of clear air. Then a doubt niggled at her, breathing on the back of her neck. *The devil took him up onto a high mountain, and showed him all the kingdoms of the world, and said, All this I will give thee, if thou wilt fall down and worship me.* But how could this be the devil's work? How could David be an instrument of Satan? No, this was God's will. She glanced at the shadowed gash of Cwmderwen, twenty-four acres, one rood and eight perches. Her home until now. But in the future lay the golden-green, the sunny pastures and rich meadows, the hundred and twelve acres of Castell Mawr, the ancient stone farmhouse with its cavernous kitchen, its cool stone dairy, its glossy cattle and flocks of sheep. And David. Most of all, David. Leah was pleasant enough to look on, tall, dark, slim – though Sarah declared she was too sharp – and in her twenty-two years she had caught the eye of one or two young men of the parish, but there had never been anyone for her except David.

All that was asked of her, in return, was to be patient. She was the owl who observed and understood. David would not put into words their mutual understanding until he had Castell Mawr farm to offer her – until his ailing father was finally laid to rest beside Mrs George in the chapel graveyard. Leah would be patient. She would not champ at such a golden bit. All proper things came in their own good time, and this would be the proper thing.

She was sorry for Mary, but what could she do?

Mary accompanied Tada to market in Penbryn. He had often requested Leah to do so, since her quick wits and willingness gave him more practical assistance than Frank's grudging support.

Perhaps he would have asked Leah now, but Mary volunteered with quiet, stubborn persistence, so Tada made room for her beside him on the trap. Leah supposed her sister was determined to visit Penbryn to make good her excuse to Flo and salve her bruised pride. If Mary had another motive, she didn't tell Leah. Since the previous day, Mary would neither speak to her nor look at her, acting as though Leah did not exist, although they shared a bed and tasks about the house.

On her return from Penbryn, still Mary said nothing. She gradually ceased to visit Castell Mawr, unless Mam bade her go on an errand, and then she returned in haste as if their neighbour's soil burned her heels and she could not bear to be near the place. Which was the truth, as Leah knew, though she said nothing. Mam looked a little grave, a little perplexed, but not unduly so. She smiled gently when Leah offered to help their neighbour Flo in Mary's place, unspoken comprehension dawning.

'Of course. You go, cariad. With poor William sinking, they must need all the help their neighbours can spare, and their neighbours will not fail them, just as they have never failed us. Go whenever they need you, Leah, like a good Christian. I shall have Mary here to help me about the house, and that will suffice.'

So Leah took Mary's place at Castell Mawr, helping with the household chores while Flo was occupied with her father. Mam was right. The Georges' neighbours certainly did not fail them. Betty Phillips was there almost as often as Leah, making herself indispensable, bossy as she had ever been at school and saving her smiles for the moment David appeared on the threshold.

'Mr George, you are wet. Let me take your mackintosh. Mr George, I declare you are quite frozen. Here, I have a warming cup of tea ready for you. Mr George, you are looking anxious. Are you still worried about that ewe?'

David was quietly polite with Betty as he was with everyone. As he was with Leah. And Betty was prettier, there was no denying that. But did he share with her the looks of silent understanding that he shared with Leah? She thought not. Jealousy was not a monster she would allow to dog her footsteps.

Mary, without being asked, accompanied Tada on the following market day too, climbing up beside him as if it were her place by rights. And so it was on the next market day and the next, the last before Christmas. They returned with a frown on Tada's face and Mary's chin set firm, though her face was as closed as ever.

'Well, wife. It seems our daughter has attracted the attention of Mr Lloyd, chandler of Penbryn. He has requested her hand in marriage.'

'Lloyd the Chandler!' Mam turned from the range in astonishment. 'But that's not possible. He married Elinor Davies not a year since.'

'Mr Edward Lloyd, the father. A widower,' said Tada. 'With two children still at home.'

'He is,' Mam looked at Mary, choosing her words with care, 'a man of mature years.'

Mary's chin set firmer. She made no reply.

'Well, and is it your wish to accept this offer?'

'It is.'

'Does your father give his consent?'

'He has not withheld it.'

'I see.' Mam smoothed down her apron. 'Is he a chapel man?'

'He attends Bethania.'

Mam pursed her lips. Leah understood the gradations of chapels in the area. Penuel, in Penbryn, was a true tabernacle of the Word, and Zion not far behind in righteousness, but Bethania, along with

Carmel, leaned dangerously towards the conceits of false prophets. However, at least it was chapel, not church. Just acceptable enough not to be an insurmountable objection to the match. Mary met Leah's eyes at last. Defiant, triumphant. She had chosen well – an aging but respectable widower of means who wouldn't waste his energies hankering after younger, prettier maids, but was willing to snap up what had been offered with such barefaced determination.

'Have you prayed about it?' asked Mam. 'Are you convinced it is God's will?'

'My prayers have been answered,' replied Mary, stabbing another look at Leah.

'I am glad for you,' said Leah. 'I wish you joy.'

Mary's wedding took place one month later. There was, after all, no need to delay, once the decision had been made. No one suspected scandal, so tongues were not set wagging. Mary spent the intervening time primly examining, altering and ironing linen and frocks that she must have been accumulating over the years, squirrelling them away in her box under the bed. Two frocks Leah had never seen before. She recognised a couple more as hand-downs, altered and refreshed, from Mrs Pritchard, the minister's wife.

'Let me help you,' said Leah.

Mary continued to fold and refold petticoats and nightgowns for a moment before looking up. 'No. I need no help, from you or anyone. Least of all from you.'

'If you feel...' What word to use? Not love, surely. 'Regard and respect for Mr Lloyd, are you still angry that David—'

'Do you think I want to listen to you babbling about David George? I have my own future to think of. I am sorry if it spoils yours.'

'It doesn't spoil mine,' said Leah. 'I am happy for you, truly. I felt so sorry—'

'Don't! Don't you dare. It is I who feel sorry for you.' Mary turned her back and resumed her packing.

'Hey. See that?' Frank nudged Leah and pointed up to the ornate plasterwork on the chapel ceiling. 'Don't let Mam look up, or she'll be denouncing the place as a temple of the Antichrist.'

'Hush. Show respect, for Mary's sake if not for the Lord's.'

Frank sank back in his pew and folded his arms with a weary sigh. They were at Bethania Chapel in Penbryn rather than the bride's place of worship because the road to Llanolwen was only metalled as far as the turning to Plas Malgwyn and Edward Lloyd was no longer spritely enough to relish the rutted last mile to Beulah. Leah studied him, stooping beside his young bride. It was the first time she had ever set eyes on him and she was taken aback to see quite how old he looked. Older than Tada. Grey-haired, bent and whiskery. He had a son and daughter of twelve and fourteen, waiting in sullen resignation to receive their new stepmother, but they must have been unexpected miracles in the last years of his previous marriage. His eldest son, Albert – already approaching middle age – had run the chandler's shop for ten years, though it was understood that the father still kept the books and the keys to the strong box.

'She'll be lucky if he's not carried out of here in a coffin,' whispered Frank, too loudly.

'Hold your tongue,' she mouthed, and he grinned. She couldn't hope for respectful behaviour from her brother but at least he was in a good humour and not sulking. Penbryn, that's what it was. He had never made good his threat to run away to sea, of course, but small sallies of escape to the local market town always cheered him up.

'One night with Mary and he's done for,' he said, barely lowering his voice.

There was a snort of amusement from somewhere behind them but Tada turned his head and all fell silent. Tada had accompanied Mary to chapel, just as he had accompanied Sarah, in silent dignity, for the sake of the family honour, but what he really thought of the match, Leah had no idea. Did he think, as she did, that it was Edward Lloyd's joylessness rather than his age that appalled? Probably not. Tada no longer seemed to know what joy was, but then he was not a bridegroom. Edward looked shrewd rather than hopeful, calculating rather than caring. Leah couldn't imagine him laughing. The same could be said of Mary. There was no hint of joy or nerves or excitement on the bride's face. No hint of anything, apart from a twitch of her eyelid. Perhaps they were too well suited. It was, in any case, Mary's choice. She may have chosen in haste, but she had done so with her eyes open.

The couple gave their inaudible assents, the pompous minister concluded, the register was signed. Leah and Frank joined Mam and the others outside to greet the happy couple as they emerged on the chapel steps. Mam was not as tearful as mothers of brides so often were, but she looked thoughtful, lost in memories as she often was these days.

Frank, of course, did not look thoughtful. If he chose, he could be a credit to the family, since he had an entire new wardrobe. All through his adolescence he had passed for a tattered scarecrow with naked wrists and ankles and bursting seams, because it didn't do to waste money on clothes for a boy who would be a different shape and size in a month or two. But at twenty, though he was shorter than Tom had been at sixteen, shorter even than Leah, it was agreed that he had stopped growing, and a decent suit of new clothes had been afforded. Good, plain, respectable and hard-wearing. They would last him into his old age, Mam said.

But Frank wasn't interested in looking respectable. He'd loosened his tie and clapped his hat back on at a rakish angle, as soon as he had escaped from chapel. Now he lounged against the railings with boredom oozing from every pore, as he eyed up the nearby shops, the passing traffic, a couple of girls, the men gathering at the door of the Red Lion den of iniquity – he studied everything other than the bride and groom, every muscle and sinew in him declaring to the world that he was no part of this family.

Leah knew better than to bother chiding him. She turned resolutely to smile at Mary in her high-necked blue frock, the short veil rising up from her hat like a cockscomb.

'I wish you all happiness, Mrs Lloyd.'

Mary had not smiled once, all day, and still she did not smile, but as she looked Leah full in the face, there was no disguising the triumph. She snapped, as if the words had been waiting for years to leap out, 'Yes, Mrs Lloyd, the *married* daughter. And now it's Leah, the sly clever one, who must stay at home and be the shackled spinster.'

Frank barked a laugh, but Leah could only stand, stunned. Stunned because she understood Mary at last. She had supposed that it was love that Mary, the plain, the overlooked, had craved all these years. But it wasn't love, or a husband or children or a home of her own she had put so much energy into fighting for, it was just escape. Escape from Cwmderwen, from her pre-ordained fate as the aging daughter imprisoned forever in a family home she detested.

Was it truly such a detestable home? Even with the love between Mam and Tada dried to a cinder, was it so terrible? Then the deeper implication dawned on Leah. She, who was so clever in many things, had not been clever enough to foresee what had been so obvious to dull-witted Mary. She was now the only unmarried daughter in the Owen family. The one who must remain, unwed, doing her duty as daughter to aging parents, until there was nothing left of her. No love or tenderness. No family of her own. No husband. No David.

She stifled a sob of pain and shock.

'Leah.' Mam was behind her, her old-fashioned bonnet brushing Leah's broad hat and there was something in her voice, something strong that had been reborn. 'Look at me.' Leah turned, forcing a false smile in response to Mam's. 'So I am blessed,' Mam went on. 'I have two daughters married, and I thank God, in his mercy, that my third will soon follow them. I know how it stands between you and David. He is a good man and when the time comes, I will give you my blessing a thousandfold. I could not want better for you.'

'But if I wed...if I were ever to wed, who would... You need—'

'I need nothing. I am content with my lot. In this life, it is my duty to tend to your father. Mine and no one else's. I am sufficient to the task. And in the next life, I trust to be reunited with my Tom, which is all I seek. Leah, you need think no more about being chained at home as my helpmeet. I neither ask nor desire it.'

'But it is my duty—'

'My prayer is to see you wed and at David's side in Castell Mawr. Promise me you will not hold back when the time comes, out of any foolish thought of duty to me.'

Having almost sobbed with pain, Leah was near to sobbing with relief. She shook in her effort to restrain her gratitude. Impulsively, she leaned forward and kissed her mother. Then she looked across to the other side of the steps where David stood. Betty Phillips, who had no business being there, was at his side, determined to loop her arm through his. What did that matter? His eyes met Leah's in a reassuring smile.

All would be well. Leah glanced round to see what Frank would make of it all. Surely he would have some wry comment to offer at her expense. But Frank had vanished.

Frank was not to be found. Tea and cake had been taken, Mary was despatched to her new home behind the chandler's shop, the trap was ready and Tada was impatient to be gone.

'I'll not wait for him. If he hasn't the grace to wait upon us, he has legs fit enough to carry him home.'

'A moment longer,' said Mam. 'There's light yet.'

'I'll ask William if he's seen him,' said Leah and hurried off to catch her brother-in-law.

William Price had attended the wedding while Sarah was confined at home, nursing young Sarah Jane who was teething and fretful. He and Sarah had weathered the disgrace of their hurried wedding and had regained Tada's grudging acceptance, but William was still wary enough to keep a respectable distance at this wedding. He watched Leah's approach with that frightened rabbit look the Owens always brought out.

'Have you seen Frank, Will?' she asked, as pleasantly as she could.

'Oh. Frank. Um.' William was twisting his hat again, his usual trick when nervous. 'Did I see him? Well—'

'Where is he?' she asked, exasperated.

'In, um...in, um...the Black Bull? I think. I don't know. Maybe.'

Leah gasped. How could he, with Mam and Tada waiting? She knew Frank had taken to drinking strong liquor when he was supposed to be about business, but he was wise enough not to broadcast the fact at home. In his parents' eyes, drink was the nectar of Satan and the entire Owen family had abjured it. No Owen permitted to cross the threshold of the Butcher's Arms in Llanolwen, even to deliver eggs. The landlady, Mrs Morgan, had to come out to collect them.

Of course, Frank drank because it was forbidden, Leah knew that. It was one of his little defiances. How often had she smelled the vile stuff on his breath, and had seen him unsteady on his feet? She had always been there, ready to shake him into steadiness, to offer him mints or aniseed balls to cover the vile smell, to swill him down if necessary, and he had let her help because his rebellion, like a child's, was only performed when his father's back was turned.

But this, on his sister's wedding day, with the whole world watching, was not surreptitious. It was a blatant challenge to Tada's authority and it would assuredly earn dreadful punishment.

'What induced the fool? If Tada hears of it, Frank will be black and blue. Did he just venture in to look, do you think, or did he stay? Will, did he stay in there? Was he drinking?'

'I…I…I–' William was obviously not going to say, so Leah guessed the answer was yes.

She hurried down the high street. Why must he choose the Black Bull? The Crown was at least partly respectable, being an old coaching inn for travellers, where even members of the clergy had been known to stay, and the Red Lion was seldom singled out for special denunciation by the temperance brigade, but the Black Bull at the end of the high street was a thorough disgrace to the town, scandal swilling around it like the foul ale it served. Every week, magistrates dealt with brawls and drunkenness erupting from its doors.

She hesitated as she approached its low entrance, near enough for the stench of stale beer and pipe smoke to envelop her. Near enough to peer in, around the figure of a woman in shameless scarlet slumped in the doorway, and see the shadowed figures, dirty boots and hunched shoulders. Near enough to hear the voices within, half mumbling, half shouting, and Frank's among them.

'Tell you, I don't give a damn. No, I don't. Not a damned thing. Why should I? Damn him.'

Leah flinched on hearing the profanity, but flinched even more on hearing the voice that replied.

'That's my boy, Frank. You go at it and to hell with all of them, eh?'

'Eli John!' Leah must have said it aloud, because the woman lolling in weariness in the doorway immediately straightened, bracing herself with an air of challenge, her blue eyes sneering as they met Leah's.

'Want Eli, do you? Look as if you could do with a proper man, you tight-arsed cow.'

Rachel Morgan, Eli's harlot as Llanolwen called her, dragged out of the middens of Swansea. She'd vanished – a year or so back – replaced at Eli's side by Dot, a sorry little wretch from Penbryn. Now Dot had vanished in turn, and Rachel was back, looking more haggard than ever for all her scarlet silk and feathers. She must be of an age with Leah, she must have witnessed the same years, but she had done so under a different sun, in a world without honour, virtue or self-respect. Harlotry was a sorry business, Leah thought, staring back at her, if her finery was bought at the cost of Eli John's company.

'I want my brother, not Eli. Will you fetch him?'

'Fetch him yourself, sour-faced bitch.' Rachel stuck out her chest belligerently.

Leah stepped back. There was no cause for the woman's belligerence, it was simply ingrained in her, her shield against the opprobrium of the world.

'Another!' shouted Eli John from within, loud, mocking, not nearly as drunk as Frank sounded. Eli, the sly malicious snake. Why – of all people – must Frank choose, for his bosom companion, the one man with whom he was forbidden to have any commerce? Sometimes Leah suspected her brother courted his own destruction.

She looked around in desperation. It was unthinkable that she, a woman of spotless reputation, should cross that vile threshold, least of all unaccompanied, unless she wanted to be tarred with the same brush as Rachel Morgan, but something must be done. She spied David, a little way along the street, cornered by Mr and Mrs Phillips, with Betty's evident connivance. David saw her hurrying to meet them, and politely tried to make his excuses, but Betty was having none of it, hooking his arm and forcefully turning the conversation in a new direction that demanded his response.

'But it can only aid your prospects at Castell Mawr,' Betty insisted, as Leah drew close.

'Perhaps,' said David, raising his hat and turning towards Leah. 'You will excuse me, I hope? Leah, I thought you had gone. Is something amiss?'

'I need your help, David,' said Leah, stepping back and willing him to follow, away from the Phillips gathering. He did so willingly, but so did Betty, determined to miss nothing.

'Tell me,' said David softly.

'Frank is in the Black Bull,' said Leah, lowering her voice even further. 'He has been drinking. He's inebriated, I can hear. And Eli John is with him, egging him on. If Tada–'

'I understand,' said David, his head near hers. 'But how can it be kept from him?'

'Will you go in and bring Frank out?'

'Go in!' David looked up at the Black Bull as if facing the legions of Satan. Then he squared up to the necessity. 'Yes, of course, Leah. It must be done, there is nothing else for it.'

'Well!' said Betty. 'Begging her neighbour to enter such a house of sin and depravity! I wonder you do not die of shame, Leah Owen.'

I wonder you do not spike yourself on your own sharp words, Betty Phillips, thought Leah, but she said nothing. She felt the shame, right enough, as she watched David brace himself and march to the door of the public house. Rachel Morgan, smiling coquettishly, pushed herself up against him as he passed. David flinched away as if contaminated, and she snarled, thumbing her nose at his back, before following him into the smoky darkness of the interior.

Hands clasped and heart thumping, Leah waited. A minute. Another minute. What had she done? Were the drunken sots within setting upon David? How could she imagine that his calm reason would get through to Frank in such a state? She took a step closer. If she must enter, for David's sake...

Betty tutted behind her.

Then David emerged, one hand firmly clamped round Frank's arm as her brother stumbled and slumped and rolled out onto the street, a gale of laughter following him.

David's colour was heightened, his distress obvious, but at least he was unharmed. Frank, on the other hand, was a mess, dishevelled, his new clothes stained and sodden and torn. His eyes rolled as he teetered to one side and began to vomit into the gutter. Eli and Rachel stood in the doorway behind him, laughing in malicious glee.

Leah looked from Frank to David in horror.

'Oh, my poor David, what a disgraceful imposition to put upon you!'

Betty was bustling forward to take his arm, but he evaded her, grasping Leah's hands instead. 'Don't be alarmed.'

'I'll never forgive him,' said Leah. 'I'll never forgive myself for asking you. I should never—'

'You did right. Don't think of it.'

'But how can I take him back to Tada like that?'

'You can't. No need. You go with your parents back to Cwmderwen. I shall take Frank home. We'll clean him up and send

106

him back to you when he is sober enough. Tell your father Frank is with me, and he'll not fret.'

'David.' Leah gripped his hands in response. She didn't need to say more.

'The nerve of the woman!' muttered Betty, but however scandalised she was, she wasn't going to surrender her territory.

Leah nodded and turned away. It was the best that could be done. She hurried back to the side road by the chapel, where Mam was waiting quietly and Tada, with impatience.

'Frank is with David,' said Leah, praying her face was not too flushed. 'They are returning to Castell Mawr together. David has a calf he's anxious about.'

'And what does he imagine that good for nothing son of mine can do about it? Frank knows nothing of anything.'

'Perhaps he hopes to encourage Frank to think about such matters,' suggested Leah. There was no actual lie in her words, but plenty in her intent. She'd not forget that Frank was putting her through this.

Tada snorted. 'I wish him success then, for I've had none.'

'It will not harm Frank to make himself useful in some small way, for a change,' said Mam. Her tone was neutral but her eyes suggested she understood the matter perfectly. She understood too that Leah was writhing inwardly in guilty discomfort. 'Why do you not go with them, cariad? I know Flo always welcomes your help.'

'Leah will come with us,' said Tada, decisively. 'Frank may not know where his duty lies, but Leah knows hers is with her mother.'

'Yes, Tada,' said Leah, and not another word was spoken on the four-mile journey home to Cwmderwen in the deepening January gloom.

1899

'Miss Owen.' David George offered his arm as a matter of course, and Leah took it as a matter of course. For three years now, he had been offering her his arm, as a public declaration of intent, though still not a word had been spoken. It was understood. Everyone understood, although Betty Phillips stood her ground and would continue to do so until that word was finally spoken.

Mam understood, of course. And Tada, though he frowned, raised no objection to the sight of his daughter on David's arm as they walked home from chapel. No objection, as long as she fulfilled her duty at home, in the house and on the farm. No objection, as long as she maintained her virtue and reputation, and Tada could be confident of that. Leah, at twenty-five, was a woman practised in patience.

'Will you not come into the village to join my parents for dinner, Mr George?' asked Betty, blocking their path as they reached the chapel gate. If the way had not been too narrow, she'd have clamped herself to his other arm.

'I thank you for your kind invitation, Miss Phillips, but I must return to Castell Mawr. The farm commands my attention, even, alas, on the Sabbath.'

'Then you shall take tea tomorrow. And your sister too, of course.'

'Thank you, Betty, I shall certainly come,' said Flo George, stepping in between them and allowing David and Leah to go on their way.

Flo, like David, was in deep mourning, but like him she looked

108

resigned rather than crippled by grief. No one doubted her love for her father, old Mr George, but his last illness had been painful and prolonged, his mind far gone, and his passing had been a kind release. Now Flo could step out into the world again, to visit friends, attend the market, busy herself with the Sunday School and reclaim her life, although at thirty-six, no one – including Flo herself – expected romance to play any part in it. But she was happy to smooth the way for her brother.

Old William George was dead, and the tenancy of Castell Mawr was now David's. Head of the family, master of nigh on a dozen men, respected farmer consulted by the estate manager of Plas Malgwyn, deacon of the chapel with his place on the big seat, David George was now his own man. All he needed to seal his place in the parish was a wife to give him a son and heir. And the wife was a possession he was happily assured of. Who better to take on the role of mistress of Castell Mawr than Leah Owen, the farmer's daughter, who already had all the skills and responsibilities that his wife would require? The neighbour who already knew Castell Mawr inside out, who knew which field produced the best wheat, which cow the most milk, which sheep the most lambs, which geese the most eggs. The young woman who was fast friends with his sister Florence and would happily share the house with her.

It was just a matter now of waiting for the proper period of mourning to end. Leah breathed deeply in contentment as they walked arm in arm along the lane a few paces behind her parents. Her patience would be rewarded soon, and it was time. In a few more years, she would be cast as an old maid like Flo. If she wished to marry, to bear David's children and clasp them to her breast, it must be now.

There was no need to speak. They knew each other's minds, well enough. But perhaps some conversation was required.

'The weather looks set fair for a day or two,' said David, as the parting of their ways came in sight. 'Your father is wise to bring in the hay now. I'll be starting on our meadows, too, I think, though my men will be at your service, of course.'

'Thank you. We must make the most of the dry weather. It will keep us busy, for sure.'

'It's the best time of the year.'

'Indeed, I fancy it is.'

Behind them, Frank, hands in pockets and dragging his feet, laughed aloud. Tada turned to glare at him.

'What is the cause of such unseemly levity?'

'I was just listening to two passionate love birds twittering about the weather.'

Leah blushed. Of course the tameness of their conversation must appear absurd to others – others too dense to understand the undercurrent in every word and gesture, but Frank had no business listening or passing comments.

'If you haven't the grace to keep your conversation decent, keep silent,' said Tada, but his frown moved from Frank to Leah, deepening as it settled on David. There was something in that frown that sent a chill through Leah. 'Do not cast aspersions on your sister. She is a virtuous daughter who knows her duty and her place, not one of the trollops you ogle in town.'

Frank's grin faded. Leah had seen him often enough, in Llanolwen or Penbryn, lounging around with Eli John, leering at the passing girls and calling lewd comments after them as if they were all like Rachel Morgan, game to be hunted and abused. He was a fool if he thought Tada had not noticed.

Tada noticed many things. Sometimes he chose to act as if he hadn't, but if they were laid too overtly before him, his righteousness was a rod of steel. Frank had felt that rod often enough. Now, Leah felt the draught of its switch come near her too, and she didn't know why.

Or did she? She met Mam's eyes, sensing urgency in them, and felt David press her hand as they walked on. They always took the high road on the Sabbath because Mam thought it unseemly to be clambering over the stiles on the path through the woods in chapel best. Leah didn't object. The longer route gave her more time at David's side.

At the milk-churns, their paths parted. David stayed, still holding Leah's arm, letting Frank pass them, winking as he followed Mam and Tada down the lane to Cwmderwen. When they were left alone, David released her arm, and turned towards the entrance to Castell Mawr, gazing through it, down over his green pastures, before turning back to her, twisting his hat in his hands, just as Will Price did when nervous. 'I have it in mind, one day soon, to call on your father and speak to him. What would you say to that, Miss Owen?'

She felt her breast swelling, pulse speeding, but she responded solemnly to his correctness, with only a twitch of a smile to show her inner exultation. 'I would say you would be very welcome, Mr George.'

'I think it's time, don't you?'

'Yes. Soon. Very soon. As soon as the hay is done, perhaps?'

His chest heaved too as he beamed at her. 'When the last of it is safely stacked, I shall call.' He clasped her hand, uncertain whether to shake it or press it to his lips. He bowed towards her. She raised her face to his.

'Leah! Daughter! Don't keep us waiting.' Tada was standing square down the lane, staring back at them.

David immediately stepped back.

Leah gave him one last smile, as warm as she knew how, and hurried on down the lane to her waiting parents.

Mam smiled, an unhappy, wistful smile, as if her attempts at reassurance were growing weary. Why that frown on Tada's brow? Why that simmering resentment in his eyes? There could be no objection to David. It wasn't possible.

Leah filled the cup held out by Amos Absalom. 'To lay the dust, Amos.'

'And it's welcome too.' Amos leaned on his scythe in Cwmderwen's meadow as he drained the cup thirstily, his shirt sleeves rolled up, the cotton dark with sweat. 'You're an angel sent by the Lord, Leah Owen.'

'I am no such thing.' She glanced up. The clouds that had begun to pile up in the west first thing, threatening rain, had dissolved into nothing and the sky was now blue, the midday sun beating down on the labouring men. 'There's an angel watching over us today though. The hay will be dry in no time.'

'Your father has a nose for the weather.' Amos helped himself to bread and cheese from the basket she was proffering. 'The master takes his lead from him, I reckon.'

'But he'll be finished first,' said Leah. David's horse-drawn hay mowers and turners would have finished the Castell Mawr meadows while Tada and his helpers were still sweating with their scythes and pitchforks. David would willingly have lent out his machinery but Cwmderwen's steep misshapen fields were ill-fitted for their use, so he lent men instead.

'Is that lemonade?' Sam Evans, another of the Castell Mawr crew, was advancing on them, trailing his scythe. 'If it is, I'll drink the jug dry.'

Leah placed the basket on the ground. 'I'm sorry, Sam. My father and Morris and Amos have drained it between them. I'll go back now to refill it. It will never do for you to be left panting with thirst.'

'Bless you!' said Sam, wiping his brow.

Leah hurried home through the swathes of fresh-cut grass, insects buzzing around her, heat shimmering up from the earth, kites and kestrels hovering overhead in search of panicking mice and voles. She was glad of the shade of the overhanging oaks as she skirted round the barley field and the middle pasture to the cobbled yard where the pig was snuffling and the door of her father's workshop stood open, creaking on its hinges. Sun glinted on the slate tiles of the house, chickens scratched for seeds and Sarah was standing on the threshold.

Sarah, plump and matronly, her face pale as a dead lamb. Her mouth was open, her lower lip quivering as she looked blindly in Leah's direction.

Leah felt something plummet within her. The blood in her veins turned sluggish. Her legs resisted her silent command to run. The jug slipped from her fingers.

'Sarah, what is it?'

'She never said a word.' Sarah's voice was a squeak. She groped for Leah's hand and began to sob hysterically.

'Mam?'

Sarah bawled louder. Leah pushed past her into the house.

Mam was slumped in Tada's high-backed chair, askew as if only the greatest desperation had driven her to such a sacrilege. Even in death she had been governed by dutiful respect for the lawful master of the house. Her mouth gaped, lips blue, and her eyes were dull and lifeless under drooping lids. One nerveless hand still clutched at her breast, caught in the pleats of her blouse.

It was Mam, but not Mam. Leah knew that, even as she dropped to her knees and clasped her mother's free hand. Not yet cold, but utterly still. She could feel instantly that there was no life flowing in the veins. Mam had gone, vanished entirely into the air, leaving only a husk behind. Leaving Leah bereft in ways she had never allowed herself to imagine.

She couldn't weep, couldn't speak. Her throat closed up. Her stomach had become a dry stone, pulling her down to drown in something thick and poisonous. Mam couldn't die. Not like this. Not without warning.

Had there been warnings that Leah hadn't noticed? How many times in the last days had she come across her, rising from a chair or stool as if she'd been caught seizing a moment of rest? How many times had she found her leaning on a table or doorframe, catching her breath? How many times had she glimpsed that fleeting look of weary resignation on Mam's face? That urgency in her words of encouragement to Leah. Or that stifled wince of pain?

Leah had seen and hadn't understood. She had chosen not to understand, because the notion of losing her was too unbearable to acknowledge. Mam was her friend, her support, her shield against...

A shiver ran through Leah, releasing the knot in her throat just enough to let out a single wail of grief beyond measure. She clasped the limp corpse in her arms and rocked for a moment on her knees. As long as she stayed there, like that, locked together with Mam, surely it wouldn't be true.

But it was true. Sixty. A good age, people would tell her, but that was a lie. It was far short of the three score and ten the Bible decreed. It was too soon. And for Leah, too late. Hope, love, future, all were swept away by this cruel thing and all that remained for her to cling to was duty, hard and dry and bitter.

First, her duty to Mam, who couldn't be left there, like a rag doll in a chair where she didn't belong. Leah released her gently and rose to her feet.

'Sarah, send the children upstairs.' She sounded cold, she knew, but it was the only way she could cope. Cold and practical.

Sarah was still blubbering, noisily, helplessly, gaping at if she couldn't understand a word.

'Sarah! The children!'

Sarah's four were huddled in the corner, as far away from the great chair as possible. Leah seized the hand of the oldest, Will, and gathered up the youngest, Maud, who was barely crawling. 'Children, up the stairs, now.' It was a bustle, getting them up the high winding steps, terrified but understanding nothing except the need for tears. Leah deposited the baby on her bed and beckoned to the others. 'Now children, I want you to stay here and say your prayers.'

'Is Mamgu unwell?' asked Sarah Jane.

'She's—' It wouldn't do to lie to them. Or to herself. 'She's gone to the Lord.'

'Why?'

'She was tired, child. She needed to rest. And the Lord promises us rest, doesn't he?

They nodded, not understanding a word that she said. She recalled her own incomprehension, listening to sermons when she was young. 'She is with Jesus,' she said, hugging each in turn. 'Be happy for her.'

Be happy for Mam, she thought, as she descended the stairs. There will be no happiness for those she leaves behind.

Sarah was still sniffling and sobbing, wringing her hands.

'Sarah. We cannot leave her like this. You will help me lay her out.'

'Oh, oh.'

'Sarah!'

They entered the hallowed parlour. The great family Bible lay open, as ever, on the draped table, along with a pair of candlesticks and a pile of bills and other papers. 'Put Tada's papers in the cupboard. Take the candles. They can come back after.' She issued orders as she reverently lifted the Bible and laid it on a cloth in the wide windowsill. Her authoritative tone kept Sarah's sobs under control, although she was next to useless, dropping half the papers.

'Come!' They returned to the kitchen. Leah gently slid one arm around her mother's shoulder and the other under her knees. 'Help me.'

'I daren't! I'm scared to touch.'

'Sarah! Mam gave you life, she protected you and stood by you in your worst moments. You will not let her down now! Come!'

Gulping a deep breath, Sarah obeyed and between them, with as much dignity as Leah could manage, they carried Mam through to the parlour and set her down gently on the table.

'This is where Tom was laid out,' wailed Sarah.

'And for that reason, if no other, it is where she would choose to lie now.' Leah closed the dead eyes and straightened Mam's limbs. She placed the candlesticks at Mam's head and feet. 'Get me new candles. The good ones. These will not last five minutes. There, that must suffice till later. You'd best send the boy for Tada now.'

Amos Absalom's eldest, Ted, was supposed to be making himself useful, weeding in the potato patch, but he had sloped off to snooze in the shade of the fruit bushes. Leah watched Sarah corner him, still sobbing and incomprehensible, although he must have guessed enough to realise there was a crisis that needed Mr Owen. He leaped to his feet and hared off down towards the meadow, caught up in the excitement.

Sarah stumbled back into the kitchen and settled onto a chair so that she could bury her face in her arms on the table and resume her hysterical sobbing in comfort. From being a plump girl, Sarah had grown into a fat woman, always looking for a chance to take the weight off her feet.

Leah gazed at her for a moment, then returned to the parlour to

116

sit by Mam's side. She didn't weep. She was empty. She tried to pray but no thoughts or words came. Through the small panes of the window, the sky shone a brilliant blue but that made no sense because there was a cloud of darkness and confusion enveloping the whole world. She needed something definite, something precise. Dust on her skirt. Tiny seed heads had embedded themselves in the fabric as she had brushed against long undergrowth, walking up from the meadow. One by one, methodically, she picked each one free. Last one tugged loose, she fixed her eyes on the far wall. The crack in the plaster was still there. It had become more obvious since Tom's death, though she hadn't noticed until now. It descended further, snaking its way through the fading pattern of dots. A snake, yes, weaving its way down, a little further every day, coming, coming ever closer, waiting to devour them all. Had it devoured Mam, or had she passed through that crack into joy? Leah wanted Matthew Vaughan there to bewitch her with his loving certainties, but he was on the other side of the world, with griefs of his own to bear, three infants dead, and then his wife. The mission had asked for prayers and Leah had offered up hers, fervently, adding a secret hope that he would be summoned home at last from such a troubled faraway land. Now she wondered whether his faith was truly proof against such woe. Had it kept him steady, despite all, confident in the love of the Lord? She had no such confidence any more. I can't remember how to pray, she thought. For him or for anyone.

The heavy dark clock on the mantelpiece ticked, filling the silence. Tick. Tick, Tick. Somewhere deep inside, though no other thoughts would materialise, she conceived a grating desire for that slow remorseless rhythm to change, to speed up or slow down or anything rather than stay as it was. Dear God, make something silence that endless ticking. The desire grew, building up to a scream, but she swallowed it down before it could escape.

That one prayer at least was answered. Alien sounds intruded into the hush. Heavy footsteps disturbed the tick tick tick and drowned it out. The heavy tread of doom. The parlour door opened and her father came in, the dark shadows of other men crowding on his heels. Tada had pulled his black coat on over his begrimed, sweat-soaked shirt. He looked down on his dead wife, his facial muscles like taut harp strings. Behind his flowing beard, his jaw was clamped shut. His black eyes gleamed beneath his beetling brows as he confronted the closed eyelids full on, for the first time since Tom's death. His own eyes gleamed, but no tears fell.

Leah wondered, in a state of utter detachment, what he was feeling. Grief? Guilt? Relief to be freed from a union that had challenged him for so long with perpetual accusation?

Or did he feel nothing at all? After a long, long moment of silence, he said 'The Lord giveth and the Lord taketh away.'

'Amen,' said the men who hovered respectfully at the door, hats in hand.

Tada raised his eyes and stared at the scripture framed on the wall. *Cerddwch yn yr holl ffyrdd a orchmynnodd yr Arglwydd eich Duw i chwi; fel y byddoch fyw, ac y byddo yn dda i chwi, ac yr estynnoch ddyddiau yn y wlad yr hon a feddiennwch.* Ye shall walk in all the ways which the Lord your God hath commanded you, that ye may live, and that it may be well with you, and that ye may prolong your days in the land which ye shall possess. 'Where is my son?'

The men looked at each other, none of them eager to spell out the truth. 'He slipped into the village for something,' said Amos Absalom at last.

They shuffled, embarrassed. The whole parish knew what the something was. It was pointless to pretend ignorance, and yet none of them could bring themselves to mention the Butcher's or the Mason's Arms or the Bridge Inn, in such a place at such a time. Frank

Owen had done what he always did, abandon his family, his land, his duty, to get drunk while other men completed his labours, and now his mother lay dead.

Tada's fists clenched and unclenched. 'They shall say unto the elders of his city, This our son is stubborn and rebellious, he will not obey our voice; he is a glutton, and a drunkard. And all the men of his city shall stone him with stones, that he die: so shalt thou put evil away from among you; and all Israel shall hear, and fear.'

The gathered men exchanged glances, appalled by his choice of text. Leah stared at him, horrified, as he turned, his dark piercing eyes falling on her. 'One at least knows her duty. My daughter. It is not for us to question the will of the Lord, but to submit and humbly shoulder the burden laid upon us. Your mother is taken from us. Now you must be my support and my right arm, even as she was.'

An invisible rope tightened round Leah. Was this not as she had been raised? To obey the scriptures, to honour her parents, to do her duty, to remember the covenant that bound her to this man, this house, this soil? She had no means to fight against it.

'Yes Tada,' she said, her throat as dry as desert sand.

David came. He smiled his sympathy when he saw Leah, his eyes full of tears and apology, but he had come, as was proper, to condole with Tada. It was his sister Flo who came to volunteer her assistance among the women. Sarah remained, but what use was she? Mary did not come, although William Price had ridden to Penbryn with the news. He brought back word that Edward Lloyd was ailing and could not spare his wife, even at such a time.

Surely he could have spared her for this, thought Leah, but she had no energy to think of the sister that she had barely seen since the wedding in Penbryn. Her mind was fixed on Mam, because beyond Mam there was nothing but an empty void. With Flo's help and Sarah's hapless flapping, she did all that was necessary, washing her mother and preparing her with sweet-scented herbs for the oak coffin. It was Leah and Flo who laid out tea cups and cold meat for the mourners when they came to pay their respects as the Reverend Pritchard conducted the service in the cramped parlour, praising the virtues of a righteous and obedient wife. Why couldn't Matthew be here, sending her home, thought Leah, aching for the comfort his words always brought. The Reverend Pritchard was upright and energetic in his certainties, but he was not Matthew. She stood with Flo on Cwmderwen's doorstep and watched as the menfolk shouldered the coffin and set off for the chapel.

Leah had stood vigil, almost without sleep, over her mother's remains, but now, watching the funeral procession wind away, Frank dragging in their wake, his shoulders heaving with sobs, the dull wretchedness of grief broke into a simmering anger. Frank had been chastised for his absence when Mam had died, but Leah too had been absent. She hadn't said goodbye. Mam hadn't waited for her. She had died without a word to the daughter she had sworn to see happy and settled. She wanted to scream in rage at Mam for abandoning her so.

She clasped her arms tightly around her breast, forbidding herself to have such thoughts. It did not do to rage against God's will.

Flo slipped her arm around Leah's shoulder. 'I see how it is for you now. It need not be so very bad, you know, what life holds in store for us. David understands how it is.'

'Yes,' said Leah. 'David always understands.'

Of course David understood. As they met on the steps, emerging from chapel, to speak for the first time since Mam's death, it was obvious from the compassion and distress in David's eyes that he understood totally.

'I am truly sorry for your mother's passing,' he said, bowing his head over her hand as he took it. 'Her loss is immeasurable. She was a good woman, a loving mother and you will miss her bitterly.'

'As will we all,' said Tada, his hands resting on Leah's shoulders. Protective. Possessive. 'But the Lord bids us plough the furrow he has set us, however clogged or stony, and we will accept his will, as obedient children.'

Leah fixed her eyes on David, willing him, for once, for one time in his life, to rebel against the strictures of custom and commandment. But the sorrow in his eyes only deepened.

'Alas, yes, your father will have great need of you now.'

'Yes,' said Leah. It was as if a golden thread that had tethered them together was slipping through her fingers until she held only the flimsiest end to keep him attached.

'Mr Owen, Miss Owen, again my deepest sympathies.' David stepped back and as if by magic, Betty Phillips was there, placing herself between them, smiling her poisonous sympathy and patting Leah's hand. 'So very sad. I grieve for you, I do indeed. Such a great loss.'

My loss, your gain, thought Leah numbly, watching her rival turn, almost skipping, to take David's arm as he walked away, head still bowed.

'Come daughter, let us go home,' said Tada, turning her firmly towards the deep dark dell of Cwmderwen.

She let the golden thread go.

She cared for the house. She dusted and polished, she washed and ironed, she cooked and baked, churned butter, milked cows, fed the hens, carried food and drink to father and brother in the fields – mostly father, for Frank was seldom to be found. Shocked into sobriety, he had made himself respectable for his mother's funeral,

121

and had wept true tears for the parent who had shown him affection, but his dutiful behaviour had lapsed before the earth had settled on Mam's grave. Leah worked in his place when needed, cutting, binding, stacking, weeding, herding. In the evenings, when not mending, she sat with her father in the parlour, his amanuensis keeping the accounts, accepting the coins he doled out when purchases were required. She who had been denied further schooling once she could read the Bible, must now read and write and add and subtract for him.

Leah tidied away paper and pencil and settled, hands in her lap, to listen to Tada as he opened the Bible and prepared for evening prayers. November rain beat against the window. A flash of lightning seared across the night sky. The candle flickered in a cold draught. Where had it found a way in? Through that crack that sometimes filled Leah's thoughts whenever she was in this room? A crack that had opened to devour others but refused to open for her.

Tada's voice rolled around the sacred words like the thunder rolling outside, but she couldn't hear. They were smothered by the beat of her own pulse. Duty. Duty. Duty. Duty.

How could she complain about her lot? Once she had longed for duties. Once she had longed to be a teacher, surrounded by books, dedicated to her charges, and when that dream had been snatched away, another dream emerged, of working at Plas Malgwyn, like Sarah, so busy and useful that her worth would be recognised and rewarded. But even that had not been allowed. She had dreamed of finding her destiny as mistress of Castell Mawr, a staunch partner at David's side, mother to his children and honoured in the parish. A futile, silly, childish dream for romantic girls. This was all that was permitted to her: menial service without end at Cwmderwen. Her duty to land and family. While Mam had lived, she had never seen her lot as a curse, in the way Mary had cursed it. Mary had fought with every fibre to break free from the role forced upon her, and where had the battle left her? Tied to a man as old as her father, who would not even release her to attend her dead mother, kept as no more than a drudge, according to the gossips in Penbryn. The last time Leah had seen Mary, two years ago – silently accompanying her husband around the market – Mary had looked blank, drawn, dumb. She had achieved nothing by her escape, so what was the purpose in Leah even thinking of resisting? *It need not be so very bad for you*, Flo had said, but Flo had accepted her role gladly, tending her father without complaint and loving him to the end. She was in her late thirties now, too old and settled to expect admirers or a new life, although there were rumours that the Reverend Llywelyn – the new minister at Soar Chapel in Felindre – had been seen talking ardently to her in Penbryn, and she had shown no disinclination to listen. Perhaps there was hope for her, yet.

But not for Leah. She knew that. Her father, though grey and grim enough to pass for one of the prophets, was still hale at sixty-two, striding out ahead of younger men, working all hours without need of rest, clean-living and Godly in his habits, as everyone acknowledged. Tada's own father had lived to be seventy-three and his mother to eighty, so why would he fall short? Leah was likely to be his handmaid for fifteen or twenty years yet, and David could not wait that long. It was a luxury he could not afford. He had duties too, to Castell Mawr, the land his family had held for generations. A duty to provide it with a son so that it would remain with them for generations to come. That was everything. That was why David was not striving to resist the constant attentions of Betty Phillips, whose pitying smiles at Leah only grew more complacent with the passing months.

There was no need for pity. Leah stiffened herself. She refused to succumb to despair. In this life she was at least undisputed mistress of Cwmderwen, of the house, the animals, the twenty-four acres, one rood and eight perches. If she were tied to it, so too was it tied to her. She had the Owen pride, the determination to keep what they had, Owen land, sealed with a covenant of blood, if not of love.

'And thou, son of man, be not afraid of them, neither be afraid of their words, though briers and thorns be with thee, and...'

The candles blew wildly, nearly guttering, as a gust of cold air swept in under the parlour door. The outer door banged shut, banged again, the latch unfastened.

Refusing to be diverted, Tada continued, his voice rising, 'Thou dost dwell among scorpions: be not afraid of their words, nor be dismayed at their looks, though they be a rebellious house.'

Another flash of lightning was followed by a crash of thunder overhead, so close the air shook and every timber in the house creaked. Like a sad jest, it was echoed by a crash in the kitchen.

Tada folded his hands together and closed his eyes, his head bowed. Leah itched to be up and investigating what chaos Frank had wreaked, surely drunk to be coming in so late in such weather. But it was not permitted to stir a muscle while Tada prayed, so she remained motionless, straining to hear oaths or inebriated singing that would have Tada wielding the stick on Frank's back. There were no oaths or songs. The kitchen was silent.

'Amen.'

At last she was free to rise. Tada strode out across the kitchen to the outer door, pushed it fast, and thrust the bolts home, too late to stop a pool gathering on the slate slabs by the threshold. Leah held a candle aloft. The cause of the crash was clear. It was not only a stool that had toppled, but Frank himself. He lay sprawled before the range, sodden, stinking, snoring like a bull, his head in a puddle of vomited ale.

He did well to be unconscious, for there was no purpose served in beating him in such a state. Instead, Tada glowered down on his comatose son, drawing deep breaths. 'Let him lie in his own filth.'

'Tada?' Leah was already bending to grasp her brother's shoulders, but she stopped.

'Let him lie, I say. He brings nothing but shame on this house and this family. Let him lie like the beast he is. Let us to bed, daughter, with prayers ringing in our ears, not the grunts and groans of unclean swine.'

'Yes, Tada.' Half of her was more than happy to obey. She had no wish to lay a finger on Frank in his present state, to grovel on the floor, breaking her back as she tried to heave him onto the settle, breathing in his stinking breath, soiling herself and fouling her clothes by mere contact with him. But she was his sister still, and though he did more, day by day, to earn her scorn and disgust, he remained her childhood companion, tied by blood. If anyone in this world had any understanding of Frank, it was her. She knew the unjust burden he bore of not being Tom, she knew how unjustified much of the anger directed at him had once been but she could not justify the contempt he delighted to show for his lot. He cared nothing for the land or the good name of the Owens and made sure the whole world knew he preferred the company of Eli John, the devil in their midst. If Eli were Satan sitting on his shoulder, Leah must be his guardian angel, and if he would not listen to her whispering, at least she could make sure he didn't drown in his own vomit.

She glanced at Tada, raising the candle so that he could see the concern in her face, but he was not in a mood to relent.

'Leave him, I say–'

As he spoke, there was a knock, a rattle on the door. Tada turned, frowning into the wavering gloom. 'Who comes calling at this time of night? Well, answer it, daughter.'

She moved forward, her pulse changing its beat at last, racing now. Who would come calling so late, in the dark, in a torrential storm? Not any of their neighbours. If they knocked at all, it would not be so tentatively. An urgent message perhaps, from Mary in Penbryn. Or from Castell Mawr. What if something had happened to David? He was a neighbour, she was entitled to be concerned.

Forcing the latch up and catching the door before the wind could crash it wide, she was expecting to see Amos Absalom's son, or a lad from town. Not this. Not a stranger, a poor beggar girl, half-starved and white-faced, wrapped in a shawl that clung to her like the pelt ripped from a seal, water pooling around her feet. Her hair dripped in rat's tails and her eyes shone in terror and desperation.

'Who are you? What do you want here?' There was something so alien, so unexpected about the creature that Leah wanted to slam the door in her face, and shut her out of sight and mind, but her Christian duty forbade it. She could not turn such a poor thing back into the storm.

'Is,' the girl stammered, her skin blue, her teeth chattering with icy cold and with racking sobs, 'does Frank Owen live here?'

'He does.' Tugging her own skirts clear of the dripping wretch, Leah stepped back, opening the door wide. 'You'd best come in, or we'll all be chilled to death.'

Maybe the girl already was. She barely managed to shuffle across the threshold.

Tada raised his candle, lighting both her and himself, a sight sure to terrify her. 'Who are you and what do you want with my son?' he demanded. 'If you are one of Eli John's harlots, be off with you.'

'No, I'm Anne. Anne Jenkins.' The girl whimpered, pausing as though she clung to a hope they might recognise the name. When it was clear they did not, she whimpered again. 'I was maid at Rhoshelyg, but they threw me out when they saw—' She raised her

126

white tear-stained face and let her hands drop, palms out, pleading. Released from her grip, the shawl slipped from her shoulders and slid to the floor. Then they knew what she wanted with Frank. She was a skeleton, barely an ounce of flesh clinging to her bones. There was nothing of her, except her belly, but there was more than enough of that.

'I begged Frank. I swore it was his, and it is, as God is my witness, but he swore back at me and Eli laughed and told me to go foist myself on another fool. I begged but they wouldn't listen. I didn't know where Frank lived, but Rachel told me to follow him, so I did. I have nowhere else to go. He threw stones at me and sent me to the Devil, but what could I do? If you turn me away, there is nothing for me except to die in a ditch. The wages of sin are death, I know.' She wailed. She wailed like a wild sea-creature, wails that would have put Sarah's to shame.

Tada's hand shook with anger, the candlelight bobbing, casting shadows like dancing devils. 'I doubt that the sin was all yours, child. That beast, lying in his filth, bears the greater guilt. And he shall pay for it. Stop your snivelling, girl. You will not be cast adrift. Leah, brew the girl some tea. Give her linen to dry herself and put her to bed. Frank has planted the seed, so he shall reap the harvest.'

Without a word, Leah did as she was bid, settling Anne Jenkins at the table with a cup of tea to warm her through, wrapping her in rough flannel, fetching a clean nightgown from her own chest, and easing the shoes from the blue feet to dry the chilblained toes. All the while thinking...thoughts whirled around her and she did not dare grasp at them. Concentrate on the matter in hand. The whining creature had been brought this low by Frank, so Frank must marry her. That was plainly Tada's intention. He left the girl to her and turned his attention on his son. No longer was Frank to be left lying in his vomit. A pail of icy well water brought him round,

127

gasping and spluttering, and Tada plucked him up before he had time to realise where he was or who was with him. He blinked in bewilderment as his eyes focussed on Anne, hunched and quivering at the table. His mouth opened in denial but Tada struck him across the face before he could say a word.

'Do you know this woman, wretched boy?'

'No!'

'You'd add falsehood to your sins? Don't lie to me, boy. Do you want me seeking the truth in the village? I don't doubt there have been plenty to witness your whoring. Tell me, you know this woman!'

'Tell him, Frank,' whined the girl. 'It's yours, I swear. There's been no other.'

She'd had no other man, and probably had not suffered Frank, willingly, thought Leah. She had been thrown out into the storm, and Frank, egged on by the evil Eli, had hurled stones at her. She had never despised her brother so much, though she had little more sympathy for the feeble girl who had succumbed without pride or resistance.

'She's nothing,' mumbled Frank. 'A slut of no consequence.'

'Though she be the whore of Babylon, you will wed her.'

'No!'

'You will not shame this family by littering the countryside with your bastards. The infant she carries was conceived in sin, but it will bear your name and you will do your duty by it and by her, or I will smite the wickedness out of you until there is no more begetting, you hear me?' As Tada spoke, he struck Frank again and again, till the blood ran down from his nose and only his father's iron hand gripping his collar kept him on his feet.

Leah stared at him, pathetic as the girl he'd impregnated. This was no marriage decreed in heaven, or even a hasty cover-up like

Sarah's wedding, but it would be a marriage. The son and heir would have a wife. A woman to be mistress of the house and tend to Tada. That was all that mattered.

The kitchen at Castell Mawr was warm and clean as ever, the smell of sickness and decay long washed away, and Florence George, no longer stretched every which way by the demands of her ailing father, looked bright, less gaunt than she had, the roses of youth back in her cheeks. Though her smile had never wavered through the years, it was more joyful now.

'Leah! Welcome. I miss your visits. Let me look at you. You look weary. Well, my baking is done and the supper is in the pot, so let us be elegant like Lady Herbert and take tea at our ease, while you tell me how things fare at Cwmderwen. Your father is well?'

'He is.' Leah steadied herself, wanting to blurt out her news. It wouldn't do. What seemed like a promise of pure bliss must be concealed behind a tale of sorrow and shame. 'He is as hale as ever in his body, but not in his spirits. You have not heard, perhaps, of Frank's disgrace?'

Flo smiled as she set the kettle on the hob. 'Again? What is it, this time?'

'He got a girl with child.'

'Ah. I cannot say I am surprised. Rather, surprised that it hadn't happened sooner. David doesn't speak of it, to save my blushes, but I know Frank is always out and about with Eli John in the worst dens of depravity in Penbryn. Alas, Leah, your brother is a sorry mess and that's the truth. Do you know the girl?'

'No. She was a servant at Rhoshelyg, over towards Boncath. She has come to us in despair and Tada will hear of nothing but that Frank must marry her.'

'Well, I am glad of that, for your family's name, Leah, and for the sake of the girl, who would otherwise suffer, perhaps more that she deserves. The world can be cruel.'

'That is true, and I am glad Tada thought to do right by her and the child, and not cast her adrift.' It would have been what many would have expected of Thomas Owen, to cast out the girl and his son with her, just as he had turned Sarah from the house in her shame. But Leah knew Frank would never be cast out, whatever sin he committed, for he was Tada's son. An unworthy son and bitter fruit compared to the boy that was lost, but still he was his son – the only rightful heir to Cwmderwen, no matter how low he sank. And his child, if born in wedlock, would seal their hold on the precious land into the next generation. A marriage there must be.

Leah paused, smoothing the cloth on the table while her heart pounded. She kept her voice steady. 'So it seems they will wed and Cwmderwen will have a new mistress.' What more could she add? *Which means I am free once more?* She had no need to add anything. Flo would understand perfectly the implications of this unexpected development.

Surely Flo must understand. But if she did, she didn't show it. She turned abruptly to the dresser, busying herself with jugs and cups and saucers, more than two refined ladies could possibly need. Having taken them down, she began to put them back again as she spoke, a slight tremor in her voice.

'And we have news too, Leah. It was to be announced at chapel, but... David is betrothed to Betty Phillips.' Shoulders braced, she turned back to face her guest.

Leah fought. The struggle within her to stay calm and dignified took every ounce of her energy, body, mind and soul, so that she could not speak for a moment. Could not let out the scream of frustration, disappointment and despair that was stabbing at every inch of her insides.

Flo came towards her, hands outstretched, eyes bright with tears. 'My dear, oh dear Leah, how I wish... I know, I know, you must... It was only yesterday. I truly believe he would have been happier to wait longer, but Betty was so impatient.'

So determined, rather. Leah would have to say something, but still she could not. If she merely opened her mouth, the gunpowder within would explode.

Flo recognised the struggle that was being fought and managed a bright smile, turning back to the kettle and babbling as she poured, to let Leah regain control. 'Well, the village will be agog with news of two weddings, I don't doubt, and we shall all have a mighty task of cooking and sewing, when Christmas is done. It looks to be a stormy winter, does it not? Though I am no weathercock in these matters. My father could always tell what the season would bring, and David... The tabby has had kittens, did I tell you? And they are already out and about. Were you not looking for another mouser at Cwmderwen?'

Embarrassed by her own chatter, Flo stopped, wiped her hands and turned back to the table, seating herself opposite Leah. 'I am so sorry, my dear. If you only knew how much I wished—'

'Wishes are for children.' Leah's voice sounded harsher than she would have liked, but at least it was steady. 'And for brides and grooms. You must tell your brother that I wish him every joy,' she almost choked on the word, 'and many years of happiness with his chosen bride.'

'Oh Leah.'

'You spoke of tea?'

'Of course. Let me pour it now.'

Leah took her cup and sipped, rejoicing that it scalded her lips, her tongue, her gullet. Why did it not burn right through her? Its heat was dissipated in an instant, turned to ice by the sound of the outer door opening behind her. She knew, merely from the expression on Flo's face, that it was David.

'Miss Owen?' His voice was more unsteady than hers had been.

Carefully placing her cup on the table, she rose and turned to greet him, offering her hand. 'Mr George, I hear from your sister that I am to congratulate you on your engagement to Miss Phillips. I hope you will both find happiness together.'

'Oh.' David blushed, hung his head, his embarrassment more obvious than hers. 'Thank you, Miss Owen.'

'I too have news. My brother is to wed as well, so I am to be ousted from my position as mistress of Cwmderwen and must find another role in life.'

Now it was David's turn to be lost for words, and he made no attempt to hide the distress racking his features. 'I—'

'And now, I must hurry away. My father will be missing me. Good day to you, Flo, Mr George.'

She walked out, dignity intact, head high. How far to the nearest trees, where she could hide among the sodden fading undergrowth and sob like a baby?

Too far. She was barely beyond the last barn of the farmyard when footsteps came hurrying behind her.

'Miss Owen, I... Leah!'

She stopped, steeling herself.

David was past her, turning to face her, tears on his cheeks, his eyes pleading like a puppy. 'Leah, forgive me. What have I done?' Was he going to drop on his knees before her?

She felt as sorry for him as her own plight would allow. She was the strong one. 'You have done your duty, found a wife at the proper time, to keep your house and... your bed. To bear your children. This is what your duty demands of you. This is what Castell Mawr demands.'

132

'I was too hasty. I don't know how it happened.'

She almost smiled. 'Miss Phillips is not a woman to be gainsaid.'

He took a deep shuddering breath, shut his eyes for a moment and then raised his head. 'It was a mistake. I always intended – you know what I intended, Leah. I should have waited. I should have kept faith.'

'No.'

'It was a mistake. I must correct it. It's only right. I must break off—'

'No!' Did he know what it cost her to say it? 'You have promised marriage to Miss Phillips. You cannot go back on your word. Does she deserve such humiliation?'

'It has not yet been announced in chapel.'

'You spoke to her yesterday! Do you imagine Betty hasn't already broadcast the news to half the world?' Her voice was growing shrill. She calmed it. 'You are a good man, David. A man of honour who strives always to do right. That is why I...respect you. You will never cause pain willingly.'

'And yet I have caused pain, to myself and to another I hold dearer than—'

'Stop! David, no more of this. You must do your duty, as must I, as must all of us. Be a good, loving husband and father, as I know you will. And,' she stopped, struggling to keep the tears back, 'be a good neighbour to me, as you have always been.'

'Leah!'

'Goodbye, David.' She stepped around him and hurried on her way, her hasty stride breaking into a run that had the breath burning in her parched throat. She would not let the tears flow. She would not. She would not. She was not to be pitied by anyone. She had self-respect and the respect of others. She had not been bought and traded from the gutter, like Rachel Morgan, or lost and lonely in uncaring service to be seduced by the force of a drunkard, like Anne Jenkins. She was strong, she was herself, she was Leah Owen of Cwmderwen and she would not weep.

1900

The lanes were decked out in bridal gear, hawthorn blossom frothing out from the fresh spring green of the hedges. Even in the deep dell of Cwmderwen, the flowers encroached with their sweet smell of death. Leah watched as Betty Phillips – Betty George as she had been now for the last fortnight – brushed fallen blossom from David's sleeve as she led him across the yard to their door. The ceremonial visit of the bridal couple after a honeymoon in Tenby. Leah and her father had paid their polite respects immediately after the wedding, and now the compliment was to be returned.

Betty was all smiles and triumph, parading her prize. Was she utterly oblivious to her husband's agonised discomfort? Either oblivious or determined to stamp it out, and when Betty was determined, nothing stopped her.

'Good morning.' Leah calmly ushered them into the kitchen.

Betty bustled in, glancing round complacently at the dark, spartan interior, the shabby dresser, the mean range, barely glowing, doubtless comparing her lot with that of her former rival. 'Good morning to you, Leah, Mr Owen.' She shook their hands as if she owned the place, before nodding dismissively at Frank's wife. Anne, already nauseous with another pregnancy, was sitting in a corner, willing herself invisible, red eyed and red nosed, nursing the baby. 'Mrs Owen.'

'It is a good thing to welcome a new neighbour who acknowledges obedience to our Saviour as well as to her lawful lord,' said Tada gravely, pressing her hand. 'Our community is blessed by such a match.'

Leah avoided David's eyes and yet was conscious that he was also avoiding hers. Was there deliberate sarcasm in Tada's words? Betty had always attended chapel punctiliously, in her very smartest clothes, but she seemed keener on observing her neighbours and the set of her hat and skirts than on the holy word, and to Leah's knowledge, she had never obeyed anyone. Betty George was a woman born to command, control and judge. It was a pity she had not been born a man. As a man she could have commanded armies and nations.

And she would not have married David.

David mouthed 'Amen,' but Betty brushed the words aside. 'I am delighted to be your near neighbour at last, Mr Owen. I know the families of Castell Mawr and Cwmderwen have always been close and that, I hope, will not change, though so much else has. We are stepping into a new world, are we not, my darling? A new century and, ha ha,' she smirked at the ring on her finger, 'a new life and new expectations. At least for some of us.'

'You are looking very well, Betty,' said Leah, coolly, laying out the tea things. 'Married life must suit you.'

'I believe it does. Well, it is what we women were created for, is it not?'

Leah poured the tea.

'May the Lord bless your union and make it soon bear fruit,' said Tada.

Betty laughed. 'Not too soon, for decency's sake. We are barely wed.' She shot one sideways glance at the baby, Mary Anne (known by all as Annie), cradled against her mother's breast.

Annie was clearly unimpressed by the arrival of the new bride. She screwed up her little face in that expression of intense concentration that heralded an imminent change of linen. Betty's nose wrinkled as the smell reached her. Annie smiled beatifically.

Leah handed tea first to Betty, then to David, meeting their eyes expressionlessly. Betty returned her gaze with defiance, but David's eyes shone with pained tears. Leah caught a short sharp stab of jealousy from the new bride. That would not do – neither the jealousy, nor Leah's satisfaction in it. For David's sake, it would not do. 'Mr and Mrs George, you must excuse me for a moment. My niece needs my attention. Go and change your apron, Anne. The baby has soiled it.' She took the baby from Anne, who offered no resistance. Left to herself, Frank's wife would cling to her child as if it were all that connected her to life, but she never argued, never dared to object when others took charge.

Safe in the privacy of the scullery, Leah let her rigid self-control slip. Her features crumpled into silent anguish. Why must she endure this? Wasn't it enough that Betty had taken David and settled herself not half a mile from their doorstep? Must she also invade the very hearth of Cwmderwen with her triumphant crowing and drag David with her like a battle trophy? How he must have dreaded this pointless visit. Best let Tada deal with them, while she gave her attention to Annie.

The child was a thing of strange wonder, she thought, gazing down on the perfect sturdy limbs as she stripped and cleaned them. Begotten out of drunken loveless lust, borne in fear and desperation, brought forth in shame and condemned for sins not her own, she should have been made in the image of her mother, shrivelled and wailing in perpetual despair. But no, Annie was as bright and bonny and beautiful as any infant conceived between sanctified sheets and hailed with celebration.

There was love still in Leah. She was not permitted to offer it to David, but she could offer it to this mite. Not that she would make a parade of it. After all, she was only the child's aunt, and an aunt who had no patience or respect for either parent. Frank had forfeited any affection she'd had for him long ago, with his lewd words and his drunkenness and infantile determination to provoke at every turn. He'd complained to her of his forced marriage and she had slapped his face. He was a feckless coward, led by the nose by Eli John, and utterly indifferent to farm or family, yet incapable of fight or flight. As for his wife Anne, Leah had pitied her plight, but could feel no pity for the girl's embrace of defeat and misery. Why had she no pride? Why did she not raise her head high and stand up to the vicissitudes of life as Leah did?

Yes, Leah despised her, but there was satisfaction, too, in the girl's helplessness. Anne had never presumed to take up her place as mistress of the house, content to remain the nonentity in the corner. Leah reigned still as the undisputed queen of the Owen kingdom. A small kingdom, only twenty-four acres, one rood and eight perches, and rented according to Man's law, but they were Owen acres in the eyes of God. Sealed with Owen blood. Acres that gave them pedigree, roots, the dignity to hold their heads high.

'Look, Annie.' With the baby freshly wrapped, Leah opened the back door and stepped out into the garden. 'This is Owen land. Do you see? The potatoes and peas? The apples and gooseberries. The trees and the meadow, the oats and barley, cows and sheep and pig and hens. Our land. Mine. Yours. They can take everything else away from us, but they won't take this with their simpering smiles and smirking comments. You hear me, Annie Owen?'

Annie, content and warmly cradled, blew a raspberry of satisfaction.

Leah gently kissed the soft brow. Reconciled for a moment to her fate, convinced that God had not abandoned her entirely, she squared her shoulders and returned to the kitchen.

'Well of course it is dreadful news,' Betty George was saying. 'But what can you expect? These heathens are all barbarians. I don't doubt our troops will settle things, but I have always said he was very rash to go.'

Leah was aware of solemn faces all around. The wedding visit seemed to have taken a dark turn.

'We go where God commands,' said Tada. 'Perils cannot be shunned if He calls.'

Leah returned Annie to her mother. 'What are you talking about?'

'Affairs in China,' said David. 'Rebellion and massacres. We must pray that our Reverend Vaughan is safe and well.'

'Has there been any word from him?' asked Leah, feeling her pulse race.

'No,' said Betty busily. 'Although the Reverend Pritchard has made enquiries of the mission. Naturally we are all anxious for news.'

Naturally. Leah sat through the rest of the visit, nodding, responding, filling cups, and all the while her mind was thinking, he will be safe. Of all men in the world, God will surely protect Matthew Vaughan, for none is so wholeheartedly devoted to Him. No other embodies all the true Christian virtues. Love, compassion, diligence, humility, faith, hope and charity. Every missionary in China may fall but God will preserve Matthew.

The news came at harvest time. The Reverend Pritchard announced it in chapel.

'Let us pray for the survivors, the wounded and bereaved, for the brave troops of many nations who are rallying to put down this foul insurgency. And let us beseech Him to grant mercy to a sorry violent world. But let us all, amidst our tears, rejoice for our beloved brother in Christ, Matthew, who is now released from his sufferings and in paradise, a blessed martyr for the Word.'

What more he said, Leah didn't hear. She accompanied her father home like a deaf mute, cut off from sight and sound. At the door she excused herself and walked across the yard, through the home field, through the long field, through the dark field, through the meadow. This was a joke. God was mocking her, mocking the faith that she had clung to all her life. Why would he allow Matthew to be murdered and yet let lesser men live? Why were foul beasts like Eli John allowed to prosper while Matthew was hacked to pieces? Martyrdom? What heavenly cause did such sickening bloodshed serve? She didn't want Matthew martyred, she wanted him coming home triumphant and joyous to Wales to tell her that God was love and all would be well.

She was at the river's edge, dried rushes rustling around her, the earth soft, sinking under her feet. Another few steps and she would be in the strong grey flood of the river. Why not take another few steps, since life held no purpose or justice?

'Heard the news, Owly?'

She hadn't seen Frank there, crouching on a stone, tossing pebbles into the river. His eyes were bloodshot, but he wasn't drunk. Not quite.

'It's all around the Butcher's Arms. Matthew Vaughan is dead.'

'Yes.'

'Futility, that's all there is. The fool hath said in his heart, there is no God. Everyone says I'm a fool. I'll say it now. There is no God.' He rose, straightening unsteadily, and she realised his eyes were red from weeping, not from gin. 'Are you a fool yet, Owly, or are you so wise you must still believe?'

She said nothing. He shrugged and ambled off.

'Yes, I am a fool, Frank,' she whispered to the river. 'There is no God.'

THE RIPENING

1905

The house smelled of babies, stale milk and burned stew. Anne was listlessly propped on the settle by the range, wheezing and coughing between croons, or were they moans, over her youngest. Baby Francis was a sickly child, unlike his older siblings, but like his mother well enough. At a year and a half, he was barely crawling, disinclined to do anything except whine.

Leah pressed her lips together to contain her urge to shout as she gazed around the kitchen, dirty pan and bowls scattered on the table, a puddle on the floor, Annie and John huddled in a corner, clothes awry, faces smeared, playing with one of the puppies that should be in the barn with its mother.

'Is this a house fit for human habitation?' Tada, behind her, was less inclined to keep a seal on his anger. 'We have not been gone twelve hours and you have let the place become a midden. Is this how you repay our charity?'

'The baby was ailing,' whimpered Anne.

Leah still held her peace. She touched the baby's brow. Too warm but not dangerously so. The child was always feverish. 'I'll give him cordial. Children, up! Take the puppy outside and then scrub your hands and faces. Now!' Annie and John scrambled up, Annie still cuddling the puppy, and sidled out hurriedly. They did not fear their aunt's anger but Tadcu was another matter. He was a stern old man who didn't shy from meting out chastisement for faults.

He ranted on now while Leah hung up her coat and hat, tied her apron and set about putting the kitchen to order. 'We have come from a meeting overflowing with the blessed spirit of our heavenly father, from amongst men and women who trembled and cried out in ecstasy at the consciousness of God's grace. We return renewed and revived in our faith, eager to be about the Lord's work, and what do we find? The woman to whom we gave Christian refuge lazes in filth and ingratitude, letting our home fall to wrack and ruin.

'I'm sorry,' whined Anne

Leah was torn. Knowing Tada's words were an ill reflection of the ardent commitment to Christ he had shown at the meeting they'd just attended, she would sympathise with Anne, if only the woman would show the slightest willingness to rise to her situation. Instead, she cowered, as she had cowered from the day she'd arrived, a kicked cur with no fight in her. She did as she was bid, like a slave fearful of beatings. Not that it saved her from them. Tada had never laid a finger on her, despite his obvious contempt, but Frank never held back, taking out his drunken rage and resentment on her whenever the mood took him. He had been forced to marry her, so now every thrashing he received from his father was passed on, with interest.

Leah had listened to the beatings, just as she was forced to listen to Frank's animal rutting – the house being so small – and there was no holding back with that. Annie and John had been born barely eleven months apart, and Frank cared nothing for his wife's soreness or fragility. There was nothing Leah could do except look disdainfully at her brother and assist with Anne's births. 'It is not proper to come between a man and his wife,' commanded Tada. 'God has bound them as one. So be it.'

So be it. Leah took the dirty dishes into the scullery, washed and dried them. Let none put man and wife asunder. Put lovers asunder, yes, with demands of duty and expectations of obedience, but not man and wife. That was the law, God's law, whether God existed or not, and she would obey it, however deadened her own soul.

144

She returned to the kitchen. Tada had had his say and was in his chair, waiting, like a judge in court, while Anne haplessly attended to the task of making tea, her eyes constantly turning to the child who was kicking feebly on the settle.

'Here, leave that to me and attend to the child,' said Leah impatiently. 'Give him a drop of the yarrow.'

The door opened and little Annie came back in, cautiously, eying each of the adults to gauge her chances of escaping censure.

'Come here,' ordered Tada.

She came, obediently, hands behind her back.

Tada placed a finger under her chin to force her head up. Her face was pink and clean. 'Hands?'

She held them out, chubby but spotless.

'Now let me hear you say the Lord's prayer, so that I may know the Devil is not in you.'

'*Ein Tada, yr hwn wyt ti yn y Nefoedd...*' Annie had it off pat, sounding properly devout as she spoke. Leah had taught her well. It was Leah, of course, who taught the children everything, their prayers, their letters and numbers as they were able, their tasks and duties. Everything but love, because that was not her place. It was for their mother to teach them love, and Anne did her best on that score, though it was a passive, helpless love. '*A'r gogoniant, yn oes oesoedd. Amen.*'

'Amen,' said Tada, patting her on the head before glowering towards the door. 'Where is the boy?'

The boy. He would never call his grandson John. The child should have been named Thomas, for his paternal grandfather and dead uncle, but no, for once Frank had demonstrated some sly energy. Before they knew it, the baby had been registered as John Francis. John for Anne's father, Leah explained to anyone who asked, though who this John Jenkins was, they never knew. Anne had only the dimmest memory of him. Leah suspected that the name had been chosen solely to annoy Tada, conjuring up thoughts of Jacob and Eli John.

The third baby had been named Francis Edward. Frank, determined that every son he begat should bear his own name – to overshadow that of his family – had threatened Francis Eli, but Leah had persuaded him to settle on the King's name instead, warning him of bloody repercussion if he went so far beyond the pale. Eli John, with Rachel Morgan on his arm, had accosted Leah in the village and demanded to know when he could christen his godchild with gin. She had stepped around them without reply and they had both laughed after her.

'I ask, where is the boy?' repeated Tada, as Annie had not replied.

'He was seeing to the pig,' she whispered.

Leah looked to the window in alarm. John was a fine healthy boy, but only four. Sturdy on his feet and old enough to see to tasks, but far too small to deal with a pig that could crush him in a trice. 'Has he gone into the pen?' She hurried to the door, opened it and drew a deep breath of relief. John, on tiptoe, was reaching over the wall of the pig pen to drop in handfuls from the swill bucket. From the eager grunting within, Leah guessed that Anne had forgotten to attend to it in their absence.

'That's good, but you must wash your hands again now and come in.'

John dropped down to run back to the pump. Like his sister, he was always obedient. Hands scrubbed, he came hurrying in and stood to attention before his grandfather.

Tada scrutinised him, frowning, then nodded slowly. 'Good boy to think of the beasts. Though your father is a wastrel and a burden on my old age, God has given me promise of a better harvest in his son. You are an Owen, boy, born to this land and the creatures upon it, to hold unto death. Never forget that.'

146

'No, Tadcu.' If John did not understand the full import of his grandfather's words, he understood that he was approved.

'Let me bless you, child.' Tada laid a gnarled hand on John's head as Leah began to close the door.

She stopped, for another figure, up from the pasture, had burst into the yard. Not Frank but young Harry Absalom from Castell Mawr, red faced and pausing, hands on knees, to catch his breath.

'They said...to bring you...Mrs.'

'Recover yourself, Harry.' Leah sounded calmer than she felt. This could only be about one thing. One thing that she wanted nothing to do with. Why must they come for her? 'Now. What is the matter.'

'Mrs George, M'm. She's started, and it's bad, and old Maggy Thomas is out with Mrs Devonald. Mr George has gone to Felindre for Mrs Llywelyn but he's not back yet, and the mistress is hollering something awful.'

'Mr George won't find his sister in Felindre. She and the Reverend Llywelyn were at the meeting with us. So I had better come, then. Give me a moment.' Leah turned back into the house. 'It seems I am needed at Castell Mawr. Mrs George's time has come.'

Tada nodded. 'Go and do your Christian duty, daughter. We shall manage without you for a short while.'

Only a short while, mind. Donning her hat and coat again, she set off with Harry Absalom across the fields. What spite life held, forcing her to come to Betty's aid in bringing forth David's son and heir, the child that should have been hers to bear. There was no help for it. She was becoming a bitter old maid and it was no more than the world expected.

The old house of Castell Mawr was humming with chatter and activity that seemed quite aimless. Nobody knew what to do. Or was it that everybody knew what to do and everybody knew differently? Rhodri Davies and Sam Evans were pacing in the yard, scratching their heads and peering in through the kitchen window. Within, Mrs Absalom and Mrs Evans were close to coming to blows over the medicinal efficacy of brandy, a dusty and untouched bottle of which had been unearthed in the pantry.

'Mrs George is in bed, I suppose?' asked Leah, as the two women stepped apart guiltily.

'Yes, Miss Owen. Millie Davies is with her, but she's swearing like a demon.'

To illustrate the point, a noise like a cow in pain emanated from the stairs, followed by a string of blasphemies roared at the top of Betty George's voice.

'I'll go up,' said Leah.

She had been up these stairs before, helping Flo with the linen and, once, a year ago, to help her dress for her wedding to the Reverend Llywelyn. Not that Leah's help had been necessary, as Betty George had pointed out vociferously, but Flo had requested her, so she had come, to adjust the veil on the bride's hat, to smooth down her soft grey dress, hand her her gloves and her posy, before hugging her one last time.

'What a palaver, when she's not going three miles down the road,' Betty had sniffed, but Flo had laughed and whispered in Leah's ear, 'The Lord answers our prayers in his own good time.'

Betty George had been forced to wait on God's timing, but not patiently, Leah thought, as she reached the top of the stairs. Three years married before she had shown signs of being with child. She had been growing very tight-lipped until then, scowling as the Owens added one child after another to their harvest.

Leah took a deep breath before entering the bedroom, one room she had never entered, though she had dreamed of it once, when such dreams were permitted. David's room. And Betty's. She found herself almost blushing as she looked towards the bed, though improper thoughts were soon washed away by the sight of Betty, swollen like a pig in nightgown and cap, grabbing the bars of the brass bedstead, teeth gritted and red in the face as she strained.

'Grrrrrrr! Damnation take it! Jesus! I'll never do this again. Awww!'

Millie Davies, the maid, leapt up with relief as Leah entered. She had a bruise on her temple. Leah looked around to see what Betty had thrown, but the room was littered with likely lethal objects, as well as softer pillows, shawls and caps. Water pooled around a bowl that had been brimful. Betty had been busy.

Leah took off her coat. She was still wearing her apron. She tested the water. 'Go and change this, Millie. It's grown cold. Is there linen?' Yes, but rumpled and scattered. She began to fold it. 'Bring some chamomile tea.'

Millie hurried off as Betty's pains eased and she slumped back onto her pillows. 'Useless girl! So, you have deigned to come, Leah Owen.'

'You thought I would refuse?'

'I don't know why you'd want to help me. I know you hate me.'

'Why? Do I have cause, Betty?'

Betty scowled, her glance flittering away. 'I suppose you take pleasure in seeing me like this.'

'I take no pleasure in anyone else's pain. Though I may take pleasure in the thought of my neighbour's joy in a child, may I not.'

'David's joy, you mean. You think he's yours, still.'

'Betty.' Leah stood over her, commanding her attention. 'You have David. What more do you want to take from me?'

'I don't know what you mean. Or are you all so holy now, having come from hearing the Reverend Joshua? You are saved, is that it and can forgive everyone?'

Leah thought back to the meeting she had attended that day with her father. With the country all around in the throes of religious ecstasy, it had been a meeting of prayer and preaching attended by a thousand and more. A meeting in which exaltation and salvation abounded and seized the souls of so many, leaping from their seats in a shrieking frenzy of agonised joy. A tide was sweeping the land, and Tada claimed that the spirit of the Lord was truly among them, washing them all with the blood of the Lamb and touching them all with grace. But Leah had felt nothing. Nothing at all. Cut off and cold, as if the words, which she would once have embraced, had no meaning for her. *There is no grace in me*, she thought. *God, if there is a God, has withdrawn His spirit from me. And yet here I am, come to help this woman as if I am still his child. If I am already damned, would it be excusable to cut her throat?*

'I'm no holier than you, Betty George.'

Betty tutted. 'Tell me about the meeting. We would have gone, of course, were it not for this. How did it go?'

'There was some excitement at the start. A novel sight for all of us, I think: they brought the Reverend up to the field in a motorcar.'

'No! Was it dangerous as I've heard?'

'Only for moles. They had intended he should stand in it to preach but it stuck fast in the mud and wouldn't move. They had to find him a box to stand on.'

'And he spoke well? Was the spirit on him?'

'There was much enthusiasm,' said Leah, expressionlessly.

'I hear that–' Betty suddenly clutched Leah as if to break her arm. 'Aaagh! Ow! The Devil! There is...I shall never...eeee!'

Leah, with her free hand, dipped a handkerchief in the lavender water that stood by the bed and bathed Betty's sweating brow. 'Calm yourself, Betty.'

'Easy for you to... Aaah!'

Leah released herself and raised the sheets, narrowly avoiding a kick from Betty. 'It's close. It will not be long.'

150

'What do you know!' spluttered Betty. 'Damned virgin spinster!'

'Careful, Betty. Don't overtax yourself. So many women die in childbirth and you are alone here, but for me.'

Even through her pain, Betty blanched with terror.

'Let us trust that my virgin spinster assistance will be sufficient,' said Leah coolly. 'Now. Push.'

The first child of David George emerged into the world with more blasphemies and obscenities than Leah had ever heard or had imagined prim Mrs George could possibly know, but the baby came through it well enough and so – despite her shouts that she was at death's door – did Betty. It was a girl, not the expected son and heir, but a healthy child.

'I suppose no need for the jacket,' sniffed Betty, once she had recovered enough to clasp the child to her breast. 'Ow!'

Leah glanced at the cradle which had been placed ready. A tiny jacket of hunting pink had been laid on it – David's, when he had been an infant. A boy's jacket.

'It's too large for a new-born, anyway,' said Leah, pulling away soiled sheets, and taking the chamomile tea from Millie, who was hovering, open mouthed.

Betty sniffed again, then forced herself to look at Leah. 'Thank you. What I said—'

'You said a great many things that must have shocked the very walls, but they are not to be repeated, now the pains are passed.'

'Not altogether.' Betty grimaced, holding her breast.

They all turned to the window at the sound of hoofs striking the cobbles.

'David is back,' said Leah. His men were gathering around to tell him the news, as he dismounted.

He came rushing up the stairs. 'I couldn't find Flo and–' He took in the scene, his child on his wife's breast, and Leah standing back.

151

She turned away as David strode up to the bedside.

'A daughter,' said Betty. 'But we'll have more.' That old strain of possessiveness was back in her voice. 'A son next time.'

'A daughter is welcome with all my heart,' said David, delicately touching the tiny wrinkled face. 'We'll call her Hannah for my mother?'

'Of course.' Betty gripped his hand, locking her fingers in his, then, nearly choking on the words, she said, 'Hannah Leah.'

'A good thought,' said David, quietly. He raised his eyes to Leah. 'You have my eternal gratitude for this, Miss Owen. Eternal.'

'I was merely being neighbourly, Mr George,' she said gruffly, reaching for her coat.

'You will stay, will you not? Eat with us? At least take tea. Millie can—'

'I must go. I cannot neglect my duties at Cwmderwen. I wish you both well, and blessings on the child.' Head high, she walked away.

An image came with her. Not of David, not the child nor the ardent preacher at the great gospel meeting, but an image of a carriage, gleaming brass and studded leather, promising all the liberty of the open road without harness or weary horse... except that it was stuck in mud and going nowhere.

1908

Leah sharpened the heavy steel knife on the rough stone of the windowsill, before turning her attention to the mutton bones and cabbage on the table. Were they all to starve? Somebody had to be busy and working, not letting the day go to waste. If she had a moment to herself she'd spend it more productively than sitting in a corner snivelling. Only a week ago, the suffrage women, Mrs Pankhurst, Mrs Martel, Mrs Pethick-Lawrence and others were addressing crowds in Haverfordwest. She'd read about it, avidly, in the *County Guardian*. That was where she would have been, listening to their arguments, if she'd had any time to herself, but she hadn't, because there was always too much to be done and she was the only one – it seemed – who had the will to do it. What would Anne do when they started cutting the barley? Sit and sob?

'That shirt won't mend itself,' she snapped, chopping furiously. 'You want your husband in rags?'

Anne, huddling in her usual corner, coughing and sniffing as ever like a sickly kitten, only sobbed louder.

Leah, hauling the big black pot across the table, refused to look at her. 'What is it now?'

'The baby.' It was like a mouse whispering.

Leah put the knife down and turned to face her sister-in-law, arms folded. There was a little bird inside her demanding sympathetic tears, but it was locked behind iron bars. Babies died. It happened all the time. Her mother had lost two, as well as Tom. What was the use of fighting against God's will? 'The child is with the Lord and you should rejoice for it. The Lord giveth and the Lord taketh away. Do you dare to rebuke God with your tears?'

Why was she doing this? She winced at her own words, appalled at their callousness, but she couldn't stop herself. She couldn't be like Flo, embracing her fate with a glad heart. She couldn't be a willing martyr like Matthew. There was no gladness in her.

Anne was crying now in earnest, the tears dropping down onto the linen she was supposed to be stitching. There was nothing to Anne except this one thing, her unbreakable love for the babies Frank inflicted on her with tedious regularity, and even there, fate conspired to heap misery on her. Like Mam, she'd lost two in the womb and little Francis Edward had finally succumbed to the inevitable doom that had been on him from birth. Even while Anne had crippled herself with grief over that, she had been carrying another child, but baby Mary had survived only a few weeks. The Lord did nothing but take from Anne Owen. They had buried Mary's tiny corpse three months ago, but still Anne wept and whimpered as if grief had become so ingrained, she couldn't escape it.

Leah wanted to shake her. It wasn't God the woman was rebuking with her tears, it was her, for her heartlessness. And the accusation was false! Locked in her own heart, in her own head, refusing to reveal itself to the world or even her family, was an agonising grief for each child. They were not hers, but still she had ached for them in their brief and painful sojourn in this world. Yet she had not shed a tear that anyone else could see. And she would not now. God knows, Anne had enough tears for all of them. Tears enough to drown the world.

'Finish the shirt, Anne,' she commanded, thrusting a handkerchief at the woman. Anne obediently wiped her streaming eyes and nose. Bright washed eyes and flushed skin. As she fought to control her sobs, another bout of coughing seized her. Leah watched a fine spray of crimson stain the shirt.

Yes, the Lord only took from Anne, and soon he would take her, too. Leah had guessed it months ago. Now it was clear. A sudden gush of contrition seized her, regret and shame for all the humiliations she had heaped on the woman, her lack of compassion, Christian or merely human. She wanted to take Anne in her arms and hug her, reassure her, beg her forgiveness.

But Leah Owen didn't do such things. She didn't make an exhibition of herself. She squeezed Anne's shoulder and gently took the marked linen from her. 'Go and lie down, Anne. You're not well. I'll bring you a cordial to sooth you.'

Anne looked up in wonder at the kind words. Well she might wonder. Were they the first she'd heard since entering that house? She struggled to rise. Leah helped her and she gripped Leah's hand. 'Annie and John.'

'Don't worry about them. They are working in the garden.'

'But,' Anne coughed again, trembling, 'you will be good to them.'

Leah swallowed. 'I will be good to them. I will,' why couldn't she say love? 'care for them as if they were my own. I swear, on the Holy Bible, no harm will come to them while I hold them close.'

The children were indeed in the garden, weeding and hoeing as they had been commanded. Obedience was a virtue in children and every child had learned it in this house, except Frank. Leah had seen to it his own offspring did not follow his example. They did as they were told. It didn't stop them keeping together, though. When their tasks forced them apart, they obeyed but, tasks done, they were back again like magnets springing together, John's hand reaching for Annie's. At eight and seven, they could have been twins, indivisible, two waifs against the world, sharing thoughts, whispers, ideas – and

155

songs. They both sang like little wrens, inheriting Tada's voice, but Leah had never heard them sing except in unison.

As she opened the back door, their heads bobbed up, looking her way. She could read their expressions and know how they responded to everyone they encountered. With Tadcu they were nervous but eager to please, for Tadcu was God. Their own father they merely tried to avoid, either his sober resentful notice or his drunken cuffs and kicks. With strangers, the children were watchful, cautious, waiting to see how the wind blew. With their mother, their faces became soft and silly, like babies, as if they clung to a fading memory of infancy that couldn't last. No, it couldn't last. Not for much longer.

But when they looked at Leah... What did their faces show when they looked at her? Confidence maybe. Certainty that she would not surprise them, but dole out instruction, sympathy, praise or scolding exactly as they deserved, no more, no less. She would dole it out brusquely perhaps, as if she couldn't be doing with small children under her feet, but she was the one who gave them all that they required. Their mother cuddled them but it was Leah who fed and clothed them, gave them tasks to do, taught them their lessons, fear of the Lord and respect for their elders. A mother in all but name.

They came obediently to her side as if she'd summoned them.

'Have you finished?'

'Yes, Aunt Leah.'

'Have you earned some bread and butter?'

'Yes, Aunt Leah!'

'Well then, go in. But be quiet for your mother's sake.'

'Is Mam unwell?' asked Annie

'She is, so we must be a comfort to her, mustn't we?'

'Yes, Aunt Leah.'

They knew, of course. Not perhaps that their mother was dying but that her life was fading as their own became more solid. It was a knowledge so instinctive that it came without shock or panic. It was what it was.

'You are very kind,' said Anne, settling back meekly against Leah's pillow. 'I don't deserve it. I have done nothing.'

No, nor have I, thought Leah, arranging a bed for herself under the sloping eaves of her cramped bedroom. *This is how I make atonement. Will God, if He truly exists, restore His grace to me? We are not saved by good works, but by His will alone, that is what we are told. Have faith – but I no longer know what I have faith in, so I will resort to this, a feeble attempt at humanity. Make amends for all the uncharitable contempt I've shown this wretched woman.*

'Don't fuss yourself, Anne. You must rest. I shall bring you some broth in a while.'

Anne groped vaguely for her hand but couldn't find it.

'Sleep,' ordered Leah. She went downstairs, passing through the room that Anne had shared with Frank, a receptacle for his drunken lust or a target for his drunken anger. Whatever the law and the Bible said, Leah could not leave Anne at her husband's mercy any longer. Through the summer and autumn, she had grown progressively weaker, the symptoms more obvious, the blood impossible to miss. Except that Frank missed it, as indifferent to his wife's state now as he had ever been. Not that he was around much, anyway. Too often washing down his own disappointments at the ale houses with Eli John when he was supposed to be minding the cows or tending the barley. Leah wondered how long it would take him to notice that Anne was no longer between his sheets.

A pot of broth was simmering on the range. She ladled a little into a bowl.

Behind her, Tada said 'You have moved the woman from her marriage bed.'

'Yes, Tada. Into mine.'

'Whom God has joined, let no man put asunder, daughter.'

'She is sinking fast, Tada. Too ill to bear Frank's attentions any longer.'

Tada frowned, black eyes glowing from the deeps beneath massed brows. 'Well, it's true, she'll be in my place soon enough.'

Laid out in the parlour, he meant – the death room – where he now slept. His bed had been moved there when Frank married, and it was just as well, because his stiffened joints would no longer carry him up the stairs. To Leah, it was still the death room and perhaps it was to Tada, as well. His own death was something he anticipated with confidence in a righteous God who would cast down the wicked and reward the elect. He would probably have slept in a coffin if he could, ready for the summons from his Lord.

'A grievous thing that she is not redeemed,' he said.

'We do not know that, Tada.'

He sniffed. 'She wallows in self-pity when she should rather welcome the approach of her God.'

'She worries for her children. But she need not. I shall see to it they want for nothing.'

'Where will you sleep then, daughter. In the barn?'

'I have made up a bed on the floor, so that I can nurse her. It will not be long.'

Yes, Anne must at least be nursed, even though she had not been afforded a doctor. It would never have occurred to Frank to send for one, and Tada had dismissed them all as charlatans since Tom's death. He would not allow anyone under his roof to be committed to a sanitorium, and Leah, after suggesting it once, hadn't argued further. She knew Anne had marked herself for death and was

158

putting up no struggle. Her body had long been ailing, but so had her mind, locked in a prison of inertia and despair that no one had bothered to alleviate. Death was the only cure to it all now, but Leah could at least make the passage easier.

'You are a Christian woman,' said Tada. Leah had acted, had argued her case and he had accepted. It was unheard of. She felt a small flutter of victory.

'Take her gruel to her, then, before you serve me my dinner. And tend to her children.' Tada settled back in his chair, nodding his approval. 'He gives the barren woman a home, making her the joyous mother of children. Praise the Lord!'

Victory vanished in the sting of his words. Who had left Leah barren but Tada?

He seemed not to notice the tears starting into her eyes.

'Yes, Tada.'

Leah smoothed down the lank, mouse-brown hair around Anne's bloodless face. The eyes were in wells of blue shadows, as if Leah's fingers had bruised the flesh when drawing the lids closed. Bruises were Anne's lot. In death, she looked more peaceful than she ever had in life, confident at last of her rightful place in this house, laid out with as much dignity as Leah could manage in the parlour.

Tada, with stubborn determination, had moved his own bed into the kitchen, assisted by Will Price, who had come from Sarah with a couple of cabbages in exchange for some potatoes, and had stayed to help. Anne must lie where respectability dictated. Leah had argued against the move. Tada had had some sort of seizure and a bad fall in the yard not a week since, when they had feared he would precede his daughter-in-law into Paradise – or the great void, or whatever was awaiting them. But this time Tada would not listen to arguments. He would sleep in the kitchen until the funeral rites

159

were over and Anne had found her final resting place in the chapel graveyard, along with the two mites who had gone before her.

He was leaning on his stick now, glaring down on the pathetic withered corpse as though he were the guardian of the holy gates, weighing up this sad sinner. Annie and John leaned closer in to Leah's skirts, and she took their hands, feeling the grief and terror rippling through them, faced at last with the enormity of death and judgement. She said not a word but squeezed their fingers in reassurance.

Tada's long beard bristled, his stooping shoulders twitched back and he looked across at the minister who had just arrived. The Reverend Pritchard bowed his head and they followed suit as he began to recite the Lord's Prayer. Leah gave the children's hands another squeeze, to encourage them to join in. Their childish voices trembled with tears, but apart from a sniff from Annie, there was silence after the Amen.

Tada looked down at John, who blinked tears away as he met his gaze, as upright as the old man had once been. 'Blood of my blood, my comfort and my pride, that this sorry woman has bestowed on me.' His eyes turned to the window and his tone hardened. 'Where is my son?'

Eyes met across the corpse. The last time Tada had asked that question, two days ago, he had been speaking of Tom. Was his mind still wandering? No, Leah could see from the glint in his eye that he meant Frank.

'On business in the village, I don't doubt,' said the Reverend Pritchard. The minister knew as well as Leah that Frank was where he always was, in a public house or puking up his guts in a ditch. 'William Price was going on to fetch him after he'd called me.' Leah felt a mirthless laugh inside her at the thought of Will tackling such a task. He usually flinched at the mere sight of Frank. 'I shall stay here and pray with you a while.'

160

Tada nodded.

Leah, feeling the trembling in the little hands she held, led the children out silently, away from the scene of death, through the scullery and into the garden.

Annie was shuddering with silent sobs, but John was silent. They had had enough of that terrible place of incomprehensible loss and simmering anger. Leah longed to comfort them but what could she say that would not trigger uncontrolled anguish? She had prepared them, prayed with them, brought them to bid their farewells. Now she must push them out, back onto the open sea, away from the rocks that would shatter the flimsy vessels of their souls.

'Well. There will be time enough for tears, I don't doubt, but there are apples to be gathered, leeks to be weeded. You have your tasks, so be busy about them. The Lord does not ask us to stand idle while we mourn.' She had dutifully brought them up in the religion that had raised her, even though she felt an outcast from it, for what else was there to give any meaning to life or death? 'Let your labour be your prayer and He who holds your mother safe in His hand will smile upon you.'

They looked at her, startled at the abrupt change of mood, but she could sense their relief that they were being given permission to escape from a thing they could not cope with. They would find the comfort they needed, and explore the mysteries they could not understand, with each other.

Leah left them to it. From the scullery window she watched them, hand in hand, trot up the garden path towards the apple tree, planted in the Revival year and productive at last. They were as she, and God – if there were a God – had made them, and she need not feel ashamed of her part. John was a strong boy, looking to be tall like Tada and worshipping his grandfather, since he could not

161

honour his father. He was naturally silent and self-contained except with Annie; seldom cowed but conscious, even so young, of his duty to farm and family. Annie was a biddable child, never sullen, quick with her fingers and her thoughts and with a promise of prettiness, though that was a blessing that would bring little benefit in this world. Sarah had been the pretty one among the Owen sisters, and look what it had cost her! Will Price was a loyal husband; never violent, that they'd heard, and six children had survived to thrive and even earn their keep, which would have been blessing enough for many but it hadn't stopped Sarah bemoaning her lot whenever Leah met her. Perhaps it would be better for Annie to be plain and avoid the temptations of sin.

'Oh Lord!' She heard Millie Davies, sent over from Castell Mawr to help, cry out in alarm in the kitchen. 'What is he thinking of?'

Leah hurried through in time to see the door flung open and Frank stagger in, eyes glazed, face flushed with drink. His appearance would have been unspeakable enough, but he was not alone. Eli John was staggering behind him, belching with deliberate contempt for the house, supporting him or pushing him. They were both still holding bottles as they grinned in wicked delight.

'Frank!' Leah hissed at him. 'You cannot! Of all times.'

'Oh hush,' slurred Frank, crashing into the dresser. 'S'true? The old devil's dead at last. Won't believe it till I see him.' Thrusting her before him as she tried to bar his way, he managed to kick the parlour door open and lurch inside, nearly sending her flying backwards onto the corpse.

'What?' He managed the one word before utter silence fell. Eli, on his heels, froze in the doorway.

The minister was holding his breath in alarm and disgust. Tada stared at his son, as he would stare at a worm. 'My son. The fruit of my loins. Has there ever been such a contemptible ingrate?' He seized Frank by the collar. 'There she lies. The woman brought into this house by your sinful fornication.'

Frank's bloodshot eyes couldn't quite focus as he gaped at his father, his face an almost comical picture of bewilderment as he grappled to understand. Whatever it was Will had managed to blurt out to him, it had not spelled out any precise truth beyond a death at Cwmderwen.

'Your wife,' thundered Tada. 'The mother of your children, bound to you in the sight of God, flesh of your flesh, and you could not even leave your filthy wallowing to watch her die. Instead you crawl here, fancying to rejoice in my death instead, with that foul carrion at your heels.'

Frank's bewilderment deepened as he made sense at last of the corpse laid out before him. Did he even remember that he had a wife?

'I had a son. A true son who would have honoured me. But I am left with you!' The old man's stiff rage suddenly broke. He raised his stick and brought it down on Frank's shoulders and back as he cowered. Again and again. 'You are no better than a beast. You have no sense of duty, no honour, no fear of the Lord. You do nothing. You leave your sister to the care of this farm. A mere woman. You are not a man, you are a curse. No wonder that you bring the stench of murdering filth with you.'

Half the blows now were being aimed at Eli, who tried to back out and tripped in the attempt. Frank, too drunk to fight back, was attempting to crawl under the table that held his wife's body. Leah, clutching Tada's arm, was desperately trying to calm her father, fearful of another seizure, as the Reverend Pritchard – recovering from his shock, pleaded – 'Mr Owen! Thomas! Remember the place, the occasion. It is enough. Let us respect the dead.'

Glowering, breathing like a bull, Tada lowered his stick, then stepped back, unsteady, reaching for his daughter's arm. She guided him to his chair and he collapsed into it.

'I'll fetch you some water, Tada.' She brought him a cup that Millie, all eyes and ears, had poured ready for her.

He seized her wrist. 'You are a good woman, daughter. My support and my right arm.'

The Reverend Pritchard nodded in agreement. 'She is, indeed. A good daughter and righteous Christian, God be praised. In that, at least, you are blessed, Thomas Owen.'

Was that what she was? She stepped over Frank as she left. He was crawling to the door, like the slithering beast he had become. Eli John, less drunk than malign, had already managed to escape.

Millie was wiping things randomly in the kitchen.

'You've done enough, Millie. Go back to Castell Mawr now.'

'But Mrs George said I was to stay and sit with you and...let her know how things are.'

Of course. Betty George would want to know every scrap of gossip. Leah was surprised she hadn't come herself, but perhaps Anne Owen's death was too insignificant for her personal involvement. Besides, she was thickening with child again, as she made sure everyone knew.

'Let your mistress know I am grateful. How is she?'

'Oh, fine as a pig in...blooming, Miss Owen. Says it will be a boy this time, she's sure.'

If Betty George could arrange such things, she surely would have done so by now, with a clutch of sons. But, as yet, her score stood at two girls and a miscarriage.

'There's no need–' Leah stopped. No need to tell Betty about the scandalous scene around the corpse. What was the point? Betty and the whole parish would know before the day was out. 'No need to put yourself out. But if you will stay to sit with me and keep

Anne company, let us make tea. The minister will be wanting some.'

'I have the kettle on and the pot ready,' said Millie proudly. Then she scowled, hearing sounds wafting through from the scullery. 'Oh those children, and at a time like this. Shall I tell them to hush?'

What she had heard was a laugh, and then singing.

'No,' said Leah. She went to the scullery door to look out. Annie and John had filled their apple basket and were sitting on the garden wall, side by side, facing into the dark tangled woods, singing their hearts out. Piping children's voices singing hymns, as if music could dispel all the misery in the world.

'Nes cyraedd hyfryd lanau'r nef...'

The hymn they had sung in chapel before Tom had received his fatal wound. Her heart clenched whenever she heard the words.

'Let them sing,' she said.

After all, it was all they had.

1912

Annie was gazing up, not at the Reverend Pritchard in the pulpit but into the nothingness of the roof. She was daydreaming, instead of attending. Leah, seated beside her, could feel the girl's concentration wandering, and a strong stern inner voice ordered her to deliver a reprimand. But a silent stubborn voice, deeper in her lost soul, commanded her to let the girl dream.

On Annie's other side, John was gripping his sister's hand as ever, but there was no dreaming in his eyes. He was wrapped in concentration, his eyes fixed on the preacher, or was it on the white-haired elder who sat below the pulpit? It was rare that Tada made it to chapel these days. He was too frail to walk and it was a struggle even to get him into the trap. Most Sabbaths now, he waited at home for his daughter and grandchildren to return from chapel and then he would have John with him in the parlour, reading from the Bible, since Tada's eyes were failing, singing the hymns and repeating the sermon as perfectly as the boy could recite it. But this Sunday, he would have nothing but to go to chapel himself. There had been a stir of appreciation as he had made his way up to the big seat. David and others had come forward to help him to his customary place.

Above in the pulpit, the Reverend Pritchard was grizzled by age and in need of spectacles, but his voice was still strong and certain as he read the holy scriptures. 'And they came to the place which God had told him of; and Abraham built an altar there, and laid the wood in order, and bound Isaac his son, and laid him on the altar upon the wood.

166

'And Abraham stretched forth his hand, and took the knife to slay his son.

'And the angel of the Lord called unto him out of heaven, and said, Abraham, Abraham: and he said, Here am I.

'And he said, Lay not thine hand upon the lad, neither do thou any thing unto him: for now I know that thou fearest God, seeing thou hast not withheld thy son, thine only son from me.'

Leah felt a chill eating her from within as she heard the words. Could he not have chosen a different reading for today's service than the sacrifice of a son? She saw Tada's eyes gleam, his lips moving as he fixed his gaze on John.

'And the angel of the Lord called unto Abraham out of heaven the second time, and said, By myself have I sworn, saith the Lord, for because thou hast done this thing, and hast not withheld thy son, thine only son: that in blessing I will bless thee, and in multiplying I will multiply thy seed as the stars of the heaven, and as the sand which is upon the sea shore; and thy seed shall possess the gate of his enemies; and in thy seed shall all the nations of the earth be blessed; because thou hast obeyed my voice.'

The minister leaned forward. 'Brothers and sisters in Christ, what do we learn from these divinely inspired words that will guide us in our lives today? What does God ask of us sinners?'

Leah didn't want to hear. She seized Annie's hand suddenly, squeezing it, and the girl looked up, startled, meeting her eyes, questioning and then smiling. They wouldn't listen. They would take their thoughts elsewhere.

Outside, the rain fell, as it seemed to have fallen for days, shrouding the world in grey. The congregation didn't linger to gossip, but hurried off, collars raised, umbrellas up, or bundled themselves into their waiting vehicles, the horses eager to be off.

'Are you ready, Tada?' Leah had brought him as far as their trap but he seemed in a dream, forgetful of where they were.

'Let me assist you, Mr Owen.' David was by her side. Betty, already enthroned in their governess cart with their children, made a show of annoyance that they must sit there in the rain, but David patiently stood with his arm ready for Tada to grip it. Tada emerged from his reverie and accepted David's help in lifting him up.

At the last moment, barely balanced, Tada let go, looking round. 'Where's the boy? I want my grandson.'

'I'm here, Tadcu.' John jumped up beside him and helped him into his seat.

Tada patted his arm. 'In thy seed shall all the nations of the earth be blessed.'

David looked at Leah, shaking her hand, his grip lasting a little longer than was necessary. 'He is failing. If you need help...'

'He has been failing for months. We cope, the children and I.'

'And Frank?' No need to ask why he was not at chapel.

'We cope, the children and I,' repeated Leah.

He nodded sympathy. She watched him hurry back to his family, then she climbed up and took the reins. They would need to get home and out of the rain or they'd all catch their deaths.

As they neared the sharp bend approaching their turning, she saw smoke belching above the hedgerow and heard the growing grumble and roar of an approaching steam lorry, bound for the quarries. She pulled in, as close as she could to the hedge, trying to calm the horse whose ears were flicking nervously. Annie jumped down to hold the horse's head, whispering to it as the lorry hove into view.

'Keep in!' shouted Leah and Annie hopped up onto the bank, bringing herself on a level with Eli John, as he clung nonchalantly to the side of the lorry, chatting to the driver. He licked his lips at her.

The horse whinnied as the vehicle rumbled closer. John jumped down to his sister's side, to still the horse and to face down the leering man.

'And down into the ditch,' laughed Eli, swinging one leg out as he passed, to catch the horse's flank. The beast flinched from the touch, but the children held it steady. Tada rose to his feet, swaying, his hand outstretched to point at Eli John.

'You! Spawn of Satan!'

'No, Tada! Sit down! You'll fall.' Leah was struggling to turn and grip him. 'John, hold Tadcu!'

John climbed up again and the lorry was passed, Eli roaring with laughter, though the driver looked uncomfortable.

David had come up behind them, rising in his seat to see if he could help.

'We are well,' called Leah hastily. 'No harm done.'

Betty tugged at David's sleeve to make him sit down.

'Annie, come up. Sit down, Tada and be still. The beast is gone.'

'Ye are of your father the devil, and the lusts of your father ye will do!' cried Tada, shaking his stick after the lorry. But John was beside him, holding his hand, persuading him to sit again. Leah urged the horse on, praying that it was the last time Tada would insist on going to chapel.

The rain wouldn't stop. All day, all night, it kept up its relentless beat, saturating the land. But work couldn't stop for the rain. Out in the fields, Leah had a mackintosh cape around her shoulders but still the rain found its way down her collar to trickle down her back. Every step was heavy with the mud caking her boots as she picked her way across the oat stubble, driving the cows and calves before her. The wet summer had spoiled the harvest. Last year it had been too dry. That was the way farming went. There was no point complaining, and yet everyone did complain. It was a part of life.

169

At the gate, Tada was waiting. He shouldn't be out in this. He could no longer manage the simplest tasks on the farm and he felt the cold even on a sunny day. She feared his soaking at chapel on Sunday would have given him a chill, although she had dried him and warmed him with hot tea and broth as soon as they'd arrived home. Now there was no need for him to be out in the rain again, but he wouldn't listen. Many things had been lost to Tada, but not his stubbornness.

She trudged back to him, the dog, Wyn Bach, winding at her feet. 'There's a calf can go tomorrow, I think.'

Tada nodded and his knuckles bulged as he grasped the gate to stop himself falling.

'We should go back to the house now. Take a dish of tea to warm you through?'

He didn't seem to hear. His eyes were wandering. 'Where is the boy?'

'At school, Tada, with Annie.' Always with Annie. John never ran with other boys.

Did Tada hear? His eyes settled on her, focussing slowly. 'You are a good daughter.'

She said nothing, tired of the repetition of this refrain. Yes, she was a good daughter. No one could fault her in that. She was a good daughter and nothing else.

Tada breathed heavily, shutting his eyes. 'I know that thou fearest God, seeing thou hast not withheld thy son, thine only son from me.'

Abraham and Isaac again. Tada had been murmuring it all night. She could have cursed the Reverend Pritchard for having chosen it. 'Yes, Tada. You fear God.'

'In thy seed shall all the nations of the earth be blessed; because thou hast obeyed my voice.' His eyes opened again and fixed intently on her. 'Have I done right by my children?'

170

A silent rage gnawed inside her. How could he put such a question to her, and how was she to answer it? He had been what her world said a father should be, the stern master of the house, providing for their welfare, watchful for sin and chastising them into righteousness. Was that doing right? 'No one in this parish would find fault with you, Tada.'

'I have kept faith with the Lord and He has kept faith with me. A covenant, yes. "For unto thee, and unto thy seed, I will give all these countries."'

'Amen, Tada. You have maintained the covenant.'

'Twenty-four acres, one rood and eight perches,' said Tada, struggling to complete the mantra. Then his hand rose to clutch his chest, his mouth opened, gurgling, and he dropped back into the churned mud and the cow muck.

'Tada! Tada!' Leah fumbled to open the gate and rushed to his side. But she knew, even before she had fallen to her knees, that he was dead.

The suddenness of it stunned her. Mam's death, equally sudden, had left her paralysed with grief, bereft for Mam and for herself. But this now merely froze her. There was nothing to feel. Did she love Tada? She had once. Of course, she must have done, as a daughter was commanded to love her father. She was bound to honour and obey him as she would have been bound to honour and obey a husband. If that was love, it had been taken for granted by both of them, binding her to him by commandment and custom. But now the bindings had been cut, like a rope snapping, and she found there was nothing there. Just an empty windswept plain and herself alone upon it.

What must she do? Whatever was required, of course, because there was no one else to do it. Except that she couldn't manage him on her own. She rose to her feet, the rain pouring down on her.

'John! John, are you there?' She shouted louder than she ever had in her life, forcing the air from her lungs. 'John!' It was a piercing shriek, expressing desperation rather than hope. She remembered her calls were futile. The children were at school and would not be home for an hour or more.

She turned back to the meadow and the footpath that ran from Plas Malgwyn to the village. She raced down to the stile where the path crossed into Castell Mawr land. If only one of David's men were in sight... Yes, there was someone, the grey silhouettes of a man and woman coming through the rain.

She raised her arm, waving. 'Help!'

The man straightened, raised a hand to his eyes to peer her way, then came on a little faster, dragging the woman with him. He didn't run, but there was pleasure in his step. Her heart stopped. Not him. Not Eli John. She could see him clearly now, grinning, sober, smartly dressed like the gentleman he could never be, come from Plas Malgwyn with Rachel Morgan in his wake, clutching an umbrella.

Leah backed away.

'Well, well, Leah Owen. See this, Rachel? The pious cow is calling me for aid. What you going to do, Leah? Fall on your knees and beg me? Try it and I might oblige. I'd dearly like to see you on your knees. Rachel will show you how.'

'I want nothing from you, Eli John.' Anger restored her self-control. 'Stay off our land.'

'Footpath. I know my rights. I always know my rights and my dues, don't you know?' He leaped nimbly over the stile, leaving Rachel to manage on her own, and advanced on Leah as if to trample her down. 'So what's got the high and mighty Miss Owen so upset?'

'Nothing of any concern to you!'

'No?' Before she could stop him he had side-stepped her to peer

172

up the meadow and the field beyond, to the open gate and the sight she had been blocking from his view. 'What's that then? Old devil's taken a fall, has he?'

She followed, desperate to stand in his way. 'I told you, it's none of your concern. You are off the path. You have no right...'

'And you're going to stop me, are you, Leah Owen?' He was into the field now, seeing Tada clearly, loping towards him.

'Don't you touch him!' Leah hoisted up her skirts to race after him, mud splattering as she ran.

Eli had come to a halt, hands on hips, grinning down on Tada. 'I wouldn't touch him to save my life or his. Except, perhaps...' He prodded Tada with his toe. 'Looks like it's too late for him, anyway. Well, well. The old man's gone to the Devil at last.'

'Take your foul thoughts and blasphemous words away. I don't want your help, Eli John.'

He laughed. 'You'll not have it. After all the ill he's done me, and the times he's raised his hand to me, let him lie there and rot for all I care.'

Rachel had caught up with him. 'Christ, Eli, shouldn't you at least—'

'Shut your mouth,' said Eli, swiping her away as he turned to sneer again at Leah. 'He's all yours, Leah Owen and to hell with both of you. Don't worry,' he added, turning his back on her. 'I'll be sure to give Frank the good news if I see him.'

Rachel shot her the briefest glance of pained sympathy before she met Leah's furious eyes and she reverted to her usual hostile sneer. She flounced behind Eli as he sauntered back to the footpath, whistling.

'Get off our land!' Leah shouted after them

Eli grinned back. 'Not your land, Leah Owen.' Rachel laughed, twirling her umbrella.

Leah stared after them, poised like a female warrior, until they were over the next stile into the woods, still whistling, still laughing, then she let herself shake and shudder. Sobs came at last, born of anger more than grief, but there was no use in tears. She looked down at Tada, at the rain soaking into his white beard, washing over his grey face, the muck splattering his clothes, caking his hair.

She couldn't leave him there. She would have to lift him on her own. And why not? She had lifted heavier. Her slim frame, which might have been called elegant in a woman of a higher social class, had grown gaunt with the years, but the muscles had strengthened with the work she had been called upon to do around the farm. She could do this. Gripping Tada under the armpits, she balanced herself to heave.

Sarah, round as a barrel, was already wailing as she squeezed through the doorway. 'Oh, oh, poor Tada, oh, what shall we do? It's a terrible thing. I don't know how I'll bear it!'

'You'll bear it easily enough.' Leah had no patience left.

'How can you be so heartless! I thought you'd be prostrate with grief.'

'Well I am not, as you see.'

'You are an ungrateful creature, Leah Owen. You were always his favourite. Can you not spare him a few tears?' Sarah had enough for both of them, though where she dredged them up from, Leah couldn't imagine. Tada had acknowledged her for the sake of the family's respectability, but he had never forgiven her the sinfulness that had brought about her marriage. And yet now she wept as if half her heart had been torn away.

'I have given him his due, and he has never had reason to complain that I fell short,' said Leah, too exhausted to react with anger or contempt.

174

'Is that all you can say? Well, I, for one, shall never get over his loss.' Sarah sniffed theatrically. 'I have come to help you lay him out.' She said it in a half-strangled voice, terrified of the task.

'It is all done. Annie helped me.'

'That sweet child? You made her do such things?'

'I made her do nothing. She did her duty, that is all.'

With the rain lifting at last, the children had come home to find Leah doing her best to clean the corpse, while her own clothes clung to her, mud-stained and drenched. They did not weep. Their grandfather's death was an awesome thing, but not a matter of grief as their mother's had been. Tada had been too stern to evoke anything in them other than profound respect, although that was deeply embedded. John bowed his head and prayed over his grandfather, a man in his piety though he was only eleven. Annie's thoughts were all for her aunt. She had heated water and fetched clean clothes for Leah, dried her hair and then stood by with bowls of water and fresh linen as her aunt dealt with the body. Anyone would think these were acts of love between mother and daughter. But neither spoke of such things. Duty, that was all it was. John was persuaded to leave his prayers and take the news to Castell Mawr and to the village. He had listened to Leah's instructions without comment but, before departing, he had paused to ask one question.

'Is the farm mine now?'

'It will be,' promised Leah, too tired to explain.

John had nodded and gone, bearing the news of Thomas Owen's death, and so Sarah had come.

'I'd have thought that Betty George would be here, poking her nose in and helping you, being such a close neighbour.' Sarah managed to whine and grumble at the same time.

'She has sent word that she will come as soon as the baby is settled

175

and Mr George is back from Newcastle Emlyn. She has promised to sit with me.'

'Oh.' Sarah looked torn between relief and indignation. It was her place as daughter to sit with the corpse, but Leah knew it was a duty that petrified her. Doubtless she imagined the dead walked at midnight. She'd be more than happy for Betty George to take her place, but still she had to resent the neighbour's interference.

Leah closed her eyes. 'If you will be useful, make some more tea. I do not have the strength.'

Sarah pouted. 'William has ridden for the doctor, you know, to sign the papers, which you didn't think of doing.'

'I would have done, but I am grateful that you thought of it.'

'Where is the girl now? Not in there, surely!' Sarah nodded towards the closed parlour door with a shudder.

'She went to check on the cows for me. I thought I might have left the gate loose.'

'Ha, and you always chiding me for carelessness.'

'I had my hands full with Tada.' Leah pushed herself up from her chair. 'Well, if you will not see to the tea, I suppose I must.'

'Oh I didn't say I wouldn't.' Sarah bustled – as only she could bustle – making much of small matters to little end. Leah finished laying out the cups.

'You will want to see him, then,' she said, as the tea brewed in the pot. Sarah fidgeted. 'To pay your respects.'

'Well...' As Leah had opened the door to the parlour, Sarah had no option but to step through into the dimly lit room. 'Oh Tada! Oh, oh, oh, how shall we manage without you? Oh I don't know what I'll do!' She was in full flood again, although she could barely bring herself to look at the corpse, his white hair washed clean, eyes closed, jaw bound up, pale papery hands laid piously across his hollow chest.

176

Leah just wanted to sleep. But there were voices in the yard, so she went out to greet the minister who had answered John's summons.

John, inevitably, was by his sister again, their hands fused. 'Children, you need not linger here. Feed the hens and then see to your tasks in the garden. Reverend Pritchard, please come in. Thank you for coming.'

The minister grasped her hand firmly between his, before ushering her into her own home. 'I wouldn't delay one moment for the sake of such a loyal and devoted servant of Christ as Thomas Owen. Your grief, Leah, must be great indeed, I know, but we shall pray together and rejoice in the certainty of your father's redemption.'

'Yes, let us pray,' she said dully.

Sometimes, it seemed that this house stored up nothing but memories of death. Or at least this room did. This parlour tomb. Had they laid out little Esther here? She couldn't remember, although the feeling of bewildered fear, surrounding the death of a baby sister when she had been a mere toddler, remained with her still. No doubt baby Esther had been laid in her cradle like Anne's lost ones. But Mamgu Owen had certainly been laid here – she remembered that. And Tom, and Mam, and Anne. Now Tada, set like a carved effigy in the coffin that had been brought from the village. One day, no doubt, she would lie here too, alone in death as she was in life. Who would sit with her through the dark nights before her burial? Annie, perhaps. Would she weep for the loss of her aunt or shrug it off, as a burden she was released from at last? We take nothing out of this world, she thought. And I shall certainly leave nothing behind.

She had nothing to leave. Not your land, Eli John had sneered, and every fibre in her had wanted to shout him down, to claim this twenty-four acres, one rood and eight perches as hers, as Owen land, a covenant sealed with their sweat and tears and their blood. But he was right. It wasn't hers. It would never be hers. The land belonged to the Herberts. The tenancy had been Tada's, the old man beside her who had given her life and then drained it dry. His support and right arm, he had called her, and that had been true enough. Right and left these last years, once his own limbs failed him. She had done all, tending to the fields, the ploughing and sowing and reaping, and the beasts, the lambing and calving and the pig killing, even while she completed her own endless, ordained tasks in the house. Miss Leah Owen, of Cwmderwen, out in all weathers, paying the rent, with no help but what the children could give her, and still it would never be hers. While she had slaved, Frank had been content to drink away every penny he could squeeze from the farm, but he was the one who would inherit the tenancy. The son and heir. That was how her father had seen the matter. Her father and the world and the God who ordained it. It must all pass to Frank, until he failed to pay the rent and forfeited it all.

Why? Because she was nothing. A crabbed and withered spinster, a dependant to be ignored. She was more likely to die in the workhouse than lie here, when her time came. Or in a ditch, gnawed by rats, or rotting in the rushes of the river. Rigid at her station at the corpse's side, she fixed on the crack in the uneven plaster. It had almost reached the floor now, no longer a hairline but bleeding dust and horsehair. The universe rending apart. It would all crumble if she failed to hold it together.

No! If it must be that the land would pass to Frank, then so it must pass to his son. John must understand that it was not yet to be his, but one day it would be. She would not let it be taken from him. John would inherit his patrimony and she would not let Frank undo the covenant.

Sitting alone, she felt her spine stiffen, her head clear. The minister had gone. William Price had ridden to Penbryn for the doctor and to take the news to Mary, if he were permitted to see her. Sarah had returned home – Leah had sent her away, unable to stand the absurd histrionics any longer. The children, wise and responsible beyond their years, were tending to the animals. Betty George would come in good time for the night watch, but for one moment, Leah need do nothing. Nothing but be still and silent, gathering her strength for the battles to come.

A moment too brief to be blessed. She heard them coming before the outer door slammed open and glass smashed. Then they burst through, Frank and Eli John, supporting each other in a sodden embrace. If Eli had been sober earlier on, he had made up for it since, and Frank must have been drinking from the moment he reached Penbryn that morning. He was foul with ale and gin and vomit, his eyes glassy, his mouth slack, only upright because Eli held him so.

'There he is,' slurred Frank. 'Old man. Look at him. Can't chide me now, can you, old man. Eh? Eh.' Leaning over the coffin, he prodded the corpse, breathing ale fumes on his father.

'For God's sake, if not your own, show some respect, Frank!' hissed Leah, flinching away from him. Frank straightened with an effort, face working while he tried to focus on her and let a groat of understanding work into his befuddled brain. Eli, behind him, was whispering in his ear, prodding him. Frank pointed an unsteady finger at Leah. 'Yes. You…You woman. You hold your tongue. Hear me. You hold your tongue. I'm the master here now. 'S'right, isn't it, Eli. I'm the master.'

'That's right, Frank, my boy.' Eli leered. 'You're the master and that ugly dry old spinster stays here on sufferance.'

Frank's finger, which had begun to wave wildly around the room, returned to its target. 'That's right! Ugly dry old spinster. You live here on my charity, so hold your...your damned tongue.'

Leah said nothing. What was the point in wasting words on either of them? Eli's malice would never change and Frank, in his sway, was beyond redemption. She pressed her lips together, looking steadily ahead, though she could feel Eli sidling up to her. She could feel his whiskers brushing her cheek, his gin-soaked breath making her skin crawl. Looking her over as he looked over all women, as if they were beasts without souls, mere flesh for his entertainment. Then he laughed in her ear, a filthy laugh.

'Ugly old spinster,' repeated Frank. 'Never had a man to show her what's what, that's her trouble. Do you want her, Eli? Take her. She's no use to me. There you are, sister. Leah. Ugly old bitch. I've found you a husband. You going to thank your brother then?'

Still she said nothing.

Eli's laugh deepened. 'Thank you for the offer, Frank. Truth be told, I've tired of that raddled bitch, Rachel and I'd fancy a taste of something new...but I must decline. Nothing new about this one. Too old and dry and sour for my taste. She'd shrivel my manhood.'

His insult had no impact on Leah and it was lost on Frank, who was leaning over his father now, head bowed, breathing heavily as though sobs were about to break out. But there was no grief involved. He was just waiting for his head to clear. He pushed himself up at last and peered around the cold dark parlour.

'This is it. Mine. All mine, and a bloody waste it is too. Damned house, damned land. Damned family. Family!' He swayed dangerously. 'I've got a family. Children. My children. Where are they? Should show some damned respect to their father for once. Not be poisoned by ugly old spinsters.' His finger stabbed back at Leah. 'What have you done with them, ugly old spinster?'

180

'They are tending to their tasks. The tasks this farm imposes on them, since there is no man about the place to do anything.'

'You show me respect, you hear? I want them here!' His finger was stabbing at the floor this time. 'Now, I say. Here!'

Silently, Leah withdrew, stepping round Eli who made no attempt to move aside for her. Her mind was working, searching for some solution to this, some way out, but nothing would come. She couldn't work her way around the immutable fact that Frank had rights and she had none. The tenancy would be his. His children were his, to do with as he wished. God's law, Man's law, all said it. All gave her nothing. She stood at the kitchen door, watching the two children bending over the chickens, confiding with each other in whispers, their thoughts on hens and death. They were not hers.

She didn't speak but they must have sensed her presence. As a child would sense its mother she thought, or wanted to believe, but that was mere fancy. They both looked up and straightened, waiting for her commands.

'Come,' she said quietly.

They came obediently to her, her helpmeets without whom she wouldn't have been able to manage the farm these last months. A sweet girl, a fine boy; that was what she would call them if they had been her own. She brushed Annie's dark curls out of sight into her cap and adjusted the black band she had slipped on John's arm. 'Your father wishes to see you.'

Their solemn faces instantly froze. There had been times, in Frank's sobriety – so rare they could probably count them on their fingers – when their father had looked them over with critical surprise and had spoken to them with a hint of bemused curiosity, as if momentarily impressed that he had such children. But mostly he was drunk, hitting out or throwing things at them if they dared to venture within his sight. He let them creep into his consciousness

181

only to complain that they were sickening brats, millstones around his neck, and they should have been drowned at birth like kittens.

They knew he had been out all day, which meant he'd passed many hours in the ale houses of Penbryn. This would not be one of those sober moments, and yet he had summoned them, wanting them in his presence. It was unheard of. Leah could see their chests heaving with alarm, but there was nothing she could do. She took their hands and led them through to the parlour, feeling them cringe at the sight of their father propped against the coffin.

Frank took a while to focus, to recall who or what they were and why they had appeared.

They said nothing, close against Leah's side.

'Your children,' said Leah.

'Shut your mouth. I didn't tell you to speak.' The surge of pointless rage shook Frank awake, into memory. 'Oh yes, my children. There he is. My son and heir. John Francis Owen. What do you think of him, Eli? No fight in him. A milksop. Is that what's she's done to my boy?'

Leah felt John stiffen, not in fear, but in anger. A silent contained anger. He was tall for his age, thin but strong as an ox. A boy in years but a man when it came to duty and hard work. Who would dare dismiss him as a milksop?

Eli glanced at John fleetingly, sober enough to recognise the inaccuracy of Frank's claim and dismissing him as a target for his malice. Instead, he sidled round Leah to get a clearer view of Annie. Twelve now and already showing a hint of blooming into womanhood. He saw the girl shrink back, caught Leah's indrawn breath and he licked his lips, just as he had done on the steam wagon. He turned to leer at Frank.

'Forget the boy, Frank, lad. You've got a goldmine with the girl.'

'The girl?' Frank stared at her, gripping the coffin as he swayed.

His face was turning a sickly green. 'Whimpering like her damned mother. She's no use to me. What use is a girl on a farm? Eh? Eh? Tell me that. Nothing but a damned drain on my purse.' His muttered complaint turned into a giggle. 'You want her? Eh, Eli? You want her? She's no use to me.'

'Something fresh and new, oh yes. I'll take her, yes, surely enough.' There was no hesitation in Eli's reply.

'What will you pay me for her, though? Eh? Tell me that. What will you pay?'

'How much are you asking?'

Before Frank could get his brain round the question, Leah snapped, 'What sort of wicked Godless talk is this?'

At least her intervention diverted Frank from focussing on the proposed terms. 'Whatever talk I choose, that's what, woman. Hold your tongue and speak when you're spoken to. When I say, all right? It's for me to dispose of what's mine, any damned way I choose.'

'With your father lying there, not yet buried? Would you call down the Lord's wrath on your blasphemies?'

Frank raised his hand to strike her, but stumbled, clutching at the coffin for support as his knees buckled. The coffin began to tip.

Eli pushed it back to steady it. He, at least, could see when the situation was getting out of hand. 'Later, eh, Frank? We'll close the deal later. When you've planted the old man.'

'Yes, close the deal. That's right.'

'I'll hold you to it, mind.'

'We'll drink on it. Seal it.'

'Aye, we'll do that. Seal it with a gin or two. No going back then, eh?' He had his arm round Frank, holding him up, wheeling him around. At the parlour door, Eli glanced back at Annie, licked his lips again and sneered at Leah, before the two of them rolled out of the house.

Leah fought to calm her pulse, to stop her breath from sawing through her breastbone. John pulled away from her, his fists clenched, his face white with anger. But Annie's fear ran deeper. It had her paralysed, her eyes blank with terror.

Leah bit her lip until she trusted herself to speak. Her voice was gruff, business-like, though she couldn't prevent it breaking. 'That's enough. Back to your tasks, or would you leave the hens to the foxes? You are not milksops, so give no one any call to think you one. There's work to be done. Off!'

She was giving them permission to flee and they knew it. John grabbed his sister's hand and tugged her until the spell broke and her breathing came out in a great sob.

'Go!' said Leah, and they were gone, back to the safety of the potato patch and the hens and the secret shaded places under the overhanging trees, where their secret lives were lived and their dreams confessed.

Leah stood motionless for a moment longer beside the coffin, then turned back to her duties, an unthinking machine, sweeping the house, milking the cows, feeding the pig, preparing the supper, till the sun was down over the steep slopes above them and darkness began to claim the house. She called the children in, and they came from their hideaway, hand in hand, fused in a protective shell of their own making. But it wasn't protective enough. She saw the same anger in John's eyes, the same terror in Annie's.

'When will the farm be mine?' demanded John.

'One day. It will be, but first it will be your father's.'

'It should be mine.'

'It will be.'

'And will I...?' Annie choked on her own request.

'You will be what you wish to be and no one will make you otherwise. Now, wash your hands and eat. All will be well. You hear me? I promise you, all will be well. Do I ever lie?'

They glanced at each other, seizing on her promise as their only anchor. They nodded and set to washing their hands. Silently, they perched on their stools to devour the bread and butter she'd cut for them.

'All right. No more tasks tonight. Say your prayers and then to bed.'

Devoutly, they bowed their heads over clasped hands, their hair touching, coiling together.

'Amen.' And then they were off, Annie up the stairs to the bed she shared with her aunt and John to the mattress and blankets on the settle by the range that Leah had already prepared for the night.

They were young. Terror and trauma and fury were not strong enough to overcome their childish need for slumber. Leah quietly cleared the table, listening as John's breathing settled into the rhythmic waves of sleep. He had always gone off like a candle snuffed, and even tonight was no exception. All was quiet.

Leah stared towards the window. The heavy clouds had brought the autumn dusk to early darkness and the window was black, but there was her reflection, conjured up on the flawed pane by the light of the oil lamp. A ghost, white-faced, less substantial than the corpse in the parlour. She had a duty to that corpse. Still, her father had claims on her. She must sit with him. That was how it always was. He was not to be left abandoned and alone through the dark night, and she had never shirked her duty. Not until now.

Betty George arrived, bursting into the cottage with a bombastic show of solemnity and officiousness. She'd had no time for poor Anne Owen, in life or death, but she would not pass up a chance to be involved at the funeral rites of a revered chapel elder. Doubtless she thought her very presence, as the mistress of Castell Mawr, would give the occasion the touch of dignity it needed. Thriving Castell Mawr, a hundred and fifty acres now, thanks to David's wise but cautious dealings. Betty George saw herself on a par with Lady Herbert, the absentee mistress of Plas Malgwyn, queen of the parish but for the want of a crown.

'Well, Leah Owen, this is a sad day for us all and no mistake, the loss of such a respected deacon and true Christian. But most of all to you, of course, for where will you be without his guiding hand and watchful care?' She sniffed as she looked around the kitchen, hoping to find fault in something, but all was spotless.

'Hush,' said Leah, nodding at the blanket-wrapped heap on the settle.

Betty sniffed again. 'Some of us, it seems, can sleep through grief, though I am sure you cannot.' Her voice was lowered a fraction, but though she still boomed, John did not stir.

'I do not have a child's need for sleep. There is tea ready in the pot. Will you take a cup?'

'I will, but first I'll pay my respects to our good neighbour and content myself that all has been done as it should be.' Betty opened the parlour door and entered with bowed head and a show of sniffing into her handkerchief, although her little eyes darted this way and that in search of something neglected.

She would find nothing, for all had been arranged with the utmost propriety. Leah watched her, feeling a crawling sensation in her palms. A desire to slap Betty George's plump cheeks. But that wouldn't do. Nor would a sharp word of sarcasm. She could not afford to antagonise the woman this night for she needed her, so she held her tongue.

Betty nodded at last. 'I see you've done a proper job, Leah Owen.' Her tone was suitably hushed now, in the presence of the dead.

'Thank you for coming to keep watch tonight. It is the act of a true Christian.'

Leah's humble tone must have satisfied, because Betty lowered her handkerchief and looked around for her tea. 'I hope I am one, certainly, and who would not do as much for a neighbour? I would have come sooner, to help, but William would not settle. You know – but of course you can have no idea – what demanding things babies are. He would not sleep but must be fed and bathed and changed and sung to, and a mother doesn't have a moment's peace.'

Three girls safely delivered and on the fourth attempt Betty had at last produced the necessary son and heir. Young William, nearly six months old, was a normal healthy infant, as far as Leah could see, but if Betty George were to be believed, he was a miracle that none but she could have accomplished. The chapel community was never allowed to hear the end of it.

'David has care of him now,' said Betty, settling herself into the more comfortable of the two chairs placed ready. 'Not that it's a man's place to busy himself with babies, but he is so very fond of his son and cannot tear himself away, some days. I hardly need a nursemaid.'

Leah restricted herself to a nod of agreement. She had seen David regard his infant son with proper paternal warmth, though she had not noticed any besotted adoration. But then, it was not her place to remark on signs of affection in him. Not even when he had raised his eyes from the baby to meet hers and had put heart and soul into that look.

Betty took her cup of tea and stirred vigorously. 'Well then, shall we begin our vigil with a prayer?'

'A prayer for courage and guidance in the dark,' said Leah, gathering herself.

Betty's eyebrows rose. It seemed a little unorthodox. 'As you wish, though–'

'I must go.'

'What? What's that you say.'

187

'I have to leave you for a while. You must keep watch alone until I return.'

'Leave me! What sort of nonsense is this?' Betty's chest puffed up in shocked indignation. There was no precedence for this – the absence of a spinster daughter at such a time – or of Betty George being given orders. Behind her bullfrog bluster, there was a gleam of panic at the thought of being left alone in that dark parlour.

Leah seized her hand before she could rise. 'Betty, you must do this one thing for me. I beg you to trust me. Do you imagine I would abandon my post unless something of greater importance than my own life depended on it?'

Betty sat back, still glaring but she said no more, watching as Leah donned her coat, fixed her hat and tiptoed up the steep stairs beside the fireplace. A plank creaked and she paused, but below her John made no move. The glow of dying embers gleamed on the tousled hair that stuck out from the blanket.

She climbed on and paced silently through to the sagging bed in the far room where Annie lay asleep. A disturbed sleep. The girl's eyelids flickered, her hand twitched on the coverlet and a faint whimper escaped with her uneven breath. Innocent as she was, she had seen enough in the village, heard enough at school and chapel, to know that Eli John was a monster. Now he was a monster invading her nightmares.

Leah laid a hand on her arm, stroking the soft skin to bring her gently out of her dream. Annie's eyes blinked open and for a moment she cringed, ready to cry out, but Leah's finger on her lips silenced her.

'Wake up, child. Sh.' She hushed the girl with soft reassurance as she lifted her from under the quilt. 'You must get dressed.'

As wakefulness got a grip, fear came with it. She had gone to sleep terrified and now she woke to even greater terror, though she struggled to obey her aunt's command.

Leah hurriedly buttoned her frock. 'Wrap your shawl round it. It's cold outside.'

Annie found her voice at last. 'Where am I going? Not to Eli John?' She crumpled, pleading, her hands clasped. 'Please, Aunt, please not to Eli John.'

'Hush. Of course not to Eli John. But you are a grown girl now. Almost a woman. You cannot be a child forever. It is time you went into service. There are plenty of other girls have done so at your age. Do you think we can afford to keep you here, sitting idle for ever more? I'm taking you to Plas Malgwyn. They always need girls there.'

Annie's mouth fell open as relief gushed out of her.

'Hurry. I don't want to be all night about it.'

'But what about John? I can't leave John.'

Leah placed her hands on the girl's shoulders, trying to be stern. 'You cannot be forever running around with your brother like children who have no cares. You must leave him. He will do well enough. I must keep the farm for him to inherit so I'll need his help, will I not?'

Panic, resistance and desperation fought in Annie's features. 'But I promised him I'd never leave him. I can't, I can't!'

'You must. There is no choice.' Leah raised her voice enough to sound angry. 'Unless you choose Eli John.'

Annie could only press her lips together to stifle her sobs and shake her head.

'Well then, come now.'

Annie followed her down the stairs, but stopped to look at the dim huddle of her sleeping brother. She pleaded with her eyes, but Leah shook her head and pushed her forward.

At the parlour door, Betty George stood watching, lips pursed in obligatory disapproval but her eyes sharp with understanding. She said nothing.

Leah guided Annie out into the chill drizzle of the night. There was no time for hesitation. Any more delay and they ran the risk of running into Frank, crawling back from one of the public houses in the village.

Two miles along the footpath, with any hint of moon or stars smothered by clouds. No light to guide their way or glint on the dark waters of the river. Annie's hand grasped Leah's as if it were a lifeline, all that prevented her from being swept away into darkness. Neither of them spoke, not until the walls of Plas Malgwyn rose before them.

'This way,' said Leah, tugging her niece away from the main path. It wouldn't do for their like to go marching up to the front door of the gracious house, even though the owners were far away. Leah led on, past stables and barns, around to the yard with its pump and clothesline, barrels and pails, overlooked by the servant's quarters. She knew the way well enough, from her visits to her sister, when Sarah had been in service. She squeezed Annie's hand, then rapped on the service door.

A gangling young man in green apron opened it. 'What do you... Oh, Miss Owen, is it?'

'It is, Arthur. I wish to speak to Mrs Thomas.'

He sniffed. Out in the village, he'd have doffed his cap to her as a respectable woman almost a lady, but here in Plas Malgwyn there were more significant hierarchies to be observed. 'You'd best wait here.'

He almost closed the door on them, leaving them in the fine cold rain that turned the cobbles of the yard to gems, gleaming in the shrouded light from a dozen windows.

The door opened again and a figure appeared: large, black, dignified, tight-corseted and tight-lipped.

'Leah Owen. Did that fool Arthur leave you standing in the cold and wet? Step inside and state your business.'

Leah accepted the invitation without hesitation, pushing Annie in front of her. 'Thank you, Mrs Thomas.'

'Well? You've not come for idle gossip, I imagine.' The housekeeper of Plas Malgwyn consulted a watch suspended on her armoured bosom. Commander of an army of servants and known for her ferocious discipline and contempt for idleness, she was virtual mistress of the house in the absence of the Herbert family who had rarely visited the house for several years. Still, she spoke civilly enough to Leah Owen.

'Will you give my niece a place in the household?' asked Leah, pushing Annie's bonnet back so that her face could be seen more clearly.

Annie, wide-eyed before the awesome housekeeper, said nothing, but managed to bob a curtsey.

'She may look young but she's strong enough, and used to hard work,' added Leah. 'Good with her needle and laundry work. Handy around the kitchen.'

Mrs Thomas stared down at the girl, neither approving nor disapproving. 'That is as maybe, Miss Owen, but this is no time to come asking me to take in your waifs and strays. I have no need for further girls, with the family away.'

Leah fought to keep calm. She drew out her purse. 'I'll pay for her keep.' The housekeeper's brows shot up. 'It's best she were away from home,' added Leah.

Mrs Thomas' eyes narrowed as she met Leah's gaze. She scrutinised the coins Leah was offering, then pushed her hand away. 'I'll keep her here tonight but that's all I can offer.' She held up her hand to silence Leah's pleas. 'I've heard they're looking for a scullery maid at The Grove. I'll have Alfred take her over there tomorrow.'

Leah drew a deep breath, shutting her eyes in gratitude. 'Thank you, Mrs Thomas. God bless you.'

Mrs Thomas pulled a wry face. 'Well, a sad business. And your father barely cold, I hear. I am sorry for your great loss. He was a good man. I trust his grandchild will be equally willing to prove her worth.'

'She will!' Leah turned to Annie, releasing her hand. 'Well, girl. Here you are. Remember, always, to work hard, obey your elders and say your prayers, to thank God for your blessings.'

Annie nodded, still barely conscious of what was happening to her. Mrs Thomas ushered her forward imperiously and the girl obediently stepped up. But then she stopped, turned, and rushed back to Leah, throwing her arms around her.

'Thank you, aunt. Thank you, thank you, thank you.'

'Enough of this silly nonsense.' Leah brusquely pushed the girl away. This was no time for foolish and whimsical emotion. No time unless she were to melt, herself, and collapse in an agony of loss which might undo them all. She stepped back into the yard and watched, expressionless, until the door closed. Then she hurried back to Cwmderwen, the darkness shrouding her grief and the rain concealing her tears.

She lifted the latch as quietly as she could, and stepped into the silent kitchen, turning to shut the door behind her, but a gust of chill night wind came in with her and the boy stirred on his narrow bed. As the latch clicked shut, he sat up. 'Aunt?'

'Go back to sleep.'

'Is there trouble? Is it my father?' How many times had he had cause to ask that?

'No, John, he is not home yet. Be still now.' She hung up her wet coat. 'Where have you been?'

192

'That is my business. Go back to sleep.'

What was it, in her voice? On her face? Something prevented him obeying. He pushed the blanket away and stood up, his bare feet curling on the cold stone slabs. 'You've been out. Where did you go? What's wrong? Is someone else dead?'

'No. No!' Sooner or later...but she hadn't wanted it to be this soon. 'Nothing is wrong. There's no trouble. I have taken your sister to Plas Malgwyn. She is going into service.'

'But she'll be back.'

'No. She won't. You cannot stay together forever, you know. It's time you parted, went your own ways. She must go into service, just as you must stay here to inherit the farm.'

Her words weren't sinking in. He was staring at her, his mouth clamped shut as if there could be no words, but his eyes bored through her, driving through her heart. Anger and betrayal. Bitter, anguished betrayal. She had snatched his one love from him and she had not even let them say farewell. How could she do otherwise? If she'd woken him to take leave of his sister, nothing short of violence would have prised them apart. She had betrayed him and now he would probably hate her forever, but what else could she have done? There was no help for it.

She dug her nails into her palms, drawing a deep breath. 'Go back to sleep,' she ordered. 'Always remember the inheritance Tadcu wished for you. You are his true son and heir, John. Take comfort in that. This farm will be yours one day. Yours. Nothing else matters. Nothing. We must all make sacrifices for that.'

Still he stared at her, then abruptly threw himself back on the settle, pulling the blanket over his head to block her out.

'So you are back at last,' said Betty George, from the parlour door. 'Leaving me here alone! I never thought to see you go gadding about, with your father stark and dead, Leah Owen.' The relief on her face was palpable. So too was the understanding in her eyes, belying her accusing words. Leah had done right. She had done what had to be done. Annie would be safe.

Frank slicked his hair down, then fidgeted with his stiff collar, not meeting Leah's eyes, but concentrating on his reflection in the kitchen window. The best she could think of him was that at least he was still capable of feeling shame. 'What's keeping them?' he muttered. 'Can't we get this over with?'

'It will be over soon enough,' she said. 'Can you not spare one day for your father?'

'Did he ever spare one day for me? Did he ever look on me with love? Did he ever listen to me when I pleaded to stay at school, to do something with my life?'

She tutted. Frank was thirty-six. Another man would have done something about his situation years ago if his resentment boiled so strongly. It wasn't duty that had kept him at home, it was mere lethargy. 'Why didn't you do something with your life, Frank? It was always your choice. If you found this place so unbearable, why didn't you leave long ago, as you were forever talking of doing so? Talking, always talking? Why didn't you just go?'

Frank stared at her, then laughed with anguish at the beams above. 'Because he said to stay. That's why.'

'And when did you ever heed Tada's words?' She must curb the contempt within her. 'So, you are free of him at last, but don't think you can walk away now. You've lost that chance. Now you will stay because I tell you to, and you will stand upright like a man, not a weak fool. Don't let the whole world hear your whining complaints.'

He laughed again, bitterly. 'Not the whole world, Leah. Just the old men of Llanolwen and Felindre and Penbryn. There's a bigger world out there, beyond this miserable snare of Cwmderwen.'

'I know how big the world is, Frank, and Cwmderwen is our part of it. Not a snare. It's Owen land and your father laboured all his life to pass it on to you.'

'Did I ever ask him to?'

'No, but it has fallen to you.'

'Fallen on me, you mean, like heavy rocks. Don't you see, Leah? This place is no more secure than the Titanic. If something that mighty can be brought to ruin so easily by a lump of ice, how do you image we'll survive the tempests?'

'With prayer and hard work. Think, if you had run away to sea as you once proposed, you might have gone down with a ship like those poor souls, but Tada's law kept you safe on land. This land, which you have inherited from him.'

'This tenancy, Leah. Sir Frederick Herbert owns the land and we are mere dandelion seeds on it, waiting for him to blow us away.'

'But he will not, for we will not let him! This is our soil, worked by our hands and it is your duty, Frank, to keep this place and pass it on to your son. His heritage.'

'My son! Now he's mine, is he? Not yours? Where's my daughter? Isn't she mine too?'

'As well you know.'

'I want her back.'

Leah took a deep breath. The parlour door was closed. Sarah preferred to shut herself in with the closed coffin rather than be in their brother's presence. But John was with them in the kitchen. John, standing stiffly by the window, his back to them, not responding in any way to their exchange. He'd said yes and no, when necessity required, but other than that, not a word had escaped him since Annie had gone. Unlike his father, though, he had no trouble meeting Leah's eyes, always with that same look of accusation.

She met his gaze now. 'John, step outside to greet the mourners.'

Without a word, he obeyed.

Leah turned back to Frank, who had slumped down at the table. 'I'll not bring Annie back.'

'She's my daughter, not yours. You had no business sending her off as a servant.'

'At least she'll be safe where she is.'

'It's a father's place to protect his child, not that Tada ever seemed to care for that.'

'A father's place? A pity you didn't remember your paternal obligations when you offered Annie to Eli John.'

Frank scowled, scratching at the table top with his fingernail. 'I wasn't serious. I was drunk.'

'Yes, and you'll be drunk again, and it will happen again. And again. And you may think it an idle joke but Eli John will hold you to it, you know he will. He is nothing but malice and you are so weak you will let him take her.'

He mumbled. 'It was nothing but a jest.'

'Eli doesn't jest. Can't you see, Frank? He'd have your daughter another Rachel Morgan, to be debauched and ruined and discarded. His only wish is to corrupt. He may have succeeded with you, but he'll not touch Annie.' Low solemn voices in the yard warned her that mourners, swathed in black, had begun to arrive. Soon the minister would join them. 'Let it be, Frank. Stand up now and be a man. Bury your father with the dignity he deserves.'

He opened his mouth, ready with a caustic response.

'For my sake, if not for his,' she added. 'Ugly old spinster that I am.'

Frank winced at the words. 'You know I didn't mean—'

'I know that you were drunk, and that demon at your elbow could make you say anything. I pay no heed to such insults, but I will have you behave like a dutiful son now, in recompense.'

Frank gave a deep sigh of surrender. He rose, bracing himself to open the door and face his neighbours as master of the house.

The house was silent. Though voices had been hushed, the mere breathing of two score men seemed to have thundered through the cramped rooms as the minister had conducted the service, but now they were gone, taking the coffin for burial, and only the two sisters and Betty George remained, lost in the sudden hush.

'He must have a proper stone,' said Sarah suddenly. 'Not like those wooden markers for Mam and Tom.' She dabbed her cheeks.

'Of course he must have one,' said Betty, emphatically. 'Such a God-fearing pillar of our community deserves a fitting memorial.'

'There is one held in readiness,' said Leah, before Sarah could take umbrage at the interference. 'Tada had Jonah Devonald engrave it more than a year ago. It was only waiting for the date of Tada's passing. It names them all, Tada, Mam and Tom, since they will all lie together.'

'As it should be,' said Betty, nodding her approval.

How should it be, indeed? Leah, taking the news of Tada's death to the mason, had seen the stone for the first time and she still raged at the memory.

Mary, wife of Thomas Owen of Cwmderwen, died 1900, aged 60.
Also the above Thomas Owen, died...
Also Thos their son, died 1882, aged 16.
'Y drygionus a wna waith twyllodrus: ond i'r neb a heuo
gyfiawnder, y bydd gwobr sicr.'
Diarhebion 11:18

In English, apart from the scripture. Of course she understood why. 'Of Cwmderwen', those were the words that mattered, his land by legal right, so the words were in the language of the law, but why couldn't he have got the date of Mam's death right? 1899. It was as if her passing were of no importance, forgotten already. One year or another, what did it matter? She had asked the mason to correct it, but he would not. And then, why had Tada not had himself named first, as head of the family, instead of interposing himself between Mam and Tom, as if determined, even in the grave, to keep them apart?

Her rage about the engraving was pointless. What did a year matter, in the face of eternity? What did the ordering of words on a stone matter, when Mam and Tom lay undisturbed together beneath it? She should not be fretting herself over such insignificant issues. Her sister was the one to do that. Like a dog with a bone, Sarah wouldn't stop fidgeting over the subject. 'All very well Tada requesting it, but how will you afford such an expense now, Leah, without Tada to keep the farm? Will and I cannot help. You have no idea—'

'It's all paid for, don't worry, Sarah. Tada saw to it. Besides, Frank will keep the farm. We are not destitute.'

Betty pursed her lips. 'There I pity you, Leah Owen, for if Frank continues as he has done, destitute is what you will be, soon enough. I know how he goes on in Penbryn.'

'We all know how he goes on in Penbryn. But now the farm will be his and I will not let him fail. It must come to John. I shall see to that. We shall have enough to get by.'

'Well, I never have enough,' said Sarah. 'But it doesn't matter how much it costs. Tada must have a fitting stone. Mam too. And I suppose you'll have Annie's wages, if it's true you've put her into service at Plas Malgwyn. I'm hoping they'll take Maudie. Though I'm surprised you sent Annie so early. Not yet twelve. What of school? You were always so strong on that, Leah.'

'She turned twelve last January, Sarah.'

'Did she? Well, you were the one for reckoning.'

'Schooling is little use to a girl,' said Betty. 'Far better have her earning her keep at last. You'll need every penny she can bring in.'

'Whatever Annie earns will be hers,' said Leah. 'It's one less mouth to feed here and that's all that matters.' She chose not to correct the idea that Annie was at Plas Malgwyn. That was what Frank thought and – thanks to Betty George's gossip – what most of the village believed. Mrs Thomas, the housekeeper at Plas Malgwyn had said nothing to deny the story, and once it got abroad that the rumour was wrong, Annie's whereabouts would hopefully be lost in confusion. Best that way, or Frank would turn up drunk, egged on by Eli John, to hammer on doors and demand her back.

'You are too soft for your own good,' said Sarah. 'I'm surprised you never wed, Leah. Men like weakness in women. The softer their minds, the better.' If she intended it as a jest, it fell heavily in the silence. Betty blushed uncomfortably.

Leah barely felt the sting. Of all accusations thrown at Leah, softness had never been one of them.

Sarah shrugged. 'Well, we're all too old and dry for men to see anything in us now.' She settled her plump rump more comfortably in her chair and sat back complacently. 'I wouldn't regret it if I were you, Leah. Children whining all the time, under your feet, always wanting food or nursing or quarrelling to drive you mad.'

'Some of us find them a blessing,' said Betty acerbically, then shut her mouth firmly, fanning her face with a gloved hand.

Then the door flew open and Mary came in.

It was Mary, but Leah only realised it after staring at her for some seconds, while the others leapt to their feet in consternation at the wild apparition confronting them.

She had been too much engaged with her ailing husband, that's what Albert Lloyd had said, coming to represent his father and stepmother at the funeral. She could not be spared. But Mary, it seemed, had other ideas.

'I've come,' she said. The words sounded strange in her mouth as if speaking were a novelty she had to remaster. She was wild-eyed, dishevelled, her greying hair a tangled mess under a fraying man's hat. She had on one shoe and one slipper, and a grimy skirt, but over it a nightdress, and over that a shawl that had wound itself into such a knot that she could not release one arm.

'I've come,' she repeated, though it was doubtful that she knew why she had come, or where.

Betty George stepped back from her in alarm, afraid of contamination, and Sarah put her hands to her mouth and shrieked.

'Mary.' Leah recovered herself, and reached out to her sister, guiding her into the house.

Mary stared round in bewilderment until her eyes fell on the old bench in the fireplace where she had worn away years at her needle. She struggled out of Leah's embrace, staggered to the bench and sat there, rocking.

'Well!' said Betty. 'What a disgraceful spectacle, and at her own father's funeral too.'

'Betty, hold your tongue,' said Leah, though she knew Betty only spoke out of panic.

'What's the matter with her? What's the matter with her?' wailed Sarah.

'Her mind is disturbed, what do you think?' snapped Leah, kneeling down by the poor woman. 'Well, Mary, *fach*, you sit there and rest. Shall I help you out of this shawl?'

Mary let Leah unwind it, but then she snatched at it, clutching it to her as she rocked. 'I've come back,' she said.

'Yes, you've come back.' Leah put her hands over her eyes. Now

Tada is dead and you are back, she thought. Was it worth it, your escape?

'Quite mad,' said Betty. 'She should be in an asylum. What a disgrace!' She held her tongue as Leah turned to face her.

'I think, perhaps, we are all mad,' said Leah.

'It's unfortunate that he allowed her to slip out,' said Albert Lloyd, back from the burying, and shaking his head over his stepmother. 'He usually takes care to keep her fast, where she'll come to no harm, but she has grown sly this last year. I am sorry that she has imposed on you in this way, but I shall take her home and see to it that she does not escape again.'

'Escape!' Leah faced the corpulent self-important man with rage. 'Is she a prisoner with you?'

'Confined, my dear, for her own safety. Would you have her wandering the streets of Penbryn, shaming the entire family?'

'Your family is shamed by your treatment of her. Can you not see she needs proper care?'

'I am sure Mr Lloyd has done his best by your poor sister,' said Betty, but David hushed her with a frown.

'He has done his best for himself because he wants to be mayor, and thinks insanity is a scandal!'

'Now, now!' flustered Albert.

'Tada used to say insanity was the Devil at work in a soul,' said Sarah helpfully.

'Tada would,' said Frank, coming in from the yard where he had been shooing other mourners away. 'So. Sister Mary's back with us then, and not before time, by the look of her. I'll thank you to leave her with us now, Albert Lloyd and you can go and dance about before the gentry of Penbryn for your supper, without fear of the lunatic in the attic. She'll be safer with us.'

201

Albert huffed and puffed, but Frank's insolent command gave him the excuse he had long sought to be free of a perennial embarrassment.

'And you, Betty George,' said Frank. 'Don't stand there lapping it all up, with that look of gleeful shock on your face. David, take her home. We'll deal with this. And you, Sarah. Off you go, because you're no more use with these things than a wet rag in a thunderstorm.'

'Oh Frank!' wailed Sarah, but she was more than happy for Will to lead her away.

David glanced at Leah, anxious and questioning.

'Yes, go,' she reassured him. 'We'll cope with Mary. Better she has some peace and quiet while we settle her.'

Shaking his head, David touched her hand, then ushered his blustering wife out.

'And after all I've done!' Betty was saying, as the door closed on them.

'Well, we're rid of them at last.' Frank unbuttoned his jacket, pulled his black tie loose and blew out his cheeks. 'Now I can go for a drink.'

'No,' said Leah. 'You don't mean that.' She was so bemused by his sudden assumption of authority that she wasn't sure if he were joking or not.

'Mm. Maybe not till we've settled what's to be done with sister Mary.'

'She'll stay here.'

'With you to care for her? Haven't you had enough of that, Leah? Caring and cosseting those who trample on you? She is quite mad, you know.'

'Life was never kind to her.'

'Or to any of us, and she was certainly never kind to you.'

202

'But still she is my sister. Just as you are still my brother, no matter what you say or do.'

He looked away. 'How do you propose to arrange this then?'

Leah thought about it. Mary continued to rock on her bench, unaware of any of them. John, standing silent by the door, watched them all, expressionless, his thoughts sealed inside him. Just as Mary had kept hers sealed inside, in her youth. Leah shook off the connection. 'I'll sleep with her, as we always did, to make sure she comes to no harm.' She glanced at the steep stairs, picturing Mary stumbling and tumbling. 'I'll keep her down here. We must have the parlour. Tada's room.' The room of death. There was nothing else for it. 'John, you can have my room. It's time you had a proper bed.'

John cast his enigmatic gaze on his mad aunt, neither fearful of her state nor pitying it, and indifferent to sleeping arrangements. Directly addressed, he replied with a shrug.

Leah helped her sister to her feet. Mary whimpered, bewildered, but allowed herself to be guided through into the parlour, lately vacated by Tada's coffin. She was still clutching her shawl, but as she entered, her eyes fixed on the scripture on the wall and she shuffled to it, touching the mottled glass. Leah pulled out fresh linen for the stripped bed. The idea of sleeping in that bed appalled her, but there was nothing else to be done.

'Here you are, Mary. You will sleep safe and sound with me. Settle yourself and be comfortable. You are home now.'

'Crack,' said Mary. She had moved on from the scripture to the crack in the plaster and was tracing it with her finger.

'Yes, we must mend that,' said Leah, trying to guide her away, but Mary was tugging at a fragment of horsehair, working a piece of plaster loose. She pressed her eye to the gap and laughed.

What was she seeing through it, Leah wondered. Was she adrift enough from reality to see those who had passed through, those that Leah could not see? Perhaps madness was a better alternative.

Mary accepted her prompting at last, and allowed Leah to strip her, to ease her into a fresh nightgown and help her onto the bed, tucking the sheets around her. Mary was passive as a baby now, but who could tell how she would be in a moment.

'Sleep,' said Leah. 'You have walked a long way. Sleep now.'

Obediently, Mary closed her eyes. Leah quietly stepped back into the kitchen.

'As ever, you manage all and leave nothing for me,' said Frank. 'Or have I a place in your schemes?'

Leah was weary of cajoling. 'You are at the heart of all, Frank, as you well know. That is my scheme for you, that you be the man I know you can be. Respected. Honourable. Head of your family and master of your house and land as you showed yourself today.'

'You mistake me for David George.'

'No, I don't. I take you for Francis Owen, who has a farm to keep, a son to bring up, a man who can walk with his head high in the streets of Llanolwen and Penbryn. You can be that, rather than a drunken sot, led into ruin by Eli John and mocked for it by the whole world.'

'Aye.' He looked soberly at his hands. 'But no one turns their back on Eli.'

'You will. We will. What can he do to harm us?'

'More than you know,' muttered Frank.

'No, he can do nothing if we choose to be free of him. Come on, Frank. Take up your proper place in the world.'

Frank laughed bitterly. 'I don't know where you get your dreams from, Leah Owen.'

'From my faith in you. My memory of how you once were. You are sober, Frank. You have done your duty today by your father, by me and even by Mary. Now do it by your son there. Come with me to Plas Malgwyn and sign the papers that will give you the tenancy, as Tada wished.'

John turned to face them at these words, though he said nothing.

Frank scowled. 'Today? Who will watch our mad sister?'

'John will sit with her and make sure she comes to no harm. If needs be, he can lock her in the parlour until we return. You will do that, will you, John, so that we can fix the lease?'

John looked from her to his father, to the range, to the beams of the ceiling, the pots on the dresser, embracing it all, his claim. He gave a nod and marched into the parlour, shutting the door behind him.

'Well then.' Leah tightened her brother's tie. 'Come with me, Frank.'

'Leah, it's late. The sun is sinking. Tomorrow, maybe.'

'There is time today. Come with me, please, Frank.'

There was a glint of a challenge in his eye now. 'To Plas Malgwyn. I'll see Annie. Maybe I'll bring her home with me.'

'Maybe, Frank.' Leah would keep talking, keep chivvying, saying whatever must be said to get him there. He was right, it was late in the day for this, but she dared not put it off till the morning, till a night of gin and ale had undone all the effort she had made to hold her brother in check since Tada's death.

'Should I not see to the cows?'

'They will wait. Their milk is low.'

Frank shrugged and straightened his jacket. 'Well, I'll do it then, if only to have a moment's peace from my shrew of a sister.'

Content, Leah fastened her hat. She couldn't trust him to go alone.

The footpath across the fields to Plas Malgwyn was bright with hedgerows aglow with berries, hips, haws, bramble and elder, and trailing festoons of bryony, all gilded by the sinking sun. Utterly different from the blind dark path along which she had taken Annie, four nights before, that small chill hand clasped in hers. Since that night, Leah's insides had been knotted in ceaseless readiness for any further catastrophe, or how else would she have dealt with the day's traumas this far? Mary was yet another problem waiting for them, and the matter of an ever-diminishing income would be with them still. But if she could just get Frank to sign the papers and settle this one matter, would she be able to breathe again? She could not afford that luxury yet.

Plas Malgwyn was glowing, soft and dreamlike, in the evening light, a peacock trailing across its smooth velvet lawns, preparing to seek a roost for the night. Its ugly squawking call split an unnatural silence. The lawns were well kept but unused. The façade of the house was gracious but the windows were blank. Leah remembered walking this way – when Sarah had been a kitchen maid – and stopping to stare with childish admiration at the ladies in white lace and ruffles, men in blazers and boaters, strolling arm in arm under parasols, until one of them had spied her watching and had shooed her away. Sir Frederick still visited on occasion, but the Herbert family hadn't taken up residence there for two years now. They kept to town, tightening their belts and making economies, so the rumours went.

It was Mr Fenston, the Herberts' steward, who was the real lord of this valley, the vice-regent to whom all the tenant farmers doffed their caps and their wives bobbed a curtsey though he was no more nobly born than they, merely the son of a solicitor in Swansea. He was a man who enjoyed his position and the dignity that went with it, but he was a shrewd businessman, too, managing the Herberts' estate without sentiment or charity. He couldn't be flattered into acquiescence. Leah ran over and over in her mind what she would say, how she would act.

Brother and sister took the path through the woods, round the side of the house, to the steward's offices. Frank was still on his best behaviour, she could tell. He wasn't talking, but he wasn't whistling, either. He looked solemn as they walked.

Mr Fenston's door was answered by a servant Leah didn't know. They were kept waiting for only a moment before being ushered into an office that made the knots within Leah tighten still further. It was such an alien room, with deep-padded leather chairs and leather-bound tomes filling the tall shelves, a Turkish rug on the floor and glittering ornaments on the mantelpiece. And a desk so huge and grand, a man could rule the Empire from it. No wonder the man sitting behind it looked so imperious, though he was balding and overweight. She and Frank must seem like threadbare beggars, standing before him.

But they were not beggars. They were respectable farmers. They had land: twenty-four acres, one rood and eight perches – or they would still have it, if he permitted – and they were the equal to any in the land before God.

Frank took off his hat. Leah nodded her head to show respect. It seemed only proper to wait for the great man to speak first. He was studying a large map spread out on his desk, and she thought he'd keep them waiting until their shins ached, but to her surprise he looked up, then rose to proffer his hand across the desk.

'Mr Owen, Miss Owen. A sad day for you both. I understand you buried your father today.'

'Yes, sir,' said Frank.

'I confess I knew little of him except when he came to pay his quarterly rent, and he wasn't a man of much idle conversation, but I understand he was highly respected in this parish. Now, I imagine, you have come to renew the tenancy. Though I am surprised to see you so soon. I would have requested your attendance in the next

207

day or two, in order to discuss the matter, but I thought to leave you to your mourning on the day of the funeral, at least.'

He spoke with modulated politeness, but his eyes were sharp, watching them, summing them up.

Leah replied quickly, before Frank could open his mouth. 'We found it best to keep busy, sir. In such a time it only deepens the wound to sit and ponder on our loss.' She caught the twist of Frank's lip, but Mr Fenston was looking at her.

'Quite so. It is the matter of the tenancy of Cwmderwen that brings you here, then. You wish to take it, I presume.'

Frank hesitated. Leah found his hand and squeezed it. 'Yes, sir.'

'Hm.' He leaned on the desk, studying the map again. 'A very small tenancy. What, twenty acres?' He reached for a ledger, but Leah spoke before he could open it.

'Twenty-four acres, one rood and eight perches.'

'Hm. The buildings have been well maintained, and the land has not declined in fertility, such as there is, but no improvements. Is there a place for such a holding, I wonder? Your neighbour has suggested that it would be more profitable to include the land in the Castell Mawr tenancy.'

Frank made a small noise that might have been a squeak of alarm or, more likely, a laugh.

'David George suggested that?' demanded Leah.

Mr Fenston raised his head to look her, one brow twitching up. 'Mrs George was the one who proposed it. A very practical manager for a woman, if I may say so. But Mr George was not amenable to the notion. He is a cautious man but that hasn't held him back from making wise choices when he thinks fit. Castell Mawr is as thriving as any farm can be in these hardened times, so I'll abide by his judgement rather than that of his good lady in this case, and leave the Cwmderwen land intact. Now...' He opened the ledger and perused it.

Frank was growing impatient, Leah could tell, beginning to fidget. One unexpected hurdle had been crossed, but Mr Fenston was not yet offering an agreement to sign. She must bring him to a conclusion soon.

'Thank you, sir. We are grateful.'

'Mm. You father took the tenancy on a reduced rate when prices had been tumbling catastrophically.'

'He always paid, sir. Without fail.'

'That's true. He was punctilious in that, to the minute and to the penny. A matter of pride and principle, I imagine.' Mr Fenston glanced up at Frank. 'You will show the same reliability and punctuality as your father, I presume?'

'Yes, sir,' said Frank, a note of irony in his tone that Leah understood, though she prayed Mr Fenston did not.

'We will be as prompt as our father, sir, I promise that.'

'Your father, I believe, eked out the income of the farm with carpentry work.'

'Joinery, sir,' corrected Leah, conscious of the exquisite cabinet-maker's art on display around her. Would Mr Fenston even recognise her father's plain solid work as craftsmanship?

'Quite so. And do you have a craft, my man? An alternative source of income?'

Leah held her breath. Frank had barely done a day's work on the farm, let alone in any other employment. Now his jaw worked as if he couldn't decide whether to laugh or cry. 'I often work for Eli John, sir.'

'The quarry master's son? Well, he has a gift for making money, I'll grant you that, if nothing else can be said for him. So,' Fenston sniffed, looking at the ledger again, 'should I reconsider the rent, now that prices have held steady for so long?'

Leah clenched her fists. What argument did she have against a rent increase, except the injustice of it, and that was not a matter of concern to a businessman. If he raised the rent, even by a shilling, they would be done for. Tada's joinery had not brought in an extra penny for two years now, since his seizure, and they were stretched to their limit. She prepared for the worst.

'No, I think we shall leave it as it is, for this year at least. As long as you fulfil your obligations and pay your rent on time, you may assume the tenancy, Mr Owen.' Fenston turned away to find the proper papers, and Leah trembled, feeling her knees giving way. Frank shook his head at her with a grin as if she were a fool to have cared. But when Fenston turned back, Leah was still and upright again, waiting with quiet dignity while Frank signed his name and the men shook hands.

Fenston nodded to Leah, then waved them away. They left, smartly, before he could change his mind.

'See what you've saddled me with,' said Frank.

'Our land is safe.'

'You're mad if you think that. We'll be out soon enough when we can't pay our way.'

'We will pay.'

'You think?' Frank shrugged, looking down the range of high sash windows into the courtyard by the kitchen. 'Since I'm now a respectable farmer, I may call upon my daughter, don't you think?'

'It's late, Frank. She'll be busy.'

'I think not.' He was striding across the courtyard to rap on the door as Leah had done only a few nights previously. A second before he did so, Leah caught a glimpse of Mrs Thomas at a window, and the housekeeper herself opened the door.

'Yes? Mr Owen, I believe. You have business here?'

'I've come to see my daughter. Entitled to, aren't I? Seeing as she's only twelve and cast adrift among strangers, who will fleece her likely as not.' The old challenge was back in his voice now that he'd escaped the iron constraints of his meeting with the steward.

Leah hurried up behind him, trying to catch the housekeeper's eye, but there was no need.

'Annie Owen is about her errands down the valley,' said Mrs Thomas.

'Oh. So I may not see her, is that it? But I may discuss terms. Part of her wages should come to me as her father, don't you think?'

'I do not discuss terms on the doorstep this late in the day.'

'Indeed,' said Leah. 'Frank, it will soon be dark. Let's go home. We'll discuss this another time.' Or better still, never. He might have forgotten about it by morning.

'Very well,' said Frank, stepping back from the door. 'But I'll have what's mine, missis. I know my rights.'

Mrs Thomas closed the door on him. If she hadn't fully understood all when Leah had called on her with the girl, Annie must have explained how things stood at home. The housekeeper would play her part in the conspiracy, although it filled Leah with agonised shame to think that even as she nudged Frank onto a new course of duty and diligence, she would never be able to trust him with his own daughter.

Frank hurried her away, walking fast into the fading glow of evening, the sun long gone. 'So I've done all you've ordered, sister and I'll tell you one thing. Eli will be mad.'

'Why? Because he cannot ruin each and every one of the Owens? Is he so desperate to see us all brought low?'

'It isn't Eli who's the desperate one, Leah. Never mind, it's done now. So can I now go and buy a drink, for if any man deserved it after this day–'

'Frank, this one night, please don't go to the Mason's Arms. We have Mary to think of, and your son and the farm. Come home this once and let us remember kinder days, when we were young, and Mam and Tada were watching over us with loving kindness and Tom was alive and—'

'Truly?' He stopped in his tracks. 'Do you really remember such a dream world, Leah?' He laughed bitterly. 'Because it was never like that for me. Not even when Tom was alive. Yes, maybe I remember seeing you carried on Tada's shoulders as he sang, and Mam tutting that he was spoiling you, his favourite. But I wasn't in that world. I was never anything but the unwanted runt.'

'That's not true.'

'Mam tolerated me, perhaps.'

'She loved you. And so did I. We were children, playing together, do you not remember that?'

'Maybe.' His tone softened. 'Chasing the chickens.'

'Making pies with the sawdust in the workshop.'

'Dropping pebbles down the well.'

'Can we not go back home and be a family for one night?'

He sighed. 'You're a fool, Leah Owen, for all you are so clever.' He mocked, but he came with her, back to the house, to supper, to soothe Mary with quiet words as she rose in a panic, wondering where she was and who they were. Home to John.

'Is my farm secure?' he demanded.

'Yes, it's done,' said Leah, and John said no more.

Was he reconciled to Annie's loss by the promise of the farm? She prayed so. John was satisfied, Mary was restored, Frank was tamed and perhaps it was possible, after all, that a page had turned. For all the burdens, old and new, that weighed on Leah, she began to believe all would indeed be well.

There was a lightness in the house, as if the sun had found its way more readily into the narrow cwm, a sense of hope and... could it be pleasure? Pleasure to have a family around her, to hear the occasional laugh, to feel a sense of ease, though she was kept eternally vigilant, watching over Mary.

Her older sister was quite mad, it was true, but not aggressive. She had become a small child, needing only food and sleep, soothed by the thought of home and safety, but ready to wander off at any moment, without aim or understanding. Leah kept her by her side, with one eye constantly on her, and it would have made her labour in the fields impossible, but Frank was there now, doing his duty. He knuckled down to work on the land with more energy than Leah had ever seen in him, and made no attempt to hide his ignorance of farming matters but sought advice from his sister and son with good humour. He tended the animals, caught a couple of rabbits in the stubble, mended a fence or two... and stayed away from the ale houses. Was this what it took to make him a man at last? The death of his father? A blessing wrapped in a tragedy.

Worries began to dissipate, leaving a golden glow of contentment, though winter beckoned. Leah bathed in it for a day or two until its source struck her and immersed her in guilt. However dry and dead her love for Tada had become, she should not be seeing his death as a blessing or rejoice that he was no longer there, with his flint-hard righteousness, his catechisms and crushing recitations of divine wrath. No longer brooding over them like the day of judgement.

She had no right to be so disloyal or ungrateful. Tada had unstintingly given his sweat and blood and tears, and – perhaps – his sanity, to give them this. Cwmderwen. Twenty-four acres, one rood and eight perches. Their own patch of paradise. But it had taken his death to release the shadow upon it. Now that Frank was no longer being condemned daily as unworthy to inherit a burden he had never wanted, he seemed content to take up his stewardship

213

of the land, though he maintained a sardonic attitude and laughed at the folly of their hopes and dreams.

John, bemused at the change in his father, began to speak again, at least to Frank, and even to Mary, sparingly, tentatively, as if he couldn't quite believe in the transformation of the family. Leah waited only to hear him sing again, to be truly convinced the spell was broken.

She would have accompanied Frank to market in Penbryn, but Mary could not be left, so John went with him. One day off school would be little harm in return for such a prize as this family harmony. They returned nursing a shared mocking secret, which Frank eventually explained with a laugh over supper.

'That boy of mine wouldn't let me so much as sniff a mug of ale. What is the point of market day, I ask you, if a man cannot celebrate his achievements with a drink or two?'

Leah smiled. 'Your son is as wise as a serpent to keep you as harmless as a dove.'

'And you are the owl watching us all as ever, Leah.'

'Ready to gobble naughty mice.'

Mary laughed, though whether she understood, they couldn't tell. Even John managed a glimmer of a smile. Frank shrugged happily and held out his cup for more tea. Maybe, thought Leah, I was too hasty in sending Annie away. Maybe I should go and reclaim her from her employer. Then we will be complete.

But it was all just a dream. Dreams end, shattered by brutal awakening. On the second market day, Leah had supposed father and son would go together again, but Frank was up before them all and had the horse harnessed while Leah was still tending to Mary. He had gone, alone, while John was still dressing.

'No need for you to miss another day of school,' said Leah,

determined to keep any hint of anxiety from her voice. 'Your father can cope well enough on his own. There's no calf to manage this week.'

John looked at her as if he no longer believed anything she said, but he shrugged on his jacket and set off for school without a word. What he learned there, she didn't know. It had been Annie who had been the keen scholar, and sometimes Leah suspected John had attended only to keep her company. But now he went alone, a solitary soul, and kept his thoughts about it – as about everything else – to himself.

The day wore on, and Leah tried, resolutely, to keep up a sense of optimism, to fight off the rising surge of gloomy inevitability. John came home from school and there was no Frank. She made supper, eaten in silence, John staring at his father's seat with cynical understanding beyond his years.

He fed the pig and watched over Mary while Leah milked the cows and rounded up the hens. Still there was no Frank.

Leah put Mary to bed, watching until her sister, curled up like a kitten in a basket, snored and twitched into contented sleep. Then she returned to the kitchen, to sit by the dying embers and wait for her brother.

Night settled. She lit the oil lamp. John took his place in the corner. Leah took hers by the range. They sat in silence, not stirring until hoofs rang out on the cobbles. Then they both sat up, alert. A man's tread approached the house. Leah dared for a second to hope, and then mocked herself for doing so. The footsteps were even. Measured. Sober. They were not Frank's.

She was not surprised by the knock before the door opened. David George was standing on the step, removing his cap.

'Miss Owen.'

'Mr George, come in. You are out late.'

'Of course. I am sorry. It is a late hour to be disturbing you. I was detained...I have been in Penbryn all day, at the market and at meetings...' He took her hand. 'I have not yet had the chance to tell you how deeply sorry I am for the death of your father.'

'You and your wife called the next day and you attended the funeral. I hardly think you were remiss.'

'But those were mere formalities. I could not say...' It was true, he could say very little with Betty George standing guard over him. But why would he need to say more? It had been enough. 'I wished to tell you, if you need anything, you have only to send word.'

'Thank you, that is neighbourly. But we are getting by. The tenancy is secure with us, though we've been told some might think it better in other hands.'

David coloured slightly, understanding the insinuation. 'Leah, I promise you, as long as I have breath, I will do my utmost to see the tenancy remains with you.'

'With Frank, David. Frank is the son and heir. He holds the farm now.'

'Yes, Frank.' David's tone became graver. 'I saw him in Penbryn.'

'At the market?'

'He was with Eli John. At the Black Bull.'

John, who had been sitting silently, waiting for prayers, rose and walked out of the cottage.

'John!' Leah called after him, but he was gone.

'I'm sorry, I should have been more discreet.' David winced. 'Leah, I saw your brother, already half drunk, at noon, with Eli egging him on. And later, I saw him outside, passed out. I tried to take him up, bring him home, but Eli had charge of him and grew abusive, so I had no choice but to leave him. I wish—'

'Hush. It's I who do the wishing, every day.' Leah sat down heavily.

216

'It grieves me to say this, but I fear he was doing more than drinking.'

'How do you mean. Women?'

'Ah. I don't doubt that. Eli had his creature fawning all over your brother.'

'Rachel Morgan, you mean.'

'That, I believe, is her name. But I wasn't speaking of women. There's a great deal of gambling done in the Black Bull, so I've been told. I heard one of the fellows laughing at Frank as the Morgan woman pulled him up from the gutter, asking him how much he owed Eli now. I suspect he's run up debts these last years, gambling debts that you know nothing about. Debts that keep him beholden to that beast.'

'Oh, Frank!'

'I regret I was alone and they were belligerent in drink, or I would have done more.'

'You did more than Frank deserves. I hoped for the best but feared for the worst, and the worst has won, as it always does.'

'Leah.' David took her hands, pressing them between his. 'If there's anything... You have only to ask. You know I will always be there for you.'

He was in earnest. This wouldn't do. She rose. 'I thank God I am blessed with such kindly neighbours as you and Betty. But you must not worry about me...us. Think of your own family and your farm. We will manage. I will manage.'

Her calm words made David remember himself. 'Of course. Well, good night, Miss Owen. Again, my sympathy for your great loss. God bless you.' He left and now that she no longer had to pretend, the pain of frustrated hopes dug its talons into Leah.

The parlour door opened and Mary was standing there, bewildered and lost, her nightgown awry. Leah's heart sank further.

How would she cope? How could she run the farm, keep the house and keep watch on Mary, without Frank to play his part?

'Come now, *fach*. Back to bed with you.' Mary was resettled, as Leah, with a will of iron, fought back tears that ached to burst out and burn her cheeks. *Why, Frank?* When she returned to the kitchen, John was standing there. He looked at Leah and said nothing. There was nothing to say.

The next morning, with no sign of Frank, John was out tending to the animals, while Leah chivvied Mary out of bed and into her clothes. She brewed up oatmeal, while Mary sat happily knitting something unspecified and shapeless. Leah made tea and stepped out into the yard, which John was swilling down.

'Come, eat your breakfast now,' she said. 'Or you'll be late for school.'

'They'll not miss me.' He filled another bucket. It was an improvement, a whole sentence addressed to her, but not what she wanted to hear.

'You need your schooling.'

'The farm needs me more.'

'I'll manage here.'

'My farm? My house? Aunt Mary? My drunken father?'

'I'll manage. I always do.'

'No. You'll fail me. This is my land. Mine. No one is going to take what's mine.' He turned his back on her and strode off into the fields.

1916

Leah emerged from the manager's office, methodically straightening her hat and gloves, and smoothing down her coat to conceal her agitation. She had paid the quarter's rent easily enough, because Cwmderwen was heading into calm waters at last, but she should have guessed that a rent rise would be the consequence. Still, they would weather it, as they had weathered all else.

Samuel Parry, the general odd-job boy at Plas Malgwyn, burst out of the servant's door and came racing towards her. 'Mrs Thomas says can you spare the time to take tea, Miss Owen?'

Leah's heart jumped. She knew what often accompanied such an invitation from her co-conspirator. She hurried to the housekeeper's room and Mrs Thomas rose solemnly, a letter in her hand. 'It came two days ago. I was in half a mind to send Sam to Cwmderwen with it, but I heard that your brother was at home and thought...'

Yes, it had come to this, thought Leah, prising the envelope open. Frank had been at home four days in a row, and that was such a novelty, the news had spread even to Plas Malgwyn. For the first two days he'd wallowed in bed, too ill to rise, and since then, he'd moped around the farm, doing virtually nothing, lost in perpetual gloom. It wasn't just the new licensing laws that kept him at home, but his lack of money. He'd have raided her purse if she hadn't watched him like a hawk. He'd only stirred himself when she mentioned the need to pay the rent. He'd demanded to take it, as innocent as a baby. Of course she hadn't let him. She'd come herself, as Mr Fenston knew she would. He no longer expected to see Frank on his doorstep.

'Thank you, Mrs Thomas.' Leah's hand was trembling as she read the letter. Fine paper, not the rough scrap Annie had used last time.

My dearest aunt

I hope all goes well at Cwmderwen and that you and John are in good health. I have a new position now. I am nursemaid in the house of Mrs Clayton in Haverfordwest, who is a very nice old lady, who has been very kind to me, and you may rest assured I am most content. But, dear aunt, we are to live in America, in Pennsylvania, and I would love more than anything to see you and John before we sail, because I do not know if I shall ever have a chance to see you both again. I know it will be difficult for you, but Mrs Clayton has very kindly assured me I may meet you one afternoon for tea, as you think it unwise for me to visit you at home. Is it possible, dear aunt, that that you could come?

Your ever loving and obedient niece, Mary Anne Owen.

Leah folded the letter, feeling the hollowness swell in her heart. Instead of facing the direst import of Annie's letter, she concentrated on lesser matters. She took the cup of tea that Mrs Thomas was holding out. 'She is employed now by a Mrs Clayton.'

'Yes, I know.' Mrs Thomas, while appearing to be regally aloof, always knew the gossip of the whole county. 'English...but a very respectable lady. Her husband was a lawyer.'

'Annie writes that she is an elderly woman, but Annie is to be a nursemaid.'

'Mrs Clayton's daughter, Mrs Strade, has an infant. Mrs Strade is recently widowed and living with her mother, now. Captain Strade was killed at Loos last year.'

'I see. I see.' Leah unfolded the letter again, determined to face up to it. 'She writes that they are to sail for America.'

'I believe Mrs Clayton has another daughter living there, in Pennsylvania. Her husband is quite wealthy, one hears. Iron or steel or some such. I am sure Annie has every hope of doing well there. She is such a sweet obliging girl.'

Leah attempted a smile. Praise from Mrs Thomas was a rare commodity, but the housekeeper was generous with Leah. She had been passing on letters from Annie for four years, keeping her aunt informed of her welfare, which was more than she would do for many in the parish. Respect for Leah and John was universal – as their ceaseless struggle to maintain Cwmderwen had begun to bear real fruit through the war years – just as any lingering respect for Frank had withered to dust.

'You will be eager to see her, I expect,' said Mrs Thomas.

'Yes. Yes I must manage it, somehow. And John, of course. He'll be anxious to see her. But–' She stopped, her mind working. It would mean leaving Frank in sole charge of the farm for a day. Could she trust him even to do that?

'You do get out and about on occasion?' asked Mrs Thomas, fully aware of the constraints on Leah.

'To market of course. And sometimes to Carmarthen.'

'How is your poor sister?'

What could Leah say? Mary was in the county asylum. She'd had no choice. For several months after Tada's death she had struggled to maintain the farm and watch over her childlike sister at the same time, but it had proved impossible. When Mary had wandered down to the river and would have drowned but for Ted Absalom's sharp eyes and quick action, she had finally accepted defeat. Everyone, Mary's stepson, her neighbours, the doctor, the minister, had agreed with Leah's decision to have Mary committed to the asylum. The only person who had doubts was Leah herself, and she was still racked with guilt about it, but what could she do? Had

Frank lived up to his duties...but he hadn't, so there was an end to it. 'She is well cared for, I believe.'

At least Mary was fed and kept moderately clean, but Leah couldn't say she was happy, any more than she could say Mary was well. If there had been any comfort in Mary's confused mind, it had been in the recognition of her old home, and now Leah had snatched that away from her. Mary was a closed book once more, whenever Leah contrived to visit her, rocking in a corner and saying nothing.

'It was for the best,' said Mrs Thomas. 'You did all you could and no one could say otherwise.' Except Leah, and Mrs Thomas was astute enough to see that. She changed the subject. 'You will be able to visit Haverfordwest, you think? I can send a letter to Annie if you wish. Would you care to write?' She indicated a writing desk as she rose. 'I have business to attend to in the laundry, but if you wish to leave a letter, I shall forward it at once.'

'Thank you. You are very kind.' Leah blinked back tears and swallowed the burning in her throat. As the housekeeper quietly left the room, she sat down at the desk and picked up a pen. A sheet of paper was laid ready.

My dearest Annie,
I am happy to hear that you have gained such a satisfactory position and that such exciting prospects await you...

At Cwmderwen, John was back at the cottage. He'd been out since dawn, working in Raven Field, clearing the scrub oak from the lower gentler slopes of the valley wall, and a pile of the brushwood was heaped by the workshop. He was cleaning his boots as she approached. When he saw her, he turned his back and went into the house.

That was unfortunate. He had been in one of his closed and uncommunicative moods since yesterday. Chapel could often snap him out of it, and sometimes hard labour, but not this time. She urgently needed to explain the matter to him but when he was like this, he would shut her out so completely that there was no talking to him. She followed him in and found Frank sprawled at the table, chin on hand, watching his son as he peeled off his dirty jacket and wound a strip of linen around his calloused palm. Not yet sixteen and John should not have to be like this, working himself like a flogged horse, dawn till dusk, breaking his back on unforgiving stone and timber.

'Waste of time,' Frank was saying. 'What are you going to gain? Another acre of worthless land?'

John made no reply. He was safe from a thrashing, at least. Frank only stirred himself to deliver those when he was drunk. Sober, he had no energy to raise a hand.

'Every rood and perch is worth something now, with the war,' said Leah, hanging her coat on the hook behind the door. 'And the price of corn rising. John slaves to make good what the Lord has given us.'

'Cursed be the name of the Lord. He'd be better off going to be a soldier, like Harry Absalom.'

'How can you say such things? Blaspheming and speaking of sacrificing your own son!'

'We come from a family that sacrifices sons. Look at him, Leah. No better than a plantation slave, when he could be walking proud in uniform.'

'Getting himself killed, like young Owen Probert, you mean? And what do you know about walking proud?'

John had gone through to the scullery to help himself to a mug of water, ignoring them. He returned, wiping his lips dry, sawdust and chippings webbed in his hair. 'Rent,' he said. One syllable.

'Yes, I've paid it, this time, but it is being raised at Lady Day.'

Frank gave a high laugh. 'Fate spits again. What reason did he give?'

'It seems the Herberts mean to sell the estate and want to squeeze its value up. Besides, land is more valuable now so we can no longer be permitted to have it so easy.' As if they had ever had it easy. 'Which means we will need the extra acreage John is clearing for more crops, – wheat or potatoes maybe – this autumn.'

'And you think that will do anything but break your backs, Leah Owen?'

'Our backs would be less broken, Frank Owen, if you would only lift a hand to help.'

'I'm better off breaking my back at the quarry.'

'And when did you last do a day's work there? At best you run errands for that beast, Eli John, like a cur at his heels. He only has to snap his fingers and—' She stopped. There was no point in this bickering. 'Can you not at least help John with the brushwood?'

'Firewood, yes, we'll not go cold, that's for sure. Half our land is wood that's not even of use for the timber they're demanding. Will you never learn, sister mine, what a futile struggle this is?'

Leah despaired of him. John said nothing. He was back outside, sharpening his axe.

The task of clearing kept him busy the next day. She could hear the axe, thud, thud, thud, and the occasional crash of gnarled trunks and branches, as he took out whatever gnawed at him on branch and root. These moods could last a week. He was still out there, slaving, when Sam Parry arrived from Plas Malgwyn with a note from Mrs Thomas. 'Tomorrow, two o'clock, at Rowland's Tea Rooms.' She slipped it into her pocket.

John had to stop work at last. The over-taxed axe handle splintered. He came back into the cottage to collect a mattock for the roots.

'Stay,' said Leah. She caught Frank eying the purse she had put down for a moment. 'There's no money for drink, Frank, and the Mason's is shut until this evening. You'll have to stay sober a little longer. Tomorrow you must mind the farm on your own if you can drag yourself out of bed before noon. I must go to Haverfordwest, and John will come with me.'

John frowned, addressing the wall. 'I need to get the axe fixed.'

'That axe has been ground down to a stump with sharpening. You can buy a new one. We'll need to go to the seed merchants.'

'I haven't cleared the ground yet.' Another whole sentence. Perhaps the spell was breaking.

'No matter. I have to speak to someone about the rent.' She sounded authoritative and neither questioned her on this necessity. It had long been understood that Leah was the only one with brains for such matters and the temper to give them thought.

John shrugged and said no more. But at least he had spoken. Leah prayed a night's sleep would finish the job and bring him back to the living world. But there was no further sign of lightening as he stomped off up the winding stair to the garret room that had once been hers, and she retired to the parlour where she still slept, though Mary had gone, leaving Frank snoring at the table in the kitchen. Two men whose moods were beyond reason, and how was she to chivvy them both? Nothing other than gin would lift her brother's spirits from the morose slough into which he had slipped, but with luck or God's grace he would at least give some thought to the beasts tomorrow, while they were gone.

And with God's grace too, John's silence would be shattered forever when he learned he was to see his beloved sister again.

John had the trap ready by the time Leah had prepared herself for the journey. She felt a peculiar, indeed ridiculous anxiety about her appearance as she glanced at herself in the spotted mirror. In her youth, rare trips to Haverfordwest had offered an opportunity to indulge what little vanity she had. She would dress in her best, put on a holiday spirit and come home with little frivolities like ribbons or handkerchiefs that had Mam tutting.

Now, Leah had no vanity left, and no desire for frivolities. She cared nothing for the place that ranked as a great metropolis when compared to Llanolwen or the little market town of Penbryn, but she cared about the meeting with Annie. Probably the last meeting she would ever have. She worried how she would appear to her niece. An old, coarse woman, no doubt. She didn't want to let her down. And she worried how Annie would appear. The last time she had managed to see her, in Fishguard just before the outbreak of the war, she had agonised about the underlying unhappiness in the girl, despite her determined smiles and attempts at brightness. There had been a gushing desperation in her all too brief meeting with her aunt, and she had looked overly thin and drawn. But her next letter had spoken confidently of a new position in a different household, and now it seemed, from Annie's latest letter and Mrs Thomas' hints, that her situation was comfortable at last. If only it did not involve a move to the other side of the world.

But she had no right to complain. Others were making far harder sacrifices, even in their little community. Martha Davies in the village had had to part with both sons, one to a mine-sweeper and one – in the army – to Egypt, while Mrs Pugh was still waiting for news and fearing the worst for a son missing in France. At least Annie would not be fighting. But then she would be sailing across the Atlantic, and Leah only had to think of the *Lusitania*...

No, this wouldn't do. Think only of this meeting today. She pinned her one brooch to her blouse and settled her hat. That would suffice. She went up to stir Frank awake and then stepped

226

out to join John. He said not a word as she climbed into the trap, just flicked the reins and they were off.

A four-mile journey to Penbryn, during which John maintained a steady silence, broken only by the occasional grunt in reply to Leah's comments about the noise and fumes of a passing truck, or the noticeable decline in the number of young men in the fields. She needed him to break this locked, barred and bolted mood before she could explain the real purpose of their visit. But they reached Penbryn, lodged the horse and trap at the Crown and were making their way to Mathias & Sons, and John was still resolutely sealed into his self-imprisonment. William Mathias, blacksmith and, more lately, motor engineer, had a charabanc for general hire and ran it weekly into Haverfordwest, which would save them the more convoluted train journey. Leah had once helped Llanolwen children to board the Mathias charabanc for a Sunday School outing but she had never mounted the monster herself before, and found herself fighting nerves as she tugged John into the assembled crowd waiting to board.

She felt him pull against her, his eyes fixed on the pavement as if trying to lock himself in place. 'John. Please. Listen to me. You are in a dark mood, I know, but this news will surely lift your spirits. I'll tell you why we are really going to Haverfordwest. We are going to see your sister.'

His head shot up and he stared at her.

'Yes. Annie! We're going to see her. She has been given an afternoon off and is to meet us.'

Still, he stared at her.

'We'll see Annie,' she repeated, desperately.

His jaw set. 'I need to get a new axe.' He stepped back.

'You can get one in Haverfordwest. After we've seen Annie.'

'I'll get one here. This is good enough.'

'John, what is the matter with you? Don't you want to see her? Your sister. She longs to see you.'

'She left me.'

'John, you know why.'

'Are you coming on board, Missis?' asked the driver. The other passengers were already aboard, shuffling and squeezing into places.

'John!'

'She left me,' said John. 'I'm getting an axe here.' He took another step back, turned and was gone.'

'Well, Missis?' said the driver.

She was desperate to follow John, to make him see sense, to slap him out of this black mood if need be, but this was her one last chance to see Annie. 'Yes,' she said. 'I'm coming.'

Hard to say if the charabanc provided more or less bumps and shakes than the horse and trap, but it was certainly noisier, and far faster. Leah held onto her hat, not trusting the pins, as the crowded vehicle groaned and ground its way up the windswept hills and over, hurtling down into green rolling countryside. A fat woman, squashed beside her, wheezed and moaned with every lurch, casting sideways glares of accusation at the small amount of space Leah was occupying.

Leah was splitting in two, one half nervous of this growling contraption and such terrifying speed, worrying with guilt that she had abandoned the farm and fretting for John and the state she had left him in. The other half gloried in the quickening of her heart-beat, the thrill of novelty, the cold air of freedom gusting into her lungs. In a beast like this she could keep going, keep going, keep going over horizons beyond all her dreams. And best of all, she would see Annie...who would indeed soon be passing horizons beyond all Leah's hopes. She wouldn't sully whatever glorious future might await Annie by regretting their parting now. Annie was safe, she would stay safe, she would be free, she would be anything she wanted.

As long as the war allowed it. South of the hills, Leah felt as if she were venturing into a different world entirely. They had been at war for two years and she had not been untouched. The newspapers were full of it, the tales of parades and embarkation interspersed ever more frequently with accounts of monstrous battles, notices of casualties and reports of tragic sinkings. The Reverend Harries who, last year, had taken the Reverend Pritchard's place as their minister, made the chapel ring with patriotic sermons exhorting duty in defence of liberty, and prayers for speedy victory. Young men had started to vanish from the land, and prices had begun to soar, which no farmer had yet complained about. Money had been raised for Belgian refugees and our brave troops, and local gossip had been rife with alarms about German spies and horrific tales of bodies washed up. All that was true, but still it had seemed at one remove, somehow, from Leah's reality. A war was being fought for her country, but the land that mattered to her was the twenty-four acres, one rood and eight perches that she had been fighting for all her life. No German atrocities or imperial designs changed that.

Now, over the hills and into another land, the war became more tangible. Twice, the rattling charabanc pulled over to allow army trucks to pass. One was filled with young men, waving at them as the passengers raised their caps and cheered. An aeroplane was sighted, the first that Leah had ever seen clearly, close enough overhead for the passengers to strain their necks peering up, with one woman shrieking that it might be Germans come to shoot at them. She was hastily reassured that it was a British craft, doubtless bound on reconnaissance out to sea. Bewitched, Leah watched the plane disappear. Once she had wanted to fly on a storm like a bird of prey, an impossible dream, but was anything truly impossible? Two boys, sitting behind her, plunged into an excited argument about the model, eventually concluding, when it was long out of sight, that it was a Sopwith Strutter. In the far distance lay the Haven, where the navy was busy night and day, and the open sea where murderous German submarine boats were lurking. There was debate whether a distant boom had been naval gunfire or blasting in one of the quarries.

The charabanc descended at last to the river, over the old bridge and set them down in Swan Square. Leah adjusted her hat, pausing to get her bearings. The town was surely the same as the last time she had visited, four years ago, before Tada's death, but it seemed different. Motor vehicles were no longer such a novelty in Penbryn as to draw comments, and even the butcher in Llanolwen now had a motor van, but here such traffic seemed commonplace, vying nonchalantly with the horse-drawn carts and buggies. There were soldiers on leave, a couple of them crippled. Young women, with skirts showing far more than mere ankles, were boldly smoking cigarettes. Flags were proudly on display, defying the Hun. A different world had taken possession of the town and she felt absurdly out of place, a country mouse.

She pulled herself together. Was she to stand there, gawping? Time to be about her business – except that she had none. Betty George would have made the most of such an opportunity but, even with money for once to spare in her pocket, Leah had no taste for fine linen underwear or the latest hats or any of the other luxuries that Haverfordwest offered. Truthfully, anything she might need could be bought in Penbryn, and the seed merchant was as good there as here. All she wanted from this day was to see Annie, and she could think about nothing else, though it was not yet noon.

She stepped up inside the Ebenezer chapel and sat there for a while, gloved hands clasped as if in prayer, though her mind couldn't fix on a God that was no longer real for her. Instead, she aimlessly counted the spindles of the railings around the pulpit and watched the sunlight edge its way along the walls, as her mind went round and round, trying to sort itself out. Every time she thought of Annie, she thought of John, too, and each rising flutter of joy was accompanied by a crash into the depths. She wanted to send herself with Annie into far places, to escape, and she wanted to hurry home, back to the confinement of Cwmderwen and repair the damage that had warped John so much. Damage that *she* had done, for hadn't she been the one who raised him? Hadn't she been the one to tear his sister away?

There was no point idling there until some helpful pastor came looming over her to offer prayers and consolation. She rose and stepped back outside. If she must wait, she might as well sit and sip tea. She set off up the steep hill to Dew Street.

Rowland's Tea Rooms were busy, too noisy for her liking, but she rejected an offer to step upstairs to quieter surroundings and settled for a table near the door. She ordered a pot of tea and sipped slowly, reminding herself that it had been a long time since she could sit and take tea like a lady without the need to jump up and tend to others, or stoke the fire, or turn the sheets, or chase the chickens off the cabbages. But then, when she thought about it, had she ever had such leisure to sit and take tea like a lady? It was doubtless a refined way to spend one's time, but it seemed a little pointless to her. She'd have been on her way impatiently if she had not been waiting for Annie.

No one paid her any heed. She was not grand enough for interest, nor shabby enough for censure. So she sat and slowly consumed tea, trying not to glance up every time the door opened. Annie would not be early. If anything, she would be late. She was in service, and

231

that meant she was subject to the whims of her employers. What if this Mrs Clayton had withdrawn the favour of a free afternoon? No point in dreading the worst, or in feeding her impatience. She must simply sit and wait.

It was not yet a quarter to two, according to the grand clock by the counter, when the door opened and a young woman walked in, peering around earnestly in search of a face she knew. She was so well grown, so modestly smart in her small hat and her pearly buttons and elegant little boots, that Leah didn't recognise her, until their eyes met and the girl broke into that smile of joyful delight that Leah recalled when the children had been offered an unexpected treat.

'Aunt Leah!' Annie rushed to her, waving wildly, causing every eye to turn, as Leah half-rose in her seat, proffering her hand. Annie seized the hand and then the other one, before throwing her arms around her aunt and kissing her on the cheek. She must have concluded, from Leah's stiffness, that such an effusive display of emotion was unwelcome, because she pulled back a little, her face questioning.

Why can't I be like her, thought Leah, urging the nut-hard casing around her to split open. Just a crack. She put her hands on Annie's shoulders and kissed her cheek. 'Annie, my dear, I am so glad to see you looking well. How are you?'

Annie's smile broadened again. 'I'm very well, aunt. And you? And John?' She looked around. 'Where is that brother of mine?'

'John...' Leah took Annie's hands again. She doubted that she'd ever had as much physical contact with the girl when she'd had care of her. 'He has urgent business in Penbryn and couldn't come today.'

'Oh.' Annie's face fell. Her disappointment that there was only Leah to meet her was understandable. It was no cause for such a stab of pain. 'Was it important business?'

'Very important.' Was that a lie? A new axe was important in some respects. 'He is a young man now, you know, and more or less in charge of the farm. And he earns a little extra for us, sometimes, working at Castell Mawr, where they've lost half their men, so you see he has great responsibilities.'

'Yes, of course.' Annie forced a smile that faded as she looked directly at Leah. 'He didn't want to see me, did he? He blames me for leaving him.'

Leah was taken aback by the simple power of Annie's understanding. She was so accustomed to navigating around the complications of John's impenetrable mind. She squeezed Annie's hand again.

'I promised him, you see, that we would always stay together, I would never leave,' said Annie, sadly. 'I never meant to, but...'

'But I forced you apart.'

'Oh! But you did right, and I am so grateful, you cannot imagine, aunt. When I remember... But John wouldn't see it like that. He's different in so many ways. A queer soul. He buries things deep inside. Like you, dear aunt.' Leah's eyes prickled with tears. 'Oh but I know how you felt underneath,' said Annie. 'I knew how much you loved us, from the way you cared for us. And I used to know how John felt too, though I don't suppose anyone else would find it easy. That's why I swore I'd always stay with him.' Her voice broke a little. 'I suppose he could never forgive me for leaving.' She gave a cough to clear her throat. 'I so longed to see him again, but it can't be helped. I cannot bear to think what would have become of me if I had stayed, and truthfully...' She paused, blushed, shook her head.

'Truthfully?'

'I was even a tiny bit relieved to be leaving John. Oh no! I don't mean that. That was wrong. I should never have said it. Of course I would have stayed with him, if it hadn't been for Eli John.'

A shiver ran through Leah. 'I understand.'

Annie hugged her again. 'And I am very sorry not to see John, but I am seeing you and that is what matters most. I was terrified you might not be able to come before we leave.'

'Will it be soon?'

'We leave for Liverpool in a week.' Annie smiled up brightly at the flat-footed waitress who had shuffled to their table with a weary sigh, anticipating yet another order for tea. 'Shall we have cake? Do you have cakes? Tea and cake for two, please.'

'Yes, m'm.'

Annie turned back to Leah as the waitress flapped away, then gasped, her hand to her mouth. 'I didn't think to ask, have you had dinner? I forgot. Mrs Clayton and Mrs Strade always dine in the evening.'

'Very grand, I'm sure. Cake will do me very well, thank you. So. You will soon be on your way to America with this Mrs Clayton. Tell me about her. She sounds an excellent employer.'

'Oh she is! A lovely old lady, very kind. I am very happy with her. At the Grove, you know, to start with, it wasn't really pleasant at all. Mrs Adams was very sharp and the cook was mean, she used to pinch me. It wasn't so bad at Belmont House except for the master trying to take liberties, but I wasn't having any of that and told him so. He took umbrage and threatened to have his wife dismiss me, but Mrs Clayton was visiting and took a liking to me and said her poor widowed daughter was coming to stay with a baby and would I like to come to her as nursemaid? You can imagine how I jumped at that.'

'I see that you have learned how to handle a great deal, for which I am thankful.'

'Well, I think of you, dear aunt, and how you always cope and don't allow yourself to be bullied.'

Leah managed a pained laugh.

'Not that I would have coped with Eli John and his bullying.' Annie shuddered. 'Though of course it would have been far worse than bullying, wouldn't it?'

'Yes, far worse.'

'I wonder that his wife puts up with it.'

'Rachel Morgan, you mean? She is not his wife. Nor even his woman, now, for I've heard she's left him, or he threw her out, or I don't know except that she is gone. Enough of those vile creatures. Tell me about this Mrs Strade, whose child you care for. How do you find her?'

'She's a very sad lady, sometimes doesn't leave her room. The doctor calls often and Mrs Clayton says it's melancholia depressing her spirits and sapping all her resilience, brought on by the birth and Captain Clayton's death. That's why we are sailing to America. Mrs Clayton thinks her daughter will recover better for the change and for the company of her sister. Mrs Strade is a little like my mother, I think, except that she doesn't have TB.'

'Yes, perhaps.' The greater difference was that Mrs Strade had a mother who understood and helped, while Leah had done nothing for poor Anne until the end.

'And little Arthur is so sweet. I really am very happy with them.' Annie smiled as the waitress set a tea tray and cake stand on their table. Two small scones, two slices of fruit cake with very little fruit, and some bread and butter, with very little butter. 'Thank you,' she said politely.

Leah took charge of the tea pot. 'You must be excited, thinking about the future, I imagine.'

'Oh yes! But fearful too. A strange land, and the voyage, which, you can imagine, fills me with more than a little anxiety.'

Not as much as I feel, thought Leah. Neither of them mentioned the *Lusitania* or submarines or mines.

'But tell me news of home,' said Annie. 'How is the farm?' She lowered her voice, imperceptibly, as she asked.

Leah instinctively did the same. Farmers had come in for much opprobrium, profiting from the war while other suffered shortages, although she felt she hardly deserved criticism. 'It would be vain to say we prospered, but we are doing well enough. Prices have risen so much since the start of the war. John... We are clearing some of the woods to gain another acre or two for crops. I have even managed to put a little aside in War Savings, though I doubt that I shall manage much more with the rent rising. The Herberts are selling the estate.'

'Are they? I wonder what will become of Mrs Thomas.'

'I hadn't thought, I'm afraid. I hope the new owners will take her on. They will need a housekeeper, surely enough, even if they have to manage without menservants.'

'I suppose the men have all signed up. The footman and the gardener at Belmont House both joined the army as soon as war was declared, and there seem to be more soldiers on the streets every day. But then, of course, they are being conscripted now. Mrs Clayton says that is the only way we are to win the war, so we must put up with it.'

'That is what many people say,' agreed Leah. It was certainly what the Reverend Harries said, but she had also listened to impassioned speeches condemning conscription in Penbryn by the Reverend Wynne and the renowned bard, Henry Lewis. She, herself, could only thank God that John was still far too young.

Annie sipped her tea daintily. 'I think it makes little sense to say we are fighting for liberty and against militarism, if we then force men to join up, whether they will or no. But Mrs Clayton says every brave Englishman should be yearning for the battle,' said Annie. 'And she means Welshmen too, I suppose.'

'Do you think they should?'

Annie gave a little shrug. 'I think, if all men were so keen to fight, why are the papers full of appeals against conscription?'

'Well, we must still have men to work the farms and factories, or who will feed the troops and make their weapons?'

'And preach to us in chapels,' said Annie, pulling a face. 'Women can do all those things, as you have proved, dear aunt.'

Leah gazed at her in comfortable amazement. The terrified sobbing child she had taken to Plas Malgwyn four years ago had grown into such a mature young woman, with a mind and judgement of her own and a readiness to face the unknown, even danger. She was everything that Leah might have been.

'Does Mrs Clayton have books?'

'Oh yes, and she tells me I may borrow any that I choose.'

'Then borrow them all. Read them all. Read everything.' Leah wanted to sing. Whatever else she had done, she had done right by Annie.

Leah made her way back to Swan Square in the golden evening light. Fortunately, it was midsummer, so she did not have to find her way through unlit streets, thanks to the fear of Zeppelin attacks – fears that Leah suspected to be a little alarmist, this far west. She had attended Annie back to Hill Street and had been greeted by Mrs Clayton, a kindly and considerate old lady, for all that she was English. She had shaken Leah's hand and assured her that Annie was much appreciated in their household and that, if such assurances could be given in such times, she would take care that Annie came to no harm.

Leah had given her niece another peck on the cheek in farewell. As she mounted the great fuming charabanc in Swan Square, she rebuked herself again and again for not having done more, for having been so constrained to the end, showing nothing of what she truly felt. But Annie must understand, surely – Annie who could understand even the workings of John's shuttered mind. Around her, weary passengers were crowding on board, laden with baskets and boxes, chattering about their purchases, and she sat with nothing but the small smiling photograph of her niece that Mrs Clayton had slipped her. One small photograph. Leah slipped it into her coat, as near to her heart as she could place it. It was all she could think of. Even the sighting of a cloud that might be an airship over the Haven did not distract her. The charabanc chugged and rattled onward, up over the hills into her own waiting world.

The shadows were long but it was still light when she was set down at last in Penbryn, which was just as well. John must have long gone back to the farm, so she faced a four-mile walk, and she wouldn't have relished that in the dark. Resolutely, she set off on the road out of town, but she had not even reached the turning to Llanolwen when a motorcar came chugging up behind her, slowed to go round her and came to a halt.

'Miss Owen.' David George jumped down and came around to her. 'You are walking back to Cwmderwen? Let me offer you a lift.' She hesitated. 'I cannot leave you to walk alone.'

Of course he couldn't. 'Thank you.' She allowed herself to be handed into the motor car. It was a two-seater Morris, far less grand than the Rolls Royce that had delivered Lady Herbert briefly to Plas Malgwyn at the start of the war, to urge all the womenfolk of Llanolwen to start knitting for the troops, but still it was the talk of the area. Were the Georges getting above themselves? If Leah had done modestly well at Cwmderwen, thanks to the war, the Georges had done very well indeed, although David always seemed slightly guilty about it.

'People will talk,' she said, as the car rolled forward.

238

David looked troubled. 'I hope we will not attract attention on the road at this hour.'

'Let them all see,' said Leah. 'And keep their wicked thoughts to themselves.' She felt strangely brazen, strangely liberated after her day in town.

David glanced at her, puzzled.

'What has brought you out in this beast today?' she asked. The motor car was kept for necessities, fuel being scarce and David being naturally cautious.

'I had to attend the tribunal, to appeal for Ted Absalom.'

'Of course. You can't afford to lose another man.'

'No, and his wife is expecting another child. His brother is already serving – they should not take all the men of a family.'

'Did you press your case successfully?'

'He has a three-month exemption, but I fear we'll lose him in the end. And what has taken you abroad, Leah, to be walking home at such an hour?'

'I've been to Haverfordwest to see Annie.'

'Ah. How is the child. She is troubled? Homesick?'

'Not at all. She thrives, no longer a child at all. She has a very comfortable position and she sails for America very soon. I am immensely proud of her.'

David smiled. 'As you should be. I fear you will miss her when she's gone, even though you have seen little enough of her these last years. America is...'

He didn't have to complete the sentence. America could be the Moon, it would be no more inaccessible.

Leah raised her chin. 'I don't begrudge the flight of my little songbird.'

David nodded, thoughtfully. She knew that none of his songbirds were likely to fly far from the nest, and nor would John, bound to his ancestral land, but Annie was free. The notion gave Leah a vicarious thrill that disturbed her, but at least it kept her mind off the fact that – instead of trudging home alone – she was travelling in style, seated next to David, his jacket rubbing against her coat, his hand so near to hers. She had an almost irresistible urge to touch it, to see if he would respond as her fancy painted...

This wouldn't do. The day had left her fey, but home was in sight and it was time to resume all the self-discipline and responsibility that went with it.

They passed Levi Morris, who stopped his bicycle to stare intently. David pressed on. She could sense him squaring up to the issue.

'Betty will be relieved to hear I was able to give you a lift,' he said. 'She wouldn't want you walking home alone.'

Leah smiled inwardly. She knew precisely how delighted would Betty be to hear that Leah had been seated there in her place. 'Assure her of my gratitude. How is young David? Still up to mischief?'

'I think he is learning to behave at last. Rather more wilful than William was at that age. But I'll be happy if either of them turn out as dedicated and devoted as your John.'

I hope not, she found herself thinking, and instantly chided herself for the thought. 'He works hard,' she said.

'None better.' David paused before adding 'And Frank? How does he fare? I haven't seen him around for a few days.'

Not rolling in the gutter, he meant. 'No, our diligent special constable Phillips takes his duties to heart. He's determined to keep the public houses to their permitted hours, so Frank is more and more confined to home. And Eli John is away. That makes all the difference.'

Eli regularly disappeared for days, or even weeks at a time. He might be too old to risk conscription, but if anyone questioned him, he claimed to be patriotically doing his duty by attending to army business. Who could tell how legitimate such business was, but it was certain that he'd make a profit from it. When he did linger in the Llanolwen vicinity, Frank was invariably with him, running his errands and suddenly flush with money, finishing up too drunk to stand, on liquor that Eli managed to obtain, despite the new laws. When Eli was absent, Frank was reduced to enforced abstemiousness, which left him morose and pathetic.

'Your brother does not deserve Cwmderwen,' said David.

Leah felt a twinge of alarm. Could it really be, after all this time, that David was angling to take over the tenancy? To buy it outright, even. Several farmers in the area had taken the opportunity of increasing profits to buy up their land, and David had already purchased fifty acres and more, although he still held the old farm as a tenancy. Betty would be urging him to bid for Cwmderwen, no doubt about that.

'Fenston should have offered the lease to you,' said David, slowing to a halt as they reached the gates of their farms. 'You are the heart and soul of Cwmderwen, Leah. He was a fool not to see that.'

Leah's pulse calmed. 'The notion was never raised. My father would not have considered it proper. Frank was the son.'

'For once I would differ with your father, for all that I respected him. Son or daughter, you are the farmer. It's true I'd wish William to have Castell Mawr when I am gone, but if he showed no aptitude or resolution for the task, or David either, I'd rather it went to one of the girls than see it fall short.'

'Well, it is as it is, and I will see Cwmderwen pass to Frank's son, since John has both aptitude and resolution.'

'He does indeed.' David gazed ahead into gathering gloom. 'Hard labour on those twenty-four acres is not the life I ever wished for you, Leah.'

They sat there in silence for a moment, unsaid words echoing around them.

'Wishes are for simpletons,' said Leah at last. 'We deal with what we are given. You have done your duty and I have done mine.' She turned away to climb down, and David immediately stirred himself, jumping out and hurrying round to hand her down.

He kept hold of her hand until she pulled it free. 'Thank you, Mr George, for saving me from a long walk. Give my warm regards to Betty.' She walked away, down the shadowed lane to Cwmderwen, knowing that he was still standing there, looking after her. It wasn't until she reached the bend that she heard the engine start again.

Frank was in the kitchen, looking happier, blood-shot eyes slightly glazed. He must have unearthed a few pennies to squander at the Mason's or the Butcher's. John was there too, sitting by the range, oiling his new axe, which had evidently already been doing good service, for his clothes were flecked with chippings.

John didn't look up as she entered, but Frank did. 'So you're back then, from gallivanting around, frittering away all my money.'

'You're the one who fritters it away, Frank. I spent a little on several cups of tea, that's all.'

'What did you buy, then?'

'Nothing. I went to see your daughter.'

Frank blinked. His eyes cleared, but his voice thickened. 'So you saw my Annie. Did she ask after me?'

'No. Not once. Does that surprise you, remembering how it was, the last time you clapped eyes on her?'

He scowled and muttered. 'She's still my daughter. Maybe I'll go. Sniff her out. Bring her home where she belongs.'

'That won't happen.'

'Why not?'

'Because you never stir yourself to do anything. But what is an even surer safeguard, you won't find her. She's going to America.'

Frank stared. Then he burst into wild hysterical laughter.

'Stop it, Frank!'

'America. You let her go to America. Ha! Well, at least one of us has escaped the jaws of this damned mantrap. Well done, Annie!' He pushed himself up, still laughing and loped out into the yard.

Silence like thick mud fell in the cottage as the door shut behind him. Leah looked at the crumbs on the table. 'Did you finish the cawl I left for your father?'

'Yes.'

'You bought a new axe then.'

'Yes.'

Leah took a deep breath. All the excitement and optimism of the day had fizzled away, like water on hot iron. She had settled Annie. She had yet to settle John.

'Annie was greatly aggrieved that you weren't there today, John.'

He said nothing.

'There has never been a day when she hasn't missed you.'

Silence.

'You and she were so tight, I know.'

He looked up at last. 'And yet she left me.'

'Should I have kept her here, John?'

Silence again.

'John, look at me, tell me. Do you think I should have kept her here to become a prey to that filthy beast, Eli John? We will vanquish Eli and his like by defeating his ploys to bring us down and by holding on to what is ours, in spite of him.'

'That's not what you did with Annie. You didn't hold her. She was mine and you took her away from me.'

He'd lit a spark of anger in her now. 'Eli's depraved desire was to defile Annie in order to debase and humiliate us, through the contemptible weakness of your father. I took from him the means to do that and you know full well what would have happened if I had not. Would you want to see Annie another Rachel Morgan? Or should I have taken you too, is that it? Should I have taken you both so that you and Annie need not be parted? No, don't look away in silence. Face me and tell me. Should I have removed you from Cwmderwen and let Eli John steal the farm that should be yours?"

He ran his finger slowly along the sharpened edge of the axe. 'No. You should have killed Eli John.'

Leah caught her breath. 'You don't mean that, John.'

'Why not? You said he's a beast. We kill beasts every day.'

'Dumb animals, yes. But for all his beastliness, Eli is a man, and killing him would be murder. Remember the commandments, John. Thou shalt not kill.'

'Tell the generals that.'

Leah felt sickened. In finding his voice at last, John had come out with such horrifying words and yet she had no answer to them. Every day, politicians and pastors were exhorting young men to take up arms and kill a reviled enemy. Could any Hun be half as vile as Eli John?

'The generals must answer to God for themselves, John, and so must we, and if I have taught you anything it is to obey his commandments. Why do you love chapel so much and yet not heed God's word? Remember who gave us this land.'

He bowed his head.

'There is a covenant, John, remember that, between you and God. Obey him, honour him, hold fast like Job and he will not permit this land to be taken from you.'

'Yes,' said John, laying down the axe and rising. 'God gives me this land and only God will take it from me.'

'Then kneel with me, John, and pray that he guides your hand in all things and keeps you on the appointed path.'

Tada's fierce faith was in him and she had nurtured it, though his God was no longer real to her. It was his grandfather's judgemental God who would bring down wrath on a world of human falseness and betrayal. Without a murmur of dissent now, he knelt beside Leah, and she remembered her father's deranged rage in the meadow, before being brought to his knees and to sanity by Matthew. If there is a God, she thought, let prayer cut through this darkness in John, for I cannot.

THE REAPING

1918

'Well say what you like, Mrs Rhys-Parker does a great deal more than Lady Herbert ever did.' Mary Lloyd from Pantglas farm buttoned up her coat as they emerged from the village hall.

'True enough,' said Betty George. 'One short visit to have us knitting comforters, and not another peep out of her ladyship. Mrs Rhys-Parker has far more patriotic spirit. Only yesterday she invited me to discuss the parcels for the troops.' A new landlord, Colonel Rhys-Parker, had taken over Plas Malgwyn, and though he was kept away by the demands of the war, his lady was very much in residence. Betty George, as the wife of the principal tenant of the estate, was keen to be seen hobnobbing with the gentry. It didn't stop her stepping back hurriedly, with the others, as Mrs Rhys-Parker – understood to be of aristocratic lineage despite her lack of title – sailed past in her chauffeured motor car. Mrs Rhys-Parker raised a hand graciously to Betty, but didn't offer her a lift.

'That Mrs Rhys-Parker does a great deal too much, if you ask me.' Sarah wheezed her discontent. 'Coming here out of the blue and telling us all what to do. I haven't the time for all these missions and flag days and what not. If we can't...' She paused as Thomas Thomas came flying through the village on his bicycle.

Thomas Thomas who delivered telegrams.

Leah stood motionless, watching with the other women, remembering the cold shock when Thomas Thomas had come to Cwmderwen two years ago, and she had stared out of the window, unable to move for a moment, convinced that it would be a telegram informing her of tragedy. Annie's ship must have been torpedoed. And then the liquifying gush of relief when she found it was a telegram from Annie herself, to reassure her that the ship had safely docked in New York. But since that day, telegrams in the village had brought only bad news. She watched the bicycle slow and come to a halt. Thomas dismounted, before the door of one of a row of terraced cottages. He removed his cap before knocking.

'One of the Absaloms, then,' said Sarah, squinting. 'Hannah or Winnie, which one is it?'

'Hannah,' said Leah.

'Oh Lord; Harry, it must be,' said Mary Lloyd. 'I don't know what to think. At least he doesn't leave a wife and little ones like Ted, but that will be small comfort to his mother.'

'He might only be wounded or missing,' said Leah.

A scream from the open door of number five told them there was no such hope.

'Oh, oh, oh!' Sarah looked ready to faint. Leah squeezed her hand, sympathising with her distress for once. Her second son, Alf, was serving in the same regiment as Harry Absalom.

Betty tutted. 'Thomas didn't stop at your door, Sarah Price, so no need for you to make such a fuss. Come along. We'd best go and see what succour we can offer the poor woman.'

Such a suggestion was beyond Sarah, who had to flap home and be comforted by Will. The others followed Betty to the row of cottages, but Ted's wife, Winnie, from the adjoining cottage, was already at the door, white-faced.

'Best leave his mother with me for now. She's too distraught for company. I'll see to it that she's not left alone.'

'Shall I fetch the minister?' proposed Mary.

'And his wife down with the influenza?" huffed Betty, who should have been the one to suggest it.

250

'He told me Mrs Harries was on the mend. I'm sure he'll spare time for Hannah.'

'If he can, that would be kind,' said Winnie. 'Yes, please ask the reverend to call.'

'If that's what you want.' Betty sniffed. 'You know where we are.' She was peering over Winnie's shoulder into the dark interior of the cottage, as if searching for another way in. 'Be sure to tell Mrs Absalom she is in our prayers. We will all rally round at such a dark time. You have only to send word. A memorial service for her son, of course—'

'Let's not discuss that yet,' said Leah. She leaned forward to kiss Winnie's cheek and whispered. 'Ted will be all right. Don't worry about him.'

Winnie drew a shuddering breath and forced a smile. 'Thank you all, but for now...thank you.' She closed the door before Betty could worm her way over the threshold.

'I'll go for the minister,' said Mary Lloyd and hurried off.

Betty sniffed. 'We'd best be on our way then, if we're not wanted.'

'We'll be wanted soon enough.' Leah set the pace.

'I just thank God William is far too young to fight.' Betty bustled along to make sure Leah didn't stride ahead of her. 'Not that I wouldn't be proud for him to do his duty for King and country.' As William was only seven, Betty could afford to be patriotic. 'Of course, your John may be called upon, when the year turns. That will be hard on you, I am sure, but we must all be prepared to make sacrifices.'

'And what do you know of making sacrifices, Betty George?' asked Leah.

Such a frontal attack invariably produced a roaring counter-offensive from Betty, but for once she merely sniffed. 'I've done my part, I'm sure and not held my children back. The girls are out with the others picking blackberries even now.' She was silent for a moment before adding, 'Maybe there'll be no call for John to serve. There's so much talk of the war ending soon.'

'They've been saying that since the day it started. They were saying, last year, how the Germans were defeated, on the run, and then look what happened. It was our boys under attack again. I'll believe it's over when it happens. And pray God it happens before John turns eighteen.' Leah wasn't relying on prayer alone. Each night she ran over and over in her mind the arguments she would bring to bear if the tribunal decided that his father was sufficient for the needs of their few acres. She would have to make them realise that it was John, not Frank, who knew how to plough, lay hedges, how to deliver a calf or judge the state of the grain. Though the upper age for conscription had been raised, Frank had been safely declared totally unfit for service. Eli John had seen to it, though Leah suspected it was actually the case. She wouldn't be surprised if it was the influenza that would carry him off. It had already claimed old Mr Williams and Catherine Bowen and her baby, and laid up several others. But maybe Frank was too pickled to succumb.

'I pray the Lord will spare your boy,' said Betty, almost sympathetically. 'And we will all be offering fervent thanks when peace comes at last. There is certain to be an election, of course, and we are to have the vote, although I don't know that I hold with it. I don't think it a good thing for women to have to trouble themselves with such matters. But I shall cast my vote, since David approves. Liberal, of course, as David does. And you will vote the same way, I am sure.'

'I shall vote for no one, as you well know, Betty. They haven't deigned to enfranchise me. I am not the occupier, merely Frank's spinster sister, living on his charity. Not fit to vote. Perhaps they fear that women such as me, without husbands to guide us, might start thinking for ourselves.'

252

'Well!' Betty humphed and snorted, before once more softening. 'It is unfair, I suppose. And I know there been little fairness in your life, Leah Owen. But you have done your duty, nevertheless. No one can deny that.'

Yes, thought Leah. No one can deny that. They heard a now familiar chug as they approached the parting of their ways. 'David is making full use of the tractor, I hear.'

'Oh, indeed, it's a Godsend, what with our workforce so reduced. There's talk of sending out prisoners of war to help, but I think these mechanical monsters are the way forward. Mind, I am less happy with the noise and fumes.'

'Indeed.' In Cwmderwen's fields, Leah was treated to all the noise and fumes of the Castell Mawr tractor, without reaping any of the benefits. David had offered, but she doubted it would serve much purpose in their small fields. 'In the sweat of thy face shalt thou eat bread,' Tada had been overly fond of declaring as he toiled with scythe and rake and the tools that Adam must have known, while modern rumbling machinery raised dust in the adjoining fields. The lie of Cwmderwen's acres seemed set on keeping them to that curse. Besides, David had already done enough, offering scarce help with the harvest and employing John for wages, whenever he could be spared. 'Well, good luck with it. I must be off home, before we are sent out collecting again.'

Leah strode off down Cwmderwen's lane. All was well with the farm, they had increased their cultivated acres, the wheat was in, yielding well, though the barley looked less promising; prices were high and John was earning extra. But she couldn't stop the nagging worries. John would turn eighteen in just three months, and they weren't merely sending young men of eighteen to training camps now but despatching them straight to the trenches. That was unthinkable. She couldn't bear to lose him, and worse, she couldn't bear the thought of how he might react if they came for him. John had no intention of leaving his land. He had matured a little in the last couple of years, and, though still obsessively devout, he was communicating a little more. He was invaluable in the chapel choir, his voice no longer a piping child's but a tuneful tenor, and the chapel elders nodded over him and shook his hand, treating him as the master of the house, for all his youth. But she knew how much his equilibrium was maintained by the adamant belief that Cwmderwen was his. His by birthright and God's will. Neither King nor country would ween him willingly away from his inheritance. For Empire, he wouldn't stir a muscle, but for these twenty-four acres, one rood and eight perches, he'd fight to the death.

As she approached the cottage, sunlight bathed the yard. The kitchen window was down and she heard masculine voices within. She was about to open the door and greet brother and nephew, relieved that they were both in a good mood, but then she heard John's voice, distantly, down in the fields, calling his dog. And from within, a laugh that she recognised. Eli John. Laughing and leering, no doubt, as he made himself comfortable at her hearth.

She stood, still and silent, listening.

'He's old school pals with the Colonel, that's the point. Always pays to keep the landlord sweet, eh?'

Frank responded with a grunt, then, 'And you say he'll pay you. How much?'

'Never you mind how much. Enough to reduce the sum owing, that's all that matters to you. You know what I'll have to do otherwise. See sense. He has the money and he doesn't want his little boy getting his head shot off. Let his toes get muddy on a farm instead of in the trenches, and Johnny boy can be a hero in his place.'

'I don't know.'

'You don't have to know, Frank. You just do as I say, like a good boy.'

'But Leah... She'll never agree.'

'Leah, that bitch can go whistle. Who's the master here, eh, Frank? Apart from me, of course. Tell her to keep her nose out.'

Leah threw the door open. 'Keep my nose out of what, Eli John?'

Frank jumped like a startled hare at her sudden appearance, but Eli, other than raising his eyebrows, made no move to rise, nonchalantly tipping himself back in the armchair, his polished shoes on her table.

As suddenly as she had opened the door, she thrust his feet off the board, a move that tipped the chair still further, and Eli went down with it. He scrambled to his knees quickly enough and up onto his feet, confronting her face to face, his nose an inch from hers, his features twisting in rage.

Leah calmly wiped her gloved hands clean and turned to Frank, whose face was an expressive study of guilt, confusion and glee. 'What stupid scheme has this creature been trying to involve you in, this time, Frank?'

'Nothing.'

'Nothing that involves you, Leah Owen,' said Eli. 'So keep your damned nose out of men's business. Go back to your woman's work. Not that you are a woman. Under those petticoats I wouldn't be surprised if—'

'If it involves John, I wish to know.' Leah continued to address Frank and ignore Eli.

'Just a proposal. Nothing. Eli...' Frank moved to the door, holding it open. 'Later, eh?'

Eli stood his ground for a moment more, then shrugged, stepping past Leah with a sneer, and slapping Frank on the back. 'At the Mason's then, when you've finished putting this bitch in her place.

And give her a slap for me.' He paused only to hawk a large globule of phlegm onto the floor before sauntering out, placing his bowler hat on at a jaunty angle.

Frank turned, a schoolboy about to face the birch.

Leah wiped down the table, then threw the cloth at Frank. 'Clean that up.'

He seemed almost relieved to be crouching down to wipe the floor, taking his time before standing again to face the music.

'What was he proposing?'

'Just a...it was nothing.'

'What was he proposing?'

'Colonel Rhys-Parker's got a lawyer friend, Jackson or Johnson or some such. He's got a son likely to be called up. Reckons, if we take him on here – work of vital national importance and all that – he'll be let off.'

'Experienced ploughman, is he?'

'Not exactly. A college boy.'

'Of course. Wouldn't know one end of a plough or a pig from another. But what would that matter if it makes his father beholden to Eli John? Is that the plan? We wouldn't qualify for extra labour, so you mean to send John in his place.'

'He'll be eighteen soon, won't he? Wanting to serve.'

'Wanting! You know John wants nothing but this farm. I can't believe this of you, Frank. You'd send your own son to the trenches, because Eli John wants to take a bribe to protect some gentleman coward?'

'Not a bribe, just payment of commission for the arrangement.'

'And that's enough inducement to you, Frank? Obliging Eli so he can make himself a nice profit out of blood money. Are you mad?'

'It's business, Leah. Good money. It will help me pay...the rent.'

'We can pay the rent, Frank. I have it ready. We have enough. We don't need to sacrifice your son on Eli John's altar.'

Frank slumped down in his chair. 'You don't understand.'

'No I don't. He'll pay you for the service so that you can get drunk in the dirtiest public houses of Llanolwen and Penbryn. Is that the deal that appeals to you? Well then, I'll give you more money. Go and drink yourself into the gutter and stay there, but leave your son alone!'

A shadow gave her pause. John was standing in the doorway. 'What are you talking about?'

'Just a mad scheme of your father, which is forgotten already.'

John was staring at Frank. 'You meant to send me into the army.'

Frank turned defensive. 'What's wrong with that? Everyone else is joining up. You don't want to be a coward, do you?'

'I want to keep my land.'

'Well keep it, then!' Frank pushed himself up and charged out. 'Keep the bloody land, if you can.'

'You're not eighteen yet,' said Leah. 'They can't make you do anything until December the second and anything might happen before then. The war might be over.'

'I don't care whether it is or not,' said John. 'They won't take me.'

It ended. Silence on the distant battlefields. In November, the Armistice was signed and Llanolwen rejoiced. Bunting and flags were raised over the High Street, bells rang out and church and chapels were filled to overflowing for services of thanksgiving. Those who mourned, like Hannah Absalom, were honoured, their dead revered.

Leah took a deep breath and felt a weight fall from her shoulders. John turned eighteen and conscription wasn't ending but she was confident now that farming skills would take precedence over the

257

need for army recruits. Peace was declared, the harvest was in, and Christmas had come. The shops were brightly lit again, the bakery full of buns, meat piled high at the butchers, dried fruits in the store. Soldiers who had not yet been discharged were home on leave, including Ted Absalom, who was cheered all the way back to his old job at Castell Mawr.

The Owens attended chapel for the Christmas morning service, even Frank, being persuaded to accompany his sister and son, in a sheepish, nervous mood. They dined on the goose Leah had been fattening, but she had no sooner cleared the plates when Frank shrugged on his coat and made for the door.

'The Mason's, I suppose,' said Leah. 'Since the Butcher's has banned you.'

Frank grunted and was gone, walking fast, hat pulled down and collar raised against the rain.

Leah shook her head. 'Well, I'll be going to Plas Malgwyn. Will you check on the animals?'

'I will,' said John, rising promptly, and was out without another word, just a whistle to his dog.

How did God mould father and son so differently, wondered Leah, laying ready her coat, hat, gloves and umbrella.

The owner of Plas Malgwyn might have changed, but Mr Fenston was steward of the estate still and would be in his office, expecting her. In her parlour bedroom she knelt down to pull the locked rent money box from under her bed.

The lock was broken. With trembling hands, she opened it. Empty. This quarter's rent and more, gone. A moment of complete paralysis, then a whirlwind of panic and fury. Frank. Only he could have done this. No wonder he had been so swift to make off. And what was she to do now? She had less than four shillings in her purse, and maybe not that if he had raided it too. She checked. No, it was still there. But what good would three shillings and fivepence ha'penny do?

She had no option but to offer Mr Fenston her three shillings and promise to pay the remainder in a couple of days. Other tenants had wormed their way out of prompt payment in the past. She had always been regular, as precise as her father had ever been, but now she must go down on record as one of the feckless ones, the unreliable tenants. She couldn't bear it, yet she had no choice. There was no point standing there nursing her face in her hands. She donned her coat, stepped into the rain, raised the umbrella and marched, head up, down to the path to Plas Malgwyn.

John, across a field, raised a hand and she nodded. No point in telling him what had happened. No point in inciting his wrath against Frank. Her brother would have enough to face when she confronted him. She would sort it. She would sort everything.

A thought came to her.

She rejected it.

But she had to consider it. Could she let her pride get in the way? It was a solution of sorts. She would have to abase herself, but it might preserve her reputation with the agent and, for John's sake, that was all that mattered. Taking a deep breath, she turned up towards Castell Mawr.

The house was aglow in the December gloom, lamps burning in the windows, children's voices echoing happily. David's eldest, Hannah Leah, fourteen and hopelessly sweet on John, opened the door to her. The family called her Annie, and Leah couldn't hear the name spoken without missing her own Annie, living and – as her last letter promised – thriving, thousands of miles away.

'Merry Christmas, Miss Owen.'

'And Merry Christmas again to you, Hannah. Is your father within?'

'He's out with the cows, but Mam's here. Will you come in?'

Leah braced herself and stepped over the threshold, prepared for humiliation.

'Well. Leah Owen.' Betty rose from the kitchen table, where she had been mending some mechanical toy for little David, her youngest. 'I didn't think to see you before chapel this evening. Is something wrong at Cwmderwen? You look ill, I must say. Are you ailing? If it's the influenza...' She was shooing her children away.

'No, I am well,' Leah assured her. 'I would...I need...I have a request.'

'Well? Out with it.'

'I wish to beg a loan of four pounds, eighteen shillings and sixpence.'

'What!'

'For the rent. I will repay it as soon as I can. Two days, no more. I have war savings that I can cash in.'

Betty breathed in deeply through her nose, swelling up with regal dignity to denounce her neighbour's financial profligacy. Then her eyes narrowed and she subsided. 'Frank, I suppose.'

Leah said nothing. She couldn't. Her throat was tight.

Betty sailed out of the kitchen, two boys trailing after her. She returned in a couple of minutes with five notes. She folded them and handed them over without a word.

'Thank you.'

Betty's emotional generosity was exhausted. 'And so I should think. Whoever heard such a thing. I'll expect that to be repaid by the end of the week as you promised, mind.'

'It will be.' Burning inside, Leah turned to go. At least the rent would be paid on time this quarter.

Frank didn't come home for evening chapel, or for bed. He didn't come home the next day either, or the next, though Leah thought she glimpsed him down Penbryn's High Street, when she went to withdraw the money to repay Betty George. Why had she ever supposed she would actually be able to save anything from the income of Cwmderwen?

Her brother reappeared at last on the Saturday, drunk of course, not looking at her, pretending to be more comatose than he was. She wasn't going to let that stop her.

'Well, I've paid your rent, Frank Owen.'

Grunt.

'And the farm is safe for another few months. I had the greater part of the next quarter's rent set aside too, but I suppose I must find that out of my savings, too.'

Grunt.

She seized his shoulders and shook him. 'Don't you dare just sit there ignoring me! You pathetic creature. You stole the rent money! Stole! From me. From your own son. Is there any lower you can sink, Frank? What did you do with it? Drink it all? You could have bought a vat of gin and drowned in it twenty times over for that sum. You can't have drunk it all away.'

'Oh, go away,' Frank groaned and curled away from her, almost falling into the fire.

'No. No! Don't play this game. What did you do with the money, Frank? Leaving me to go begging from Betty George!' She slapped him.

He looked up at her, trying to glare, trying to be angry, but instead his face creased into a whine. 'Why couldn't you just let it go?'

'What do you mean? Let go a theft like that? Seven pounds, Frank! Our security.'

'Let the rent go. Let the farm go. Why do you always have to fight for it?'

'Because it's ours! Because it will be John's. What did you do with the money?'

'I gave it to Eli John. All right?'

Leah stepped back, fighting down the anger that was ready to explode out of control. 'What is he going to do with it? Invest it for you? Use it in one of his crooked schemes? With you as his partner, is that what he told you? Are you really such a fool?'

'I used it...' Frank sat up, then sank down again, his head in his hands. 'I owed him. I used it to pay him back.'

'You... You owed Eli John seven pounds?'

Frank's head sank lower.

Leah turned cold. 'More than seven. How much, Frank?' When he didn't answer, she shook him again. 'How much do you still owe?'

Frank was crying. 'He says if I release the farm, he'll release me from the debt.'

'Why? What would he gain by that?' Leah couldn't believe what she was hearing. 'Does he think to take the tenancy himself? He's never done a day's farm labouring in his life. If we ever did lose this land, David would almost certainly take it on. Fenston would offer it to him without a second... Oh, but your foul Eli John doesn't really care who has it, as long we lose it, is that it? You – you fool, Frank Owen. That vermin! You know what a cruel creature he is, how malevolently he holds grudges, how he ruined Tom Davies' business because of some slight. How he put the Beddoes out of their cottage because Harry wouldn't sell cheap to him. You know he uses you only to bring us low, and yet you – you grovel before him! You wretch! Tell me. Don't snivel. How much do you owe him?'

Frank seemed to be trying to curl up into a ball. 'He wants it now. He says—'

'How much?' she screamed.

'A hundred and twenty-eight pounds.'

Leah had never fainted in her life, but she thought she was going to do so now. Had she heard aright? She couldn't have done: It wasn't possible. 'Say it again.'

'A hundred and twenty-eight pounds.'

'No!' How could Frank owe such an impossible amount? He couldn't have drunk... Gambling. David had warned her before that Frank was involved in worse than drink at the Black Bull. And not merely gambling, which was dreadful enough, but gambling with a monster who doubtless cheated at every opportunity and never missed a chance to tighten his stranglehold on his pathetic victim.

'Tell me again.' She forced the words out, needing to hear it repeated once more.

'A hundred and twenty-eight pounds, all right?' Frank looked up, pleading. 'That includes the interest owing.'

'Is that supposed to make it better?' She couldn't breathe. A hundred— No, no, no. She was going to wake up in a moment. Then she looked at the nightmare that was her brother and knew there would be no waking. She sat down heavily and lowered her head to let the roaring cease. What was to be done? There was nothing that could be done. They were destroyed. She could sell every scrap they had and there still wouldn't be enough to pay such a debt. With any other creditor, she might have pleaded for terms, for time to pay in instalments – except that there was no paying such an amount in her lifetime, and Eli John would not be interested in terms. He wasn't in this for profit. He was in this to see the Owens in the dust.

And it would be John in the dust with them, after all she had promised him, after all she had fought for. She couldn't betray him again. It couldn't be allowed to happen. And yet there was nothing she could do. Nothing.

'When does he want it?'

'The end of the month,' said Frank. 'Said I relinquish the farm by the thirty-first or he'd break my arms and legs. Just business, he says. Can't let anyone get away with not paying.'

'Your good friend, Eli John.'

'That's right, my good friend, Eli John.'

'He's never been your good friend, Frank. Can't you understand that, even now?'

He shouted, a wail. 'Of course I understand. But what can I do? I'm at his mercy. I've been at his mercy for years. Why do you think I stayed here, enduring Tada's scorn? Why do you think I didn't just walk away? Because he told me to stay. He ordered me to stay, to be a millstone around Tada's neck. To make Tada look on while he wrapped me up in his web.'

'But why did you have to obey him like a whipped cur? You could have run, Frank!'

'I was a whipped cur! I owed him. Always, I owed him. Not as much as now, but I always owed him, and no one runs from Eli John. Believe me, no one. I've seen him gouge out a man's eye for trying it. He'd kill me if I didn't come to heel. He's come near to it before now.'

She stared at him, the bitter response hovering in the air between them. There was no need for her to voice it.

'Yes!' howled Frank. 'Better if he had. But what can I do?'

Leah stood up. Watching him grovelling, whimpering, defeated, the anger in her hardened into steel. She would not do the same. She would fight. Somehow, she would fight.

She had to get out. The air in the cottage had turned to sulphur and brimstone. She was suffocating. If she didn't get out, she would die.

John was across the yard, his back to her, surveying something in the barn. Had he heard any of it? Dear God, she hoped not. If they were brought to ruin and his inheritance lost, he'd hear about it soon enough. She hurried up the lane without a word to him. Where she was going, she had no idea. If she walked to Llanolwen, to what end? To beg help from Sarah who never had a penny to spare? If she walked to Penbryn, what then? She could cash in the last of her savings certificate and have, what? Seven or eight pounds? What was the point? Yet she must do something. Left or right, she couldn't think. Should she just walk blindly in circles?

Blind and deaf. The motorcar coming round from the village caught her unawares, though it made enough noise. She looked up, blinking, as it stopped. It was David and...no, not Betty. Thank God. She couldn't cope with Betty, not with this. It was his sister Flo, Mrs Llywelyn.

'Leah! What a delightful...' Flo's eager greeting dried up, her sweet face all concern. 'Leah?'

David had jumped down. He grasped Leah's hand. 'What is the matter? What has happened?'

She could say nothing. She must look like a ghost, from their expression of alarm.

'Has there been an accident?' insisted David. 'Is John hurt?'

'No,' she managed. 'No accident. It's nothing.'

'It is something, that is clear enough. Tell me, please, Leah.'

She couldn't hold back the sobs any further, her hands over her face. 'Oh the shame of it! The fool, the fool.'

'Frank,' said David, as if no further explanation were needed.

Leah nodded. Flo had climbed down now and was holding her other arm. 'You are in shock, my dear. We can see that. You must come down to Castell Mawr with us–'

'No! I must...I don't know what I must do, but I must do

something.' As if from afar, she saw herself whimpering in defeat just as Frank had done. She forced herself straight. 'Frank has incurred debts.'

'To Eli John, I suppose,' said David, anger in his voice. 'He may not be the only one Eli's sought to ruin but he's surely his most willing victim.'

'His weakest, you mean.'

'You have all the strength your family needs, Leah.'

'But little use that is now. Eli is calling in the debt. He wants payment by Tuesday.'

'I see. I imagine there's little point attempting to reason with him. How great is the debt?'

Leah had to attempt it twice before she could say it. 'A hundred and twenty-eight pounds.'

There was a sharp intake of breath from David.

Flo gave a more voluble gasp. 'Oh good Lord, but how could Frank have run up such a monstrous debt!'

'I'm sure Eli spared no effort to bring it about.' Anger was getting the better of Leah again. 'He means to have the farm taken from us, but I will not let him. He must take what I have for now, and then whatever I can raise.'

'Yes. Of course.' Flo was soothing her, exchanging glances with her brother, who was saying nothing, merely thinking. 'But now you are in no state to do anything. You must come back to Castell Mawr with us and—'

'No, I can't face Betty at the moment. No. Please. You go on.'

'Out of the question. We can't leave you here, can we, David?'

There was a moment's pause before he spoke, calmly, distantly. 'Go home, Leah. Think no more about it today. There is nothing you can do. We shall see you at chapel tomorrow, where we shall pray that God sends you deliverance in your hour of need.'

266

'Yes,' she agreed, deflated. 'I can pray, if nothing else.'

David was staring ahead. 'Come to Castell Mawr on Monday, please. In the afternoon. Two o'clock. Betty will be at Plas Malgwyn but I shall be there and we shall discuss the matter.'

'I don't want—'

'But I do want. Monday, Leah. At two. Now go home.' He was already handing his sister back into the car. Returning to the wheel, he touched his cap and drove on, his face grave, deep in thought. Flo's hand was on his arm.

Leah stood watching the car descend the broad track to Castell Mawr. Pray, said David, but though he might have faith to move mountains, she had none. God, if there was a God, would not help her here – unless he sent a lightning bolt to strike down Eli John. But apart from prayer, what was there? David was right in one thing, at least. There was nothing she could do. Feeling dead inside, she turned back down the lane to Cwmderwen.

Frank took himself off again that evening and didn't reappear on the Sabbath. Leah attended the chapel services as usual, with John by her side. He was silent, in that ominous way he could be since she'd taken Annie, but there was less of the sullen boy about him now. His stern features were set rigid and he did not step forward to join the choir as usual but remained by her side, his eyes fixed on the pulpit and the cross above it.

He had overheard her argument with Frank, she was sure of that, but she couldn't bring herself to discuss it with him. Him or anyone else. Betty George was on David's arm as usual, as the family emerged from chapel, a clutch of children following them in smart Sunday best. Betty nodded at Leah and opened her mouth to speak, but Leah nodded back and turned away. She couldn't bear Betty's crowing or that distant coldness in David's demeanour. Why hadn't she kept her secret shame a little longer? The hollow prayers that she had offered in chapel and in every waking moment echoed back at her from a barren vault.

She lay awake all night, waiting for Monday, for the meeting with David that would resolve nothing, because nothing could be resolved, but still she must go through the pretence of hoping. One more day of vainly ransacking her brain for remedies to a mortal ailment. One more day and then ruin.

She dished up cawl for John's dinner, but she could face none herself. There was some still in the pot for Frank if he deigned to appear. Dishes cleared, she set off for Castell Mawr. Not by the footpath but up to the road. It wouldn't do to arrive ankle deep in mud for a formal indictment preceding the day of execution.

Bethan Absalom, who helped in the Castell Mawr dairy, opened the door to her, bobbing a little curtsey as if Leah were a lady, not a pauper about to be utterly destitute. 'Mr George is back, m'm. Said you'd be calling and I was to show you straight through to his study.'

Study. Office. So formal, so severe. Not a homely chat in the kitchen. She entered, half expecting to be kept waiting.

David was standing by the window, dressed smartly for business, not for farm work. If her spirits were not already at the bottom of the abyss, they would have fallen further. Discuss the matter, he'd said: the only thing they could discuss was the surrender of the tenancy to him. Castell Mawr would devour Cwmderwen, as Betty had long ago advocated, and she would have no option but to agree. Better he have it directly than that Eli John should snatch it from them, but either way, she was destroyed. John's inheritance was lost forever, and she would be branded traitor once more.

David turned from the window and hurried to her, taking her hand and guiding her to a chair. 'I have been to town,' he said, without further greeting.

268

She sat, looking up at him bleakly. 'To see your solicitor?'

'The bank.' He opened a box on his desk, a box no different to the one Leah kept beneath her bed, and drew out a bundle of papers bound by brown tape. He held it out, and when Leah did nothing, he pressed it into her hand.

She stared at it, trying to take it in. Pound notes, brown and green and under them, large white notes. Notes that she had never held in her life.

'One hundred and twenty-eight pounds,' said David.

'I can't take this!' Her hand shook.

'It isn't a gift, Leah. Not charity. It's a loan, nothing more.'

'One I could never hope to pay back.'

'I believe you will, or will do your best. Cwmderwen has been prospering, and in time—'

'In a lifetime, I couldn't pay this back.'

'Consider it a mortgage on the farm. If our lifetimes are not enough, John will repay the remainder to William. I have faith in his determination and hard work.'

She could only shake her head. 'It's too much. I can't take it. You cannot afford to part with such a fortune.'

'I can. Not only for your sake, Leah, and for John's, but for this community. I will not stand by and see another family ruined by Eli John. I have little respect for his father, but at least Jacob John managed honest work, for all his vices, until the rheumatics laid him up. Eli has no such saving grace. He is a cancer in our midst. I have a fair idea what nefarious schemes he's been involved in, here and around the county, what illicit deals he has negotiated, what cruel pressures he's been bringing to bear on honest folk. And worse deeds too, I suspect. One never knows, but that woman of his hasn't been seen for several months now, and there are some who suspect foul play. I didn't only visit the bank this morning, I spoke too with

Colonel Rhys-Parker, concerning Eli John's activities. As a magistrate, he can press the police to look into Eli's suspect dealings, and high time, too. It's my duty as a good citizen to stand up to him, and this money, this loan, is a part of that stand. And who knows, if any part of Frank's debt is proved to be questionable, we might yet recover it in court.'

She looked up at him, her eyes swimming with tears, unable to speak, her mind still unable to encompass this reversal of fortunes. It was impossible.

'You prayed, did you not, that God would send you deliverance?' said David gently. 'He sent you a friend.'

She clasped his hand between hers, the notes locked in their fingers. 'You should not—'

'God knows, I should,' he said, coughing to clear his voice. 'It's the least I owe you, Leah.'

Her grip tightened. 'Did Flo—'

'Yes, I discussed it with my sister. She understood perfectly that we could not let Eli John destroy you. She offered to contribute twenty pounds of her own, but it was not necessary. I have sufficient funds. This is mere business. Credit to a neighbour who will undoubtedly repay the loan in time. You know I never take risks.'

Leah took a deep breath to steady herself. If this were no delusion of her fevered brain, then she must be clear-headed. Business, he said, so she must take it as such. 'It must be official. In writing. I must sign an undertaking to repay – in time. And... and Betty must be told about it. I will not do anything in a corner.'

'No,' He concurred, steadying himself also, releasing her hand. 'It will all be in order.' He drew out a sheet of paper and sat down to write, his pen flowing steadily across the page. 'A formal loan of one hundred and twenty-eight pounds to Miss Leah Owen of Cwmderwen, Llanolwen, and to her nephew and heir, John Owen, of the same, to be repaid in,' he looked up at her before resuming, 'fifty years from this day, thirtieth of December 1918. Does that satisfy?'

She nodded. Every penny, from now on, would go to repayment of this loan, even if she had to starve herself.

David signed the paper, then turned it for her to add her name. She did so.

He opened the study door. 'Bethan, may I call on you to sign a paper? Merely a matter of witnessing a transaction.'

'Oh!' Bethan looked flustered, wiping her hands on her apron as she sidled nervously in. She picked up the pen as if it were a serpent ready to bite, added a scrawl where David indicated and put the pen down hurriedly. 'Will that do, Mr George?'

'It will. Thank you, Bethan.'

When she had gone, he blotted the paper, folded it neatly, and slipped it in a drawer. 'There. Are you comfortable that it is all above board and official? Signed and witnessed.'

'Yes. Yes, thank you, David. Thank you from the bottom of my heart. God has indeed sent me deliverance in a friend more than my faith deserves.'

'We always have and always will be friends, Leah.' He smiled sadly. 'You must always rely on me, in the future, even if you could not in the past. Now,' he shook himself, 'will you take tea to seal the deal?'

'No. Thank you, but no, I must get back to Cwmderwen. I need to think.'

'You'll not let Frank have any suspicion of the money?'

'No! Indeed not. He'll know nothing of it. Even though it's his debt I am paying, I couldn't trust him not to lose some of it in the Mason's before he ever got to the quarry.'

'Good. Will you allow me to accompany you to see Eli John?'

'No. Thank you, but I would prefer not.' She had heard enough of Eli's obscene and blasphemous insults not to want them inflicted on David.

'But you must not go alone. You will need a witness. And I've seen evidence of the violence he can inflict when he's crossed. He'll not be pleased with this payment.'

'I am sure he will not. But I shall not go alone tomorrow. John will accompany me.'

'That is good.' He showed her to the door and solemnly shook her hand.

She turned to go.

'Oh, and Leah—' She turned back. 'Betty already knows. I told her my intention before I went to the bank. She approves.'

Leah blushed. 'God grant me always such good neighbours.'

'Amen.'

In her room at Cwmderwen, Leah paced, nursing the bank notes to her bosom. Their presence burned. She would not trust them to the rent box with its broken lock. Was the cabinet beside her bed any better? It was like keeping a live grenade in the house. It was no good. She couldn't bear it a moment longer. She had planned to visit Eli John early in the morning, but she wouldn't wait. It must be now, though the midwinter sun had already set, and cold, wet darkness was claiming the land.

'John.' She returned to the kitchen where he was sitting, staring into the fire. 'I need to go out. I mean to see Eli John. Will you accompany me?'

'Yes.' He stood up. She had expected him to question, to point out that it was too dark, to ask why such a visit to such a man could possibly be desirable, but he merely said yes, as if already prepared.

They climbed up to the road in silence, emerging from under the

272

deeper darkness of the trees into a dim, damp, lingering light that would itself soon fade to blackness, for the moon was old and wouldn't rise till the early hours of morning. Hurrying while they could still see, they turned towards the village. The lane to Y Garn quarry turned off the road just beyond the chapel, before the first houses of Llanolwen, climbing up over the open hilltop above the village before descending between two quarries, one disused and flooded, the other near to exhaustion. A third, a little way below, was still productive. Even now, at such an hour of winter darkness, men were at work. Engines growled, the ring of hammers echoed around, with an occasional shout, and lamplight gleamed like distant glow-worms on slate walls.

Eli dabbled often enough in quarry business – the sort that involved bargaining, not sweat – but he hadn't taken his father's place as manager at Y Garn. Jacob had retired when his limbs had given out, and was living in a cottage on Penfeidr farm, where his respectable cousin regularly lectured him on the virtues of sobriety and prayer. His post at the quarry had passed to a gruff Scotsman who now occupied the manager's house, down by the lower quarry, within sight of a row of slaters' cottages. Eli had commandeered a house, surrounded by trees, just above the higher pits, where his comings and goings could go unnoticed.

It was a looming mass in darkness, a solid house, well built but without grace. Leah recoiled at the sight of it. Nothing but this debt would have persuaded her to approach it. She almost wished that she might find it empty, but there was a faint light glowing through drawn curtains.

'You know why I am here, John.'

'Yes.'

The answer didn't surprise her. She stiffened her resolve and rapped on the door.

In any other house of this standing, Leah would have expected a servant to open the door, but not here. Eli lived alone. Rachel Morgan had come, gone, come and gone again, as dependency and desperation dictated. She had last been seen a few months ago, in a caterwauling brawl with Eli outside the Butcher's Arms. David had said people suspected foul play, but no one had made any effort to search for the missing woman. The unlamented harlot. No woman had been fool enough to take her place. He'd had a man too, Jack Jones – groom, clerk and general factotum – but Jones had been conscripted into the army in October, despite Eli's conniving attempts to keep him out, and had not yet returned. One woman – too big and brawny for any man to argue with – came in each day from Felindre to clean his house and cook his dinner, but she stayed no longer than needed. So Leah would have to wait for him to answer his own door.

There was silence within for a while, then heavy footsteps. The door swung open and Eli John stood there.

Eli John the dandy. He was dressed in a brocade waistcoat and his silk tie was fastened with a gold pin, his pugnacious chin was cleanly shaved and his oiled hair neatly combed. But all the elegant touches in the world couldn't disguise that calculating, mocking sneer in his eyes.

'Well, well, Leah Owen. So that snivelling brother of yours has sent you, has he, bitch? And the welp, too. Thinks you can find a soft spot in me with your mincey-wincey pleading. "Oh, Mr John, have mercy on us. A poor spinster and a motherless orphan."'

Leah's revulsion at the thought of this meeting vanished. Face to face with Eli John, she found a strength within her, born of her knowledge that he couldn't touch her inner soul, no matter how hard he tried. Her spirit was stronger than his, her contempt greater than his, and she exulted that he knew it. He hated her for it. Now he would be brought low, his spite foiled, and it would be at her rejoicing hand. Tada had done wrong to blame him and his father for Tom's death, but she would never forgive him for his spiteful corruption of Frank.

'You hope to hear me beg, Mr John? I am afraid you will be disappointed. I have come to speak to you about the debt you claim my brother owes you.'

'Claim?' He sniggered. 'You think I concocted a fairytale? I imagined the debts?' He turned and led the way into a living room furnished for a gentleman: upholstered chairs, a fine clock on the mantelpiece, gilt-framed paintings on the wall, brandy and cigars on the table. Eli John had done very well for himself, as everyone knew. Still sniggering, he opened a tall cupboard, revealing a great iron safe, worthy of a bank. He nonchalantly drew a bundle of keys from his pocket and moved to insert one into the lock. Then he stopped, with a knowing laugh, turned instead to a great mahogany desk and pulled a drawer open. Leah found herself staring into the barrel of a cold, black Webley revolver.

She kept resolutely calm, though she reached for John's hand to reassure him. His hand, though, remained clasped to his side, unmoved by the threat.

'Just in case you and the welp have ideas,' said Eli, stepping back to the safe, unlocking it with his free hand. As the heavy door swung open, Leah could see it was stuffed with bundles of papers.

'Where are we?' said Eli, in a conversational tone. 'Ah yes, these. Here you are. Try this. You recognise Frank's writing?' He held up a torn and beer-stained scrap, with a barely decipherable scrawl, though '£5' was legible enough. 'Ah no, it's hard to read on this one. Frank might as well be a pig writing with his left trotter when he has a gallon of gin inside him. But what about this one?'

He produced a second sheet, a formal promissory note for

twenty-five pounds, signed with the perfect copperplate hand that Frank had mastered at school. 'Clear enough?'

'I don't doubt that my brother signed papers.'

'Plenty of them. Would you like to see them all and calculate the full amount? How good is your arithmetic? Frank's was always good, I'll give him that. Never could figure out odds, though. Far too impetuous when it comes to gaming. I could have warned him he was ruining himself...but I didn't. Why? Because it amused me to watch the fool sink ever lower into a cesspit of his own making.'

'I know what you've done to Frank, and to God alone knows how many others,' said Leah. 'I wouldn't waste your breath boasting of it. I know the sum Frank owes. One hundred and twenty-eight pounds. I ask you this, as a courtesy, on the chance that you might be willing to redeem yourself in some small way: will you release Frank from his debts?'

Eli grinned. The grin broadened until it seemed to eat his face. 'Never.'

'Will you reduce them?'

'Never.'

'What, then, is your wish? Make it clear, please, with John here to witness precisely what is said and done.'

'I wish Frank Owen to repay me in full by tomorrow midnight. Every penny that he owes me. There, have you got that? One hundred and twenty-eight pounds in full. Not one farthing less. Either pay or relinquish the tenancy of Cwmderwen. Leave your damned hovel and your sad little acres and let me watch you take to the road like the penniless beggars you are and have always been, with all your pious arrogance trailing in the mud and shit where you belong. Let me see that and then I'll let him off his debt.'

Leah thought that John would speak, but he said nothing. Not a hair on him stirred. He simply stood rigid at her side, letting her do the talking.

'And that is your final word, Eli John?'

'Yes. My irrevocable ultimatum.'

'Then here is the repayment.' Leah produced the bundle of banknotes, still in their wrapper and held them out. She had not counted them. David had been true to his word, she was sure of that.

Eli stared at the notes in her hand. 'You are...they are not real. You're lying.'

'Do you not know a five pound note when you see one? This money in exchange for those promissory notes. John, stoke the fire. I wish to see all Frank's debts burned before my eyes.'

John seized the brass poker, stirring the flames in the fireplace till they roared.

Eli's features turned dark with pounding blood, his lips wet with spittle. 'I'll not accept your money, Leah Owen. I have no dealings with you.'

'It's Frank's money, as you demanded, and here is John to witness that the debt is paid.' Still she proffered the bundle, her other hand extended for the proof of Frank's folly. She stared at the revolver still pointing at her, refusing to be cowed. 'This is no trick. This is the payment you demanded to release my brother from your foul bondage. You must accept it and if you will not, I shall return tomorrow with a police officer who will oblige you to comply.'

The dark crimson of anger faded from Eli's face. If nothing else, he was a businessman, without compassion or unprofitable pride. Money was money. His eyes narrowed as he surveyed the bundle, calculating its value. His spiteful desire to ruin the Owens might be foiled, but he would come out of it with a healthy profit. 'Very well. Count it out. Let me see that it's the precise amount. One penny short...'

Leah broke the wrapper and counted out the notes, Eli's beady eyes following her every move. 'One hundred and twenty-eight pounds.' She kept her hand clamped hard on the pile. 'When I see you burn all Frank's debts.'

He shrugged as he withdrew more papers from the safe, shuffling through them and counting some onto the table, just as Leah had counted the bank notes.

Leah watched them, adding up the sums. Ninety-three pounds, ninety-eight pounds... And the last one, 'Thirty pounds interest, Francis Owen', one hundred and twenty-eight pounds. Eli stepped back.

'John,' said Leah. 'Burn them.'

John picked up the papers and thrust them into the fire, prodding them with the poker as they curled and crumbled in the flames. When there was nothing left but ash, Leah removed her hand from the bank notes.

Eli scooped them up, smirking as he thrust them into the safe. 'Earned it on your back, did you, bitch? God help the men so desperate they'd poke you and pay for it.'

'I am not Rachel Morgan.'

He laughed. 'No, you keep your temper. Not like that diseased whore. But don't go thinking it will save you. You've paid off Frank's debts this time, but there'll be more. You know there will. And sooner or later I'll have you out of your hovel and begging.'

'Not while I have breath.' Head high, Leah walked out, out of the parlour, out of the hall, out through the open door, into the biting cold of clean air. It was done. It was finished.

'While you have breath.' Eli was following her. She felt the muzzle of the revolver touch her neck as she strode down the path. 'And how long will that be, bitch?' He was whispering in her ear. 'Ask Rachel what I'm capable of. When you are cold, I'll have Cwmderwen and everything else you hold dear.'

'Is it true then, what they say, that you killed her?' Leah turned to face him, ignoring the gun that was almost in her face. He wouldn't dare shoot. Not out in the open. The quarrymen would hear the shot. Eli wasn't such a fool.

No, he didn't shoot. Or reply. The revolver clattered to the ground as he crumpled, like a rag doll. She stared at him, twitching at her feet, making guttural groans, then up at John, who was holding the poker in both hands. He wasn't looking at her, but down at Eli, and as she watched, he raised the rod and brought its heavy brass knob down on Eli's face.

'John! Stop!' Leah flinched back in horror, but John didn't stop. He brought the poker down again and again until there was no more twitching or groaning, no face, no recognisable head. Forcing herself forward, when every nerve urged her to back away, she tried to grab John's arm and stop him, but he was an automaton and she was half-paralysed with shock. At last he stood back, breathing heavily, lowering the gory poker as he stared down at the mess. He was neither terrified, nor gloating. Emotionless.

'John.' She struggled to find words. 'John! You have... What have you done? This is—' It was a nightmare. 'He would never have dared to shoot me—'

'He wanted to take the farm,' said John, calmly. 'No one will take the farm from me. It is mine by a covenant with the Lord.'

Leah's veins froze within her. Her father's words rang in her ears, dripping with blood. Did John understand that he would hang for this? That thought stirred her into life, at last. Whatever horrors crowded into the corners of her mind, she could not let that happen. John could not hang. Yet the way he stood and spoke, acknowledging his deed as if it were righteous, she could imagine him standing proud on the scaffold, waiting for the Lord to intervene and prevent his execution. She had prayed for deliverance

279

and God had sent her a good friend. Now she had no choice, she must be God's agent in her turn and defend her boy.

'John, we cannot leave him here. He'll be found, come daylight, and we are sure to be suspected. I cannot allow you to be arrested. We must dispose of him.'

John frowned, then nodded. 'Yes.' He looked around, saw a garden shed and strode to it, wrenching open its door. He emerged with some sacking and rope. 'I shall dispose of him.'

She watched him wrap up the bloody mass that was Eli John, willing herself to bend and help but she couldn't. 'What will you do?'

He looked around again, taking bearings. 'The quarry. Stones. He'll sink.'

'Yes,' she whispered, watching him prepare to heave the bundle up. 'Wait! The gun, too.'

John nodded, pulling the sacking open sufficiently to thrust the revolver in, then he rewrapped the body and heaved it onto his shoulder. Leah watched him stride off into the trees. Only then did her knees give way and she sank down on the rain-soaked path, covering her face and moaning like a wounded animal. What had they done? What had they done?

Lowering her hands, she looked, willing it all to have been a dream. But there was the path before her, awash with blood, glowing crimson in the light from the open door. The rain thinned it, causing it to flow in all directions, but it would take more than that to rinse it away. She must act. She pulled herself up, trembling, and – on shaking legs – sidestepped the gore. The door of the house yawned open to greet her. A darkness seemed to envelop it, despite the light of lamps and flickering flames. There was a listening silence: she felt she must step softly for fear of raising vengeful ghosts, but she had to go in.

280

There was a scullery at the back. A pump and a pail. She filled it, again and again, heaving the water over the path till it was clear of all but rain as the blood drained into the black earth on either side.

She returned the pail to the scullery and paused by the parlour. The fire was dying down. Where was the poker? She found it out on the grass beside the path and ran it under the pump, wiping it convulsively before returning it to the fireside.

The safe still stood ajar. Eli must have been so determined to have the last threatening word that he had not stayed to relock it before chasing her out. She swung the door open. She had to reclaim the money, or it would be evidence that they had been there.

What money though? There were bundles and rolls of bank notes, at least twice as much as she had paid down. Which were hers? She couldn't think. She scooped them all into her bag. And then there were the papers. Stacks of them. Frank's debts had been burnt, but how many other despairing souls were shackled by promissory notes kept in that safe? She'd burn them all, free everyone. Would that atone a little for what had happened? Scooping them up, she fed them into the fire, watching them disappear into nothingness, feeling her heart beat like the hammers in the quarry. She couldn't tear her eyes from the flames until she was sure that every scrap was gone. A sheet had slipped to one side at the back of the grate. She would have to touch the poker again to draw it into the embers.

'He's gone,' said John. He was standing in the doorway, his hawkish features underlit by the flickering flames and the oil lamp. He was splattered with blood. The sight brought a scream to her throat, but she smothered it. Eli's jacket was hanging on the door.

'Put that on to cover yourself,' she said. 'And wipe your face.'

The jacket was broad enough but too short. It would have to do. At least it would conceal the stains on his shirt. When he'd finished, she took another deep breath. Never had she been so close to total collapse. She must not succumb. 'Let us be gone, too.' She followed John out and automatically shut the door. If only she could shut out what had happened. But she couldn't. She would never shut it out.

They tramped back in silence – and in pitch darkness, now – but John seemed to find his way as though guided by an invisible hand, over the hill and down towards the chapel. There were lights twinkling in the village, and the sight only increased Leah's simmering hysteria. How could life be carrying on as normal; neighbours sitting down to supper, children being put to bed? Or were they lined up at their windows, peering out to catch a glimpse of two murderers?

Murder. The worst of crimes, the worst of sins. She seized John's arm. 'Let's go into the chapel. I need to pray.' She had been praying, she realised, all the way down the road, but she needed to feel herself standing before some seat of judgement, a cross looming over her.

'Yes, let us pray,' said John, as though it were perfectly natural.

The chapel was empty; cold, but not quite dark. A lamp, turned low, stood by the pulpit. Leah slipped into a pew and dropped to her knees, covering her face, trying to block everything out, trying to find words beyond 'What have we done, what have we done?' Forgive us our trespasses. Even when they include murder?

But then John's voice rang out, echoing round the chapel. 'Heavenly father, I thank you for walking beside me, for guiding my hand and putting your strength in my arm to bring mine enemy low.' He was standing before the pulpit, his face uplifted, his hands raised high.

Her John, thanking God for what he had done. He lowered his arms and looked at her. 'Amen.'

'Amen,' she repeated weakly. There were no prayers left. She meekly accompanied him back to the chapel door and took the arm he offered as they descended the steps to the gate. The road before them was suddenly illuminated as a motorcar came by. David George, with Betty beside him, smiling graciously as they headed for the village. David nodded, with unspoken reassurance, as the car chugged past. What were they seeing? Miss Owen and her nephew come to pray for strength and courage before the trial of their visit to Eli John tomorrow? Not blood splatter. Not white guilty faces – for there was no guilt on John's face.

She must not think about this monstrous new side to him. She must merely think of what she must do to save him from the hangman's noose. She must put aside all horror, panic; all convulsive guilt, and think. Think. Plan. Do whatever was required. As they walked home, it became clear to her. They had seen no one on the road this evening until they had emerged from the chapel. David and Betty would have no reason to believe they had been anywhere else. The debt was due tomorrow, so she would go tomorrow, without John. She would take the money, as if ready to pay, and be seen countless times by quarrymen on their way to work. She would say that she had knocked and there was no reply so she had come away again. It would be true. There would be no reply. If Eli's battered remains did come to light, she would take the blame. She had gone alone and killed him. It would not be an absolute lie; she had brought about his death.

The rain eased and ceased as they walked, replacing it with sharp wind and dry reason. Perhaps John had spoken some horrific truth in the chapel. Perhaps God had indeed guided his hand, just as he had guided David to come to her aid. It was all part of the deliverance for which she had prayed, and now everything was resolved. Frank was no longer threatened with impossible debts, David's money could be repaid without too much delay, all being well; the farm would be safe. And Eli John was a monster. A murderer, himself; he had killed Rachel Morgan and probably others, too. His death was a just God's will.

She felt shame gnawing at her as she allowed herself these thoughts. Whatever justice God had in store for Eli John, it was not her place to deliver it. She no longer knew if a just God, or any God, were real but she knew that Hell was opening up beneath her feet.

Safely back in Cwmderwen, she lit the lamp and forced herself to look over her coat and skirt. A speck or two of blood on the hem of the coat and a spray on her sleeve, but the dark cloth was sodden with rain and could be scrubbed clean. John was another matter. 'Change your clothes,' she said. 'Burn those. Burn that jacket. Burn it all.'

Without a word, he did as she bade. She watched the flames leaping up in the back yard. Flames of Hell. They died down soon enough. She heard the pump gushing in spurts as John rinsed his hair and face spotless. In fresh clean clothes he returned to the kitchen.

'Shall we read, aunt?'

'What?'

'The Word of the Lord.

'The Word? Yes.' For God's sake, let us bury ourselves in Scripture.

John opened the great family Bible and the darkness in her deepened as he read.

'Lord, how are they increased that trouble me! many are they that rise up against me.

'Many there be which say of my soul, There is no help for him in God. Selah.

'But thou, O Lord, art a shield for me; my glory, and the lifter up of mine head.

284

'I cried unto the Lord with my voice, and he heard me out of his holy hill. Selah.

'I laid me down and slept; I awaked; for the Lord sustained me.

'I will not be afraid of ten thousands of people, that have set themselves against me round about.

'Arise, O Lord; save me, O my God: for thou hast smitten all mine enemies upon the cheek bone; thou hast broken the teeth of the ungodly.

'Salvation belongeth unto the Lord: thy blessing is upon thy people. Selah.'

Leah was up before the first hint of grey smeared the night sky. She felt her coat. Hung by the range, it had more or less dried, but there were damp patches still where she had scrubbed hard. Still, there was no blood visible by lamplight. She would have to trust there would be none by cold daylight. She took out the money that she had blindly stowed in the cabinet beside her bed. David's loan – and more. Far more. Eli's money. She didn't dare think how much. She stared at it, seeing it dripping in illusory blood. Its very touch burned her. Put it away. Hide it. All she needed now was the one hundred and twenty-eight pounds David had lent her. With trembling fingers, she counted it out and slipped it back into her bag. She was going, as she had planned, to pay off Frank's debts. Eli would not be there to receive it, but still she would go through the pretence of visiting him on business.

Dim light was seeping into the sky as she set off up the lane to the road. It was bright enough, by the time she reached the chapel, to see that there was no danger of going unnoticed on her morning trek. Quarrymen who lived in the village were tramping up the hill, and others too; villagers who would normally have no business at the quarry. Leah was swept along and found herself walking beside

Ifan Davies, recently discharged from the army and back at the village butcher's shop.

'Seen them marching up there,' he said. 'Like the Hun were waiting over the hill. Had to go and see, didn't I?'

'Who was marching?' asked Leah.

'Policemen. Two dozen of them, Sarah Price was saying, though I only saw six. Still, haven't see the like since the tithe protests.'

'Policemen?' Leah's heart was missing beats. 'Why are they here?'

'Some say break-in at the quarry. Others say a lorry was stolen. Mind you, Kathryn Lewis reckons it's murder.'

Leah tried to keep calm. No one in the village knew anything – that was clear – and ignorance was never a hamper to gossip, but Kathryn Lewis had hit upon the truth. Eli's murder must have been discovered in the night. John's attempt to make sure he sank had failed and the corpse must be floating on the dark waters of the flooded quarry for all to see.

She wanted to flee but she had no option but to walk on, with the other curious sightseers.

'Oo!' A woman some way ahead turned and nodded knowingly back at them. 'Eli John, then. Well it would be, wouldn't it? What did I say?'

A crowd was gathering at the entrance of the short track leading to Eli's house, even the quarrymen lingering to see, rather than hurrying on to work. But they couldn't get close to the house itself. Two uniformed policemen were standing guard at the gate, preventing access and refusing to say a word. Leah could see the front door wide open, policemen passing in and out. One appeared from around the back with a covered basket. Why were they fussing with the house? Had they brought the body back there? Pulling free from the crowd, she walked on, down the hill to the narrow neck where, with a few steps to the left, she could peer down into the flooded quarry. The waters were dark, oily, broken by shattered slabs of rock, timbers, rusting submerged machinery. Nothing stirred. There were no policemen on guard on the winding path down to the bottom of the pit, or at the top of the cliff. There were no ropes and poles and tackles that might have been used to pull a body from the black water.

She turned back, bemused, and walked home. What could she do now except get on with life, do all the things expected of her around the farm, make the dinner, feed John? The money that David had given her was in her bag. She was carrying it as if it were nothing. One hundred and twenty-eight pounds. Yesterday, it had been salvation. Today, it was a curse she just wanted off her hands.

She was in half a mind to turn aside at the milk churns and walk down to Castell Mawr, to return the money, untouched. *I tried to give it to him*, she'd say, *but he wasn't there, so you can have it back*. No good. He'd say she should hold onto it. Eli might be out today but he could return at any moment. Frank's debts were still to be paid and how could she tell him she knew that Eli was never coming back?

This would never end. How long must she sit on this heap of blood money? It was punishment. So be it. She returned to Cwmderwen, hung up her coat, donned her apron and set the kettle on to boil. Then she slipped into her bedroom in the old parlour, shut the door and set about opening a seam on her mattress.

Rip, rip, rending the fabric apart. She looked across at the wall, at the crack that had now reached the floor, lateral splits spidering to either side, a section of the plaster billowing out like a sail, ready to crumble and fall. She had been mistress here so long, but she had never had that crack repaired. Why? Because it symbolised what she knew in her heart, that this house was built on sand, and nothing would hold. Their world had always been splitting apart and now it was rent in two. Others had escaped through that crack, but not her. All she had was ruin.

Grimly, tucking all the money – David's and Eli's – into the mattress, she began to resew the seam.

The next day, Frank was back, shame-faced in front of his sister but eying every shadow cautiously for fear some thug employed by Eli John might be lying in wait to break his legs.

'Don't worry, you're safe,' said Leah, bitterly, slamming a pot on the table.

'They're saying in the village he's gone.'

'Yes, they say that.'

'Reckon he got wind the police were coming for him and scarpered before they got there.'

'Is that so?'

'Your David put them onto him.'

It was true, of course. David had said he'd spoken to the colonel. Whatever information he'd passed on, that must account for the early morning police raid, not the discovery of a mutilated body. She should be relieved, but she was beyond that. 'Have you seen your son?'

'He's trimming hedges in Dark Field. Seems in a high mood.'

'Oh, does he?'

'Thinks we're safe, I suppose, because Eli's not around and the year's gone, but nothing will make us safe. Eli will be back and—'

She turned, brandishing a ladle. 'Eli will not be back!'

'You can't be sure of that.'

'I am sure. Believe me, Frank, I am sure of that, if nothing else in life!' She glared at him as he gaped. 'Do you understand what I am telling you? I went to see him last night, and I know he will never return.'

Fearful comprehension dawned on Frank's face. 'You... Where is he?' he whispered.

'Tangled in the debris at the bottom of Hengoed quarry.'

'My God. My God.' He didn't know whether to cringe in terror or rejoice. 'But the debts. His father will find them.'

'There is no more debt.'

'I signed chits.'

'Burned. You are free.'

He stared at her in wonder – still taking it in – then burst into tears, like a child.

She put the ladle down and sank on a chair. There was relief of sorts in confessing, even to Frank, but he could not absolve her. 'You are free,' she repeated. 'And I...I am damned.'

Could that be concern creeping into his features? He wiped his eyes, then his nose. 'You did it for me.'

'No, Frank, I did it for John, God help me.'

'Does he know? About the debt and the...other thing?'

'Oh yes. He knows.'

'But then,' Frank drew up another chair and sat staring at his hands, clasped between his knees, 'you shouldn't have–'

'Shouldn't have done it? No, I should not. I should have let us fall into ruin. Better that. I see that now.'

'No.' He looked up. 'I meant you shouldn't have to bear it. You won't. You mustn't. It was for the farm. For John. Because of me.'

'Not just you, Frank. Because of everything.'

He leaned forward and took her hand. 'Things will be different, now. I'll be different. I promise.'

'Oh, please! Don't make promises that you know you won't keep.'

'But I will. I swear. You don't understand how... I'm free. You freed me. He was a demon on my shoulders. I know it. I was so weak. I always was. Not strong like you, Leah. But not any more. I swear. I'll do anything you say. There'll be no more drinking. I'll take the pledge.'

'You took the pledge when you were five, Frank.'

'Yes, but I was a child, told what to do. But now... I promise, not another drop. I'll work. I swear I'll work. I'll make this farm pay. I'll do anything you want. Just tell me what to do.'

What could she tell him to do? Wind the clock back to a time when John played innocently with his sister and Frank could have been a proper father and Cwmderwen could have been a house of love and respect and hope? 'Just...do whatever is needed, Frank. Do whatever you can and when you fail, don't come to me. I can't pick up any more pieces. My soul is cracked and emptied. I have nothing more to give.'

March 1919

'Mary.' Leah took her sister's hand to try once more. There was no resistance, but no recognition, either. There had been no recognition in Mary's eyes in the full hour that Leah had been sitting at her side. With her free hand, she continued to sort laundry. Quite how she was sorting it wasn't clear, but she was shifting garments from one pile to another – and back again. A supervising nurse had twice stopped, tutting, to remove some of the clothes and pass them to another patient who was sorting more rationally, muttering as she did so.

Mary showed no signs of ill health or ill treatment, though she was grey-haired and pallid like a creature kept too long indoors. She looked neither happy nor sad – merely blank – as if she had taken her mind off into another place, long ago.

'Mary, I must go now. And I want you to understand. If you are in there somewhere, please understand. I am sorry I have not been able to visit you more often these past years, but this is my last visit. If all goes well, we are going away. I cannot take you. They wouldn't let you come with us, because of the way you are, so I shall never see you again, but I need to save John. I want to say goodbye properly. Can you understand? Can you forgive me? Will you look at me just once and say goodbye?'

But Mary didn't look at her. She hadn't said a word. The nurse claimed she never did.

There was nothing more to be done. Leah leaned in to kiss her sister on the cheek. That, at least, did elicit a response. Mary flinched. Sighing, Leah rose. 'Goodbye then, Mary. I shall always remember you in my prayers.'

Mary continued to sort laundry.

Leah made her way through the maze of corridors to the entrance of the hospital. It wouldn't do to keep David waiting, since he had been good enough to spare her the bother and expense of the train journey. She was in good time. He had not yet arrived, so she sat on one of the long benches in the hall, lost in her own thoughts.

Murder. She couldn't escape it. No matter how evil Eli John had been and no matter how much cleaner the world was without him, murder was wrong. That was etched so deeply in her soul that she could never think otherwise, and yet John had committed murder without a qualm, without guilt. She had done this to him, binding him with blood and sinew so closely – to their twenty-four acres, one rood and eight perches – that he could not see the light. She could see no way of excising that blindness from him, except by taking him away from such poisoned roots. They would have to leave Cwmderwen.

It was odd how – the moment she had reached that dread conclusion – weights dropped from her like tethers from a great ship launching. Not the weight of guilt – that would remain forever, but the weight of Cwmderwen, of barren, pointless duty; of obligation to Tada and his obsessive dream. They would be free, like birds on the wind, free to go wherever they liked; be what they liked, start afresh, washing the venom from their blood. In a new country, breathing new air, John could be released from the shackles she had rivetted to his strange mind. America. They would go to America, where Annie was. If they released the farm and sold all they had – the livestock, the fodder, the straw, the tools – they would have enough for steerage passage and a little to see them on their way in the new world. John and she were hard workers, and even Frank had pulled his weight since the horrors of the new year. He was a reformed man…

No, he wasn't. She wished he was, but she couldn't pretend. He'd go for days without touching intoxicating liquor and then he'd fall from grace and roll home drunk again, only to be contrite and full of promises the next day. He was enthusiastic for the American scheme. She would just have to pray that he would keep sober enough to see it put into effect. Just as she would have to pray that when she explained it to John, he would understand how right it was.

All that was required was to undo all the indoctrination she had helped to imprint on him since birth. How was she to accomplish that miracle? There must be a way. If she only used the right words, at the right moment, playing on his piety and speaking of God's will, she could surely bring him round. It would have to be soon. She had been putting it off and putting it off, but time was running out. Lady Day was approaching.

With a creak of brakes, David's car pulled up outside on the gravel. No longer the two-seater Morris. With the war over and austerity in such matters no longer obligatory, he had exchanged it for a larger Ford that could, at a squeeze, carry the whole family of parents and five children.

'Miss Owen.' He was always carefully formal in public places. 'How is your sister?' He opened the passenger door and his eldest, Annie, scrambled out and into the back to join her sister Martha.

'Mary is unchanged.' Leah allowed him to hand her in. 'I am afraid she was completely unaware of my presence.'

'I am sorry to hear that. I hoped for better. Perhaps your next visit will be more fruitful.'

'Perhaps,' said Leah. She could tell him nothing. Not yet.

'Let's be on our way then.' He half-turned in his seat. 'Martha, sit still, or I shall put you off and you will have to walk.'

'Annie is kicking me.'

'I'm not!'

David turned around fully to face them. Both girls sat still, hands in their laps.

'Sorry, Tada.'

'Good.'

They were off, the girls entertaining themselves singing hymns on a journey interrupted only once, when sleet began to fall and David stopped to put the hood up.

'I wouldn't want you getting wet, Miss Owen.'

She smiled in reply. She didn't care if she were wet or dry. Or cold. There were rugs piled ready in the car against the icy weather and snow flurries that had swept back after a lull of damp mildness. She allowed David to tuck a blanket around her, clasping her coat close. Her coat, unstained except for the stains she couldn't eradicate from her imagination. There was agony in this, sitting next to David, feeling the occasional touch of his arm, her skin alive to his nearness, and yet her feelings trapped inside her, forbidden to show themselves. Of all that she would lose in moving to America, David was the one real regret, but at least she would be cut free from these bitter-sweet bonds, no longer tortured by his untouchable closeness.

'...and Flo will be coming. I hope we'll see you there too.'

She mustn't drift off into private thoughts. It was imperative to keep up innocuous conversation. William's forthcoming birthday party. Would she still be there? 'If I can, I shall come, of course.'

David studied the road ahead. 'Perhaps you can trust Frank to take care of the farm for a few hours, and John can come too?'

'Oh yes!' said Annie. 'Do bring John.'

Leah swallowed. 'We'll see.' Trust Frank? No, she knew she would never be able to trust him fully, however hard he tried, and he was trying. He took work at the quarry, when it was offered, and some of his wages had come to her for the secret fund towards their great escape, although some also disappeared down the gullet of the Mason's Arms. She had locked up what he gave her, along with the remaining war savings she had cashed in and the pennies and shillings she had managed to save each week by feeding them all on scraps and air. Their worldly wealth. A miserably small amount compared with the fortune that still remained sewn into her mattress. She would have to do something about that, soon. How, though, to raise the subject now, with the girls in the back of the car?

They had turned onto the road to Llanolwen before she ventured to mention the loan. 'I must speak to you, David. On a matter of business.'

He concentrated on steering. 'There is no rush.'

'With you incurring such expenses as this motorcar, I think there is. I must clear the books. I don't believe Eli John is coming back.'

David smiled. 'I very much doubt if we'll ever see him again. And there is nothing for you to fear if he does reappear. It's clear he must have had warning that the police were coming, and he burned any evidence of his nefarious dealings before he fled. Colonel Rhys-Parker told me the police found a strong box emptied. And there was evidence of...' He glanced back but the girls were engrossed in examining their purchases. 'They found blood.'

'Blood!' It caught her unawares. Surely the rain and her efforts had washed away the blood.

'Spots of it on a dress, upstairs. I presume it belonged to that wretched sinner he kept.'

'Rachel Morgan.'

'Yes. Not that anyone spares any grief for a woman of such ill repute–'

'Do they not?'

295

David nodded. 'You are right. It is not for me to judge her sins, but God, and I fear she stands before him now. So, if Eli is ever rash enough to come back to Llanolwen, he will be arrested and Frank's foolish debts will be of no further consequence.'

She sighed.

He took it for a sigh of relief. 'You have nothing to worry about. Cwmderwen is safe.'

'Then I shall settle my debt to you very soon. Though money alone cannot repay all I owe you, Mr George. And your wife.'

'It's no matter.' He slowed as they approached the milk churn bay and edged the Ford onto Cwmderwen's rutted lane.

'No! Stop here, please,' she insisted. 'I cannot let you inflict our lane on this magnificent chariot.'

'It will take the strain.'

'No, please. I am grateful beyond words that you could take me to Carmarthen today, but I insist, I shall walk the last part. Take your girls home to their mother and thank you again.'

He agreed reluctantly. 'As you wish.'

She allowed him to hand her out. 'I shall visit you very soon and settle everything.'

Solemnly, they shook hands and he returned to the wheel. She watched him reverse the car and turn onto the Castell Mawr track.

'We're in a chariot!' squealed Martha as they sailed out of view.

Late dawn and Frank was in the barn that had served as joiner's workshop, shaking his head over the saws, planes and chisels that Tada had used, as if he had half a mind to make something.

'You're no woodworker,' said Leah. 'We'll sell them with the rest. Morris Jones will take them.'

'For little enough. But we should get a decent price for the beasts, shouldn't we?' Frank spoke more in hope than judgement.

'We'll get whatever price we can. They must go this week, before rent day.'

'And you were always the one determined to fight to the death to keep this place, Leah.'

'Yes, to the death, and death followed. It was the wrong battle. You were right, Frank. You were always right. This place is a curse, not a promise. It's souls I must save now, not this farm. We cannot stay here and be clean.' She looked up to the rafters, down into the gloom of the barn, at the assembled tools, plough, scythes, sickle, rakes, drill, yokes, hooks...half of them too antique even for the Owens to value. But there were bits and pieces that would bring a reasonable price. 'We'll get whatever we can, and with your earnings and what's left of my war savings, we should have enough. Well, let's not stand here dwelling on it. Take those tools now to Jones' workshop and see what he'll give for them.' She helped Frank gather Tada's tools into a sack and heave them onto his shoulder. She stood a while, watching him head off down the fields to the footpath. Helpful. Eager. Willing. All too late. She pulled herself together and turned towards the house.

John was standing before her.

She hadn't heard him. His sudden appearance made her jump. 'John, what are you doing here?'

'Enough for what?'

'What do you mean?'

'You said we should have enough. Enough for what?'

Now it was too late, she knew she should have spoken much earlier, let the seed drop quietly and germinate in its own good time. Let him ponder and pray and, in time, come to understand the wisdom of her plan. But there was no time left now. She had to do the best she could.

'Listen to me, John. I have prayed about this – long and hard – for many months, seeking divine guidance, and I believe that God has spoken to me. He has smiled upon us through the war, holding us safe, has he not? In his name, we have worked this land hard and achieved such miracles, and now it is time to reap the reward that he has held in store for us. Something bigger and better. A new challenge. A new land.'

'What do you mean? What new land? Rent more?'

'I mean a new country. America, where Annie is. That is what God is offering us. There is land in America. Farms far bigger than Cwmderwen. We could—'

'No.'

'Think of it, John. Instead of twenty-four acres, we might have a hundred. Or more. Our own land and Annie—'

'This is my land.'

'There is so little of it. It was given to us so that God might test us here, to prove that we are worthy. We are not like the Georges or the Lloyds. We will always struggle here, but even so, we have never shirked. God intends that we should prosper, and we shall never do so while we remain at Cwmderwen.'

'This is the land God gave me.'

'Yes. But now, in reward for our fidelity, he is preparing a better life for us in America. I hear his voice summoning us.'

'No. You lie. You always lie. He doesn't speak to you. He speaks to me. He bound us to this land. Cwmderwen. Twenty-four acres, one rood and eight perches.'

'It wasn't God who gave us this land, John.' She couldn't stop herself letting the bitterness spill out. 'It was the Devil, I swear. All it has ever taken from us is blood, blood and blood. It eats us alive. Tom, Mamgu, Tadcu, your mother, your brother and sister; it drove Mary mad, it destroyed your father, it almost destroyed Annie, and now see what it has done to you. Driven you to murder, John. Murder! Can that have been the hand of God?'

'God will strike down all who threaten to take this land from me!'

298

'No, God does not condone murder, you know that. Thou shalt not kill! God is offering you forgiveness, freedom, a clean slate, a chance to start again and be clean and whole. We must leave, John, before this place destroys us all. Come Lady Day—'

'No.' He said it stubbornly, but calmly, as if explaining to a wayward child. 'There is a covenant between God and me, which he will not permit anyone to break. He will destroy anyone who attempts it. This is my land. If you try to prise it from me, I shall crush your skull as I crushed the skull of the beast, and God will guide my hand in doing it.'

'John!' She stared at him, less in terror – though she could feel the sincerity in the threat – but more in horror that he was capable of such a thought. 'What sort of God is it that urges you to such unspeakable acts? It's no God that I recognise!'

'No, for you recognise none. You are unknown to God, an outcast from the throne. It is the God of Abraham, the God of Israel, the God of righteousness. My God. Tend to your house and your duties, aunt, and pray for grace, but do not attempt to thwart me, or God will strike you down.'

He strode off before she could say another word, and she was left standing in the yard, her last hopes of salvation for any of them crumbling around her.

She wished he had crushed her skull.

She was at the kitchen table kneading bread when Frank returned. He had gone early, to the carpenter's shop less than a mile away and now it was far gone noon. Gone closing time at the public houses. He looked satisfied and shifty at the same time.

'Did you sell the tools?' she asked, without looking up from the dough.

'What? Oh. Yes.'

'Where's the money?'

He sniffed, fumbling in his pockets and dragging out a note and a handful of coins which he laid on the table. She glanced at it between thumps. A ten shilling note and...five, maybe six shillings? 'I'd expected a guinea at least.'

'Yes, well, they were worn, some of them. He said–'

'Don't bother. Whatever he really paid, I'll never be told. You'll have spent some of it in the Mason's.'

'I just thought I'd best clear the slate.'

'Add to it, you mean. Why not add yet more? There, take it all. Go and drink yourself sick. You might as well.'

'Leah, I promise you it was only one beer. Just one.'

'Lie as much as you like. I don't care. It's no use any more.'

'What's "no use"?'

'Anything. The money. You might as well spend it. We're not going anywhere. John won't go.'

'Oh. But you can persuade him, Leah.'

'No. I can't. There's a louder voice in his ear, shouting me down. He will not listen.'

'We knew he'd be reluctant. He needs time. Anyway, he can't stay if I say not. The lease is in my name, isn't it? If I say we go—'

'Say it and he'll probably do to you what he did to Eli John. God is in his right arm.'

Frank flinched. The days when he had belted his son were not so far behind, but he had done so in the drunken delusion that John would never dare hit back. 'You mean...Eli... Was it John?'

'What do you think? That I dealt the blows?'

'No. But...no. So, is that it? We don't go to America?'

'No. We don't go. We stay and we pay the rent next week and we carry on until he kills us or they hang him. One or the other or both. That is our life from now on.'

300

Frank stared at her. Useless, hopeless Frank. He scooped up some of the money. 'I'll take this, then.'

'Yes, Frank, you take it. Do what you like.' She slapped the dough back onto the table and turned away.

Lady Day. A third consecutive day of torrential rain that had the yard awash and the little brook that trickled down their cwm foaming white. John, his hair still damp from his labours, looked up from his dinner. 'You'll pay the rent.' It could have been a query, a reminder, but Leah knew it was an order.

'Yes, I'll pay the rent.'

He returned to wiping his bowl clean.

'I'll take it,' said Frank, slurring the words.

She didn't bother replying. She cleared the table, then went to fetch her coat and hat. The cabinet by her bed showed signs of scratches around the lock. Frank had been trying it again. Once he'd realised that their plans were dashed, he had slithered back into his old ways with a vengeance. No Eli John to egg him on, now. He was his own scourge and would always be so. At least he hadn't managed to break in, this time. She unlocked the cabinet door.

The rent money was there, safe and sound, along with the savings that she had accumulated for America. Useless, now. Let Frank drink it all away if he would. Nothing mattered any more. Just as long as David's banknotes were still safely cocooned inside her mattress. She had meant to return them before this, but she had been so numb after John's threats that she had done nothing. It was time she dealt with it. Ripping the mattress apart again, she groped within, and pulled out the money.

All of it. David's one hundred and twenty-eight pounds and Eli's secret hoard. How had she forgotten about that? By blocking it out of her mind, along with so much of that terrible night at the end of

301

the year. Tainted spoil. She sat on the bed, looking at it. What was she to do? She hadn't counted it; she didn't want to count it, but she could see that it must be at least another hundred. Two perhaps. A fortune big enough to buy Cwmderwen outright, and good stock, machinery, new clothes. Cwmderwen could be made anew, the covenant sealed forever. Except that it was a cursed covenant binding them to cursed land, and it would be bought with cursed money, cursing them forever more. No, it had to go. If they must linger on here, in this corroding inheritance of death, let it consume them entirely and blot them out forever.

What to do with the money then? Hand it to David, when she returned his loan? Or to Mr Fenston at Plas Malgwyn, when she paid the rent? How could she, without explaining its source and revealing all? Leave it in the chapel, perhaps, to be found and devoted to good works of charity? No, either its discovery would cause an outcry, investigations, questions, or some less than Godly member of the congregation would hide it away for his own gain, unaware of the curse upon it. Better it were lost forever. Drowned. Yes, that was what she would do; she would cast it into the river.

She pushed the bundles of notes into her bag, then pulled on her hat and gloves and passed out, through the kitchen, into the yard, without a word. She felt John's eyes boring into her as she raised her umbrella and shut the door behind her. Down to the footpath, over the stile into Castell Mawr land, up to the old farm house. It wasn't just the rain that made the walk a trial. Her feet dragged as if they were shod with lead. Her legs resisted at every step. But she was there, on the doorstep of Castell Mawr, and Betty was greeting her with a look of smugly censorious superiority.

'Well, Leah Owen, we thought we might see you today, it being Lady Day. Have you come to repay our money perhaps, since my husband insists Eli John will not be requiring it?'

'Is David at home?'

'Mr George!' Betty snorted, then looked her over, softening at what she saw. 'He's back from Plas Malgwyn. I'll send William for him. Will!'

Her eldest son popped up from another room. 'Go fetch your father from the sheep. Tell him Miss Owen is here.'

Sturdy young William ran off, leaving the two women facing each other.

'Don't stand there, dripping. You'd best come in,' said Betty. 'Dry yourself. It's a foul day to be out.'

'Is it?' It could have been thunder and lightning or a driving blizzard, for all Leah cared.

Betty was rubbing her hands, working the fingers together. A gesture of nervous anxiety. What had she to be anxious about, safe and sound here in the home that might have been Leah's? 'You'll take tea.'

'No. Thank you.'

'Well then.' Betty plumped herself down by the fire and took up her knitting, like a knight taking up his shield. 'Can't stand gossiping all day.'

'No.'

Footsteps hurried outside and the door opened. David strode in, dumping a lamb in front of his wife. He shook the rain from his jacket, wiped his hands on a cloth and whipped off his cap. 'Miss Owen.' He sounded out of breath. 'Betty, will you see to it?'

Betty had already put her knitting down and was gathering up the mewling new-born creature. She might posture as the grand lady of the parish, but she was a stalwart farmer's wife who knew what was expected of her. 'I'll deal with the lamb. You speak to Leah.'

David ushered her through to the study. 'What is wrong, Leah?'

'Wrong? Nothing is wrong. I have come to repay the loan, that is all. I am sorry that I didn't come sooner, but there was so much to do on the farm.'

'Of course.' He frowned, unconvinced. 'But there's something more.'

'There's nothing more.' She opened her bag, cautious of too much spilling out, and produced the notes that she had counted out in readiness. 'Here it is, one hundred and twenty-eight pounds. With my gratitude.' Bitter gratitude. If she could turn the clock back, she would never have accepted the loan, never have tried to pay Frank's debt, never let John be stained with such sin. Better that they be reduced to landless beggars.

'Leah.' David took the money, laid it to one side as if it were of no importance, and seized her hands. 'I can see your spirits are deeply troubled. I am your friend. Tell me. Please.'

'There is nothing to tell, David. We go on, along whatever road awaits us. That is all there is.'

'Yes.' He sighed. 'It is true. Our paths are set. And sometimes the road seems hard, but we must have faith that all is as God wills it, and trust to his judgement, not our own.'

She looked at him directly and caught a faint blush at his own platitude. What God had willed for David George had not been so very hard, though he played at regrets. He had a good wife, fine children, a prosperous farm and a secure future. Whereas Leah...

She stepped back. 'As you say, David. God dictates, with a vengeance. I must go. I have the rent still to pay.'

'Of course.' He looked disturbed, confused. 'Let me accompany you. The path is flooded in places.'

'There is no need. I know where the river floods. In this weather and season, your sheep need you more. Thank Betty for her forbearance. Goodbye.'

She turned and walked away, into the rain. Betty, by the open

304

bread oven, said something as she passed, but she didn't hear. Didn't want to hear.

She returned to the footpath, following it as it dipped down towards the river. A river that, in summer, glided somnolently through meadows, weaving around lush islets, its banks beached by gravel where cattle stood to drink or wade. But now, with all the heavy rain, it was a churning gunmetal surge, rushing in waves over hidden obstacles, flecked with yellow foam and swirling detritus. The river was devouring the sodden meadows on either side, leaving trees standing half-submerged. In places, the water swilled across the footpath, and she had to pick her way up into the adjoining fields, the soil saturated and squelching beneath her boots, her body automatically finding a way, while her mind raced around in numbing circles that led to nothing but darkness.

A copse lay ahead. The path usually skirted it, but the water was already lapping around the lower stumps, so she diverted higher. The trees had not been coppiced for a couple of years and the shoots were long and sturdy, snagging her umbrella. She heard it rip and lowered it. There were no leaves as yet to give shelter, so she surrendered herself to the rain, finding passage where she could through the thick growth.

Ahead of her, something moved. Fast.

Alarm instinctively swept through her. Footpads held little terror for her when she was carrying nothing, but today she had the rent and more. Much more. Thank God that she'd already returned David's money. If a thief took the rest... No, she didn't want to surrender it to a thief. She wanted to throw it in the river, that was it. She had forgotten, but now she was determined again.

She stopped, shading her eyes against the rain, and a figure rushed forward. Someone was fighting through the tangled wood towards her. Someone visible in a way no footpad would choose.

Rachel Morgan, in a plush coat of dark green, trimmed with fox fur, diamante buckles on her mudded shoes, a diamante clasp attaching pheasant feathers to her hat. An elegant town lady, bedraggled and the worse for wear. The rain had smudged the paint on her face, but it didn't dim the glittering glare in her eyes.

'Leah Owen. I knew you'd pass this way today.'

'You're dead.' The idea did not disturb Leah. Sooner or later she would find herself among the departed. It made sense that it was today.

'Dead? I'm not dead.' Rachel looked as if she'd been near enough to it, though. 'No thanks to that bastard. He tried. He would have killed me, I swear, if you hadn't come calling.'

Leah couldn't make sense of her words. 'What are you talking about?'

'I was there, wasn't I? Upstairs, where the bastard left me. Knocked me out, took out one of my teeth, but I came round. In time to hear you downstairs, you and your boy. In time to see you do for Eli John out there on the path.'

The images of that night swept back over Leah. Her pulse began to race. 'I don't know what you mean.'

'Yes you do, liar. You good Christians aren't supposed to lie, are you? Or murder people. Not that I blame you for that. You saved my life and I hope he rots in Hell. I'd have danced around the bastard if you'd left him lying there. But you didn't. Threw him over into the quarry, did you? Is that where they'd find him if they went looking?'

If they went looking. If Rachel tipped them off.

'Why would they look?' Leah could think only of calling her bluff. 'They thought you were dead and no one went looking for you.'

For a moment, a flash of pain crossed Rachel's ravaged face. Then

306

she gave a harsh laugh. 'What do I care? I didn't wait for them to find me. I took what he had, stashed upstairs, twenty pounds and more, and I ran. It set me up for a while, that money.' She came closer to block Leah's path, pushing branches out of the way, stumbling on rocks and snags hidden by leaf mould. 'But now it's all gone. Things didn't turn out. Bastards. They tricked me out of it and now I need more. You've got it, I know. All that money he kept in his safe. It should have been mine. I deserved it after everything he did to me. So I want it now, and you'd better give it to me, or I'll go to the police and tell them how I saw your John beat Eli's brains to a pulp with a poker.'

'No!'

'I'll do it, if you don't give me the money! You want to see your boy hanged? That's what they'll do. Hang him by the neck until he's dead. So give it me. It's quarter day. You're going to pay the rent. You must have that much at least. I need it. Give it me. I don't care how much, just give it to me!' Rachel suddenly lunged forward, grabbing for the bag Leah was carrying.

If she hadn't lunged, if she had only continued to threaten, what then? Leah might have paid. It might have made perfect sense for her to be free of Eli's blood money in that way. Let Rachel have it in recompense for all that she had endured at Eli's hands.

But Rachel did lunge and Leah instinctively raised her umbrella to ward her off. It caught Rachel on her breast. Not a heavy blow but in a tender spot. With a squeal Rachel floundered back, shoes slipping in the mud and sodden undergrowth. She lost her balance, staggered, clutching wildly at air and went down, backwards. There was a crack. An egg smashing on the side of a bowl.

Leah stood, heart thumping, waiting for her to rise, but she didn't. She twitched, her eyes fluttering blindly, then she stiffened and sank back, subsiding into dead leaves as if she had suddenly decided to go to sleep. Leah threw herself onto her knees, frantically waving her hand before blue eyes that didn't see, touching the face that didn't stir, groping for a hand, pulling the glove off, searching desperately for a pulse. There was none. No, no, no. How had this happened? She tore leaves away from under her and found the sharp-edged boulder that had smashed into Rachel's skull. This couldn't be. It was some evil jest by fate, making Rachel fall in that spot, in such a way, skull smashed just as John had promised to do to Leah. No, no, it was all wrong. It should be Leah's skull smashed, not Rachel's.

It was too much. Leah couldn't take any more. She hadn't wanted this but there it was, mocking her. Like all of life, screaming in mockery at her. And this wouldn't be the end. There'd be more, and more and more. It would never end. Eli John had been murdered and because of that, Rachel Morgan was now dead and someone else must have seen, or even be watching her right now, and it would go on and on and on and there'd be no end to it until everyone was dead.

She held the cold hand and looked down at the painted face, tears streaming down her cheeks. She was supposed to despise this woman. Eli's whore. That's what people called her. Harlot. Strumpet. A woman of ill repute, reviled and damned. But what was the difference between her and Leah, except for chance and circumstance? If they had been changed at birth, would their lives have been any different? One condemned in the city slums, one imprisoned in a rural anchorite's cell. One labelled a sinner from birth, bought and defiled and discarded at will, and one hailed as a righteous spinster, pure and Godly. A woman of unimpeachable repute. Except that it was Leah Owen who was stained black with murder – the true sinner – not this poor wretch.

There was a small child inside her, screaming 'It's not fair!' And the weary adult in her replied, 'Nothing is ever fair. There is no God. There is no justice. Rachel Morgan is dead and she should be alive. Leah Owen is alive and she should be dead.'

Yes, only death would bring an end to it all. She had fought, she had slaved, but nothing she had ever done had come out right. Everything was bent and twisted and doomed. Now what? Was she to stand by while Llanolwen folk slung this body into a pauper's grave, rejoicing to be rid of a wicked woman and hailing Leah as a heroine for the nudge she gave her? It wasn't right. It shouldn't be like that. It was unjust. Rachel was the innocent one, not Leah. But it was Rachel lying there with her head in a pool of blood. Time to put the balance right.

Leah pulled herself up, and staggered, struggling through briars to the water's brink. First the money. The damned money. She fumbled in her bag. A five pound note. There! In a second it was just a sodden white speck on the heaving flood. Another. Gone. A handful more. Confetti on the water, soon sodden to pulp. A roll of notes. And another. She groped in her bag for more, lost her balance, grasped at a branch and put out a foot to brace herself. The water rose around her boot, topping it and she could feel its lethal strength. It wanted her. Why was she fighting it? She wanted it to take her too, didn't she? It was time to end it all and be free forever. No more Cwmderwen and its endless pointless toil, no more watching Frank drink himself to death, no more watching Betty George preen herself in the life that should have been Leah's, no more watching John warp into evil insanity. No more thankless struggle, no more duty. Just nothingness. Sleep.

It would be so simple. She need do nothing except take one more step, release the branch, let herself go.

She took the step.

And then she stopped. Her grip on the branch tightened, resisting the surge that was pressing now at her knees, impatient to sweep her away.

No.

No; she never surrendered, she was a fighter. All her life she had been a fighter and she wouldn't stop now. She had fought the wrong battles, that was all. She had fought for Tada's dream, and it had been nothing but a millstone around her neck. She had fought for Frank, and what had he ever done to help himself, the brother who had let her down time and time again, and always would? She had fought for John, her nephew, the son she hadn't had, and he had grown to be a murderer, threatening to crush her skull. What of her own dreams? Why had she never fought for those? Teaching. That had gone like a spark on the breeze. David. She had ached with dreams for him, her one love, her one true friend, and now he spoke of God's will as he complacently consigned her to her lot. America. That was her dream, the salvation she had prepared, and John had flung it back in her face. Why must she submit? Why must she always be the dutiful woman?

She had had enough of duty. There was one battle that she had fought and won. Annie. Annie was alive and whole and free and beautiful. That was where Leah belonged. She would do it. She would go to America and leave others to fight the lost battles.

She dragged one foot free of the water. Then the other. A twig snagged at her hat as she threw herself back from the brink, tearing it free and tugging her hair loose. The hat tumbled down, snatched by the water that swirled it away. It caught on a submerged bough, just out of reach. If she hooked it with her umbrella... Once more, she nearly lost her footing. The umbrella was out of her hand, gusting out to settle like a ship on the water, circling its way downstream. Nature was making a fool of her. Let it. Let the hat lie.

Plain black felt with a bit of black ribbon the only trim, brim turned up like a general on the field of battle. But not her battle. Not any more.

'Keep it!' she shouted at the river. It was a dutiful woman's hat. Leah Owen's hat, gone on the flood. In a flash she saw what she must do, for herself and for the wretched Rachel Morgan. She struggled back through the thickets to the body of the sorry woman. A woman who should at least receive in death the respect that she had been denied in life. That at least she could do for her.

Kneeling, she fumbled to unbutton Rachel's fox-trimmed green coat, and gently, as if afraid to wake the sleeper and cause more pain, she raised the smashed head, neck, shoulders, to ease her clothing from her. Then she stripped, every scrap. She didn't feel the pouring rain hissing on her naked flesh. She didn't shiver with the cold. She was too fired up from within as she donned Rachel's clothes. Rachel's hat, with its jaunty pheasant feathers was hanging, snagged on a hazel branch. She set it onto her own soaking hair. A harlot's hat, and now it was hers.

It was a struggle, redressing the corpse in her own respectable linen and wool, but her fingers were steady now, unfastening and fastening buttons, ribbons, stockings, stays.

At last it was done. She stood looking down on Leah Owen. They were sufficiently alike, tall and thin. Rachel's hair was almost black, a shade darker that Leah's, and her eyes were blue, not brown, her chin weaker, her cheek bones less pronounced, but still they could have been sisters. And now they were one. Leah Owen – spinster of Llanolwen, name, body and soul – would be consumed by the river, and Rachel Morgan would go on, to America, to Annie, to live the life both women should have had.

She found the strength to drag the body down to the water. Strength enough for anything now, because she was free.

Unshackled. She stood for a moment in prayer to a God in whom she did not believe.

'Let judgment run down as waters, and righteousness as a mighty stream. God, let Thy righteous stream take this righteous woman to thy bosom.'

She thrust the body out into the flood. It dragged. She prodded it loose, nearly overbalancing as she watched the body float away, swirled round and round as the roaring currents took it. If it were found, battered and swollem, when the floods died down and the river released its burden, it would be taken for Leah Owen, a virtuous and dutiful woman, sadly missed.

That was it. She had nothing left of the woman she had been, except the bag. She hadn't thrown out all the money. There was some left, forty or fifty pounds, maybe. Fortune enough to see her into a new life in a new world. Clasping the bag to her, Rachel Morgan turned, off the line of the footpath, up towards the high road, striding into the rain.

HARVEST HOME

1922

David George saw his wife and daughter outside the store and pulled up to the kerb. Betty looked, as ever, slightly affronted that the day was not entirely hers to organise. 'What are you doing here?' she asked as he climbed out.

'I came to let Sarah Price know what happened. She couldn't attend.'

'Humph. Couldn't attend the inquest of her own brother. Well? How did it go? What was decided?'

'As we expected. Accidental death.'

Betty snorted. 'And what else could it have been? A waste of time, if you ask me.'

'There were questions to be answered, Betty.'

'What questions? Nonsense. Frank Owen was drunk and met the end he deserved.'

'Perhaps.' David methodically pulled his gloves off. 'But there are always doubts to be settled in such cases.'

'Such as?'

'Will Griffith said that Frank was not so very drunk when he left the Butcher's Arms.'

'If that was so, it would have been the first time since Leah died.'

'True. But that's what Griffith claimed. Frank had told him he was clearing out, going to America as Leah had wished.'

'What utter nonsense. As if Leah would ever have dreamed of such an irresponsible fancy. She knew where her duty lay. Or at least she did until she succumbed to the Devil and committed–'

'Betty, hush. We both swore at her inquest that she must have slipped and been swept away. It was ruled an accident, not suicide.'

Betty sniffed. 'Well, we shall see, but I do know—'

'Yes, we knew what a state she was in when she came to see us. That is something I shall never forget, or forgive myself for; that I let her go! But I refuse to believe she committed such a sin as self-destruction. Leah was a good woman.'

'Oh, she always did have you wrapped around her little finger. Lending her an outright fortune...' Betty growled uncomfortably, seeing David's expression. 'Poor woman, accident or no, she deserved better.'

'Yes.'

'But I won't believe there was any doubt about Frank's death. He was drunk and he fell under the wagon. What else could anyone claim?'

David said nothing. With his daughter standing by, he had no wish to repeat the evidence of the driver Levi Morris, who claimed that Frank had seemed to stagger out from the lane as if pushed, and there had been a look of terror on his face even before he had turned to see the heavily laden quarry wagon thundering down on him. Levi was given to exaggeration; to lurid tales, and was known to be fond of a drop or two himself, which made him occasionally see things that weren't there. His original claim had grown in telling. However, when he was called to give evidence at the inquest, he had left out the part of his story that he'd told the first time around; about glimpsing a dark horned figure.

'All I can say is, Frank Owen is dead, and the world's a better place for it,' said Betty.

'But poor John,' said Annie. 'He's all alone in the world, now. Shall I visit him to comfort him?'

'Only with me at your side, Hannah Leah,' said David, partly amused, partly alarmed at her partiality. John was a God-fearing, hard-working upright young man, but was he what David wanted for his daughter? Young Sidney Lloyd over at Pantglas, who had been showing an interest, would be more suitable perhaps. A better match all round... He felt guilty that he allowed himself such thoughts. John was a good man. David had sworn to himself to take care of him, for Leah's sake, and Leah would surely have welcomed such a match. Her beloved nephew and his daughter, the families brought together at last.

The very thought of Leah brought a lump to his throat. He coughed. 'Are you ladies done?'

'I still need to visit Mrs Devonald about that dress. Will you give us half an hour?'

'Yes. Half an hour will be fine.' He watched wife and daughter head for the dressmaker's cottage, then he turned and walked down the road, past the last houses, to the chapel. He turned into the graveyard and walked down the rows of graves, to the one that bore the name of Owen.

Mary, wife of Thomas Owen of Cwmderwen, died 1900, aged 60.
Also the above Thomas Owen, died 1912, aged 76.
Also Thos their son, died 1882, aged 16.

Y drygionus a wna waith twyllodrus:
ond i'r neb a heuo gyfiawnder, y bydd gwobr sicr.

And now, between the old English inscription and the Welsh scripture, the words that David had commissioned to be added, though Betty had sniffed and tutted.

Also Leah Owen, their daughter, died 1919, aged 45.

He had wanted to add more, some eulogy or word of love and worth. But Leah would not have approved of that. She had never been a woman for sentiment.

He stood there, leaning on the stone awhile, his eyes closed, praying. His heart, he swore, had been bleeding since her battered corpse had been found. But no, he must be strong for his family, and for the nephew that she had given so much for.

Would John need his help more, now that he was alone at Cwmderwen? Perhaps less, truthfully. And he would not remain alone. In time, he would find a wife, though David prayed not Annie. A woman to share his toil and respect his strengths and quiet dignity. A woman who did not seek effusive professions of love, for John was too self-controlled for that. He had faced his beloved aunt's loss with the silent stoicism of unwavering faith. A strong man, for all his youth. He had been equally unmoved by the fate of his father, though David could not blame him for that. John had given one-word answers at Frank's inquest, and had said nothing at all on the journey home, until David had set him down at the gate of Cwmderwen.

Then he had spoken. 'Thank you, Mr George.'

'Will you be all right, John? You know where we are. You are not alone.'

'I am not alone. God is with me.'

'Amen, John. Never doubt that.'

It must be a profound faith that was sustaining him, he thought, now. God's hand upon him.

'Leah,' whispered David. 'I let you slip through my fingers and I failed you in your darkest hour, but I will watch over John in your name, for he is safe in the Lord as you surely are.'

On the highest pasture of Cwmderwen, John Owen looked out over his land, his hands raised to embrace it all. The tenancy was in his name now. Times were hard. Prices had plummeted. Farmers were facing ruin, but he would not, because there was a covenant twixt him and God who gave him this land. Him and him alone.

He returned to the house and opened the door to the parlour, long empty of the iron bed and any trace of Leah. He stood at the table, his hands resting devoutly on the great Bible, his eyes shut. 'I thank you, Lord God that you are with me, my rod and my staff, a guide to my hand to smite my foe and crush him beneath the wheels of justice, even as you hurled the beast back into the abyss and drowned the false Jezebel. Thy will be done. Amen.'

Opening the holy book at the page where births and deaths had been inscribed, he picked up a pen and scratched out the names of Francis and Leah Owen.

Leah was the aunt who brought up Gran and your grandfather, when their mother died. My gran came over to America with another aunt, Rachel, whom I don't remember because she died the year after I was born (1955) but my mother knew her well, as a very spirited old lady. I know there was some mystery about her which Gran would never tell but hinted at. She may have been a governess perhaps, with some sort of scandal. She certainly encouraged Gran to become a teacher and she would help the children with their schoolwork. She and Gran used to speak Welsh together apparently, which is how my mother picked up some, although it never rubbed off on me.

I know very little about any of Gran's other relatives, except that she was fond of her brother John, your grandfather, and I am sorry to hear that he met such a tragic end, Sarah. I wish I'd asked Gran more about her old life when she was still alive, but alas it's too late now.

I enclose a photograph of my grandmother, with her aunt Rachel, my grandfather, and my uncle Jonathon, outside their house in Allentown. My mother is the baby Rachel's holding, so it must have been taken in about 1930. They all look very happy, don't you think, despite the hard times? Gran had a full life and her twelve grandchildren remember her fondly.

Looking forward to hearing anything you discover about life at the old homestead. I do love family mysteries.

Kind regards

Lea Olsen Hayes.

321

ABOUT HONNO

Honno Welsh Women's Press was set up in 1986 by a group of women who felt strongly that women in Wales needed wider opportunities to see their writing in print and to become involved in the publishing process. Our aim is to develop the writing talents of women in Wales, give them new and exciting opportunities to see their work published and often to give them their first 'break' as a writer. Honno is registered as a community co-operative. Any profit that Honno makes is invested in the publishing programme. Women from Wales and around the world have expressed their support for Honno. Each supporter has a vote at the Annual General Meeting. For more information and to buy our publications, please write to Honno at the address below, or visit our website: www.honno.co.uk.

Honno, D41 Hugh Owen Building, Penglais Campus, Aberystwyth University, Aberystwyth, Ceredigion SY23 3DY.

We are very grateful for the support of all the Honno Friends. For more information on how you can support Honno, see: https://www.honno.co.uk/about/support-honno/